The
Caperton Project

By
Ronald D Renshaw

Published by Raspberry Ridge Publishing
Jefferson, Iowa

ISBN 9798729583096

Copyright 2021 by Ronald D. Renshaw

Cover Art and Design by Cody Renshaw
Cover Photography by Ronald Renshaw

Dedication

I dedicate this manuscript to the memory of my wife Kris. She was a great wife and mother and brought joy to all who knew her. I wouldn't be where I am in life without her.

Acknowledgements

I would like to thank my brother Don for tirelessly reviewing the manuscript and making many useful suggestions.

My son Cody did most of the cover work and is a genius with computers. He also reviewed the document and made suggestions. His wife CT contributed the eye of a professional photographer regarding the cover arrangement and colors.

I thank my granddaughter Ryenne Bentley for posing as Tara Lapley for the cover photo. She is the same age as that character in the book and is a perfect model. I also thank her mother Rachel for assisting with the photo shoot.

I must also thank my son Josh for use of his first name as a character in the story, though the character is nothing like him, and my daughter Randa for her enthusiastic support.

My daughter Robin and my granddaughter Audri also reviewed one of the later drafts, as did my daughter-in-law Casey. My son Brady reviewed an early draft and commented. My sons-in-law Dan and William helped keep my computer and printer working and I am grateful beyond words.

Ronald D. Renshaw

April 2021

Chapters

Prologue

Sam Brashear threw his suitcase into the trunk of his car and strode to the front door of his empty house. The town had been full of extended family members; he was the last one residing in the area. The house, once the scene of so many joyous events, family birthday parties, kids' sports celebrations, neighborhood get-togethers, was now empty.

He closed and locked the door out of habit. In this small town there was no need to worry about someone stealing from a neighbor. Then he hurried to his car where his wife already waited. Without looking back, he sped out of town. He dreaded what he might see if he looked in his rearview mirror, so he kept his eyes on the road and kept driving, staring straight ahead.

He really didn't have a destination in mind. Getting far away was all that mattered. He was thankful that Jay and Cheryl had moved out after college.

Sam, his wife, and their car were never seen again.

Years passed...

Chapter One: The Country Road

Jay Brashear struggled on foot along a hot country road. He felt exhausted and his shoes scraped against gravel with every step. A distant cloud of dust caught his attention as he crested a hill. At first he only gave it a perfunctory glance as he proceeded down the sloping gravel road, occasionally slipping on some loose rocks. Something caused him to take a second glance at the cloud, almost involuntarily. The mid-summer heat was oppressive, and any unnecessary physical activity brought forth additional rivulets of perspiration.

It was turning into a really bad day. His car had stalled, and Jay could think of no alternative but walking to the next small town. He tried but couldn't quite recall how long he had been walking. His cell phone's battery was inexplicably dead, and he was sure he had left it plugged into the charger in the motel room the previous night, as he always did. Perhaps the cloud of dust portended an approaching vehicle, but Jay noted that the cloud was a good distance off to the left of the country road and didn't seem to be moving.

Jay stumbled over a rut in the road. This brought his gaze back down to his feet. He had grown up on a farm and had done a lot of walking along country roads, so he knew how easy it would be to trip in a rut in the road and sprain his ankle. That would only make it more difficult to find help.

When he raised his head back up again, he was shocked to see that the dust cloud seemed to be actually just over the next hill. It had the appearance of a typical wind-blown collection of farm field soil particles, but it dawned on Jay that there was no perceptible wind, which explained the overpowering heat, but turned the dust cloud into a mystery.

Jay quit walking. He stopped thinking about the ruts in the road. He even ceased to be aware of the constant heat. As sweat beaded up on his forehead he stared up the next slope. He sensed that something wasn't right. He wanted to turn and run, but for some reason his legs didn't obey. His feet felt heavy as he continued to plod his way up the hill.

Jay tried to puzzle out what was so troubling, but his mind seemed to have slowed to the same pace as his feet. He observed in a detached manner the full view at the top of the hill. It wasn't a cloud of dust. The last thought he was able to formulate came from deep within his subconscious: "Not again!"

Now it was growing dark. Jay stood beside his rented SUV and placed one hand on the door. He glanced over his shoulder, still in a half-awake daze and smiled. It was an incongruous sort of half-smile, he knew. He shouldn't be smiling at all. He should be screaming in terror. He tried to focus on the terror. It was beginning to slip away from his mind like a dream might upon first awakening. As his mind cleared of the unpleasant thoughts, his fear was replaced by a feeling of complete calmness. He felt in his jeans pocket to verify that the key fob that would unlock the door was still there.

The next thing he realized was that he was driving in the direction of the last town he had passed, Millardville. He was vaguely perplexed, but no longer alarmed. It was morning once again.

Darkness had always been Deke Fraley's friend. He had an uncanny ability to see better in the dark than most other people. But, he had never been a morning person and had always experienced difficulty getting to sleep before 1:00 or 2:00 in the morning. On weekends he often slept all day and stayed up all night. His high school academic performance had subsequently suffered, since he often fell asleep in class. He scraped by and his graduation the previous year had liberated him.

Deke was fortunate to land a job as a night watchman at the carton factory on the outskirts of Millardville. He felt totally relaxed roaming the fenced-in grounds around the warehouse where the cartons were stored prior to shipping. While some people might feel nervous about moving around in the dark amid the shadows cast by the spotlights that topped each building, Deke was completely comfortable. He often fantasized about getting a job in the far north where it was dark for half the year. At least he could then experience total bliss for weeks at a time. Sunlight made him feel anxious.

But Deke's reverie this time was interrupted. He heard something as his route took him past Warehouse Number 8. Probably nothing, he thought, but it would be best to check it out. Number 8 was the building that was nearest to the blacktop road which led off into the wooded area on the south side of the town and you never could tell when some dumb kid would be out cruising late and would get the urge to climb over the chain link fence and see what sort of trouble he could get into. Since it was close to the road, they could get in and out fast without being seen.

Sometimes several rowdies would climb the fence and find a place to do drugs. Deke's predecessor, whose recent promotion to a supervisory position had resulted in the job opening that led to Deke's hiring, Fred Merchant, told him that he had more than once caught high school kids spray painting graffiti on the back of a warehouse, visible to the road.

Of course, Deke never admitted that he had tried this diversion himself a couple of times and had even been nearly caught by Fred himself once after his school's homecoming game. That had been two years earlier. Now, he was the one trying to guard the buildings. Deke bit his lower lip and gripped his flashlight as he approached the rear of Number 8.

As he neared the corner of the building, it suddenly occurred to him that he could be wrong. This might be something other than a dumb kid scaling the rattling fence. It could be something less serious, maybe a raccoon or a large rat. He figured the light from his flashlight would frighten away whatever or whoever was making the racket. He only worried briefly that it could possibly be a gang of thieves trying to break into the building, but cardboard cartons didn't seem like something that would attract thieves.

There had recently been some thievery at various farms in the area and some animals had been killed. The flashlight had a nice heft to it and could be used as a club, if necessary. And, if he couldn't frighten whatever was back there, he was prepared to make a dash for the office, where he could phone for help. Once again, he wished he had a cell phone, but neither he nor his mother could afford one. Deke was quite thin and a fast runner. Though he hadn't seriously considered participation in any high school sports, he knew that he could run fast.

As he edged along the building Deke slowed both his steps and his breathing to the point at which he began alternating deep inhalations and slow expirations with each careful placement of his feet on the concrete path that edged the warehouse. He readied the flashlight in his right hand, his thumb caressing the switch button nervously. He was clutching the flashlight so tightly that his palm began to perspire in the heat of the July night.

His mind no longer pondered the peacefulness of the darkness. He felt the same sort of excitement that he used to feel when stalking prey during hunting season, when his father used to take him into the woods outside Caperton in search of pheasants. The difference this time was that he didn't yet know the nature of his prey. Nor did he know for sure if he would remain the hunter or somehow become the prey himself.

"Ya jest never know," as old Fred used to say. Deke smiled to himself as he recalled those words, but the smile faded quickly.

The faint sound that first fixated his attention on Number 8 now sounded again. Deke sensed that something was rustling the weeds along the fence. The growth inside the fence was trimmed weekly, so whatever was around the corner must be just outside the fence. Somebody preparing to scale it, or maybe just some large rodent rummaging in the overgrown grass where the warehouse crew sometimes threw their lunch scraps. Deke didn't know. He paused to try to analyze whether the chain links were beginning to rattle. Some new sound had definitely been added to the weeds' rustling.

Deke sucked in an involuntary breath. It was the fence! Someone or something had clearly taken a grip on the links along the bottom and was beginning to ascend it, slowly, but steadily. It could be human or maybe a cat or some other animal. Deke still wasn't certain.

The rattle of the chain links continued. Deke could sense that the would-be trespasser was moving higher with each shake of the fence. The intruder's progress wasn't rapid, but quite deliberate. Deke was tempted to peek around the corner and end the mystery, but the thought struck him that he really didn't have an effective plan of action, in case this turned out to be a dangerous intruder. Should he leap into the open space between the warehouse wall and challenge the intruder? Should he race back to the guard house and call for help?

Before, he had always just happened upon relatively harmless four-legged creatures and had been able to chase them away. Because of the recent farm vandalism incidents, he'd abandoned his previous nonchalant approach to his nightly rounds, but since nothing bad had actually happened, he suddenly realized that he wasn't as prepared for this confrontation as might be required.

Then it suddenly dawned on Deke that there was something peculiar about the way the fence rattled. The climber must be quite small, he noted, since the fence was not shaking loudly. It was most likely an animal or, perhaps, a child. By the sound, any animal shaking the fence that way would need to be rather lightweight.

Deke recalled that he had first scaled this very same fence when he was in sixth grade, a skinny little twerp who had sneaked out of his house on Halloween night to tag along with some neighborhood kids in defacing various unguarded buildings around town. Never got caught either, Deke smugly reminded himself.

Actually, it was the other kids who were vandalizing the warehouse. He merely watched from the fringes of the group, then sneaked back home. But, still, for young Deke Fraley it was an adventure.

The fence was eight feet high. The almost negligible rattling continued. Deke felt better, now that he had convinced himself it was either a kid or an animal, although he found the thought of a four-legged animal scaling a chain link fence perplexing. At any rate, the sound from around the corner of the warehouse indicated that whoever or whatever was scaling the fence had just about reached the top.

Deke, clenching his teeth, chose the aggressive approach. He hit the flashlight button and hurled himself around the corner while simultaneously shrieking out what he hoped sounded like a karate style scream that would strike terror in the intruder. He began swinging the flashlight wildly as he landed in the space between the fence and the back wall of the warehouse. Kid or animal, he thought, this should be effective in scaring it away.

At that moment, the area behind Warehouse Number 8 lit up in a pale green glow.

Deke hated morning sunlight. He hated the glare in his eyes that signaled the end of another blissful night of darkness. Mostly, he hated the fact that throughout his life daylight meant responsibility, the necessity of rising from slumber to meet the demands of someone else's schedule.

This time, however, it was different. Deke felt immeasurable relief when he realized the light came from the morning sun. As his vision cleared, he shielded his eyes from the glare and realized that he was propped in a sitting position against the back of the warehouse.

He focused momentarily on his wristwatch, long enough to confirm that it was broken. He recalled something about the fence and shot a quick glance at it before the thought that he must have dozed off hit him hard and he decided he had better race back to the guard shack before anyone noticed he was away from his post.

He realized that he no longer was holding the flashlight. He looked around and finally found it on the outside of the fence! He tried to recall how it had ended up out there, but an annoying buzz in his ears suddenly made careful thought impossible. He haltingly made his way back to the office to clock out.

Dr. Tyrone Williamson was puzzled. He sat at his office desk with the computer screen in front of him. He had just seen Nicholas Dunbar, a patient in his late forties who seldom had any medical complaints. In fact, there was only one previous entry for Mr. Dunbar, a routine physical exam that was needed for insurance purposes. That was five years ago.

But now, his office visit was for a very unusual reason. After pausing for several minutes, the doctor began to make a brief entry: *Patient complains of inability to sleep and a constant buzzing in his ears plus a burning sensation in his eyes. Physical exam notable for triangular indentation at base of skull. Patient couldn't explain it. Sent to hospital for lab work and x-rays. If negative, need neuro consult.*

Pushing his chair back from his desk, the doctor removed his reading glasses and ran his fingers through his neatly combed, slightly graying hair. Nick Dunbar had suddenly clutched his head at several times during the exam but didn't seem to know he had done it. He had continued to speak in a flat monotone while grabbing at his temples, forehead, and the back of his head, as though he were in great pain. Ty thought the patient sounded robotic. There was no emotion attached to the apparent pain he was feeling.

Turning again to the computer, he inserted a brief comment: *Patient claims to be going to bed earlier than usual, sleeping later than before and still awakening exhausted.*

Perhaps, the doctor thought, there was depression. A mental health evaluation might be a good idea. Or, the patient could have apnea, ceasing to breathe for short periods of time in the midst of sleeping. A sleep study may be called for.

Ty's contemplation was interrupted when his nurse, Jean Ruehle, came to his door to announce that there was a walk-in patient. He glanced up, sighed heavily, and then pushed himself up from his chair.

"You're going to want to see this patient," Nurse Ruehle added. That was an unusual comment for her to make, he thought, and she didn't usually allow a walk-in to interrupt the appointment schedule. Emergency patients were directed to the hospital emergency room when there was no opening in Ty's schedule.

As the doctor reached the hallway outside his office, he noted that Jean had led the unexpected patient to an examining room. The man, appearing to be in his late thirties or early forties, was already sitting on the edge of the exam table when Dr. Williamson entered the room.

The patient was wearing a yellow tee-shirt and faded jeans. He was slumped forward, his hands clutching at his head, first in the front, then at his ears, then at the base of skull. Except for these movements, the patient remained motionless with his eyes closed. He uttered no sounds. As the doctor approached, the patient clasped his hands around his ears. The doctor's eyes were drawn to the back of the man's head, where, just at the hairline, he was surprised to note what seemed to be a perfect triangular impression. Just like Nick Dunbar...

Jay Brashear opened his eyes and looked at the doctor. For a second he had difficulty remembering where he was. He knew that he had been on his way to visit his old childhood buddy Paul Sloan, who lived in the country outside of the small village of Caperton, where Jay had grown up. He had exited the Interstate highway at the Route 128 exit, followed it to Millardville, and picked up the old gravel road just on the south edge of that small town.

It had been years since Jay had visited his boyhood hometown. Jay remembered making a few turns as the paved highway became a blacktop, then a gravel road.

Then, he recalled being in his rented SUV and driving back into Millardville. He didn't know why he came back. But, as he neared the town, the odd burning feeling in his head had grown into a blinding headache. He stopped at a gas station and asked for directions to the nearest doctor.

The attendant had suggested the hospital emergency room, but Jay had insisted on the nearest doctor, so he found himself pulling into the parking lot outside Dr. Williamson's office, just a couple blocks from the gas station.

He threw the car's door open as he entered the parking lot but failed to remember to reach back and turn off the engine. He also left the door open. He then stumbled blindly into the waiting room, collapsing against the receptionist's desk, where the nurse had rushed to assist him. She quickly led him to an examining room and called for Ty.

"I am Dr. Tyrone Williamson. You may call me Ty," the doctor began, holding out his hand. Jay didn't respond. When the patient didn't respond, the doctor continued. "And your name is...?"

Jay's face remained blank.

Ty kept his composure. "What seems to be the problem?" he continued, though he thought he knew the answer.

"I...I don't really know," Jay finally blurted out, surprising himself at the tremor in his voice. A *Real Estate Salesman of the Year for Central Ohio* should have more self-confidence, he observed to himself.

"There's something wrong in my head, a constant buzzing. It's driving me crazy!"

"What about this indentation on the back of your head?" Ty asked, though his calm voice disguised a rising nervousness that he felt in his stomach.

Jay reached with his right hand to feel the spot the doctor had touched. "I don't know..." he began, then continuing, "Oh, right—it's from a bug bite."

Jay rubbed the spot for a few seconds. Then, he dropped his hand back into his lap. The comments sounded rehearsed to Ty, like prefabricated excuses.

"Bug bite?" Ty queried, trying to visualize the event. "The impression is covered by an orange scab and appears to be a perfect triangle."

Ty thought it must have been made by a man-made object, perhaps a medical instrument, but a bug bite seemed unlikely to leave such a symmetrical scab.

He paused for a few seconds, then continued. "Did you seek medical treatment?"

"Medical treatment?" Jay responded in a monotone.

"Would you mind if I contact your doctor?" Ty inquired, forcing his nervousness down and using as calm a voice as he could. His patient just stared blankly.

Now Ty was curious. Maybe this man had some sort of brain injury and didn't remember his own name, or the name of his physician, or how he suffered the injury. Perhaps whatever caused the neck scab also caused amnesia.

Ty had always been intrigued by mysteries, which is one reason he went into medicine. He found the similarities of the strange medical problems of Nick Dunbar and this anonymous patient to be a compelling mystery to pursue. He also thought this man seemed familiar but couldn't figure out why.

Leaving the patient sitting on the edge of the examination table, Ty went to his office. He paced back and forth for a minute or so, deep in thought, pondering the mystery. Why was the man unable or unwilling to give his name? What was the connection between the medical conditions of Nick Dunbar and this mysterious patient...?

Nurse Ruehle rushed into the room. "He's gone, Dr. Williamson! I tried to stop him, but he just pushed past me and bolted out the door."

Ty wheeled and dashed for the waiting room. Not finding the patient there, he then hurried to the front door just in time to see a silver SUV screeching out of the parking lot. Ty raised one hand in a futile gesture to signal his mysterious patient to stop. It did no good. After a moment Ty dropped his arm and slowly walked back into the building, shaking his head.

A few blocks away, Kathy Fellner was sitting in the front seat of her car. She had a Department of Family Services investigation form attached to the clipboard resting against the steering wheel. She was trying to collect her thoughts in order to make a concise and objective entry. She only needed to make a few brief notes that she could expand on when she got back to her office.

She had just completed a visit to the Mayes family to see if they had followed through on the steps she and Mrs. Mayes had discussed during her last home visit. At that time, Lola Mayes had agreed to take little Carla to the public health clinic for her routine examination so she could begin kindergarten. Davey, age ten, was to be signed up for the second session of summer day camp to give him a chance to develop his social skills among other children his age and to give his mother a respite from the stress of raising the children with no help from their fathers.

All fine and good, Kathy thought, as she made a few notations on the Department of Family Services form.

"Objectives met for Carla and Davey. Good." She put the clipboard on the seat next to her and bit her lower lip.

Kathy had found that little Kimberly was back in the Mayes' home. The three-year-old had disappeared several weeks before the subsequent *Amber Alert* and police search had met a dead end. Mrs. Mayes was distraught but was unable to offer any help on where her youngest child might be.

Kimmy had apparently wandered away while Davey was supposed to be watching her. A ten-year-old watching younger siblings was not considered appropriate, for just such reasons as were made obvious by Kimberly's case.

Her mother confessed that she had left her children in the care of her cousin Julie, but an emergency came up and Julie had turned the care over to Davey. Lola didn't mention that Julie had admitted that the *emergency* was actually the need to drive to the nearest store for a carton of cigarettes.

She claimed that she had only left the house for about a minute, but when she returned, Kimberly was gone. Lola had returned shortly thereafter and discovered that Kimmy was missing. Lola had challenged Julie about Kimmy's disappearance. Davey had no explanation and just stared vacantly in response to his mother's questions. The police who were summoned had no better luck with Davey. Carla had been difficult to arouse from her sleep. Neither knew what had become of their sister.

Then, after the fruitless searching over the next several days, Davey suddenly volunteered that Kimberly's father, whose place of residence was unknown to the rest of the family, had knocked on the door around 11:00 PM and had taken his daughter to live with him. He hadn't taken any of her clothing or toys. He had simply scooped her up, told Davey to lock the door behind him, and left.

At first there was much public concern about the abduction. Efforts were made to locate Kimmy's father in his last known city of residence, but Jeffrey Dubold could not be found. He had apparently pulled off one of those parental kidnappings that were becoming all too common and had, at least temporarily, gotten away without leaving any clues behind.

Lola Mayes had eventually calmed down, but the incident left the family in a state of increased tension. DFS had previously been involved, due to some comparatively minor issues, but this event with Kimmy had resulted in a level of disruption uncommon for even this family.

Finally, after extensive effort and supervision by DFS, the children were again receiving adequate care and life was returning to what passed for normal.

Now, this! Today, without any warning, when Kathy knocked on the door, Mrs. Mayes answered, and she was holding Kimmy by the hand. Lola didn't even offer an explanation, at first.

"Kimmy's back?" Kathy blurted out. "What happened? Did Jeff bring her home?"

"No. She's just back," was Lola's markedly unemotional response. "Woke up this morning and there she was, asleep on the bed next to Carly."

Kathy was dumbfounded. She had seen a lot in her twelve years of professional social work, and it took a lot now to shock or surprise her. But this did not make any sense, especially when Lola confirmed that the doors had been bolted from the inside all night. Lola had no idea how Kimmy had been returned. She had heard no noises, no voices. It had just happened.

Lola's unemotional reaction seemed almost as amazing to Kathy as the fact that little Kimmy was back. She gently patted her own bulging tummy, thinking that when her baby was born, she would never let him or her out of her own care. It had taken ten years since her marriage to Lee for her to be able to carry a baby this far and she would never be able to be as unemotional about her child as Lola seemed to be.

Kathy stopped patting her protruding abdomen and let her hand rest heavily just above her own navel. She pressed down slightly, feeling a prompt kick in return, almost as though she and her baby were communicating in some special way.

She scolded herself quietly for her unprofessional, judgmental attitude toward Lola. It was not appropriate for her to apply her own values to others who had grown up in different circumstances, different cultures. Of course, this neutrality did not apply when it came to basic care and safety issues and that is why Kathy felt so strongly about the Mayes family situation. She knew that the family was walking a tightrope when it came to meeting basic needs of food, shelter, and emotional well-being.

But, despite all this, despite the fact that she knew she needed to maintain a professional attitude in working with this family and others in similar circumstances, Kathy felt a deep-down pain that people could treat their children so indifferently. Beyond basic needs of physical care that their families seemed nearly unable to provide, where would these children receive the kind of attention that would elevate them beyond this limited life they knew? What would keep them from repeating the mistakes of their parents?

Again, Kathy scolded herself for her assumptions about the cultural values of the Mayes family.

Kathy felt another, stronger kick. "No, little one," she whispered. "You will never have to experience such pain. Never. I will protect you. You will never have to go through what little Kimmy has been through."

Kathy would soon face a startling awakening.

Jay slowed his car to make the left turn onto the gravel road. He felt a legitimate sense of déjà vu. After all, he had made this same turn only a few hours earlier. At least, he assumed it was the same day. The buzzing in his head had intensified after he left the clinic.

He couldn't recall why he left the doctor's office or even how he found it in the first place. Even trying to recall what had happened caused the buzzing in his head to increase in intensity, to the point at which he thought his head would explode. Jay fought to ignore it. He was determined to make it all the way to Paul's house outside Caperton this time.

He vaguely recalled being on this road before, but he had no idea why he had turned around earlier. But the memory of the desperation in Paul's voice when he had called Jay a couple days earlier urged him on.

Paul was a longtime buddy, and he couldn't let him down in this moment of need, even though he had no clear idea what Paul's problem was. He had refused to discuss it over the phone. Jay slapped his hands to his head in an effort to clear away the buzzing and then completed the turn, speeding down the country road.

Up ahead was THE HILL. Jay didn't recall why, but he felt that he had to make it over that one rise in the road in order to reach Paul. He made it to the bottom of the slope and reached down to shift to a lower gear. As he did so, there was a sudden flash that seemed to explode from somewhere inside his SUV, which left a greenish glow that completely filled Jay's vision.

Jay heard his car engine die. The SUV stopped immediately, not even coasting forward from momentum. The green glow seemed to envelope him like a neon air bag and he suddenly sensed that he was being buoyed forward in the midst of that light.

"Am I dead?" he heard himself ask.

A distant voice, like the echo of a whisper, seemed to reply.

"All will be well."

Jay immediately realized that it would be. Then his mind began to grow dark for the second time that day.

Chapter Two: Caperton After Dark

Caperton seemed to sink into the darkness as the sun fell in the west. The streets of the tiny village, never crowded at any time, were always empty after the blast of the village fire alarm from atop the Main Street hill at six o'clock sharp. The alarm was originally installed to warn of an approaching tornado or as a signal to nearby farmers that it was mealtime. There didn't seem to be any legitimate need for it now to signal the farmers, though it was still used as a tornado warning. Nobody had bothered to reset the alarm now that it was no longer needed to alert people of the time. It was as much because of tradition as it was lassitude.

Most people probably view small towns as having perhaps a few thousand residents. Anyone living in a town the size of Caperton would scoff at that notion. They know what a small town is. In fact, they know that there are some other towns even smaller. Caperton was basically four blocks wide along the state highway and seven blocks deep.

It is often said that in a small town everyone knows everyone else, but even in Caperton this was not true. People tended to keep to themselves and only sought out their neighbors when necessary. A small town's residents, at least those who had lived in the area for most of their lives, mainly knew their close neighbors and any relatives who happened to live nearby. They might have a nodding relationship with a number of others, but that doesn't mean they really knew one another.

Most streets in town terminated at a fenced-in farm field. They were planted in corn or soybeans or left fallow. The brick three story schoolhouse stood along the eastern edge of the town. It had been there since early in the twentieth century. Since the consolidation of three small towns into one school system back in the 1960s, the Caperton school had housed grades 5 through 8. The small towns of Caperton, Reginald and Bond were spaced about equally apart from one another, so the powers that be dubbed it the "Triangle School District."

Most people moved away from these small villages after finishing their schooling, but the ones who remained, or returned after college or military service, made up the social structure of the communities. Their social institutions reflected in microcosm those in the bigger municipalities around the state.

Though at one time the three small communities had thrived and had their own movie houses, grocery stores, libraries, and clothing stores, by the Sixties their populations had dwindled so much that many of the remaining stores existed primarily to service the needs of the local farmers.

There was a church in Caperton, plus one tavern and two grocery stores. For other resources, the locals would travel to Millardville and other larger towns. A railroad track along the north side of the town had once been a lifeline bringing in supplies and luxuries from far away, but now it served mostly as a place for the local children to investigate.

Things were much slower than they were just a few decades ago. During World War II and the Depression and even more before the thirties, Caperton had been a bustling community. Saturday nights were set aside for socialization in the downtown area, in the tavern café or grocery store, even just on the street when the weather was warm enough.

Gradually, all such activities had died away. The improved

highways and automobiles made it easier to reach more robust communities. Quality medical care was available in Millardville. Even better care was found in Spring City about an hour north of Caperton.

As the night began to clamp itself around the edges of town, however, on this particular evening, there was an unusual level of activity. A town meeting had been called and a small clump of automobiles and pickups were slant-parked on Main Street up against the curb in front of the little-used building that once was a meeting place for a VFW chapter back when the town's population was much larger.

It was a two-story brick structure which long ago had ceased to have any real use for its upper floor. Before it was a meeting place for the VFW, it had once held the town's police headquarters and the two-cell jail. Since that time, the police force had gradually shrunk to one person and one of the jail cells had been turned into a storeroom.

A mismatched collection of wooden and metal folding chairs had been lined up in precise rows; only four rows were needed. Men in blue jeans and baseball caps bearing the logos of farm implement and seed corn companies and women in simple patterned tops and pastel pants filed into the single large room and quietly seated themselves. Most of the crowd were over the age of forty. There was no talk; the meeting's purpose was too serious. They turned their full attention to the pudgy figure standing at the front of the room.

Mayor Ralph Osgood fidgeted nervously, alternately checking his wristwatch and glancing at the door to make sure he didn't start while people were still arriving. The mayor was unaccustomed to running formal meetings; the city council usually just met over a few beers next door at Paige's Bar and there was no need for any procedural mumbo-jumbo. In fact, since there were only four council men, or council persons, since Judy DePriest was one of the officials and Ralph always wanted to be politically correct, most decisions were made by a nodding consensus rather than a formal vote.

Now, Mayor Osgood, who preferred that formal form of address, but few people actually called him by it, would need to conduct a meeting of the entire town, or at least the portion that could be present on this warm midsummer evening. People lately had become less willing to travel after dark. Ralph secretly hoped that few people would show up, but by the 7:00 PM starting time, he was disappointed to find that the chairs were all taken and there were even a few people leaning against the walls along the sides of the room. There were a few quiet interchanges of small talk, but not many.

"Uh, let me get your attention," Osgood began.

The room grew completely quiet, which somewhat startled the Mayor, since at previous town meetings he had struggled to attain that goal. He smiled nervously as he scanned the small crowd seated before him.

"This meeting of the Caperton community is now in order."

The mayor hoped that this sounded official enough to impress the stranger who had silently slipped into the building through the back door, out of view of the audience. Mayor Osgood was acutely aware that this visitor was a big city type and would be accustomed to formality. He didn't want to embarrass the citizens of Caperton. Mostly, however he didn't want to embarrass himself. He paused for a moment to try to frame another official sounding comment to explain the purpose of the meeting.

Before the nervous mayor could continue, however, and much to his relief, a lanky man in the front row unwound his frame slowly, turning like a corkscrew as he rose, until he was half-facing the other audience members and also Ralph. By the deep tan of his arms, which protruded from his rolled-up sleeves, it was easy for any stranger who might be in the room to see that he was a farmer.

The tall man swept the cap from his head in the same graceful manner in which he had arisen from the chair, revealing unkempt black hair that was flecked with grey and was crowned by a bald spot at the back. It was Dale Tooney, who farmed a large acreage several miles to the west of Caperton, actually closer to the equally small town of Hartford. He had been a star of the basketball team back in high school, a fact which still earned him respect nearly 30 years after he graduated. Mayor Osgood had been a senior the year that Dale began high school.

"Good evening, neighbors," Dale began. "I want to get past these formalities and cut to the matter we all came to discuss."

Osgood wondered if he should rule Dale out of order. Ralph didn't know much about the *Rules of Order* for meetings, but he knew that formalities needed to be observed, at least to the extent required to prevent the meeting from dissolving into a raucous mob, with everyone trying to out-shout everyone else. But he was too nervous about trying to regain control of the meeting, so he merely gestured to the tall farmer and muttered, "Go ahead, Dale."

"Our town and the farms around it seem to be getting a lot of attention lately. A lot of unwelcome attention. You all have either heard about it or experienced it yourselves. Yeah, I know that most of you are having a tough time believing all of this, but I have enough firsthand experience to tell you straight up that it's true."

"It's got to be those city people!" Minnie Boyd growled from her chair in the back row where she sat, not to avoid attention, but to keep an eye on her neighbors, whom she didn't trust.

She stamped her old wooden cane on the floor between her orthopedic shoes. "They've come to Caperton to try and take advantage of us and we won't stand fer it!"

Ralph shot a perturbed glance at Minnie, which quieted her to a mere muttering. He dared not say much to her about her crotchety outburst; after all, she was his mother-in-law and he needed to keep peace in the family. Also, the mayor mused, she could be right, at least partly. The visitor who remained at the back of the room in the shadows next to the small storeroom might even be here to confirm Minnie's suspicions.

Dale, a man known for getting along with everyone, acknowledged the validity of Minnie's freedom of speech.

"Could be, Minnie," he replied. "However, whatever it may be, it's doing some big-time damage to our farms and it's scaring the kids and we need to get some answers. Now, you all know I'm not the violent type, and I don't even care too much for hunting, except an occasional pheasant, but I have a shotgun and I have had about all I can stand, so if we don't get some answers, I may blow me up someone or something."

Even as he said this, he chuckled to himself. He knew that nobody in the room really believed he could perform such an act. They all must think he was exaggerating for effect. If only his neighbors knew the truth, they would be shocked.

Dale glanced at Jim Higgs, another farmer, in the front row, who gave him a nodding acknowledgment. Dale's threat seemed all the more serious, given the steady monotone in which it was delivered. A low murmur began to spread around the dimly lit room. Satisfied that he had made his point, Dale wound his lanky frame back down onto his chair.

Osgood knew that he should say something, but he couldn't think of any mayoral sounding statement that he could use to regain control of the meeting. Before he could do more than stammer a few incomplete phrases, the stranger emerged from the shadows and strode confidently along the space between the folding chairs and the concrete block wall and stopped at the front of the room, a few feet to Ralph's right.

He held up one hand, his first finger extended, until calmness returned. His face held just a brief hint of a smile, his eyes closed slightly as though he were staring into the glare of some car's high beam headlights, rather than the 60-watt light bulb that hung naked from the ceiling on a length of partly frayed electrical wire. He was wearing a tailored, dark blue three-piece suit, despite the heat and humidity. He removed his wire-rimmed glasses and put them in his inside coat pocket. He ran his hand over his forehead, brushing an errant lock of hair back into place along his receding hairline. He turned first to the left, then to the right, finally stopping to face the mayor.

"Let me introduce myself. I am Dr. George Huit of the Federal Rural Safety Program. I have been sent here by my superiors in Washington to speak to you loyal citizens, the backbone of our country, in regard to some recent occurrences in this area. We want to reassure you that everything is alright, that your safety is protected."

"Never heered of you!" grumbled Minnie with another stomp of her cane. "Never heered of no Federal Safety thinga-ma-callit, neither!" Ralph groaned quietly.

Dr. Huit smiled benignly, his squint intact.

"Well, we like to think that we do our job so well that most people don't need to ever hear about us. We're the ones who make sure you're drinking water is safe after a natural disaster, or even a manmade one. We certify the safety of structures after an earthquake. We're the good guys. We're a subsidiary of the Department of Homeland Security. We're on your side and we don't see the need to toot our own trumpets."

Huit knew that this small town was too far off the beaten path for anyone to dispute his claims. He smiled slightly, inwardly pleased that these yokels seemed to be accepting everything he said.

"So, what's your make of what's been happening 'round here?" Dale queried, crossing his arms and leaning back in his chair. For added emphasis, he slapped the cap back on his head.

"Well, we heard from our sources that you folks were having some problems, so I've been sent to hear from you about what you have been experiencing."

"Big city claptrap!" Minnie shouted, pounding her cane extra hard on the wooden floor. "Send some dudified fool in a three-piece suit to help and he asks us questions! WE should be the ones askin' and he durn well better have answers!"

Mayor Osgood felt he had better smooth things over with the government representative, even if Minnie was his wife's mother.

"Now, Minnie, we must show some hospitality here and treat Dr. Huit with respect."

Dr. Huit lifted one hand, palm out, and waved it gently toward Ralph.

"That's alright, Mayor. Minnie has a legitimate concern. I simply wanted to let you people know that we will listen to your complaints and not just rush in with predetermined answers that don't always fit the situation. You people are what this country is all about and we people in Washington need to pay attention to your concerns."

And then divert your attention to something else, he thought to himself, his smile curling a bit more at the edges of his mouth.

"Well...then, we'll tell ya, Doc," Dale responded, unfolding his arms and leaning forward intently with his hands on his knees. He turned his head to stare directly at Huit. He squinted his eyes in response to Huit's squint, but Dale's expression conveyed contempt, not interest.

"We've had our crops damaged and our livestock slaughtered in very mysterious ways. We wake up in the morning and find burned areas in our fields. We figured it was teenagers, but we ain't found no footprints."

"Give it to 'im!" Minnie interjected, for once not stomping her cane for emphasis. Ralph put one hand over his eyes and groaned softly, again.

"What we want to know is, what is causing all this? Is something or someone zapping our cattle and crops with laser beams? Are Army copters landing in our fields? Are big city gangs tryin' to scare us poor country hicks?" Dale's last word dripped with sarcasm.

"Wait, Dale!" sounded a high-pitched voice from the back row. "What about the lights in the sky? Huh? Be sure to ask about the lights in the sky!"

It was Peter Lapley, known to all as "Petey," commonly considered the town fool, a consensus opinion that no one felt the need to debate. He also doubled as the town drunk. It was a small town.

"Well, that's right, Doc," Dale continued. I didn't think we needed to bring that up, since they don't seem to do us no harm, but..."

"Yes they do, yes they sure do!" interrupted Petey. "They scare me, and I don't like it."

Dale shot Petey a dismissive glance and continued. "As I was saying, these lights have been seen flashing across the sky, mostly at two or three in the morning. I ain't seen them, but Petey here sees 'em when he stumbles over a rock or his own feet and lands face up in his yard after a night out."

This comment resulted in a short burst of snickering from the townspeople, but this was a serious meeting and it died down quickly. Petey took no offense. He just looked bewildered.

"I have seen the lights," observed Mary McGee, who had been sitting stiffly in the second row. "I was up with my six-year-old, who had the flu, about a month ago. I happened to glance out her bedroom window, just to see if my ten-year-old had put his bike back in the shed. He's always leaving it in the driveway and my husband gets so angry about that. He says he gets a bad headache from it. All at once I saw something that looked like a star or planet, a brightly lit circle in the sky. But it was different. It was moving from west to east, then it suddenly stopped, held still for a full minute or so, then moved back to the west. Then, it began to go real fast and just, well, it just vanished!"

"See? I told you so!" squeaked Petey. "Didn't I tell you? I'm not crazy!"

Dr. Huit had been standing with his hands in the pockets of his suit coat. Now he pulled out his right hand and began to slowly stroke his chin.

"I see," he said thoughtfully. "This does seem to be unusual. Does anyone else have anything on the lights?"

A well-dressed man in the front row had been listening intently all evening. He straightened his necktie, raised his right hand as if volunteering, and rose to his feet without being called on, though it required three tries for him to do so. He buttoned his suit coat as if this would restrain the prodigious paunch that overlapped his belt. With his left hand he brushed back his thinning mixture of gray and blond hair and then clasped both hands behind his back. He jutted his chin forward with an air of superiority that was somehow additionally stressed by his long, ski-slope nose.

"Dr. Huit, I am Reverend Alvin Selkirk, Minister of the local True Faith Believers Church. Many of those present are my parishioners. Most are, actually. You will excuse me if I emphasize at this point that we are a God-fearing community. We do not put our faith in the government; only the Good Lord can deliver us from evil and He will do so in His own good time. We did not ask for your help. We did not ask that you come here."

He paused and peered over the top of his glasses at Ralph, since he suspected that Ralph had actually asked for help.

"If there is turmoil in our land, we must bear it and if tribulations issue forth, we must repent and pray for deliverance."

As he slumped back into his chair, he grunted, "It is a pity that we did not open with a word of prayer this evening." He raised one eyebrow and again peered momentarily at the mayor, who seemed to be cowed.

"I asked that Dr. Huit come here," Osgood confessed defensively. "I'm sorry about the prayer matter, Reverend. My mistake. You are quite right."

No use in getting on the bad side of both Minnie and the Lord the same night, he reasoned. *The Lord* was Ralph's secret nickname for Selkirk. He smirked to himself. He wouldn't ever dare to say it out loud.

"Actually, ladies and gentlemen, our agency has been aware of your situation for some time," Huit offered. "We were only too glad to accept your mayor's kind invitation. You see, what you people have been experiencing has sometimes led to panic in less sophisticated areas of this country. We knew that you would not be as superstitious as others, but we wanted to be sure you had a clear understanding of what's going on here."

"Superstition is the devil's playing field," the seated minister sighed, adjusting the glasses perched on his bulbous nose. He glared at Huit over the rim.

"We totally agree," responded Huit, striking the air with his raised right hand. "So, let me resolve your worries by letting you in on what's been happening."

At this point, Dr. Huit walked to the rear of the room, once again edging along the narrow pathway between the folding chairs and the wall. Two farmers who had been leaning against the wall scurried out of his path. The audience turned their heads to follow him. He stepped through the rear door, holding it open with his right heel as he retrieved a tripod on which was perched a flipchart bearing an official looking government emblem in the middle of the first page.

He edged his way back to the front of the room, again displacing the two men, who tried to flatten themselves against the concrete block wall to make room for him as he dragged the tripod along behind him. He set it down next to the perplexed mayor and smiled with his usual squint. Reaching into his vest pocket, he pulled out what appeared to be a ballpoint pen. However, with a flick of his wrist, the pen extended to become a pointer.

Huit glanced once at the audience before flipping over the first sheet of the tripod. On the next page was the picture of a squat-appearing metallic object, with what seemed to be very abbreviated wings and a small glass canopy.

With the tap of the pointer and an upward snap of his jaw, Huit proclaimed, "This is the TS 824 experimental warplane, the highest tech military machine in our arsenal, the best hope of our future defense. It flies at amazing speeds, can hover in mid-air and is totally silent. It is equipped with stealth technology. It has all the latest weaponry, including some still experimental proton beam guns."

Huit glanced around the room to see if everyone was

accepting this information.

"Is this what I saw?" asked Mary McGee.

"I believe it is, ma'am," Dr. Huit responded. "The government had been testing the TS 824 and a renegade pilot stole it and has apparently crashed it in a local farm field. We have been trying to locate it for a couple of weeks now, but it has a masking capability that is designed to make it almost invisible."

"What does that have to do with the crops and spooked cattle?" Dale asked pointedly.

"That's right!" squealed Petey, leaping to his feet. He looked around sheepishly and quietly sat down again. He often spoke up at inappropriate times, and after he spoke he worried if this was another one of those times.

"For that, we apologize," Huit replied. "The traitor apparently tried some target practice in this area before he crashed the plane. Don't worry about it. The government will fully reimburse all legitimate damage claims. Very generously, in fact. In return, we ask only that you agree to keep this all very hush-hush. The payments will need to be in cash, to avoid unwanted publicity."

Some members of the audience stirred restlessly. Reverend Selkirk spat out, "Money is the root of all evil, my friends! Don't be tempted!"

"I believe the actual warning is 'Love of money is the root of all evil'. Money itself isn't evil," Huit said with a smile that bordered on a smirk. Selkirk sniffed with contempt.

"How do we know it won't happen again?" queried Dale skeptically.

"How? How? How do we know?" Petey was once again on his feet, bobbing up and down with each syllable he spoke.

"And what in truckleberries is in it fer the rest of us, the ones who don't have farms?" Minnie added, once again stomping her cane for emphasis.

Ralph Osgood had moved away from Huit, having given up any pretense of being in charge of the meeting. He stood in the shelter of the old rusty jail cell, which had not been used in decades, and chewed nervously at his fingernails as he followed the discussion.

If he wondered what a truckleberry might be, Huit didn't give any indication. "Well, we have considered that. We will be working with your city administration to devise a way to help your community recover from this. If that means we would pay for some community improvements or some monetary compensation for emotional trauma, we would find that to be only fair."

"The water pump at the top of Main Hill could stand replacing," suggested Joe Paige, owner of the town's only tavern and also the Water Commissioner.

"We could maybe repave the streets and put up official street signs," added Judy DePriest, Street Commissioner. "Of course, we would need to name the streets first..."

Not to be outdone, Town Marshall Carl Johnson, added, "It would be awful nice to have a new patrol car and not have to use my old Chevy. It just isn't much good for police type work. Its muffler is so noisy, I really ought to give myself a ticket!"

Carl was noted more for his wit than his law enforcement skills, but in Caperton there was more opportunity to employ the former than the latter. Carl chuckled at his own joke, then cut it short as an idea lit up his face.

"Maybe we could even hire a deputy or two, so I could maybe take a vacation sometime. Then I could spend more time with my boy Cody."

"Yer an idiot, Carl!" Minnie spat. "You wouldn't know a criminal if he pulled out a shotgun and robbed you in broad daylight."

Minnie didn't really dislike Carl, but she still held a grudge against his grandmother who had at one time stolen her fiancé, several decades ago. There wasn't much wealth or valuable property in Caperton, but grudges could be passed down from generation to generation. Minnie was a one-person conservation corps when it came to preserving animosity.

A low murmur began to spread in the room as people started to discuss other ideas of how the town could use any money the federal government gave to them.

"My friends," he began, "we must not bicker. We are all God's children…" The minister began to rise again from his chair with much more difficulty than previously; he actually threw himself forward and then tried to regain his balance before he fell; that is why he sat in the front row.

Suddenly the door at the front of the building crashed open. All eyes turned immediately in that direction. Reverend Selkirk froze in his half-risen state. Mary McGee gasped involuntarily. Mayor Osgood backed up against the bars of the jail cell.

Dr. Huit, despite the suddenness of the occurrence, maintained his cool demeanor as he turned slowly to face the open door.

For a few seconds nothing happened. The blackness of the night outside seemed to be crowding into the room. Carl Johnson edged his right hand down to his hip and tapped his fingers nervously on the butt of his ancient revolver which had been passed down from the previous marshal, who had received it from his predecessor and so forth. Its exact age was unknown.

The sound of metal scraping upon metal broke the silence. Then came a call from the darkened doorway. "Someone come and give me a hand."

The townspeople relaxed in unison, Reverend Selkirk collapsing heavily back into his chair. Carl removed his hand from his holster.

"Why can't this town get with the times and install a ramp?" demanded the voice from the doorway.

Carl and Dale sprang into action and quickly edged along the wall until they reached the open door. Both stepped out into the dark and returned immediately, hauling and tugging at a wheelchair, its occupant clutching tightly to its armrests, his thin lips squeezed together, his face wearing an impatient frown.

"It's Paul, it's Paul!" Petey sang out from the back of the room, again bouncing up and down with each word.

"Idiot..." Minnie muttered in Petey's direction.

After awkwardly maneuvering the chair through the doorway, Carl and Dale set it down carefully in the front of the room, a few feet from Huit. Paul Sloan, its occupant, shook his upper body vigorously to straighten his clothing before reaching down to wheel himself closer to the tripod displaying the picture of the experimental aircraft.

Ralph released his grip on a jail cell bar, which he had been clutching to counter an urge to flee the building and stepped out from the shadows. Now that he knew it was Paul Sloan, he felt at ease enough to resume his mayoral responsibilities.

"Dr. Huit, let me introduce Mr. Paul Sloan. He's certainly one of our leading citizens and has had experience with experimental aircraft. Paul, this is Dr. George Huit from Washington, D.C."

Ralph's renewed presence of mind did not stretch far enough for him to recall the name of Dr. Huit's agency. Paul ignored the mayor's inaccurate description of what he had done while in the Army.

"From the Federal Rural Safety Program," Huit offered as he extended his right hand toward Paul.

Paul cocked his head to the right, like a curious parrot, and eyed the man from Washington. He took the offered hand and gripped it with a firmness that Huit felt was somewhat hostile. Only Paul's winning smile, for which he was known in the community, diluted this first, negative impression.

"Sorry I'm late, folks," Paul began with an upward thrust of his jaw. His smile widened with a warmth known to everyone present with the exception of the federal bureaucrat. "Had some trouble with my van. Engine trouble." He emphasized these final two words with a jerk of his head to the left, in the direction of Dr. Huit.

George Huit didn't miss the obvious reference to himself, though he had no idea what Paul Sloan might mean. Paul gave the right wheel of his chair a quick push forward and spun around to face Huit. Placing both hands on the chair's armrests, he pushed himself into a fully upright sitting posture. He stared directly at Huit.

"I've been listening at the door for a few minutes. I heard the 'explanation' you tried to sell these people. It's just not the truth. I know it and you know it. On the way here tonight, I was followed..."

Petey shouted out, "By who?"

"Not a *who*, a *what*. Something flying. It sped up when I did, it hovered over my van when I stopped. Then, my engine died. I opened the door to the van and leaned out. Above me was something that didn't at all resemble your photo here."

Paul gestured toward the tripod. "I watched it for a minute, and it watched me. Then, it started moving away and suddenly just disappeared. It's what Mary McGee saw. I believe it's also been spooking livestock and leaving strange patterns in the fields. It's not any TS 824."

Paul's demeanor changed into contempt as he glared at Huit. Then, he continued. "Friends, what we have here is a genuine UFO."

As the citizens of Caperton were meeting in the town hall, not all was as usual in the small town. Just four blocks away. which was actually halfway across town, three small figures huddled in the protective cover of darkness behind the McGees' garage. They felt safely out of sight there, since the rear of the garage bordered on a corn field at the edge of the village.

"Your dad didn't see you sneak out?" asked Joey Paige in a loud whisper.

"No way!" Doug McGee replied with some irritation. "Can't you ever speak in a quiet voice?"

Lindsay DePriest tugged her baseball cap lower on her forehead and punched Joey in the shoulder. "Doug's right. Shut up. Let's go."

She crouched down low and led the way, single file, as the three moved from the shadow of the garage to the fence that divided the McGee's property from the farmland belonging to Calvin Dunn.

"Forgot my flashlight!" Joey blurted out, nearly in his normal loud speaking voice. He briefly rummaged through the contents of the backpack he carried with him. It was filled mostly with candy and chips from his father's bar.

When his fingers touched something metallic he excitedly seized it and pulled out a cell phone. He punched an icon and turned on its flashlight; a bright beam lit up the weeded area at the base of one of the fence posts.

Both Doug and Lindsay shouted at him to turn off the light, so he switched it off. But he instead swiped the screen to bring up the photo option and held it over his head; a touch of his finger resulted in a small, but bright flash that lit up the annoyed faces of the two other kids.

Doug felt like shoving Joey, but merely crouched lower and glanced back at the rear of the house. His father had looked in at his room and said goodnight to what he thought was his sleepy son. What Darrell McGee didn't realize was that Doug was still fully dressed under the covers. His mother would have suspected something, but his father was too tired to take the energy to do anything more than open the door a few inches to offer a perfunctory goodnight wish.

As soon as his father went back downstairs, Doug had padded a couple pillows into place under the blanket in an approximation of the shape of a sleeping ten-year-old boy and then climbed out his bedroom window and edged down the back porch roof, which left him only a short drop to the ground. By the time he had tiptoed to the back of the garage, Joey and Lindsay were already waiting for him.

They only paused briefly on their mission when they had to pick up Joey when he clumsily tripped over a broken stalk that lay across their narrow path. Joey's reputation for clumsiness was well-deserved.

After two minutes of nearly silent progress, with just the rustling of the stalks of corn in the slight breeze, Lindsay slowed to a halt, holding her arms away from her sides, palms turned back, a signal for the boys to halt behind her.

Doug readily froze in his tracks. Joey, watching the dirt path at his feet, crashed into his companions, knocking all three to the ground and simultaneously breaking off some of the cornstalks. He dropped the cell phone he was carrying in his right hand, and hastily crawled on all fours to retrieve it. He rose to his feet and spun around, but bumped into Doug, who was intent on following Lindsay's lead.

"You idiot!" Doug snapped, punching Joey in the shoulder.

Joey showed no emotional response to this insult. Having a chance to get out of his house with other kids was a rare occurrence that he didn't want to spoil by taking offense at anything Doug might say.

Lindsay ignored the boys as she kneeled on one knee between the rows. "Quiet! Now!" she hissed.

Taking for granted that her word was law within the small group, she pushed herself to her feet and pointed wordlessly in the same direction they had been heading.

"There!"

Doug shoved Joey to get his pudgy friend's body off his legs. "You weigh a ton, Paige!" he gasped as he gave one more shove.

Joey rolled away, this time bumping over some cornstalks on the other side of the dirt path between the corn rows. Some of his candy and a few gumballs escaped from his bag and rolled up to a stalk of corn. Joey quickly dived after them and hurriedly shoved them into his jean pockets.

"Put that cell phone away!" Doug hissed. Joey tried to do so, but his jean pockets were tight and now were full of candy and gum, so he just continued to hold it.

"There!" Lindsay repeated, even more insistently. The boys scrambled up beside her.

"I don't see nothing'...." Joey muttered, barely suppressing a yawn.

Lindsay frowned, fighting an urge to correct her pudgy friend's grammar. Instead, she took a breath and frantically waved her right hand toward the clearing just beyond the cornfield. "Look!"

As Joey bent to dust the dirt from his jeans, his two companions squinted into the darkness ahead.

"Ripped a hole in my jeans..." he mumbled, bending over to get a good look at the tear and probing it with one finger. He momentarily lost his façade of calmness. "And this thing on the back of my neck hurts!"

He rubbed a sore at the base of his skull. "All your fault, McGee. You knocked me down on a rock. Dad'll really yell at me for this."

Doug ignored Joey, as he often did. Joey was always complaining and blaming other people for his problems. Sometimes he was such a nuisance that Doug wondered why he even put up with him. But, in a town as small as Caperton, there weren't a lot of choices for friends.

Lindsay had been his friend since Kindergarten. She was always willing to play catch or shoot baskets, so among the boys of the town she was "just one of the guys". And she was a real take charge person. Doug appreciated her friendship, though he occasionally found her to be a bit overbearing.

Lindsay shot her right arm out and grabbed Doug by the elbow, digging her fingernails into his skin. It was all he could do to avoid screaming in pain. She pulled him forward to a spot beside her. Doug was about to pull free of her grip when he saw the light.

Just like the first time the three had done this, there was something glowing in the sky over Calvin Dunn's farmhouse.

Just as before, it was moving about erratically. Once again, it seemed at first to be heading directly for the trio. All three dove to the ground, even Joey, who had at last followed Lindsay's pointing finger.

"D'ya think it will stop in the field this time?" Joey pondered aloud.

Doug didn't bother to shove Joey this time. "Watch!" he shot back.

The light seemed to grow larger as it zigzagged in the direction of the three children. As it came closer, the three could at last discern that there was a solid object within the light, but they couldn't tell precisely what it was. Just when the kids were certain it was chasing after them, it veered away at the last moment and instead circled back toward the farmhouse, coming in low and close to the building.

The three were now flat on their stomachs, well hidden in the corn, watching the scene through the drooping cornstalks. Blue and orange flashing lights alternated with the yellow and red ones the youngsters had already observed. Despite the object's movements, there was no detectable sound. The three children instinctively held their breaths.

Joey broke the silence.

"What...do...you...think...it...will...do?"

He enunciated each word as if speaking slowly and clearly would make his voice sound softer and thus placate his friends. Lindsay punched him in the shoulder, anyway.

Doug's eyes were fixed on the object. This was the greatest adventure he had ever experienced, so he was determined to take in every detail. The three had been coming out to this cornfield about once a week since Lindsay had first noticed the object. She had told her parents, but they only laughed at her and said it was just a helicopter or star or airplane, then told her not to trespass on Mr. Dunn's property.

For that reason, the three had resorted to secrecy. Lindsay was the naturally curious type. She was a straight A student who sometimes exasperated teachers with her constant questions and irritated her classmates with her serious demeanor and disinterest in the minutiae of daily life. She didn't have a lot of friends, but she didn't see the need for them. She was just determined to do her own thing and didn't care what anyone thought of her.

Joey was along mostly for the companionship. He was an only child of a single father, who spent most of his days running the family business, Paige's Tavern. This left Joey on his own at home, a small four room frame house a block east of the tavern. He had television and an old video game. His father supplied him with a wide array of snacks, which he purchased in bulk from the company that supplied the tavern. Consequently, Joey was both lonely and a bit overweight. His social skills weren't well developed.

When Doug told him about the lights and asked him to come along that first time, Joey was more than ready, both for some adventure and the chance to bring along a supply of candy and chips from his father's business. All this exercise would make them hungry, he reasoned, and he would have a chance to both solidify his friendships and to pig out.

For Lindsay, and almost simultaneously for Doug, their hiding place among the corn rows suddenly seemed very inadequate. Neither could get a really clear view of what was happening after the object descended toward the farmhouse. The barn partially obscured their vision.

Joey, however, was busy sorting through the candy and chips in his backpack. He wasn't clear on why Doug and Lindsay suddenly got to their feet and began moving forward.

He was puzzled but was able to completely unwrap one candy bar before lurching to his feet and stumbling after them. He dropped the wrapper to the ground—something Lindsay would never do because she valued the environment and something Doug would never do around Lindsay, since he was afraid she would punch him and, even worse, launch into one of her twenty-minute lectures about taking care of the planet.

The cornfield sloped down gently from that point before rising again to form a crest on the far side of the field, near the farmhouse, which was set atop the rise. Lindsay and Doug shuffled down to the low point of the field and were already on their way up the other side before Joey could reach the dip.

For a few moments, the ridge blocked their view of the light emanating from the object. By the time Joey could catch up with his friends at the top of the rise, they were again on their stomachs in the midst of some tall weeds near Dunn's apple orchard, gaping in wonder at the sight before them.

Joey glanced up, fell to his knees, the strap of his backpack slipping through his fingers and spilling an assortment of Baby Ruths, Ding Dongs and Doritos into a rut left by the farmer's tractor. The half-eaten Hershey bar in his mouth was dissolving and began dripping down his chin onto Lindsay's baseball cap as she sprawled in awe just in front of him. She didn't notice.

"My god!" Doug exclaimed even louder than Joey's previous whispers, temporarily forgetting his mother's command to never swear.

A large, roundish, metallic looking object, almost as big around as the farmhouse itself, was suspended motionlessly above Dunn's barn. From underneath it there suddenly and soundlessly flashed a beam of pale green light, which reached out through the darkness to anchor itself at the other end to an upstairs window of the house.

A small black slit appeared at the origin point of the light.

"Wh...what is th...that?" Lindsay stuttered in a chilled whisper.

"There's somebody in that light!" Doug exclaimed in a squeaky voice that surprised even him.

"They're coming down the light like it's a ladder!" Joey sputtered as drops of chocolate colored spit splattered against the back of Lindsay's left shoulder.

"More like an escalator..." Doug corrected.

A corner of the barn and a large oak tree next to the house blocked their view of the full light beam. They could see what appeared to be three or four small figures moving effortlessly, floating downward in the silver light, but the edge of the barn kept them from seeing exactly what was happening as they approached the house.

Within moments the small figures had reversed their direction, emerging once again into view. They were now rising toward the hovering object, but they were accompanied by a much taller figure, who slumped between them.

Joey figured this was his chance, so he stood up and took a photo. Lindsay gasped and Doug groaned, "Get down, you lunkhead!" Joey complied, dropping to both knees behind Doug.

As the figures vanished into the same slot from which they had earlier exited, the beam quickly pulled back into the same opening and the slot zipped shut. The object dipped lower on one side and then began to glide silently in the direction of the three observers.

Doug jumped to his feet and spun around to run, gasping, "Let's get out of here!", but he immediately tripped over the kneeling Joey and both collapsed into the weeds. Joey again dropped his cell phone but scrambled to pick it up.

Lindsay, despite her usual cool demeanor, also felt a surge of panic, but she had the presence of mind to grab each of her friends by their clothing, Joey by his shirt collar, Doug by his right shirtsleeve, and yanked them both to their feet. She gave them both a shove in the direction of the cornfield, then joined them in a mad dash for shelter amid the stalks.

There was a sudden flash of light that seemed to physically knock the three off their feet. Lindsay felt herself flying through the air until her body smacked into a row of corn, mowing down several stalks. Doug was lifted into the air and then slammed down into a clearing somewhere in the middle of the cornfield. He rolled over and over until his body bounced off something large and solid. His last thought before he closed his eyes was that he had been thrown against a tree stump.

Joey had just managed to reach the fence when he felt himself lifted up. The cell phone flew from his grasp and landed just beyond Dunn's property in the overgrown weeds at the base of a fence post. Then he felt nothing.

Time passed. Doug opened his eyes. The morning sunlight seemed somehow very unpleasant to him. He found that he was in his bedroom, tucked in with a pile of pillows. He had a vague, uneasy feeling that something disturbing had happened, but he couldn't quite recall what.

He felt that the answer was just outside his grasp. He felt groggy. He remembered his plan to sneak out of the house the night before. His mind offered the explanation that he had been so tired that he had fallen asleep on his bed in the midst of arranging his escape, and he accepted that as the answer.

That explained why he was still fully dressed and was even wearing his shoes. However, it didn't explain why the shoes were muddy. He stared at his right shoe for a couple seconds and shrugged. Then, he stood up and wiped the mud on the bottom edge of his dresser.

"Doug! Lindsay's here to see you. Aren't you up yet? It's nearly ten o'clock."

Fifteen minutes later Doug and Lindsay were on their way to the Good Buy grocery store, which was located on the south edge of town, along the blacktop road that edged the north side of Mr. Dunn's farm. Mary McGee had given them some money to buy her a gallon of milk. She had told them they could use some of the change from the ten-dollar bill she gave them to buy themselves a treat of their choosing, so the two ten-year-olds set out cheerfully.

"Did you see the ballgame on TV last night?" asked Lindsay. The two shared an interest in their favorite team, the Cubs.

Doug answered without pausing, "Yep. Good game." Then

slowing his pace a little, he tried to recall who won. His mind was strangely blank.

"I think I must have gone to bed early," Lindsay commented. "I can't remember what happened in the game. I asked my mother this morning how it came out and she said she didn't think the game was on TV."

"I usually watch the games with my dad," Doug responded. He halted completely and turned toward Lindsay. "It's kinda funny. I remember him telling me goodnight..."

"So, why's that strange?"

"My father doesn't usually do that. It's something my mother always does. She was gone somewhere last night but I don't remember where, or why."

Lindsay had also stopped walking. She didn't understand why Doug was so disturbed because his mother hadn't told him goodnight.

"Oh, shut up, Doug. After all, Joey Paige doesn't even have a mother to tell him goodnight and he doesn't complain."

"It's just odd, that's all. First I didn't watch the game with Dad, then I went to bed so early, then Mom didn't tell me goodnight. When I woke up, it was so late. And I think I had some sort of bad dream last night, but I can't even remember it. I'm telling' you, Lindsay, it was a weird night."

The two resumed walking. Doug crammed his hands into the pockets of his faded jeans. He checked absently to make sure the ten-dollar bill was still there.

"I don't know if I had any dreams, bad or good, last night," Lindsay resumed after a few seconds. "But it was real strange. I somehow got chunks of chocolate stuck in my hair. Look at my cap. It even has chocolate gunk all over it. I wonder how that happened. I don't even eat chocolate. I'm allergic to it."

Doug nodded, recalling that her mother always sent non-chocolate treats to school on her birthdays, but he had no theories on how the chocolate got on her cap.

The two were within sight of the small grocery store, still walking on the south side of the road, where there was no sidewalk. They were just about to cross over to the other side, where there was a sidewalk that led to the store's parking lot, when Doug happened to glance down into the grassy ditch between the road and farm field. He nudged Lindsay and pointed.

"What is it?" Lindsay queried as both edged down the slippery incline. "It looks like a bag of some sort."

Doug reached the red and yellow object first and grabbed it with his right hand, slipping the rest of the way into the ditch as he did so. Lindsay hopped the last couple feet and landed opposite her friend, seizing the bag with her left hand. A brief, though friendly, tug of war ensued.

"It's a backpack!" Lindsay asserted as she gave it a firm yank.

Doug pulled it back his way, even more assertively. "Give it here! I found it first!" He shifted his grip to one of the shoulder straps.

At this moment the flap of the backpack flipped open and a

jumble of its contents flew into the air, landing in a semicircle between the two contestants.

"Hey! Candy bars and chips!" Doug shouted triumphantly. "I hit the jackpot!"

"Shut up! It's mine, too!" Lindsay responded testily.

The two threw themselves upon the spilled goodies and rapidly scooped them into two piles, one for each of them, as they each struggled to scoop together more than the other.

"Wait, Doug," Lindsay said as she stopped gathering the contents. "Whose book bag is this? Is there a name on it? We really should return all this stuff to whoever lost it."

"Shut up, girl! We...I found it, so it's ours. I mean mine. and we..er...I'm gonna keep it."

Even as he spoke, Doug poked one foot in the direction of the empty backpack, deftly flipping it over in the grass. Lindsay bent to examine it closer.

"It's Joey Paige's," she stated with authority as she straightened back up. "I wonder how it got way out here. Let's finish our errand for your mom and then go give this back to him."

"No way!" Doug responded. But then, he flipped open the flap of the bag with his left hand and dejectedly stuffed in his armload of treats. He knew that Lindsay was right. She always was. Joey was sort of a friend and it was such a small town that he couldn't afford to make an enemy of even someone as weird as Joey.

Lindsay followed Doug's lead and dropped in her treasures, reaching down to retrieve a couple candy bars that Doug had fumbled into the weeds in his effort to stuff his armful into the bag in one smooth motion. Doug felt a tinge of embarrassment at his clumsiness.

Lindsay closed the flap and snapped it shut, looped one strap over her shoulder and started back up the incline to the road. Doug frowned and followed her. Why was she always so good and smart? He groaned to himself.

Half an hour later the pair had lugged the heavy jug of milk back to Doug's house and were on their way toward the center of town, where the Paiges lived. Lindsay was holding the brightly colored backpack in her right hand.

As they neared the small house, they noted that the old dark blue Chevrolet that belonged to town cop Carl Johnson was parked in the gravel driveway next to the house.

Joey's father was leaning into the car, apparently making some point to the town's lone law enforcement officer, whom the two young friends could now see was holding in his hand the microphone of his ancient CB radio. Carl hoped to get a modern radio or at least a cell phone, if Huit made good on his promise.

As Lindsay and Doug approached, they slowed their steps involuntarily. Joe Paige suddenly whirled away from the car to face them. Doug jumped back. Lindsay shifted the backpack to her left hand. Both stopped so suddenly that they kicked up some of the gravel.

"You two seen my boy Joey?" Paige asked plaintively. "He...he wasn't home last night when I got off work." Then noticing the red and yellow backpack, he shot out a hand to seize it. "It's his backpack! Where did you get it?"

Lindsay and Doug stammered out their brief story, the part they could remember. Carl Johnson, who had now climbed from his car to listen, then radioed to the county sheriff's office to ask for assistance in searching for Joey.

Carl then quickly herded the two children and Joe Paige into his car and jumped in. His tires spun noisily, spitting out gravel to each side and raising a cloud of dust as the car backed out of the driveway.

In only a minute the car had careened through the lazy late Saturday morning streets of Caperton. It came to a halt along the edge of the Good Buy parking lot. The kids pointed out the area of the ditch where they had found Joey's backpack.

Carl did a cursory check of the ditch, then went back and leaned against the car until, twenty minutes later, a county patrol car appeared in the distance and, after rapidly traversing the last mile of the blacktop-covered country road, came to a sudden halt facing the small-town cop and his party.

The deputy got out and Carl directed him to the spot. They spent several minutes stumbling around the edge of Mr. Dunn's cornfield. After spending a few minutes in muffled consultation, the deputy climbed up the embankment to his car and questioned Lindsay and Doug for a short time. Then he placed a call to his office at the county seat.

"Tell Sheriff Post that we have a kidnapping here in Caperton. I'm going to gather up some town people and search the area. Send some help. Bring the bloodhounds."

A couple of hours later a deputy sheriff found the Hershey Bar wrapper Joey had discarded. It wasn't clearly Joey's, but the fact that his backpack was loaded with candy and chips led the searchers to consider that it might be a clue.

When they couldn't locate Dunn at his farmhouse or anywhere in town, they put that together with the fact that Joey was missing and Sheriff Post declared Mr. Dunn to be a "person of interest."

Dunn was rather quiet and reclusive, even more so since his wife had taken their daughter and left him a few months ago. Though they had no proof or motive, the working hypothesis was that Dunn had kidnapped Joey. During the next few weeks, no additional clues were uncovered concerning the whereabouts of either.

Joey was gone.

Chapter Three: Pseudocyesis

Ty Williamson sat in his favorite booth by the window at the Bluebird Café in downtown Millardville, sipping a cup of coffee. It was Thursday morning, and his office was closed. He glanced at his watch and at the nearby front door of the small eatery. Wally was late, as usual. Renee, the waitress, hovered nearby, awaiting Wally's appearance. Business was slow and she knew the two doctors always met at the small café on Thursday mornings.

Dr. Wallace Hunter was Ty's closest friend. They had gone to medical school together in Spring City and had kept in close contact throughout their subsequent internships and residencies. They had even married women who were cousins to one another. Wally had met Cheryl at the wedding of Ty and Dana.

After five years of marriage, Cheryl gave up on Wally's disorganized ways and divorced him. Shortly after that, Dana's pursuit of a journalism career took her to another state, but Ty's practice in Millardville was already established. They tried a long-distance marriage for a while but knew from the start that it would be a challenge.

Eventually, Dana's skill as a reporter took her up the ranks and she landed a job at the main office of NBC. A couple of years later she was investigating a mysterious event in the Rocky Mountains, in which an entire village had vanished and she herself disappeared. Ty rushed out to the site where she was last seen, but no one could find her.

After a couple of years, he just had to accept that she was gone, probably forever. He threw himself into his medical practice. He continued to keep their wedding photo on his office desk.

After his divorce, Wally moved his practice to Millardville and found an office a couple of blocks from Ty. Wally did his best to help his friend adjust to life without Dana, but only time gradually eased Ty's pain.

Ty and Wally met every Thursday for coffee and, to deliberately avoid the stereotype, played basketball at the Y, rather than golf out at the Tall Oaks Country Club on the edge of Millardville. Wally didn't have the patience for golf.

If only they could have pursued the same medical specialties, they would have made a great team, Ty often speculated. But Wally had decided to become an obstetrician and Ty had gone into family practice. They occasionally had patients in common but adhered to strict rules of patient confidentiality unless their patients specifically requested that they share medical information.

Today's rendezvous at the Bluebird was not totally casual. Wally had phoned Ty to ask if he would mind including some professional discussion on this particular Thursday. This was totally against their unwritten agreement to avoid such discussion, but Wally had been so insistent that Ty had finally relented.

At last, the bell on the door jingled cheerily as Wally pushed through it. Even as Renee, buoyant as usual, rushed up to take his order, Wally veered to the left and plopped down in a chair at Ty's table. Renee scurried after him, pen and order pad in hand, but Wally waved her off with a gruff "the usual" and leaned forward in his chair, palms flat on the table. Renee smiled fetchingly at him, but he didn't notice.

"So, what's up, ol' buddy? You seem a bit..." Ty began.

Wally cut him off abruptly. "It's one of my patients, Ty. There's something unusual going on and I want your input."

Wally ran his right hand across his forehead, pushing back the unruly lock of hair that was always falling over his eyes. This had become a nervous habit and Ty recognized it as a sign that his friend had a serious concern.

"That bad, huh?" Ty quipped. Ty recalled the same intensity when Wally had first talked to him about Cheryl's request for a divorce.

"Well, it's got me stumped, Ty. This patient has been a regular of mine. She's had two previous pregnancies, both miscarriages. Now she is finally getting close to the delivery date. Everything has been fine. Baby seems to be quite robust; mother is in excellent shape."

"So, what's the problem, then?"

"She, the mother, has started complaining of strange feelings. She says there is a nearly constant buzzing in her head and that it feels like her eyes are on fire. She's become very agitated, grabbing her head, moving her hands all around as though she's trying to keep it from exploding..."

Upon hearing Wally's description of the symptoms, Ty's demeanor immediately changed. His look of calm tolerance of his friend slipped from his face and was replaced with increasingly intense concern as Ty digested his friend's statements. He had been leaning casually back in his chair, but shifted forward and leaned toward Wally, bumping his coffee cup with his left elbow.

Ever-alert, Renee rushed over with a cloth to wipe up the

spilled coffee, and then refilled the cup. Ty's lips squeezed tightly together, his eyes squinted, he fastened his complete attention on his friend.

"What's the matter, buddy?" Wally asked, leaning back in his own chair as if expecting Ty to attack him.

Ty took a couple seconds to respond, clenching his jaws, which Wally had seen him do many times when he was contemplating difficult matters.

"Does this patient have a symmetrical, triangular impression at the base of her skull?"

Wally nodded. "That's caused me the most concern. She says she doesn't know how it got there. She's also extremely tired, despite adequate sleep. She's taking the vitamins I prescribed. Have you ever seen anything like these symptoms?"

"Dunbar," Ty muttered to himself. "and the other guy."

"Other guy? Are they patients of yours? Were you able to come up with a diagnosis or treatment?"

"No. Identical symptoms to one another and seems like this pregnancy patient of yours may have the same thing. I couldn't get the walk-in guy to tell me anything, but he did look vaguely familiar..."

Wally put his hands on the edge of the table and pushed himself to a standing position. He reached into his hip pocket and pulled out his wallet, extracting a few bills, which he dropped on the table.

"Let's go," he said. "We need to do some research on this condition."

Ty glanced briefly at the wallet his friend held, since usually Wally wouldn't have any cash and Ty would need to pay. The wallet was flipped open to the photo section. Ty reached out suddenly, blocking Wally's effort to close the wallet. Ty pointed to an old, creased photo from his friend's wedding that Wally had laminated and kept in remembrance of a happier time.

Ty seized the wallet and held the photo up to Wally's face.

"It was this guy!" He pointed at the first of the photos.

"That's Cheryl's brother, Jay," Wally said, following Ty's finger to one of the four groomsmen lined up behind Wally in the photo. "You met him at the wedding."

"Well, I haven't seen him for years," Ty explained a bit defensively, "but I am certain it's the same guy. He came into my office a few days ago without an appointment. He had shorter hair with a bit of gray in it, but I'm sure it's him." Ty shoved the wallet back into Wally's hands and turned toward the door.

Wally obediently followed his friend out the door as Renee swooped down upon the deserted table. Snatching up the small clump of bills, she gave the door a quizzical glance as she began clearing away the untouched cups. As usual, she smiled as Wally rushed past her.

Laurine Fraley awoke early the morning after Deke's experience at the warehouse and immediately eased her slender body out from under the single blanket on her bed, as she did every morning. Before her bare feet slid into her well-worn slippers, she realized that she hadn't heard Deke return home after his nighttime shift.

She worried about her son and the dangers he could possibly encounter while patrolling those warehouses. Who knew when some total lunatic might decide to cause trouble? Someone had tried to burn down the library a couple of months ago and there were those recent farm vandalism incidents. The world wasn't safe anymore.

Laurine padded down the hallway, her steps so light that not a board in the old floor even squeaked or groaned. Just as she raised her hand to rap on her son's door, she heard a sound from within. It sounded like Deke's voice, but a bit muffled. He seemed to be mumbling something over and over.

Laurine quietly turned the doorknob and pushed the door open a couple of inches. She didn't even need to strain to hear her son's words, which were quiet, but clear.

"No! No! Please don't! Stop! Take me home!" he pleaded.

Laurine edged the door open a bit more until she could see her son, who was propped up at the head of his bed, his eyes tightly closed. Her usually pale complexion faded nearly to white as she realized her son was in big trouble.

Deke had his hands clasped over his ears, but suddenly moved them to the back of his skull, then to his eyes. Without hesitation, she decided to seek medical attention for her son.

Twenty minutes later, Deke sat stiffly in the chair of the waiting room while his mother conferred with the nurse on duty in the Millardville Memorial Medical Center emergency room.

His head still buzzed. His neck hurt and his stomach felt bloated. He had not felt this ill in years, which is why he hadn't resisted when Laurine insisted on taking him to the hospital. Dr. Williamson's office was closed on Thursdays and Deke agreed that he couldn't wait any longer to seek medical help. He didn't know if he could take it any longer.

The ER physician finished examining a teenager who had broken his arm jumping from a freight train on which he had hitched a ride.

"Kids!" He muttered to himself as he approached Deke, his brow appropriately furrowed to indicate concern.

"I'm Dr. Garris," announced the heavyset, balding physician. "What seems to be your problem today, young man?"

Deke ordinarily would have resented being called "young man." He was, after all, out of high school and working fulltime. However, he felt so terrible that he didn't even think about taking offense at the remark as he would have if he had felt better. A wave of nausea curled its way upward from his intestinal tract as he hunched forward and clutched his arms around his knees. He started to speak but changed his mind. He feared he would vomit if he opened his mouth even an inch.

"He seems to have some form of flu, Dr. Garris," the nurse volunteered, seeing that Deke couldn't or wouldn't respond. Laurine gently placed a hand on her son's shoulder and nodded in agreement.

Following a cursory examination of Deke, Dr. Garris emerged from the curtained partition within which his patient now reclined on a hospital bed. His original look of concern had never left his face.

"Mrs. Fraley, I want to admit your son for observation and further testing. I don't quite know what he has, but the symptoms don't match with any flu symptoms I have ever encountered. All he was able to tell me was that he had been taken for a ride that was very fast and *jerky* to use his term. I'm especially concerned about the buzzing he reports in his head and the triangular impression on the back of his neck, just below the skull. He seems unable to focus his eyes. It could be an infection from some sort of insect bite. We may need to bring in a neurologist to do some further tests."

Laurine smiled weakly. She was somewhat confused about the ride Deke had reported, since Deke had no close friends who would have offered him a ride. She followed the gurney that transported her son to the second floor of the hospital where a small room awaited the new patient.

In spite of her increasing joy at the thought of having a baby, Kathy Fellner had been feeling ill. Her entire pregnancy had gone smoothly, and, in fact, she had never felt so alive and energetic. Then, without any warning, she had awakened one morning with an uncomfortable stiffness in her neck and the vague sensation of a low humming sound that she seemed to hear from inside her head.

But more than her physical discomfort, Kathy felt herself somehow weighed down by a heavy emotional burden. She just couldn't figure out why, but she felt deeply depressed and fearful.

Dr. Hunter had told her to expect emotional ups and downs, but now all she was feeling were the downs. Just when she had anticipated feeling in top spirits as her due date approached, she had an unshakeable sense of foreboding.

Lee Fellner shared his wife's concern, even though she hadn't voiced it. Kathy was usually quite forthright about her feelings, maybe even too forthright, Lee felt, though he told himself that was part of any marriage. During each of her previous pregnancies, she had remained reticent about her own health. Or, rather, with each pregnancy since the first one. With that one, ten years earlier, Kathy had been outgoing and talkative, obviously thrilled until that dark morning when the hemorrhaging had begun.

Then, with the passage of time and with each hope-dashing failed pregnancy, Kathy had become more and more unwilling to openly discuss the baby and how she was holding up. Lee figured it was her way of avoiding the emotional letdown of a possible miscarriage, so he accepted Kathy's quiet moods.

However, this time it had been different as the months passed and each positive report from Dr. Hunter hinted that, at long last, the couple would successfully become a family.

Lee had seen Kathy smiling at her swelling abdomen, heard her whispering to the life within. Kathy had seemed to be nearly ready to burst out with the joyfulness he had not seen for so long. Any day now, Lee told himself, I will be able to join her in this often-delayed exuberance that other couples had experienced. He and Kathy both looked forward to the time when it would seem so natural.

Now, however, Lee knew that something was wrong once again. He asked Kathy, but she wouldn't admit it. She became withdrawn and sullen. One day she seemed to be glowing internally, the next day the light seemed to be dim.

Lee even remembered the night before the change. He had slept the soundest sleep he could remember, but Kathy told him in the morning that she had had nightmares about being taken somewhere and the baby being taken from inside her body. As she revealed her dream, she burst into uncontrollable sobbing and he had been unable to console her.

Kathy had gone again to see Dr. Hunter, or Wally as most of his patients called him at his own insistence. It did seem natural since he seemed so warm and friendly. Wally had checked the baby and checked her, but he could offer only encouragement. Everything was fine, he said.

Perhaps she just had a case of jitters about the impending big event. The joy of imminent motherhood was just momentarily overshadowed by the responsibility Kathy knew would be involved. After all, Wally reminded her, she had spent ten years seeing the dark side of pregnancy, maybe she didn't realize how good it could be.

Wally's efforts to encourage her did make Kathy feel better for a few moments, but the humming sensation had not subsided, and she soon felt the darkness closing in again.

Kathy went through that Thursday mechanically, dreading every minute, hating what she found in successive visits to homes that didn't really deserve to be called homes.

Roger and Denise Cayman were living with their maternal grandmother, who fed them and clothed them, though she did neither too well, but age and arthritis seemed to have sapped her of the ability to really care for the children.

Danita Yost and her two children were living in a homeless shelter and were facing a bleak future. Andy Pendleton tried to provide for his large family, but his lack of education and borderline intellectual capabilities largely negated his best efforts and the family seemed to be in perpetual chaos.

Following the next-to-last home visit, Kathy collapsed into the driver's seat and clutched at her head. The humming was always there now. Whenever she finished a contact with a client, its presence seemed to escalate. Only one more visit and she would call it a day.

The Mayes family. Kathy's puzzlement regarding Kimmy's disappearance and sudden reappearance had already receded into the back of her mind. Today, she wanted to wrap things up as best she could before her impending maternity leave, so her substitute worker, Tonya Belding, would have a relatively clean start with the family. She had to make sure Lola had taken Carla to buy new shoes for school. She also wanted to make sure the landlord had repaired the roof as he had promised.

Kathy knocked on the dilapidated screen door which, she noted, still had one missing hinge. Davey ran to the door from within the gloomily dark living room, his bare feet slapping on the wooden boards of the uneven floor.

"Guess what!" Davey shouted breathlessly. "Our mom says we're moving far away real soon! To a place where we won't be poor anymore and where we'll always have everything we want!"

Kathy grimaced. Lola was always moving and always promising her kids a better life, but each move seemed to only push the family deeper into the maze of poverty.

Kathy had known Lola when Davey was just a baby, and this was probably the eighth or ninth hovel into which they had relocated since then. Kathy feared this move would put the family into an even worse neighborhood, or maybe Lola was moving in with another man, something she had done periodically, usually finding herself soon afterward the victim of abuse and in search of new housing.

More work for Tonya. Kathy told herself that she should have known that she would be unable to leave her sub with a clean slate when it came to the Mayes family.

Lola emerged from the front bedroom, leading Kimmy by the hand. Right away Kathy sensed that something was different. Lola's usually dull façade was absent. Her face seemed to be aglow with excitement, though her eyes seemed unfocused. Little Kimmy shared the same bright countenance as her mother. Kathy experienced a sudden violent pain as her unborn baby delivered a swift kick to her rib cage.

Before Kathy could ask Lola about Davey's comment, Kimmy released her mother's hand and walked calmly up to her. Kimmy placed one hand on her swollen abdomen and issued a cooing sound through pursed lips. Kathy felt her baby settle into comfortable inactivity. Kimmy held her hand in place for a few seconds, then removed it, ceasing her peculiar vocalization. Kathy did not know what to make of this.

"Davey tells me you plan to move," Kathy began.

"Davey! I told you not to tell anyone!" Lola admonished her son, placing one hand firmly on top of his head. Davey's arms dropped loosely to his side and his face seemed to lose its animation. He stood stiffly next to his mother.

Kathy shifted her weight to her left foot. The humming in her head again intensified. Her legs suddenly felt weak. A growing numbness began in her feet and gradually moved upward. The strap of her purse slid down from her right shoulder and her fingers clutched ineffectively at the leather flap as it dropped to the floor. Kathy felt faint. The edges of the room seemed to be closing in on her like fog in an old movie.

"What's happening to me?" Kathy thought she heard herself asking, but her voice seemed to issue from a distant corner of the room.

Her vision narrowed until her eyes fell upon little Kimmy. All she could see as the darkness closed in was the little girl's face, still glowing in that uncommon way. But Kimmy's features seemed to slip gradually out of place. Her eyes became narrow slits, dark and piercing and deeply recessed. Her face seemed to become quite pale, almost white. Kathy could no longer focus on anything but the little girl's eyes, which now seemed to be two red, glowing orbs. Kimmy's very fine hair seemed to have become even thinner.

How odd, Kathy noted groggily.

"It will all be well," Kathy thought she heard someone say, but the figure before her didn't have a visible mouth and she didn't exactly hear the words. It was more like she just found the words inside her own mind. *"Give yourself up to us."*

Kathy felt herself falling backward, but she didn't hit the floor. Instead, her feet seemed to rise as her head went back and she felt buoyed as if she were supported by a pool of water. Only, it was more like a pool of light: soft, green and totally filling her consciousness until nothing else remained.

Then, for Kathy Fellner, the darkness came.

Back in Ty's small office, Wally impatiently ripped the medical file from Ty's hands as soon as his friend held it out. He withdrew his reading glasses from his shirt pocket while he slid into a chair next to Ty's office desk. As his friend pulled another chair up to the other side of the desk, he completed reading the brief notes.

After a few seconds, Wally looked up at Ty.

"Jay was always a real nice guy, good family man, sincere. He and I always got along, even when his sister and I were ready to kill each other. But why would he be driving around by himself in this area? None of his family lives here anymore."

"Jay had the same symptoms as my other patient, but his labwork and other tests came back negative, after he had already left. And the similar problems seem to be troubling your patient..."

"Kathy Fellner," Wally volunteered, completing his friend's sentence, an old habit that often annoyed Ty.

Ty was just contemplating the possibility that he was breaking rules related to confidentiality by even discussing the cases with Wally, when Wally added, "Whatever is going on around here seems to be turning into an epidemic. We need to see if we're the only two docs in town who have seen this."

Ty grabbed the two medical records in one hand and headed for the door. Wally paused for a moment to call his office, asking his partner, Joe Degan, to have Kathy Fellner's file ready for him to pick up on his way to the hospital.

"Glen Garris is on duty in the ER today," Wally called ahead to Ty as they hurried across the parking lot to Ty's Mercedes, passing Wally's older model Ford truck on the way. "I'd bet he'd know if any similar conditions have been reported in the last couple of days."

Glen Garris emerged from a curtained off examination space in a corner of the large emergency room, his heavy frame nearly filling the aisle between that area and the adjacent screened off area. Wally and Ty were waiting, charts in hand.

"Yep. Got one of those right here. Came in just a short time ago," Dr. Garris volunteered after hearing what the two doctors wanted. "Kid's in bad shape, though. He seems to be out of touch with what's happening around him. I think he's experiencing hallucinations. His poor, ol' widowed mother is worried sick about him. I've called in a neuro consult and Dr. Niemeyer has examined him, recommended lotsa tests, but we don't know anything yet."

Suddenly the emergency room doors burst inward, and the three physicians turned to see what was going on. A rather tall, thin man was cradling an apparently unconscious woman, hurrying in obvious panic toward the nurse's station in the middle of the room.

One nurse sprang to a curtain next to the doctors and hurled it back out of the way as another ushered the frantic man and the woman he was carrying into the cubicle, where the man gently placed the woman on the waiting examination table. Even as he carefully put her down, the man turned toward those around him and pleaded for help.

"My wife!" the tall man called out in desperation. "Help her. Help her, please!"

Garris hustled his bulky form across the room with a speed that belied his heft and age. Doctors Williamson and Hunter trailed after him, though they were careful not to get in the way of the ER staff who were hurrying to and from the exam room. Carts of electronic equipment, IV stands and various trays of shiny metal instruments were rushed to the curtained-off space.

Amid the frantic, but professionally orchestrated bustle, one nurse managed to lead the distraught husband away from his immobile wife. Wally caught a glimpse of him as the nurse led him past the nurse's station. He looked familiar. Then, as the busy group hovering over the wife parted for a moment, he saw the face of the unconscious patient.

It was Kathy Fellner.

Wally promptly moved to the examination area, informing Garris of the identity of the patient and his involvement with her. Ty waited for a few minutes to assure himself that there was nothing that he was needed for at the time and edged his way through the automatic doors and into the waiting room.

He found Lee Fellner huddled nervously on the edge of a plastic chair at the intake desk, trying to give the clerk all the pertinent information about his wife's medical history and insurance coverage. The clerk asked questions in a business-like monotone, trying to calm down the man in the chair.

Ty could see that it was all Lee could do to remain seated and try to give coherent responses. He kept glancing back toward the doors leading to the ER.

Once Lee had been released from the clerk's interrogation and was told to have a seat in the waiting room, Ty stepped forward to intercept him. Ty quietly introduced himself as a doctor and a friend of Kathy's obstetrician and assured Lee that his wife was in good hands at that moment. He calmly asked Lee what had happened.

"I told the nurses in the Emergency Room and this insurance girl," Lee replied, motioning with his head in the direction of the intake desk. The panic in his voice was obviously ebbing. "I received a call from someone Kathy was visiting as part of her social work job. The woman said my wife had fainted and she didn't know what to do. I advised her to phone for an ambulance, but she seemed flustered and couldn't even give me her complete address."

"I got the approximate area from her. She said it was close to McCarty's Bar, and I drove over there from work. I drove up and down the streets until I found Kathy's car. The lady who had phoned me led me into her house. Kathy was on her back on the couch. She was really groggy, barely conscious. I got her into my car and drove her here, since it was only three or four blocks away."

"Did she say anything during the time it took to reach the hospital?" Ty asked. He was beginning to worry about the emotional state of the agitated husband and hoped that keeping him focused on specifics might help him to calm down.

"Yes, yes. She kept moaning and saying something about her baby..." Lee paused briefly, then corrected himself.

"Our baby. She kept saying, 'Not my baby!' or something like that. I don't know. She's had several problem pregnancies. I don't know..."

His voice trailed off into a low murmur.

Ty led Lee to a chair in the waiting room. There was only one other person present, a janitor who was mopping listlessly among the chairs. A television was barely audible at the front of the room, but nobody was watching it.

Ty probed a bit further. "Has Kathy had any medical problems lately?"

Lee had been staring at the floor between his feet. At this question, he lifted his head and stared directly into Ty's eyes.

"She's had a buzzing in her head. Nonstop, she says. Oh, and she pointed out an impression on the back of her neck, just below her skull. I wouldn't have seen it, but she pulled her hair away from the spot. And she kept clutching at different places on her head."

He paused and moved a little closer to Ty's face. "Do you know what this all means? Is there a problem with her, or the baby?" The panic in his voice was again rising.

"Not that I know of, but something seems to be going around lately. We'll need to wait a few minutes for Dr. Garris and Dr. Hunter, see if they've been able to sort it out. Meanwhile, you need to calm all the way down. You can't help Kathy if you're incoherent."

Lee straightened up in the chair and took a deep breath. "Of course, you're absolutely right, Dr. Williamson."

Just then, Wally pushed open the ER door and motioned to Ty. Lee gave a nervous nod as Ty excused himself and hurried over to where his friend waited. Wally put one hand on his taller friend's shoulder and looked up at him. Lee stared intently at the pair from his chair, straining to hear their words.

"What's wrong, Wally?" asked Ty. "You look like you've seen a ghost! Good lord, you're pale!"

"It's the baby, Ty," Wally began. He paused as though to marshal strength to continue. "The baby, Ty. It doesn't make any sense. The sonograms didn't show any problems. It just doesn't make any sense."

Ty had never seen his friend so flustered. "What doesn't make sense?"

"Ty," responded Wally, "I have never seen this before. I heard about it in med school; it's something called pseudocyesis."

He paused for a moment, dropping his gaze to the floor, then, looking up again, he added, "A false pregnancy."

"Ty, there is no baby."

Chapter Four: Hilltop House

Paul Sloan's residence had at one time been an orphanage, located on a small rise in the middle of the county, amid the clumps of trees that separated the flat farmlands. The building was accessible only by a gravel road and it was hidden among the woods. It was far from any large city and not adjacent to any of the several tiny villages that dotted the rural landscape.

It was an extremely large building, once the home of thirty or forty children under the age of sixteen, in addition to the two adults who ran the place with the help of a small and devoted staff. The proprietors, who had been Paul's grandparents, resided in the north wing.

It was of special significance to him that he had been able to purchase this abandoned property from the county. He had not been born yet at the time it was left empty when his grandparents died within a month of each other, and the few remaining residents were sent to foster homes.

His father had regaled him with tales of growing up in the large building surrounded by dozens of playmates. Though Paul found the solitude to his liking, he could not imagine why his grandparents had ever wanted to live in the old mansion, which they had given what Paul thought was a rather unimaginative name, *Hilltop House*. However, the name came to be associated with the orphanage, so it made for good publicity.

Paul had come to tolerate seclusion. It had helped him become physically independent after he found himself paralyzed below the waist. Following high school, he had gone to college for a couple years, but didn't feel happy there, so he dropped out and enlisted in the Army. He fully expected to pursue a military career, as his father had done.

Paul was excited when, after only a few months, he had been assigned to a top-secret job. He had multiple interviews with the brass before his selection. Things seemed to be going well. He was sent to a special school, at a "secret" training site in the mountains out west. He was promoted to corporal upon completion of that program. His subsequent assignment had been to supervise a small squad that retrieved crashed experimental aircraft in the mountains outside his home base.

One day, there had been a jeep accident on the way to a crash site. At least that was what he had been told; he could recall nothing of the incident. Paul awoke in the base hospital, no longer able to use his legs. He was given a medical discharge.

He had tried to recall the accident, but the only memory he could dredge up from deep in his mind was a vague image of colored lights along the dirt road where the crash occurred. He had experienced periodic nightmares since then, usually involving shadowy figures, but these had eventually faded away.

At first, he had lived an aimless existence. Then he decided to use his disability settlement to buy the old mansion and rehab it. Once he was done with that, he again had no plan, but eventually began to experiment with electronics and found that he had a knack with computers.

In a few months after moving into the mansion, he had accumulated a large collection of the latest computers and related equipment and was beginning to pick up freelance jobs involving computer technology.

Paul had been encouraged to pursue his vocation by his childhood friend Jay Brashear, who had also been his roommate for the short time he was in college before joining the Army. Although the two friends no longer lived in close proximity, Paul always felt they had an almost psychic link and even years and miles couldn't dim their friendship.

Of course, they had another link.

Just before entering the Army, Paul had become engaged to Jay's sister Cheryl, but their separation during his assignment to the lonely western base and the subsequent emotional turmoil Paul experienced after the accident ended that relationship. Cheryl had gone her own way, had married some doctor, and Paul lost track of her. He still thought about her from time to time, but he knew there was no point in it. He and Jay never spoke of her. Jay realized it was a sensitive topic for Paul and Paul preferred to avoid discussing the stressful aspects of his past.

Paul had felt very safe and secure in his isolated wooded hideaway. He needed little and bothered no one and no one bothered him, at least not until a few weeks ago. That's when the trouble started and that's when Paul realized he did need a friend, after all. That's when he had contacted Jay.

Paul had been working late one night on a program to enhance global satellite positioning technology. When he thought he had worked out all the bugs, something strange had happened. He had everything in place for a trial run, when his computer screen began to sizzle and caught fire, just inches from his face.

Paul had pushed himself away from the desk so violently that he overturned his wheelchair. When he rolled himself over to his stomach and raised his head to observe the burning equipment, he discovered that the fire had gone out. In fact, he could see no evidence that it had even occurred, and he didn't smell smoke.

The screen, however, was glowing a fluorescent green.

By the time Paul had righted his chair and pulled himself up into it, the glow was gone, leaving him wondering if he had hit his head when he fell and if he had imagined it. He resumed his place at the computer and was just about to begin his test again, when a series of black images appeared on the screen.

Paul thought something had scrambled his computer. To Paul. the figures resembled hieroglyphics. As each line of the markings fell into place, the screen rolled down and a new line began. The digits came faster and faster, until the screen was filling up and rolling at an amazing speed.

Paul was unable to fathom what had happened. He stared intently at the screen until its blinking march of hieroglyphs began to slow, eventually changing to a few uneven zigs and zags. As Paul continued to stare, he became aware of an uneasy feeling, a sort of déjà vu. The strange figures looked vaguely familiar to him, but no matter how he concentrated on them, he couldn't recall why.

Finally, with a shrug, Paul decided that the best he could do at the moment would be to print off what he had and look through the pages. In a few minutes his high-speed laser printer was humming energetically as it spewed sheet after sheet of the strange symbols into its tray in rapid succession.

Paul retrieved a handful of the first printouts and flipped

through them before placing them on his nearby oak desk, trying to find a familiar marking or pattern.

He was just about to give up when one page caught his eye. He thumbed back through the stack until he at last located it. He carefully extracted the page from the middle of the growing tower of paper, being careful to mark the location in order to replace it when he was done looking at it.

As he slid the page out, he realized with a start that the ink of the printer had created a pattern, clearly a picture of something. On closer look, he realized it was a picture of a person. Then, upon holding the picture upright in the light of his fluorescent desk lamp, Paul felt a sudden jolt.

The person whose face was produced by the printed symbols was clearly that of Cheryl Brashear.

Meanwhile, out in Colorado, Cheryl Hunter dodged through the summer downpour, splashing to her car which was parked on the far side of the grocery store parking lot. Rain was somewhat rare in this area, but when it did rain, it came down hard. The two bags of groceries clutched in her arms swayed awkwardly as she ran. Curse that bag boy for loading so many heavy items at the top of the bags!

Just as she slowed at the rear of her older model car to begin fumbling for her keys, once again telling herself that she should have taken them from her purse before leaving the store, the contents of the bag in her left arm lurched forward from momentum, and bread, eggs and a jar of pizza sauce tumbled out, bouncing off the dark red fender of her midsize automobile and crashing to the pavement. Pizza sauce mixed quickly with egg yolk and ran under her car, carried by a river of rainwater.

Cheryl stomped her right foot in frustration, which was another mistake, since the rain had soaked the paper bag that she still held precariously. The bottom of the bag was soaked and broke open, dumping a mixture of salad dressings, uncooked sausage, bread and various spices, a soap opera magazine, and bananas into the river of slop at her feet.

She had just managed to retrieve her keys, since she no longer had to worry about spilling anything, and they now slipped from her clutching fingers and bounced under the car parked next to hers. Soaked to the skin and locked out of her car, Cheryl slammed the few remaining groceries onto the pavement and kicked at an apple as it rolled by on its way to join her keys.

Well, she thought, why should today be any different? Her entire life had pretty much gone like this, lousy. She was still recovering from her divorce from Wally, which had basically ruined her life, even though she had come to acknowledge, in her quieter, more honest moments, that it had mostly been her fault. Bad temper and having grown up getting everything she wanted, thus becoming a spoiled brat, had led her to frequent conflicts with nice, easy-going Wally Hunter.

Shortly after she learned of her parents' disappearance, her marriage had collapsed. It had been the last straw for her emotionally. After the breakup she decided to find a job far away from Millardville, so she had just headed west on I-80, taking any exits that caught her interest. She had always been protected, first by her parents and by her big brother Jay, then by Wally. She decided to just take the plunge into the unknown and see where she came up.

She did obtain employment at a couple spots in Nebraska, but after a few months at each place, she felt restless and moved on further west. She eventually drifted to this small town a few miles from an Army base near the Rockies and was able to land a job as a civilian clerk at the base.

"Need some help there, neighbor?"

The friendly voice came from a tall man with thinning blond hair, who was now standing next to the car under which her keys had disappeared.

Cheryl knew him by sight, her neighbor at an off-base apartment building. He was a lieutenant. She hadn't really met him, though they had a nodding and waving sort of relationship.

The man got down on his knees to search under his car, then sprawled flat onto the asphalt to reach even further. Then, with the front of his shirt and slacks totally soaked, he pulled himself back from under the car, climbed back to his feet and held out a jingling set of keys.

Cheryl smiled weakly, not sure what to say, other than a squeaky "Thanks" that escaped her lips. Then she cleared her throat and held out her right hand and added, "That was very gallant of you...neighbor."

She had seen his name on the mailbox outside his apartment but didn't want him to think that she was snooping.

"John Lundy." The tall man responded, confirming what Cheryl already knew, while trying to dry his hands on his soaked shirt, before extending the right one hesitantly. "Sorry. It's a bit muddy."

Cheryl reached out her hand, anyway. "My name is Cheryl," she began, but he interrupted her.

"I'm John Lundy..." then realizing that he had already introduced himself, he blushed and bent down and began gathering Cheryl's spilled groceries from the paved surface.

"...Hunter," Cheryl finished, following after John as he retrieved the items and held them up to her. She opened her trunk and began tossing them in. At last, John finished his task and stood up again.

"I know. I've seen your name on your mailbox," he said with a rather sheepish grin. Cheryl smiled, realizing that her qualms about privacy weren't shared by everyone, though she definitely felt flattered that he had taken the trouble to check on her name.

The rain made it less than comfortable to stand and talk, so they each got into their own car and headed for their apartment building. Once there, John merely waved goodbye as he lugged his bags into his apartment.

Cheryl opened her trunk and looked despairingly at the pile of cans, boxes, and bottles, the ones that hadn't broken. John had tossed the broken ones into the dumpster beside the store. She had a momentary feeling of disappointment that John had hurried inside so quickly. She had hoped to speak with him some more. She realized that she didn't have any close friends.

Just as she was feeling sorry for herself about this, however, John reappeared with a sturdy cardboard box and began unloading the trunk's groceries into it. He then followed her along the covered walkway until they reached Cheryl's apartment. Though John declined Cheryl's invitation to come in and talk some more, they did share some information about one another, and he departed with a cheery smile.

Cheryl learned that John was planning to make the Army his career; he'd already put in several years. John mentioned that he was divorced, to which Cheryl responded, "Oh, I'm sorry to hear that," but her slight smile betrayed her.

John merely nodded acknowledgement when she mentioned her own marital status. John also had no close relatives. He had lived with distant cousins after his parents were killed in a car wreck when he was four years old.

John smiled a slight smile as he turned to leave. Cheryl thought quickly and suggested that they could carpool to work. He said that would be nice, but his hours varied, and he could not know beforehand when he would be called into work or how late he might need to stay. As he walked away, he mentioned that on stormy nights he almost always had to work late or go in early the next morning.

It was quite stormy that night with much lightning, with each flash followed a few moments later by loud, bone-jarring thunder. Cheryl looked out into the parking lot a couple times and saw that John's car was still there.

The thought crossed her mind that perhaps John told her a lie to avoid having to ride with her into the base. She felt a weighty depression beginning to descend upon her. As she went to bed, there was a tremendous clap of thunder that shook the entire building. She tried to sleep, but the driving rain hitting her bedroom window kept her awake.

She couldn't quit thinking about John Lundy and what he had said about stormy nights. She shuffled down the hallway and down the stairs and unlocked her front door, opening it a crack to see if John's car would be gone. It wasn't. However, parked behind his car with the engine running was a jeep.

She heard distant voices and, being curious, wrapped her robe more snugly around herself and edged along the canopied sidewalk of the apartment building until she was within twenty feet of John's place. As she came closer, she noted that his front door was open. She took a deep breath, and crouched low to listen.

"Come on, Lieutenant Lundy! We have to go! You know the rules. They sent me to get you when you didn't report on time. If I don't bring you back with me, I'll be the one facing the consequences."

"Listen, Sergeant Rader, I'll take full responsibility for my actions. I just can't do this anymore. I've met someone and now I think I have a reason to live. Go tell the Colonel and everyone that I just can't continue to face this!"

Cheryl was shocked at the intense fear in John's voice. He seemed to be near tears. Why was he so upset? She wondered if she was the *someone* who gave him a *reason to live*, though it took her aback to consider that John had read so much into their brief encounter. But what was putting his life at risk?

"I've done this for seven years, Rader. Seven! That's longer than most guys have lasted. Can you understand the stress I'm under? It ruined my marriage and Jolene took the kids with her that night she left. That's part of the reason they only recruit single guys now, like you. I couldn't tell her what my job was and she wouldn't believe me if I did. Secrets like that destroy marriages. They ruin lives. They cause people to explode and hurt others."

"Now, every time they say on the weather report that there is going to be a storm, I start trembling. The pills they give me help a little, but after a few hours, they are no longer effective. Every time it thunders now, I scream! I scream, Rader! Don't you scream?"

Cheryl had never heard anyone so shaken. Why did the weather bother her neighbor so much? Sure, thunder and lightning frighten a lot of people, but this was way beyond fright.

"Nope," she heard the sergeant respond with no terror in his voice. "It's just a job to me, Lieutenant. Don't bother me none, sir. I just do it and keep my mouth shut. That's all the military and THEY ask. I've become so used to this job that I don't even think that it's unusual anymore. All in a day's work, I say."

Rader paused and looked Lundy in the eyes. Then he resumed in a plaintive tone, "Now, let's go. Ya haveta at least report in. Maybe they'll let you take some sick leave when they see what a wreck you are. I've heard of them doing that for some guys who give this too much thought. You haveta look at it as just a job, Lieutenant. Just a job. Of course, I've also heard of guys who screw it up or who tell people what they do, and they disappear. All the job really is, is recovery. Like when one of our experimental jets crashes."

"But I'm beginning to think it's not always *ours*! I think maybe they've recovered something from a crash, and they are getting new ideas from what they have found," John shouted back. "The higher-ups know stuff they aren't telling us, Rader, I'm sure of it!"

There was a pause and Cheryl could hear John's voice. It was gradually calming down. There were a few seconds of silence.

Finally, he just sighed and said, "Maybe you're right. And I'm in too deep for them to just let me out. I've heard rumors about memories being erased. I think that's what I need. Why don't they just let me out and wipe out my memory?"

John's voice began to trail off.

"Lieutenant! You know there's only one way out. THEY have got to let you out and THEY ain't hardly ever let anyone out. And, if they do let you go, you go out changed. You won't really be you anymore. And you won't even know why. You become a loner without close friends. We've all been reminded of that over and over. And, if THEY learn you have any close relatives or friends, like that woman you mentioned, THEY'll take care of them, too."

Rader paused, then added, "Besides, I'm not sure there is a THEY. I think it's just the Army's way of keeping us quiet about the strange flying machines we've seen crashed out there. I ain't never seen any of their pilots out there, just their wrecked stuff."

Cheryl heard Rader's voice trail off to a whisper. Then there was silence for a couple minutes and she heard footsteps approaching the doorway from inside John's apartment. She quickly ducked back into the shadows as John and Rader exited the building.

The end of the parking lot was well-lit by a pair of large street lights, so she could clearly see John's face as he dejectedly stumbled toward the waiting jeep. John was now in fatigues and was carrying a belt with a holster and canteen under one arm. He had a look of resignation and defeat. His shoulders slumped and his eyes were trained on the ground. He seemed to be biting his upper lip and his hands were clenched and trembling.

Cheryl couldn't determine if he was scared or angry. Maybe both. The two climbed into the jeep and sped away.

It was still dark, sometime after 2:00 or 3:00 in the morning, Cheryl was sure, when she again heard the sound of a large truck slowing to a stop in the parking lot below her bedroom window. Cheryl had been awakened by the sound, but she had really not been sleeping well. John's voice and Rader's words had somehow left her feeling very on edge, unable to fall asleep for long.

She wasn't even too sure what it was that worried her. Certainly, she had never heard such a distraught voice as John's. That, by itself, was very unsettling. But, what Rader had said had also left her quite uneasy.

Who were THEY, that pronoun the sergeant spat out so forcefully? What assignment did these men have that was so undesirable, but that they couldn't even resign from or be excused from?

She rose from her bed, grabbed her robe and descended the stairs. She again opened the door and looked toward John's apartment.

A sudden flash of light jolted Cheryl awake. She found that she was in her own living room, stretched out on the couch. The light through the window gave her the impression that it was late afternoon. She felt as though she had recently been concerned about something, but it slipped from her mind as she tried to concentrate on it. She arose and walked to the kitchen to glance out the window there.

"That's odd!" Cheryl said to herself, noting the open trunk lid on her car. She hurried out her front door to check on this, only to discover that her laundry basket was resting upside down in the trunk. A few pieces of clothing were scattered around the trunk. After staring at the open trunk for a while, she gathered up her clothes and closed the trunk.

She couldn't even remember going to the laundromat.

She felt a stinging sensation on the back of her neck, near the hairline, but ignored it after the thought, "*It will all be well*" entered her mind.

Chapter Five: Peter Lapley's Wild Ride

Caperton sizzled miserably in the mid-summer heat. For several days hardly anyone had ventured out in the middle of the day. Unless absolutely necessary, nobody was hurrying anywhere. The farmers, of course, did what work needed to be done. A few children roamed around trying to find something interesting to do. One group formed a club for the sole purpose of catching and releasing garter snakes. They kept track of how many they had caught, but they had no way of knowing how many they had already captured before. They called themselves *The Snake-Catchers Club of America.*

These same kids occasionally played baseball, but in Caperton it wasn't really possible to find enough interested companions to play a regulation game, so they took turns hitting flies to one another in a vacant lot and playing catch.

Most kids just stayed inside out of the heat and humidity. One eleven-year-old did find a cell phone on the edge of Calvin Dunn's abandoned cornfield and was overjoyed to find that it used the same charger as one his older sister had at home.

There were two topics of conversation other than the heat whenever any adults ventured out to go to the tavern or post office. There was the minor mystery of the abandoned rented SUV that was found parked in the middle of a cornfield with the engine running. Paperwork found in the glove compartment revealed it had been rented two states away by someone named Jay Brashear, but no one recalled that he used to live near Caperton. Paul, of course, knew, but didn't see the point in sharing that information with the people in town.

The main mystery, however, was the disappearance of Joey Paige. It had been several weeks now, with no further clues. His father had resumed operation of the tavern, but Joe's heart continued to leap into his throat every time the phone rang. It could be a call that his son had been found, he knew, but the news could be good or bad. The more time that passed, Joe realized, the less likely it was that the news would be good.

From time to time, Carl Johnson or Sheriff Post's deputies would stop in to let him know that nothing new had been discovered about Joey's disappearance. There was also no word on Calvin Dunn.

Peter James Lapley, known to everyone as *Petey* had lived in Caperton all his life. He had grown up there, made it through eighth grade, and worked only when the mood hit him. He had managed to meet and, somehow, convince a nice young girl from the nearby village of Reginald to marry him. Margie and Petey had three children, all in grade school.

Margie was a warm and patient person, the only combination that seemed possible for someone who was married to Petey, who spent most of his time playing pool and drinking beer at Paige's Tavern with a few friends who had only a bit more ambition than he did. They all had jobs; he had no steady employment. Still, after every serious transgression with the law or the bottle, Margie would take a deep breath and welcome her errant husband back.

The kids, unfortunately, were victims of small-town bullying and had few friends. But Margie always did her best to soothe their feelings and protect them.

Then, one blazing morning that August, Petey did something amazing that surprised the entire town. He was out all night on a Saturday, which was not uncommon. It would have been more amazing if he hadn't been out. But when he showed up the next morning, he wasn't drunk. Margie just opened the back door and found him perched on the railing of the porch.

"So, you're back, then?" she asked, cocking her head to the side as she surveyed him from the back door.

She continued to shake the dust out of the rug she was holding, even as she stared at her wayward husband. She found it odd that he had enough balance to maintain his position.

"I am more than back!" exclaimed Petey, throwing his head back and smiling. "I've been places."

Margie cut him off. "I know where you've been, Petey. Carousing around..."

"Boy have I!" her husband interrupted, shoving himself off the railing and spinning around to face her.

She involuntarily took a step back. Margie ceased shaking the dusty rug and edged further onto the porch. She wasn't accustomed to anything resembling sobriety in her husband after one of his all-night benders. Also, his voice sounded different, not squeaky, but calm and low pitched.

Margie took a couple of steps in her husband's direction to get a whiff of his breath. Usually, she could smell the liquor from several feet away, but this time she couldn't detect any. The thought crossed her mind that she didn't know how to relate to a sober husband on a Sunday morning.

"Margie, you just won't believe where I have been! I have been..." he paused and pointed skyward. "...up there."

Margie felt her world slide back into place. Petey was speaking nonsense, as usual. He must be drunk, even if she couldn't detect any odor. All was right with the world, after all.

"Yep. Up there with THEM!" Petey continued, jerking his thumb repeatedly in the air. "Up, up and away, Margie! They took me for a joy ride in the sky!" Petey twirled around in a circular dance, still with his head tilted and his thumb pointing upward.

Margie's brief sense of relief did a nosedive. Her slightly unbalanced husband had either discovered a new drug to replace alcohol. or his mind had finally lost its mooring. She wasn't sure which explanation would be easier to accept.

Just at that moment Mayor Ralph Osgood pulled his older model Cadillac into the entrance to the Lapley driveway which ran along the edge of the house all the way to the small garage located just past the back porch. Ralph emerged quickly from the car, not even pausing to close the door, and, hearing Petey's voice from the back of the house, proceeded directly to the back porch. As he rounded the edge of the house Margie could see that Ralph had something serious on his mind.

"Petey! Gotta talk," Ralph squawked hoarsely.

He seemed to Margie to be more rumpled than usual, as though he had slept in his lightweight white summer slacks and faded purple polo shirt. Ralph stopped by the steps leading up to the back porch. He looked up at Petey and slapped both hands down on top of the back porch's railing.

"Yahoo, Ralphie! Did you hear about what happened to me last night? Am I a lucky dude or what?"

"Petey!" Ralph glared. "What happened last night didn't happen!"

Osgood turned to Margie, neglecting the nonsense sentence he had just uttered. "What did Petey say to you?" he demanded, still glaring, still tightly gripping the porch rail.

Margie was flustered by the mayor's unusually decisive tone. She, and everyone in Caperton, had grown accustomed to the mayor being very docile.

"Petey said something about going up in the sky with 'them'," she responded, jerking her right thumb upward in imitation of Petey's gesture.

Margie was unaccustomed to having to explain her husband's behavior. The one advantage to being married to the town drunk is not having to explain his weird behavior. Everybody knew the cause and accepted it though usually shaking their heads in pity for Margie and the kids.

"But, don't you see, Petey," Ralph's voice turned plaintive, "you can't just go around talking about that sort of thing! People will think you're crazy!"

"Hecko, Ralphie! They already KNOW I am. That's what I like about being me. I don't have to make excuses for who I am."

To Margie that sounded like a quite adequate response. After all, she'd been accepting that justification for years.

"But Petey!" Ralph said, "You can't expect to go around

acting like this! What were you doing up on the water tower, anyway?"

Ralph Osgood's voice betrayed his own fear and uncertainty. Margie turned toward the two men with a look of shock.

"Mayor Ralph! I woulda been bigtime scared if I hadn't already been up so high with them."

"Wait a minute. You were up on the water tower, Petey? You must have really gotten ahold of something strong this time!" Margie's voice betrayed concern.

She was beginning to wish that she had found her husband face down on the lawn, as usual. "You could have been killed!"

"Got down okay, din't I?" Petey challenged, jutting his chin out at his wife in half-serious defiance.

Ralph placed his right foot on the first step leading up to the porch and leaned toward Petey.

"But Petey, don't you remember our meeting that night with Mr. Huit at the town hall? We ended up agreeing to his request that we keep quiet about all the strange things around here, national security and all that! You can't go around telling everyone that you got a ride on a UFO! Someone who wasn't at the meeting might hear you and spread the word. Before you'd know it, the newspapers would pick up on it, or the radio station over in Millardville and then the whole deal would be off."

"No new police cruiser, no new water pump, no repaving of our streets, no street signs, all that!" Ralph sounded desperate.

"Hecko, Ralph! That's all about that flying thing that Huit guy talked about. That isn't what I was in. I was in a real, actual flying saucer! It took me up right into its inside when I left Paige's last night. Then, it zoomed off into the sky, with me inside."

"Petey, dear, you just had too much..." Margie began, placing a sympathetic hand on the back of his neck.

"Yee...ouch! Don't touch me there!" Petey screamed, pulling away. He pushed his wife's hand away and replaced it with his own.

"What happened to your neck, Petey? Margie queried, again approaching him with her hand raised, reaching for his hand, which he had now rested tenderly on the spot at the base of his skull.

Petey removed his hand. Margie and Ralph could now both make out a large red spot where his hand had rested.

"Hoohah! Ya shoulda seen them guys! They tried and tried to poke me there with some sort of metal thing, but I kept moving and they couldn't get a clean shot at me. Couldn't hold me on that silly table of theirs, neither!"

Ralph looked at Margie, his mouth dropping open, then he turned again toward her husband.

"You mean that some space aliens kidnapped you and tried to cut you up?"

Over the years, under the influence of various lubricants, Petey had come up with some whoppers, but this was getting to be one of the bigger ones. Unfortunately, Ralph was beginning to fear, it could be true.

"Them funny looking little guys sure botched it on my neck. I think they were getting kinda mad at me, too. I wouldn't hold still, and they couldn't figure out how to stop me from running around their old flying machine."

"C'mon, Petey. How did you really mess up your neck? Probably scraped it while climbing through a barbed wire fence, right?" Ralph's tone was now gentle skepticism.

"Nope, May-or Osgoody! Them funny looking guys did it. I have proof, too!"

Petey plunged his hand into his right front jeans pocket. As his wife and the mayor watched, he slowly extracted it, until, clutched in his fingertips, there appeared a blue metallic object somewhat resembling a large pencil. He held it aloft in triumph.

"It's real light-weight. The end is sharp. I used it to open a beer a few minutes ago. It slit the can like paper. I'm gonna be real careful with it. And that was the only beer I had, Margie. So don't get all upset."

Petey turned toward the metal garbage can just to one side of the porch. He fished around in it until he found a recently discarded soup can. With a quick motion, he stabbed the metal object into one side. It slid effortlessly into the can and out the other side. Petey grasped the pointed end very carefully as it emerged from the opposite surface. He pulled lightly on it and drew it the rest of the way through the can, much as a tailor would pull a sharp needle through a piece of cloth.

The two witnesses stared dumbly at Petey, who merely held up the device and smiled broadly.

"Oh, there was one other thing that happened that I gotta tell ya about!" Petey looked first at the mayor, then at his wife. His smile took on the fiendish look that both recognized as Petey's usual skunk-drunk grin. "I got to drive that thing!"

"I don't know where you found that sharp piece of metal," began Ralph, "but your story is getting to be ridiculous. You'd better go sleep this one off before you hurt yourself or someone else." He turned as if to walk away.

"I ain't a bit drunk, Ralpho! I may have been when it all started, but those yahoos didn't even offer me a beer. Some hospitality, huh? And they're the ones who interrupted my usual Saturday night routine. So, I was in no mood to be poked at or ogled by their squinty eyes. I just jumped down from the table they had put me on and pushed them all down. They don't hardly weigh nothing. I was knocking them down, left and right."

"Since they couldn't stop me, I began exploring the place. I found a bunch of blinking lights and decided to have some fun. I just began putting my hands over the lights and we began to zigzag around. AND zoom! We shot away faster than a flea hops. Then, I put my hand on another light and we came to a sudden stop. It was odd, though. The stop was immediate, but no one lost their balance."

"I just kept on laughing an' those big heads just ran around like ants on a paper plate at a picnic. And every time they tried to pull me outta the driving area, I just pushed 'em away. I may have hurt some of 'em, even. Finally, I just got tired of it all and let them drop me off on top of the water tower. Boy, did they hightail it out of there!" Petey's voice trailed off into a high-pitched cackle.

Margie and Ralph looked at each other skeptically. The

mayor shrugged in frustration and turned to walk back down the driveway.

"Oh, and one other thing! This is important, real important!"

Ralph reluctantly slowed his pace and turned again to face Petey.

"On board that flying saucer," Petey added in a suddenly serious tone, "they have people! Human people! They're knocked out or something, kept in rows of glass and metal tubes. Some were on tables. I saw them just before they hauled me out of there. And..." Petey leaned over the porch rail to look straight at the mayor, "...one of them was that Paige boy!"

A couple blocks away, in one of the mobile homes in the trailer park across from the schoolhouse, a young woman sat before a console and listened with a look of alarm at Petey's last comment, picked up by a listening device she had placed atop her mobile home.

Near Washington, D.C., in a suburban office building, a man wearing wire rimmed glasses also listened.

Elsewhere, in a windowless room, two deep, dark, unblinking eyes stared at a green glowing screen and also listened.

Chapter Six: Charles Keller, MD

Marla Brashear pulled her small, bright green Kia into a service station at the first Spring City exit. She was tired from the drive, having been on the road since 4:00 AM; it was now 5:00 PM. The stress of recent events kept her going, however, along with about a gallon of strong coffee that she had consumed. Finally, however, the fatigue was catching up to her and she found that she didn't have the energy to push the car door open and fill her gas tank. She leaned forward against the steering wheel and closed her eyes.

Jay had discussed with her his concern about Paul Sloan, and she agreed that he should go help his oldest friend, but he hadn't phoned for several days. Then Paul had phoned to say Jay had never shown up and she began to really worry. The police also called about Jay's rental car being found and she knew she had to do something. She arranged for her sister to stay with the kids, and she left early the next morning.

She didn't know if she could find her husband, but she had to do something. Jay had been gone now for three weeks; he had told her that he would only be gone three or four days. And, he hadn't phoned her, something he had always done when he had been gone in the past. He'd even call her every day from his office. Now, whenever she tried phoning him, the call went directly to voice mail.

The state police had been alerted all along the route from her home to Caperton. There had been no signs of her husband. The Fillmore County Sheriff's Department had promised to investigate, but they were already preoccupied with an investigation of a kidnapped child, so their resources were stretched thinner than usual, a deputy had told her when she called. It was a small county. At any rate, they had not phoned her back. The state police did phone her occasionally but had no useful news.

Marla had needed to fill the car's gas tank, so she had pulled off the interstate at a combination gas station and convenience store. She also had another purpose. She had a picture of Jay with her. She had checked the online banking statement which showed that Jay had used his debit card to buy gas at this very gas station, so she knew that Jay had been here. Perhaps the photograph of her ever-smiling husband would trigger a memory, and someone might know where he had headed from this point. Jay, a good realtor, liked to chat with strangers and it wouldn't be unusual for him to discuss his plans with the gas station attendants.

It had taken Marla a while to gather up the energy to pull her exhausted body from the driver's seat, but she finally took a deep breath and threw open the door, climbing out in almost the same motion. She first filled the tank of her small car before turning to stride into the store. A few minutes later she was back in her car, headed south on her way toward Millardville. The station manager had tried to help but had no memory of Jay. Marla was disappointed, but it had been a long shot.

She dwelt on this disappointment for only a brief time, allowing her mind to wander. She hadn't been to this area since the funeral of Jay's aunt twelve years earlier. She remembered being pregnant at that time with Rosie, who was now an older sister.

Jay had never been interested in living around Caperton, believing it was a dead end, especially after the disappearance of his parents. He had, rather, accepted her father's offer of a job with his real estate business and he was expected to take over ownership when her father retired in a year or so.

Things had been looking good lately. Jay was the manager of their son Ritchie's baseball team, was known throughout their city as a man that others could count on. There had even been talk of him running for city council, a suggestion Jay always just laughed off. When Jay told her that his old friend Paul had phoned with a call for help, she wasn't thrilled with Jay leaving home, but she knew he was the type to always help out his friends. He had to go. That's just the way he was. She was glad that her younger sister Paula was able to take care of Rosie and Ritchie to allow her to launch this search for her missing husband.

At last, the highway signs began to mention Millardville, and Marla eventually came to the exit. Once she left the interstate, she knew she had to look for the state highway that led to Caperton. She slowed slightly to scan the scenery ahead, looking for a road marker. She glanced in her rearview mirror as she slowed, to make sure no one was immediately behind her. She didn't notice anything at first, but a small, bright object in the distance caught her eye, sunlight reflecting off a car, she surmised.

But, just as Marla turned her attention back to the road ahead, there was a sudden blinding glare in her driver's side mirror. It seemed impossible, but the car she had seen in the distance had already caught up with her. It must be going well over 100 miles per hour! The silvery vehicle drew even with Marla and slowed just long enough for Marla to glance at it as it stayed even with her for a few seconds. Marla expected to see some wild-eyed teenage driver flashing obscene hand signals at her for driving so slowly.

That wasn't what she saw, however, and as the vehicle cut abruptly in front of her, as she felt her car being nudged from the road, all she could think was, "That's not a car!"

Then there was a grinding of metal and a flash of green light and Marla realized she was about to be involved in a serious accident. Then, everything went black.

Laurine Fraley had lapsed into a routine. She would go to her job at the supermarket every day and stop by the hospital to see Deke during her lunch break. After work, she would return to the hospital and keep a quiet vigil until darkness fell, then drive home. Deke had slipped into a coma and the neurologist had no idea why. All testing was negative, revealing no internal problems. There was simply no known reason for this to happen.

During the past couple days, however, Laurine began to sense that her only child was beginning to rally. He seemed to be trying to speak. She was convinced that he knew she was there in the room with him. She spoke back to him when she felt he was trying to communicate, doing all she could from her end to bring him back from his darkened world. She felt that she was reaching blindly into an unlighted tunnel, stretching with all her strength to find his hand in order to pull him into the light. It was a mental stress that left her physically exhausted, but she knew that she was the only one who could do it.

Day after day, night after night, Laurine found herself dealing with the terrible loneliness and frustration of this dim nightmare. She repeatedly slipped into a swirl of memories of the past, of her husband's death in this same hospital five years earlier; of the time Deke broke his leg on that motorcycle he had saved up to buy, spending several days on this same floor; of that one glorious moment, even further in the past when she herself had been here to bring new life into the world.

Then, coming out of her state of reflection, she found herself next thinking of her son's life. He had always been a bit of a loner, having few close friends, a fact attested to by the lack of visitors to his hospital room, other than Laurine herself and a one-time perfunctory visit by Deke's boss, Fred Merchant.

When possible, Laurine kept the room dark. She knew that her son would find the atmosphere more conducive to recovery, since he had always enjoyed night. She herself had never understood this fondness for the nocturnal, but she had at last come to accept it, the same way she accepted his apparent lack of a need for close friends or the fact that he was left-handed, which resulted in her husband Karl's ongoing battle to make Deke learn to do everything with his right hand.

All in all, Laurine had finally concluded, it was a good thing that her son was different and that he seemed to have no qualms about it. Someday, she was sure, he would grow to be self-sufficient and successful, if only he could overcome his current problem.

Then, one evening, Deke suddenly sat up. With his eyes closed, he turned his head to the left as if to look at his mother, who was sitting in an armchair across the room. Laurine had sprung up immediately and moved toward Deke. For a few seconds Deke didn't move; he just continued to face her. Laurine was stroking the side of his face, softly speaking words of comfort, trying to reassure him that he would soon be well. Still, he didn't acknowledge her presence, didn't open his eyes, just sat in the middle of the hospital bed, head turned, back straight.

Abruptly, Deke spoke, still not moving. *"It is the truth of the universe: all will be well. What is, is."*

Then, his left arm suddenly shot out in a sweeping motion, catching his mother by surprise and knocking her off the edge of the bed and onto the floor.

She clutched instinctively for the bed sheets to break her fall but succeeded only in knocking a lamp and a vase of flowers from the table next to the bed. She hit the floor hard and screamed out in pain.

As she scrambled to free herself from the tangled sheets, Deke slid off the bed, stepped over her, and exited the room. She heard rapid footsteps in the hallway. A few seconds later, the night nurse rushed into the room and stopped to help Laurine to her feet. Laurine realized that she had hurt her left leg when she tumbled onto the hard floor and the pain kept her from standing. She collapsed onto her son's vacated bed.

The nurse looked past Laurine, who was half sitting, half lying on the bed and suddenly noticed that the comatose patient was missing. She had assumed that he would still be in the bed and that only his mother required immediate attention, but she was now shocked to find that he was no longer in the bed.

In rapidly increasing panic, she clutched at the various tubes and the wires leading from devices that had been monitoring the patient's vital signs, but were now hanging loosely above the bed, as if to confirm what her eyes already told her, that the patient was gone. Then, executing a lightning-like about face, she raced from the room, her clipboard dropping to the floor behind her.

Within five minutes a thorough search of the floor was organized, then the entire hospital was searched.

Laurine awaited results of the search from the emergency

room, where she was being treated by Dr. Garris for a badly bruised patella. Despite all the efforts of the hospital staff, Deke was not found. The police department was notified, since there was much concern about a person of Deke's medical condition wandering around the city, but there was no sign of him.

Laurine was dropped off at her house by Sergeant Mikulsky of the Millardville police department. Another policeman drove her car home and parked it in front of the house. Mikulsky helped her check the house to see if Deke had made it home, but he wasn't there. Mikulsky asked Laurine for a list of Deke's friends, but that request only drew a blank stare from his mother. Deke had never really had any friends.

Kathy and Lee Fellner returned to Millardville after a three-week vacation trip to Canada. Lee had taken Dr. Hunter's suggestion that this might help his wife recover from the shock of her phantom pregnancy. Kathy, however, continued to be sullen and depressed.

Lee worried about her constantly. He greatly regretted that he couldn't be more supportive, but he also couldn't convince himself that the baby had never existed. He had felt it move when Kathy had enthusiastically placed his hand on her stomach one night. Both Kathy and Lee had experienced this thrill. There was definitely a life inside her.

At last, Kathy agreed to see a psychiatrist and Wally had arranged an appointment with Dr. Charles Keller. Kathy and Lee were seen initially as a couple and then separately in later sessions.

Dr. Keller had been in practice in Millardville for the past five years, since moving there from a suburban Denver practice. He had hoped to find a more peaceful life away from the metropolitan existence he had always known, and while Millardville wasn't exactly a rural village, it wasn't plagued by traffic congestion, crime and pollution.

His practice was good, but clearly not overwhelming. This suited him fine, since he had time to work on his version of the "great American novel," which for him consisted of a morality tale situated in the West. Dr. Keller wanted to paint a picture in words of the fragile state of the human psyche and to emphasize the need for simple forgiveness and the importance of family if civilization was to have any chance to advance.

He had experienced this need himself during a brief marriage to a fellow student while he was in medical school. He realized that his wife and he could have resolved the issue if they could only both accept their own guilt in the failure, but his wife moved away before he could repair the damage.

He was struck by how much forgiveness could have helped heal the rift, and how beneficial it would have been to view themselves as a family, but his wife's response made it clear that he would need to work on the issue without her. He would have to find a way to forgive himself.

Part of the process for him was to write his novel, which had begun during his residency. It was a slow and difficult effort, but he never abandoned it through all the years he had been in practice as a psychiatrist.

He felt that he was well on his way toward the achievement of his goal when the Fellners' case intervened to sidetrack him.

Kathy's emotional pain quickly engaged Dr. Keller's professional interest. He did not need to probe at all to determine that she felt an overwhelming guilt about the loss of her baby. It was clear that she was clinically depressed. She was having great difficulty moving forward with the necessary grieving process.

As he spoke calmly with Kathy, jotting down occasional notes on a pad resting on his lap, the doctor began to realize that Kathy had had problems all her life and that she usually suppressed her memories of past traumas. There were the previous miscarriages, of course, but she was also reluctant or unable to discuss her own childhood.

She seemed like two people Keller mused as he wrote up his notes later. On the surface her affect was very flat, and she was emotionally inhibited. She had trouble even getting to her appointments. Lee would accompany her to the door of the office, then wait outside after nearly having to push her through the doorway. The doctor would meet her at the door and lead her inside, for she seemed unable to enter on her own. At other times, once the sessions began, Kathy would show momentary sparks of anger directed at him, her husband, and Dr. Hunter.

But there was one comment Kathy made in passing one day that caught the doctor's attention. They had been reviewing the home visit to the Mayes family, which seemed to be the flashpoint of Kathy's descent into deep depression. Kathy recalled entering the home and repeated to Dr. Keller how she had begun to feel herself growing faint and saw Kimmy's face grow pale, and she thought she heard a voice.

"The voice said, *'It will all be well,'* but it hasn't been," Kathy sighed as tears began to streak down her cheeks. Keller wrote down her comment.

It was a couple weeks later when the psychiatrist, skimming through a professional journal, came upon an article dealing with hallucination. The author had been working with patients who reported hearing voices. Most of the examples cited in the article referred to the content of these messages as "nagging" or "giving suggestion."

However, one patient stated that the voice she heard merely conveyed a soothing message: "*It will all be well.*"

Keller stared at this sentence, not being able at first to recall why it sounded somehow familiar. In a moment he had jumped from his desk chair and scrambled to a file drawer in his outer office. He began flipping through Kathy Fellner's file until he found what he was seeking.

He traced a finger down the page until, about halfway, he found the spot where he had dictated an exact quote: "*It will all be well.*"

When Kathy had come for her next appointment, Dr. Keller led her into his office, as usual, while Lee retreated to the waiting room.

"I want to talk with you today about something you said a few sessions ago," Keller began. "Tell me more about the voice you heard, the one that told you 'It will all be well.'"

Kathy sat back in the comfortably padded office chair and brushed her hair back from her forehead. "Is that important?" she asked. Aside from the irony of the statement she could find no reason to attach any significance to it.

"It could be," the doctor replied. "I'm struck by the fact that your exact words were 'the *VOICE* said.' Why didn't you say 'Lola said' or 'Kimmy said'?"

"I don't know. I had started to feel faint, and it just seemed that I heard the voice, that it just came to me from all around the room. Or wherever I was."

"Wherever you were? Weren't you in their living room?"

"I'm not sure. I just had the feeling that I was somewhere else. Like in those dreams I used to have when I was little."

"What dreams?"

"I used to dream that I had been taken prisoner by faceless monsters. The rest of the dream would be very vague. I'd always wake up screaming and struggling with those horrid captors."

Charles paused in his note taking. He thought about pursuing her childhood dreams, but when he asked her a clarifying question, her face went blank, and she refused to answer. Finally, he spoke. "Do you recall anything else after fainting at the Mayes's house?"

"No. Everything just went blank. The next thing I remember was waking up in the car, with Lee driving."

"Lola had called him to come get you?"

"I guess so. It's odd. They don't have a phone. She must have gone to the neighborhood bar to call. But it seems to me she took a long time to make the call."

"Why's that?" Keller leaned forward in his chair.

"My home visit was at 10:30 and I got there at exactly that time. I like to be punctual. I'm pretty sure I fainted almost as soon as Davey let me inside. But, they say I got to the emergency room at 12:30. Lee says he left to get me as soon as he got off the phone. It's a 20-minute drive at most."

"Did you ever check with Lola to see what happened?"

Kathy fidgeted in her chair. "No. Now that I think about it, the whole thing seems strange. After the emergency room, I was admitted for observation. I was in really bad shape, maybe even worse than now. Lee went back to the Mayes's house to get my purse, which I had apparently dropped there. No one answered the door. A neighbor said they had moved. How could they move that fast?"

Kathy's response had delighted Dr. Keller in one respect, since she usually had responded in phrases and short sentences, with little affect. The slight tone of puzzlement in her longer than usual reply showed that she was opening up a bit. At least he hoped it was a portent.

But the time lapse she mentioned worried him. This was new. Kathy attached no obvious importance to it, but the possibility of hallucination in combination with apparent unconsciousness could imply many things: drug use, perhaps, or seizures, or a brain tumor.

Lee had told Dr. Keller of the buzzing sound Kathy had described to him so many times. But Kathy no longer complained of it. Keller sensed that the buzzing, the voice, and the missing time were somehow intertwined with Kathy's entire emotional upheaval. He had to investigate further.

"Kathy, how would you feel about hypnosis? I think it would help unlock some things you aren't dealing with consciously." He paused to see if she had any reaction.

When she didn't, he continued. "I just want you to be able to relax enough to review the events of that day. I think it would help in getting to the source of your distress if we could know the details of how things happened just before you went to the ER."

Keller reached back to place his notepad on his desk. He then pulled over a chair identical to the one Kathy occupied. He clasped his hands together on his knees and leaned forward to make eye contact with his patient over his glasses.

"I, I guess it's okay," Kathy responded in a flat, emotionless voice.

She didn't understand why Keller was focusing on Lola, the time of day and all the trivia related to her home visit and trip to the emergency room. She had never been hypnotized before, though she had volunteered to undergo it at a bridal shower for a friend. She had found out she wasn't the type who made a good target for hypnosis. She didn't think Dr. Keller would have much luck with her. But, if it could somehow help, she would give it a try.

Dr. Keller had Kathy lean back in her armchair, which reclined when she gave it an extra push, as he had instructed her. He dimmed the lights slightly and she soon found herself feeling totally relaxed as Dr. Keller continued speaking to her in a calming tone. He had her relax her entire body, one muscle group at a time.

The next thing Kathy was aware of was the doctor's voice saying, "Well, that's all for today."

She was puzzled about why he gave up so quickly.

"Kathy, you did fine. We made definite progress."

"But you weren't able to put me under..."

"You responded very quickly, Kathy."

She noted that he was now seated behind his oak desk. After a few minutes of closing comments, Dr. Keller opened the office door and escorted his patient out to her waiting husband, while advising her to make a follow-up appointment with his secretary.

Once the Fellners had departed, he rushed back to his office. He flicked on his tape recorder, an older model that he had been reluctant to replace, running it back a short distance. He punched the stop button abruptly, then hit the one marked *Play*.

Then, removing his glasses and cradling his chin in one hand, Charles Keller leaned forward to listen to the voice of Kathy Fellner describing what had really happened to her baby daughter.

Chapter 7: The Hermit of Hilltop House

Paul Sloan had become a near recluse, leaving his rambling country home only when he needed to purchase groceries. He spent his days with his computer equipment, trying to unravel the mystery of the strange communication that he had received.

Over the past few weeks, he had come to the unsettling conclusion that what he had said at the town meeting in July was very accurate. The area was under siege by UFOs. He clung to this belief despite the skepticism the gathering had expressed that night.

Encouraged by Reverend Selkirk's reluctance to believe in UFOs, some of the townspeople ridiculed Paul's statement of his conclusions. Paul had finally spun his wheelchair around with a single, quick twirl of one wheel and had, this time without assistance, exited the building. He would probably have felt humiliated if it weren't for the fact that he was so concerned about what was happening. Also, he knew that what he was asserting strained the normal bounds of credibility.

Paul left town in his van that night, feeling depressed by his inability to sway the townspeople. Halfway home, he noted that he was being trailed by a silvery white flying object that zigged and zagged all around his vehicle, as if to mock him, then vanished abruptly.

It had taken Paul some time following the incident with his computer to begin to accept what was happening. At first, there were unusual occurrences that he passed off as coincidence, like when his electrical power failed at exactly the same time for four nights in a row; or when he would be awakened at night by flashing lights outside his window.

What really got his attention, however, was the impression that soon developed that he was being harassed on purpose and the conclusion that he then reached that whoever was responsible intended him harm. He tried leaving home. He took long trips out of town to try to escape his tormentors. But, the lights followed him, even seeking him out in motel rooms in far distant locales. Finally, he just gave up and stayed home.

Paul did not consider himself a person who scared easily. He had dealt with the spinal cord injury he had sustained with what he felt was real grit, even bravery. He had always been the type to face life squarely. But he felt he had used up all reasonable options for dealing with all this on his own.

That's when he had contacted Jay. Jay had always been his friend, since they met in kindergarten. Jay had helped him through some of his toughest times and had been there for him after the accident, even when Cheryl failed him. And now, Jay had vanished. He had, according to Marla, started on his way to see Paul, but he never made it.

Then, one night, when Paul sat down to work at his computer, the flashing signals began again. Just as before a myriad of unrecognizable hieroglyphs dashed and darted before him across the screen of his monitor. This time, however, the printout didn't have Cheryl's likeness. It had Jay's.

Somehow, Paul wasn't surprised. He feared that whoever was sending the signals knew where Jay was, but Paul was not sure he wanted to learn what had happened to his friend. Paul also pondered the possibility that the unidentified sender was involved somehow with Cheryl.

Paul had tried to reach Marla, in the desperate hope that

she knew more about what had happened to Jay. There was no answer at her home phone, so he tried the number he had for her place of employment, the county courthouse.

Someone at that number told him that Marla had been injured in a car accident and she was still unconscious in a hospital in some midwestern city. After a pause, Marla's supervisor, the County Clerk, came on the line and informed Paul that Marla was at the hospital in Millardville.

"It's a funny thing..." the Clerk continued.

"What's funny?" Paul retorted with some irritation. To Paul, more than many, there was nothing funny about vehicle accidents.

"No, no, don't misunderstand me! I mean funny in a peculiar way," replied the Clerk in an apologetic tone. "A driver in the other lane said that Marla's car had just seemed to lift several feet off the ground and then flip over into the ditch...like it had been sucked up by a giant magnet and then dropped."

Paul didn't like the sound of that description. Lately, he had trouble believing anything anyone told him. George Huit, for example.

There was a pause, then the Clerk added, "They say Marla briefly regained consciousness in the ambulance and insisted that a car forced her off the road. But, the other driver, the one who witnessed the accident, said only that he thought he saw a bright silver flash before Marla's car left the road, like the reflection of light off a shiny surface. Now, that's an odd sort of thing for someone to say, when there were no other vehicles in the area."

"Not really," Paul interrupted. He thanked the Clerk and set the phone back down on its charger.

The next morning Paul had driven to Millardville Memorial Hospital with the aim of visiting Marla, but when he got there, she didn't recognize him. Though he tried in several ways to explain exactly why he knew her, all she kept saying was, "I'm sure you're a very nice man, but I just don't know you." After about half an hour of this, he gave up and returned home.

Paul was sitting at his kitchen table that evening, having just completed his evening meal. He was mulling over the frustrating contact with the wife of his best friend. Just at that moment, he heard a crash that seemed to come from the west wing of the mansion. He wheeled himself around instantly and gave both wheels a simultaneous shove with the heels of both hands, propelling himself down the passageway toward the spacious room he used for his computer work, which at one time was the living room of the orphanage.

In only a couple of seconds, he had shot nearly effortlessly from one end of the tunnel-like hallway to the other and emerged into the central room. He glanced quickly around the main room, noting that all his electronic gadgets seemed to still be in place along the edges.

Then, to his left, he detected the quick movement of something darting into the hallway that led to several bedrooms along the west side of the building, where Paul himself had established his own bedroom. It was the part of the building that had been reserved for the families who ran the orphanage, and Paul understood that his grandparents had lived in that wing.

He pulled a large flashlight from the bookcase by the door,

and launched himself forward along the edge of the hall into the shadows that lined the south wall. He rested the flashlight on his lap where he could reach it in a hurry.

All at once the lights in the large room flickered and died. Paul was left in the dark. His visitors must be back. He clamped his hands down quickly on the wheels of his chair, coming to an immediate halt and reached down to switch on the flashlight.

Nothing. The light didn't work.

Without a second's pause to dwell on this frustrating development, Paul gripped the handle of the flashlight tightly and stared resolutely into the darkness ahead. In just a few seconds his eyes began to adjust to the darkness. His heart, he now noted, was beating heavily.

For what seemed like a long time nothing happened. Then, in the doorway of the bedroom he used, Paul was able to discern the figure of a man. The shadowy being at first appeared to crouch in the doorway, then it edged forward toward Paul, who sat unmoving in the middle of the central room, his fingers tightening on his makeshift weapon.

Suddenly, the intruder leaped forward and made a dash toward Paul, who used his left hand to whip the wheel of his chair forward, causing the chair to make a lightning like turn toward the right. Simultaneously, he swung the flashlight in an upward arc.

There was a solid crunch as it collided with the jaw of the intruder, who then collapsed on top of Paul, tipping the chair onto its side. Both tumbled out and slid across the floor, slamming into the large desk where Paul kept his printer.

Ending up on top of his foe, he searched the immediate area with his hands until he located the heavy flashlight.

He started to raise it overhead to strike his opponent again, when he realized that the intruder wasn't moving. Paul pushed himself up on one hand to get a look at the attacker. Though the lights in the room remained off, a faint river of moonlight found an entry through one un-shuttered window and the two combatants had fallen into its path. Paul squinted his eyes to enhance his focus. His assailant began to stir; he tightened his grip on the flashlight and lifted it overhead, just in case.

The face of his enemy was human, Paul realized with relief. For the split second before the attack, he had considered the possibility that it wouldn't be. In fact, it appeared to be a slight and rather young man, with longish dark hair. Paul noted that he was wearing one of the shirts from his bedroom closet.

The stranger's eyes blinked open. It seemed to take him a few seconds to recall what had happened. In sudden panic, he tried to pull free from Paul, whose weight of more than 200 pounds kept the younger man pinned to the floor.

"Just hold it right there, buddy!" Paul commanded as authoritatively as he could. He waved the flashlight to back up that warning.

The young man pinned below him then quit struggling. Paul noted by the faint light from the window that he appeared confused. When he was sure that his opponent was calm, he used his powerful arms to push himself up and away, collapsing back against the big wooden desk. The young trespasser now appeared quite docile.

The darkness of the room was suddenly split with a slice of

green light, followed immediately by a flash of red. Then, abruptly, the lights of the room came back on. Paul knew the routine quite well, having experienced it several times in the past few months. His visitor shrieked and pulled himself into a fetal position.

"No! No! Leave me alone!" he shouted.

Paul was startled momentarily, but then realized how familiar he himself was with that terror.

"They won't leave me alone! They're always coming after me! Why can't they just stay away?"

Paul pulled his chair upright, locked its brake and began to struggle up into it. The frightened figure on the floor continued to huddle against the side of the old oak desk. At last, when Paul sensed that he was calming down, he decided it was time for some questions and answers.

"So," he began, "who are you and what are you doing here?"

The intruder unknotted his body slowly and pulled himself into a sitting position against the side of the smaller printer desk. He still appeared frightened, chewing nervously at the knuckles of his left hand. Paul began to feel some sympathy for this boy, who only moments earlier had seemed like such a threat.

After a pause, Paul cleared his throat. "I'll ask again. Who are you? Why are you in my house? Why are you wearing my clothes?"

Paul noted that the lad was tall, but quite thin and the clothes were very loose on him.

The young stranger glanced up. "I, I'm not sure who I am.

All I know is that I was running from them lights and I saw your buildings out here and hid in your shed last night. Then, tonight, I sneaked out and found a way into your house. I didn't have clothes. That is, all I had was some sort of pajamas; I didn't even have shoes. I need clothes if I'm going to escape from those lights."

"Well, you may have noticed that my clothes are a bit large for a skinny kid like you. But why are you running? I am familiar with those lights. I've seen them, I've also been chased by them. It does no good to run. If they want someone, they'll get him."

"That's just it. I don't know why I'm running. All I know is that I'm scared to death and I have to get away. Sometimes I feel like they're sort of herding me, playing some sort of cat and mouse game with me. It's like they get their laughs out of seeing me scared!"

Paul knew the feeling. He began to sense a kinship with this frightened youth who huddled, a few feet in front of him on the floor, trembling. He, too, had tried to escape, only to eventually come to the conclusion that he could not. He did not understand why he was being pursued. What possible use could these, whoever or whatever they were, have with him? What use could they have for this kid?

"I'm Paul Sloan," Paul said, his face relaxing to a smile. "If we're going to share in this grim game of theirs, let's at least try to work together. Maybe we can help each other."

"Okay," the youth replied somewhat hesitantly. "But what can we do?"

Paul leaned back in his chair and folded his arms. "We'll support each other, that's what. Maybe we can't escape or chase them off, but at least we will be in this together."

Paul extended his hand to the young man, who then pulled himself to his feet and shyly walked the few steps to offer his own.

"Strength in numbers, y'know?" Paul said.

As the stranger took his hand, Paul noticed a plastic band on his wrist. Paul turned the plastic band until he could make out the printing on it. He realized that it was a hospital name band.

"Well, then, welcome to my humble home," Paul pronounced in exaggerated graciousness. "Glad to meet you, Deke Fraley!"

Chapter Eight: Rader's Challenge

Sergeant Theodore Rader leaped to his feet when the cell phone on the table next to his cot started to ring. There could be little doubt about the reason for the call. The sky behind the mountains had been full of thunder and lightning for hours.

Before he even reached for the phone, he grabbed his combat boots from their place by the foot of his bunk and began tugging on his left boot with one hand as he grabbed his phone from the charger with the other. Outside, the roll of thunder that had accompanied the ring of the phone continued to intensify.

"Sergeant Rader here..."

"Code R," was all the response Rader received. It was all he expected.

A minute later, Rader had completely dressed and was bounding down the stairs that led from his barracks room to the parking lot, where his jeep awaited. Several other residents of the building were also moving toward parked vehicles. As usual, and as required by regulations, they were fully fueled and ready to go.

Rader, compactly built and muscular, five feet nine inches, 220 pounds, had measured his stride perfectly and was able to leap the last few feet and land in the driver's seat with one hand gripping the steering wheel and one foot on the accelerator pedal. As he landed on the seat, he grabbed the high-powered night vision binoculars that he'd left on the passenger seat and looped the strap over his head. His right hand automatically gripped the gearshift. In an instant he had the engine revving and was pulling out of the parking space.

As he pulled out of the parking lot well ahead of the other Army vehicles, Rader smugly congratulated himself on his record time in responding to the emergency call.

The darkness of the night was compounded by the heavy, tumbling storm clouds that struggled above. Occasional lightning provided a counterpoint to the crashing thunder underneath the roiling tumult. Rader hummed along in his small, olive green vehicle. He'd been in the Army eleven years now and had been hand-picked for this job eight years earlier.

He was not the type to reflect much on anything in his life, but he found himself doing so this night. He had performed this same drill so many times in the past few years that it all seemed routine. He recalled how, at first, he had been astounded by the nature of the mission. He remembered the initial recovery mission in which he had participated after months of classroom training that prepared him only in a very general way for what he would be doing.

That first trip out into The Forbidden Zone, as it was called, had left him somewhat in shock from what he had seen. The rest of the crew didn't seem to be perturbed by it, so he soon came to accept this aspect of his job as just a part of Army routine. Now, to Teddy Rader, it was just a job, extremely sensitive, top secret and all that, but still just a job.

He suspected that there was something very strange about the wrecks he and the others recovered. For one thing, they had some very strange writing on them, and the interiors were not always spacious enough for adults to occupy, but he knew he wasn't allowed to ask questions, so he pushed his thoughts aside.

Rader's reverie ended abruptly as he sighted the driveway

to Headquarters. He steered the jeep into its reserved slot and vaulted effortlessly from his seat and sprinted toward the front door of the two-story red brick building. Other vehicles were, by this time, pulling into the parking lot, each with similarly somber occupants.

A caffeine propelled corporal scurried out to open the doors of the larger arriving vehicles. Everything was moving in its usual, clockwork fashion. Within ten minutes of the initial phone call alert, both Recovery Teams A and B were assembled, seated before Colonel Webber, the officer in charge of the team, in the auditorium of the headquarters building. Usually only one team went out on an alert, but for some reason the Colonel had called out both teams this night.

Webber's opening comments, however, surprised Rader.

"Tonight, gentlemen, we have a different mission. We are going out into the Forbidden Zone, as usual, but this time our recovery task will be highly urgent. There has, again, been a crash. However, this time it is not just one of our craft or one of theirs. It is not just a matter of bringing back fragments of the wreckage or even the bodies of our flyers. Tonight, there will be a medical detachment accompanying you."

"The purpose will be explained to you when you open your sealed orders as we near the sites we have been told to investigate. I will take one envelope and Lieutenant Lundy, leading Team B, will have the other. When we near our sites, we will split up, then continue for precisely ten minutes, at which time I will fire a flare. That will be the signal for both teams to open their orders. The lieutenant and I will then open the envelopes and follow the instructions within."

This was highly irregular, the sergeant thought. He was puzzled by the change of procedures, but quickly reminded himself to trust that the Colonel knew what he was doing.

Rader glanced around. Lieutenant Lundy was present, which he hadn't noticed, apparently free of the panic that had gripped him during the previous alert. The Major who usually led Team B had been injured in a car wreck, Teddy had heard, but he had also heard a rumor that the major had "cracked up," which was becoming a more and more common problem.

Lundy must be taking temporary control of his team until a permanent replacement was found. This conclusion left the sergeant a bit nervous, since he knew that Lundy was emotionally unstable. Rader thought he detected fear in Lundy's eyes and in his posture as the Colonel dismissed them and they all headed toward the vehicles that were idling outside.

A minute later Rader found himself jolting over the ruts and rocks of the restricted base road that led into the Forbidden Zone. Colonel Webber was seated beside him, holding a large, sealed envelope. He had a grim expression frozen on his face. He didn't speak during the ride, except to urge the sergeant to greater speed. He kept his gaze fixed firmly ahead.

Immediately behind the jeep in each team came a new entry into the Recovery Teams' usual parade of military vehicles, an ambulance. Rader found this addition a bit perplexing, since there were never any survivors at the crash sites. There were rumors about the reason for this. Rader's own belief was that the recovery teams' dispatching was delayed while a top-secret squad checked out the wreckage. That explanation seemed rational to him.

If there were ever any survivors, that other crew whisked them away to some private medical facility, probably to be sure they wouldn't talk about what they had experienced to anyone who did not possess the appropriate security clearance.

"Sector 8H," Colonel Webber announced.

He pointed to the right leg of a Y branch in the road and Rader obediently cut the wheel in that direction. Lundy split his Team off onto the left branch. He was in the jeep leading Team B, bouncing along next to his driver, Specialist Hubber.

The ambulances were the second vehicles in each Team's order of march. In the back of each ambulance were three physicians, appropriately attired in the white smocks of their profession. Lundy was curious about their presence on this trip. He had never had physicians in the convoy before. He'd had what he assumed was a thorough indoctrination, but never had been told of the possibility that ambulances would be part of the lineup of vehicles. Perhaps the envelope he clutched would clear up everything.

The small caravan of Team A approached a hill and slowed to a crawl as Colonel Webber consulted his map. He finally pointed to the left and Rader shifted down as he edged his way off the pavement and down through the ditch that separated the gravel road from the flat sandy land at the base of the hill. The ambulance and trucks trailed behind him in a slow snake-like procession.

Lightning flashed behind the hill, followed a pulse beat later by a bone rattling clap of thunder that struck Rader with such a physical force that he feared for a second that his internal organs would suffer injury. He involuntarily took his foot off the gas pedal; Webber at once admonished him to step on it.

Just as he did, however, the jeep died. He immediately tried to restart it, since he knew that Webber's temper was short, and he wanted to avoid one of his boss's outbursts. But, the jeep would not respond, not even with a sputter or grind. Rader squeezed his eyes shut in anticipation of the profanity which he expected to be released.

But Webber only whispered, "Oh my god!" He checked his watch and added, "Get the flare gun and go to the top of that rise and fire it! Now!"

Rader assumed that he was to fire the flare to alert the other team that they should halt and check their sealed orders. He stepped out of the jeep to retrieve the flare gun case from the back seat. As he did so he suddenly recognized that all the lights of the trucks behind him had apparently also been doused and that all the military vehicles were stopped dead in various stages of descent from the road.

Rader removed the flare gun and turned back to the colonel, only to find him seemingly mesmerized by the nearly constant bolts of lightning that danced just beyond the crest. The Colonel's face appeared ashen each time lightning briefly parted the curtains of darkness; also, his driver noted that Webber's mouth had fallen open and stayed that way through several flashes of lightning.

Rader followed his gaze until his vision also became fixated upon the same spot as the Colonel's. The lightning had become so frequent that it gave the impression of a bank of alternately flashing, multicolored floodlights.

The sergeant pondered for a second that lightning didn't

usually come in colors. Suddenly, however, his contemplation ceased when it struck him that the lights were moving upward toward the sky as if climbing the other side of the hill. As Rader began to ascend the steep hill, he looked up.

Silhouetted atop the hill, with the flashing-colored lights behind him, was a kneeling figure, leaning on one arm with the other arm raised as if in supplication. Rader lifted his binoculars. Then, involuntarily, he took a step backward, unsure what to do next. This was unexpected. He had become accustomed to fire and smoke at these recovery sites, and even the unrecognizable charred corpses that the team had to pull from twisted wreckage, but there was something about these lights and the apparently injured person that terrified him. It took him a few seconds to figure it out.

The kneeling person didn't look human.

It seemed too small, and the upraised arm was too frail, ending in a hand with only four appendages. On previous missions, collisions and explosions had been discovered much longer after the event, after the sites had cooled. This time it appeared that the accident was very recent and there was a nauseating stench in the air as fires raged out of control. Rader had smelled burning flesh before, but he had never experienced this odor.

That thought shook him out of his contemplation. He had a job to do. He loaded a flare into the gun and began to struggle up the steep hillside with the flare gun clutched in his right hand, in response to Webber's order. He understood that he should climb to the top of the rise in order to get the best launch site for his flare, so it could be seen by Team B.

What he would do about the kneeling figure would have to be determined when he got there.

A few miles away, Team B's trucks had also stalled, and John Lundy had immediately stepped out of his jeep. As the lieutenant surveyed the convoy stretched out behind his jeep, his driver, Specialist Hubber, sat numbly staring at the dashboard gauges, trying to fathom what had caused the sudden halt.

All the drivers and their passengers began climbing down from their vehicles. There was another extremely loud explosion of thunder off to the east, accompanied by simultaneous forks of lightning. Lundy called back to his driver to get the Colonel on the radio. Hubber tried a couple times, then looked at the lieutenant with a shrug.

Lundy scowled and muttered a threat that Hubber could be court-martialed for insubordination if he didn't get through to Colonel Webber. This wasn't the first time he had been frustrated by an underling; early on, as a new second lieutenant, he had encountered a jovially lighthearted private from Georgia, who didn't take guard duty seriously.

When the private leaned his rifle against the guard shack, Lundy had crept up behind and snatched the weapon, shouting "Aha! Gotcha! You're in big trouble now!"

He had expected the private to quiver in fear and beg for forgiveness, but he merely smiled. Lundy felt that he wasn't being taken seriously and he was flustered. With his ruddy complexion even redder than usual, the lieutenant handed the rifle back to the soldier.

"Don't let it happen again!"

Now, with the entire convoy of trucks stretched out behind

his jeep, Lundy began to worry. He needed to assert his authority, so the soldiers behind him would treat him with respect. Webber had given him an opportunity to lead; he didn't want to look foolish again.

Why had the engines all died simultaneously? Why couldn't Hubber reach Team A on the radio? Since this was the first time there had been two teams sent out, there was no protocol for addressing this problem, at least as far as the inexperienced officer knew. If Team A was having some sort of trouble, maybe Team B should go to their aid, but not being able to contact them left the inexperienced Lieutenant unsure. This was just the sort of situation that caused him to fear dealing with the crashes.

Back at the site where Team A waited nervously, the lights behind the hill suddenly blinked out completely, trapping the soldiers in the moonless dark. There was a horrendous screeching sound, like metal scraping against rocks. Then the lights resumed, brighter than before. The engines of the Army trucks roared back to life. Those that had been left running in gear when their engines stopped, lurched forward and then died.

Specialist Tucker made a frantic dash for his wrecker and clambered into the cab in time to place the truck in reverse and back up onto the pavement, thus averting its tumbling down the embankment.

At the same moment, Team B's vehicles also restarted. John Lundy spun about in mid-stride and made a dash for his jeep. He had made his decision.

He instructed Hubber to turn the jeep around and head toward the direction of the lightning strike, which he was certain was the location of Team A.

By the time the specialist could manage this maneuver on the narrow, bumpy road, the ambulance had already executed a U-turn and pulled out to pass his jeep. One of the doctors, sitting in the passenger seat, barked at Lundy to get the team moving.

Lundy felt like he had felt with the private from Georgia; nobody gave him any respect. He ordered Hubber to step on it and pass the ambulance, which nearly caused a collision on the narrow dirt road. As his driver struggled to keep the vehicle on the road, Lundy gave the doctor in the ambulance a condescending smile.

Just as Hubber managed to pull in front of the ambulance, there was a flash of blinding light so bright that the drivers who had not yet turned around and were facing the lights were rendered temporarily blind. Lundy, seated next to Hubber, shuddered as a slowly advancing fear began to climb up his spine. That flash somehow shattered his barely recovered stability. He screamed for his driver to step on the accelerator, which the driver did, soon leaving the rest of the convoy far behind.

In only a couple minutes, Team B had backtracked to the point at which the two teams had split apart. This time they turned onto the other fork and sped along it. As they neared the hills that seemed to be the location of the lightning, the trucks of Team A were silhouetted by the flashes in the sky. Lundy noted a figure clambering up the hillside a short distance from the Army vehicles, clutching what to him appeared to be a handgun. His panic increased. He didn't like this. He didn't like this at all.

Something bad was about to happen, he was sure. He just had a bad feeling. He signaled Hubber to floor it and he began yelling for the gunman to halt. Weapons were a violation of the protocol, which the soldiers referred to as

The Deal, that THEY had established. The punishment for carrying one into a recovery zone could be severe. Lundy recalled that clearly from his orientation.

As soon as Hubber braked at the bottom of the hill, the lieutenant leapt from the passenger seat and began scrambling after the gunman. It didn't occur to him that the man could be merely trying to get to higher ground in order to launch a flare.

"The DEAL! The DEAL!" the Lieutenant shouted hoarsely as he stumbled across the dry terrain. Colonel Webber had regained his composure and was loping along ahead of him. Rader was nearing the top of the ridge. It began to rain. The wind picked up. He couldn't hear the Colonel's voice from below.

"Stop that man!" Webber barked. As he stumbled forward toward the hill, slipping on the ground that was beginning to turn to mud, others recognized the problem and joined him in a race to stop Rader.

But Theodore Rader had a lengthy head start and, besides, was in the best physical condition of all the team members, and he had already crested the hill. He looked around for the injured figure but couldn't see him. A clap of thunder drowned out the shouts from Lundy, Webber and the others. As far as the sergeant knew, Team B was a couple miles to the south.

Rader lifted his right hand, prepared to fire off a flare. Suddenly, the loose gravel at the top of the hill gave way and he found himself sliding down into the valley on the other side. He began to tumble downward, hitting his hand on a large boulder as he did.

With a sudden flash, the flare shot from the gun, which was

now pointed downhill, in the direction of the crash scene.

The initial flash of the flare revealed a solitary figure clinging to an outcropping on the steep slope, a dozen yards downhill from Rader. As he slid down the slope, the sergeant just had time to see the individual desperately clinging to the edge of a large boulder, see his glowing red eyes and large head, his grayish white skin.

Then, even as the sergeant slid to a halt in a sitting position against another boulder, the flare exploded with a searing white flash. An ear-piercing screech echoed off the surrounding hills.

Rader was temporarily blinded by the flash, but when he regained his vision the figure on the boulder was gone. At the bottom of the hill, in the gully formed by the hill and a rise on the other side, Rader perceived several figures scurrying about amid a clutter of twisted, dully gleaming material that he assumed was the wreckage of a flying vehicle, though it didn't look like any metal he had seen in any Army aircraft.

Rader regained his feet. He stood for a second in shocked amazement. He had shot the injured figure!

The flare gun slipped from his fingers and clattered down the hillside to the crash site. His eyes followed its path until he was able to just barely discern a crumpled body resting at the bottom. As the other team members crested the hill behind Rader, they each paused momentarily to take in what they could of the scene below. The darkness returned rapidly as the fires caused by the flare died out.

One of the doctors paused long enough to give Rader an icy stare and then led a team of stretcher bearers down the hill.

Colonel Webber reached the summit as Rader turned away from the doctor. He ripped off his baseball-style fatigue cap and hurled it to the ground at Rader's feet. Rader stared blankly at the officer.

"You idiot! Do you realize what you've done?" the Colonel screamed, seizing the sergeant by the collar. "You have violated the PROTOCOL!"

Rader gulped. Beads of perspiration began to collect on his forehead. He felt a shiver shake his entire frame. He stared helplessly at Webber.

"Don't you see, Rader?" Webber screeched. "What if you killed one of THEM?" Webber stepped around the sergeant with the intent of descending the slope..

Rader's mind was swimming. Were *THEY* really aliens? He'd always suspected it, but then suppressed those suspicions. But now?

Then it hit Rader. The enormity of possibly killing one of THEM washed over him. In all these years he had never actually seen one in person, unless...maybe...those charred and featureless bodies.

The rumor of their presence had been commonly bandied about by the enlisted men. The recoveries always involved experimental aircraft, manned by humans, sometimes shot down by THEM or damaged in collisions. The entire protocol was based on an agreement that, if the humans didn't make THEIR existence known, THEY would not embark on a program of mass extermination and THEY would share some of the secrets of THEIR advanced technology with humans.

The full purpose of THEIR presence was top-secret.

It was assumed that the truth would cause widespread panic. That was why the government refused to admit that THEY were real. There was even a secret agency based in Washington, D.C. and in the capital cities of most nations whose primary purposes was to cover up THEIR existence.

It had initially been a shock to learn this, but members of Rader's squad had been handpicked because they could keep this huge secret. The results of actually killing one of THEM could be devastating. No one knew for sure how THEY would respond. Rader had always been able to ignore those things.

Suddenly the reality of it all hit Rader like a mortar shell. The sergeant began to giggle nervously, uncontrollably.

"Shut up! Shut up!" Webber shouted, whirling himself about to face the shadowy hillside where the other team members were stumbling about with flashlights, trying to locate Rader's victim. "You'd better hope everything is okay! You had better pray that no harm has been done!"

Webber stopped and spun about and started down the slope again, pulling his own flashlight from his belt as he descended. Rader stood staring after him for a few seconds, then slowly sank to his knees, clutching his arms across his stomach, which had begun to churn. His head began to roar. With each throb of his pulse, a distant voice seemed to grow louder and louder from somewhere within his skull, indistinct at first, but eventually emerging into Rader's full awareness, the words he had spoken to a reluctant and frightened John Lundy just a few days earlier: "Just a job...just a job...just a job..."

Then, Rader vomited violently.

Chapter Nine: The Sleep Study Mystery

Nicholas Dunbar had about reached the end of his physical endurance. He felt himself growing more exhausted each day, though he had started going to bed earlier each evening. He now found himself in bed by 5:00 PM.

His wife Louise had become increasingly worried about her husband's health; they had been married for 26 years and he had never had any serious medical problems. But, every time she mentioned her concern to him, he would either ignore her or snap back some sarcastic response. Lou feared it must be a brain tumor or stroke.

Then the MRI Dr. Williamson had ordered was done. The doctor had called Nick to his office to discuss the results. Nothing showed up on the film, which Dr. Williamson had described as a "three-dimensional x-ray."

Lou was relieved, but her husband remained just as worn out, just as irritable, just as sullen. He was unable to work most of the time at the paint store the family owned in Millardville. Their oldest son Clint had taken over day-to-day operation of the family business. Some days Nick even refused to leave the house. Clint and Jenni could no longer bring over little Oliver to see his grandfather. Neighbors were beginning to talk. Lou had begun to consider taking her two youngest children and going to live with her sister Sheila in St. Paul.

Nick had tried to explain to his family what he was experiencing, but he felt they didn't believe him. He knew that he was seldom aware of sleeping at night, but he also realized that he must be sleeping more than he thought he was, since he had several times found himself staring at the lighted digital clock in the middle of the night abruptly aware that several hours had passed since the last time he checked the time. Apparently, he had fallen asleep, but just didn't recall any sense of drifting off gradually. And he always awoke abruptly as if someone had doused him with cold water. But, if he was sleeping, it certainly wasn't restful, replenishing sleep.

Lou had become frantic. Her entire life seemed to be unraveling. She could no longer communicate with her once easy-going husband, a man everyone in town had seemed to know and like. Denise and Timothy were no longer able to have friends drop by, since Nick had begun to have unpredictable rages that sometimes concluded with screaming ejections of everyone from the house. She was unable to convince Nick to make another appointment with Dr. Williamson, so she phoned the doctor herself to express her concern.

Dr. Williamson came up with a suggestion. "Let's line Nick up with the University Medical Center Sleep Disorder Clinic in Spring City. They may be able to find a reason for your husband's sleeping problems."

So, there they were, finally. Lou had been a bit scared of the idea of going to the big city, but Nick had glumly agreed to cooperate. Clint closed the paint store for the day and volunteered to do the driving, since Lou was terrified of the city traffic and Nick was so overly tired, he couldn't be trusted to drive.

They managed to find the clinic, which was actually in a medical building across the street from the hospital. The receptionist checked Nick in and then directed the family to the adjacent waiting area. Clint found a magazine on a table and sat down to browse through it. There was an article on unidentified flying objects, which he found interesting.

His father slumped into one of the molded orange plastic chairs next to his son and immediately leaned forward to rest his forehead in his cupped hands, a position that had become habitual. Lou sat on the other side of her husband, gripping his arm.

Finally, a small, thin man with a patch of disheveled red hair approached the trio. The white, unevenly buttoned lab coat he wore, along with the dark rimmed glasses settled on the end of his nose gave him the appearance of a kindly, but forgetful, college professor. Nick remained sullen but allowed Dr. Baines to lead him away to his office. The doctor returned to the waiting room a few minutes later.

"I am Dr. Howard Baines," he said as he held out his hand. "I have studied your husband's medical reports that Dr. Williamson was kind enough to send me. There is one thing that puzzles me."

He stared directly into Lou's eyes. "It's that triangular impression on the back of your husband's neck."

Lou was perplexed by the tone employed by the doctor, which seemed to imply that the impression had some medical significance.

"Well," Lou responded, "Nick told me that he had spilled some paint on his neck and he had an allergic reaction to the paint thinner he used to clean it up."

Dr. Baines straightened his slight frame and tilted his head to one side. "I see." He began, rubbing his chin with his left hand.

"There is a reason I asked about this. Mr. Dunbar is my fourth patient this month with a triangular mark at the base of his skull. They all complain of a constant buzzing in their ears. They all report significant lack of sleep. I thought maybe we had happened upon some sort of invasion of poisonous insects or spiders that led to all these same problems, but each patient had his or her own explanation for what caused the mark. They all told me immediately where it came from. One woman told me her cat had scratched her. A man who works in construction said that he was hit on the neck by a board with a protruding nail. Another man from a town near where you live said he knew that he'd been shot with a pellet from the gun of an irate neighbor."

Lou stared blankly at the doctor. Clint pulled himself from his chair and approached them. Dr. Baines, now sure that he had their full attention, continued.

"One thing that puzzles me is that when he initially went to see Dr. Williamson, he had no idea where the mark came from. Were you aware of the mark and the event that may have caused it, at the time it happened, I mean?"

"Well, I did notice it in mid-July," Lou reflected, "but Nick just shrugged it off. It wasn't until a week or so after he went to see Dr. Williamson that he mentioned the paint thinner accident."

Clint spoke up, "Mom, you know I work with Dad every day down at the store and I don't recall ever seeing an accident. In fact, Dad spends most of his time doing the paperwork, ordering supplies and so forth. I'm the one who mixes the paint, stocks the shelves and helps the customers; he stays in the office in back. He doesn't even remove his suit coat, even when it's hot and humid. He always says it's important to present the right image to the customers. I'm the labor and he's the management, that's how it goes. At least it was until he got so bad that he couldn't handle it anymore. Now, I do everything."

"Then, why the story? That's what I wonder about all these patients. I've spoken with other families and heard similar stories and encountered similar discrepancies. We seem to have an epidemic of prevarication."

Dr. Baines ran his fingers through his already tangled hair. "I guess this doesn't matter, but once I began noticing the marks at the base of the skull, I couldn't help but wonder if there is some connection with sleep disturbance."

"Pre...what?" asked Lou.

Clint leaned in close to her and whispered, "It means lying, Mom."

"Well, Dr. Baines," Clint turned his attention to the doctor, "were you able to help those other patients? Did you find out what caused their problems?"

"No, I did not. But, I had hoped to do so in follow-up visits with some additional testing. I had received some new computerized equipment that I thought would help with my diagnosis, but I was unable to use it on those patients."

Clint looked puzzled. "Why was that?"

"Because," Dr. Baines sighed, "they have all disappeared."

Nick Dunbar spent two nights undergoing the sleep study. There was an electroencephalogram, cardiac tests and a brain scan. Dr. Baines's staff had worked hard to schedule them all close together so he wouldn't have to commute from Millardville so often. Those tests were daytime events; he spent the nights in a quiet room, under the benign gaze of a video camera, wired by electrodes to various machines. The first night he had trouble sleeping, but by the second he was quite exhausted and was accustomed to the room, so sleep came readily, for the first time in months. Lou and Clint returned home after Nick was settled in for the first night.

Dr. Baines now had his first chance to use the new computerized equipment on one of the *buzzheads* as his irreverent young lab assistant Greg Bowie had labeled the patients who complained of the constant humming in their skulls. There had been a small, but noticeable increase in the number of such cases recently. Greg had helped Dr. Baines hook the new patient up and had entered the basic identifying information and health history into the computer.

The first night, because of Nick Dunbar's restlessness, the computer evaluation was not successful. The second night, however, Gene Baines grinned in satisfaction at Greg Bowie and gave him a thumbs up sign when the special equipment verified that Nick had entered the deepest stage of sleep.

The computer began to record all the information from the various attachments to Nick's body, such as heart rate, respiration and brain waves. After half an hour of uneventful recording, Dr. Baines slapped Greg on the shoulder and bade him goodnight. Bowie could call him if there was any need for his input, but everything seemed fine with the patient, so it appeared that the young technician would be in for his usual boring nightshift job of watching the computer do its work.

The sleep study clinic had been set up, deliberately, in an isolated part of the building. The other offices and examining rooms in that part of the building were dark and vacant at night, giving the sleep center the advantage of being apart from all the irksome noises that might interfere with its need for nighttime peace and quiet.

This night, also, Nick was the only patient being studied, so Greg Bowie soon found himself to be the lone person awake in that part of the building. He was accustomed to this, however, and had no trouble concentrating on his job of watching the electronic wizardry of the equipment hooked up to Nick Dunbar.

Mostly, the job entailed an occasional need to reattach an electrode that had come loose when a patient turned over while asleep. Greg also made periodic notations in the patient chart, if an unusual event occurred, such as the person awakening and requesting a blanket. He also checked the equipment and verified its functioning every hour on a checklist attached to his clipboard.

Greg always re-read his entries toward the end of his shift just to make sure he had recorded everything in clear language that was in no way vague. Early in his experience with Dr. Baines, Greg had put down a comment for which the doctor had requested clarification when he read it hours later and Greg had been unable to recall what exactly he was trying to say; since that time Greg always reviewed his notes before Dr. Baines saw them.

This night seemed to have gone well. *"Midnight: patient drifting regularly in and out of the various sleep stages, monitors all functioning well. One A.M: patient turned over to his left, technician had to reattach cardiac monitor, all computer readings normal. Two A.M: check of the computer readings reveals prolonged period at deepest sleep level. Alarm bell rang, technician checked patient, reset alarm."*

When Greg read the last entry, he was shocked. He didn't recall the event happening. It would take an unusual event to set off the alarm, such as prolonged apnea or cardiac irregularity. Usually, the technician would check on the patient, readjust the face mask or some wires and all would be well again.

He re-checked his clipboard. The 2:00 AM entry was the most recent entry. There should have been entries at 3:00 and 4:00. Maybe he just forgot to make entries, but he didn't recall anything after the 1:00 entry and certainly didn't remember an alarm sounding. He decided to rewind the video of the sleeping patient to see what had happened during the missing time between 2:00 and 4:30. Otherwise, Dr. Baines might conclude that he had indeed fallen asleep at the console.

Greg rewound the recording to the 1:00 AM time period, then hit the forward button. He sat nervously on the edge of his chair as he waited. For a while nothing much showed up. Nicholas Dunbar lay motionless, his chest moving rhythmically as he breathed. The date and time appeared automatically in the lower left corner of the screen.

Greg hit the fast forward button, releasing it periodically to check the time. At last, he came to 2:00 AM. He leaned forward even closer, holding his breath. The patient on the screen continued to sleep. He wasn't moving at all.

Suddenly, Greg noticed what appeared to be a flash of white along the edges of the bed, on all sides at once. He could see the wires dropping away from Dunbar's body, as though plucked off by invisible hands. Then, there was a quick glimpse of something white, or perhaps light gray, and an oval, narrow and dark.

Next, the screen went totally black.

Almost immediately, it returned, but the time in the corner indicated that it was now twenty-six minutes after four.

Greg's hand shot to the phone. Dr. Baines would have to see this now, for certain. Greg had evidence that something had malfunctioned in the electronic equipment, and his boss would want to know about that.

After a short conversation with the slightly agitated doctor, with profuse apologies, he convinced Baines to come in early to view the film. Then, after hanging up, he turned back to the video screen and rewound it to the 2:00 AM time. He watched the film over and over, trying to identify what knocked the electrodes loose and what the whitish blob was that appeared just before the blackout.

He couldn't decipher it, after four or five tries. Then, he tried advancing it a few seconds at a time. Still, the wires slipped from the sleeping patient for no apparent reason, but the white blur around the edge of the bed seemed to be darting in toward each of the electrodes just before they came off.

Then came the narrow, slanted shape.

Even at the slowest speed, Greg couldn't determine what it was. He ran it through again. As he neared the point at which it appeared, he stopped the recording and began advancing it a frame at a time. At last, the narrow, black line appeared, rising from the right lower corner of the screen. Then, as the frames advanced jerkily across his line of vision, Greg suddenly found himself staring into two narrow slits of darkness, which seemed to be sunk into the larger white oval.

A long, thin hand, though Greg could see that it wasn't exactly a hand, crossed in front of the oval, seeming to reach for the video camera.

Then, for the last few frames, Greg again could make out what he now understood to be eyes. They didn't blink and seemed to Greg to be staring deeply into his soul.

Suddenly, startlingly, a bright red glow appeared in the middle of the blackness. The eyes came closer and closer, until the blackness obscured the screen.

Then, the image of Dunbar reappeared with "4:26 AM" in the lower left corner.

Greg shivered and turned away from the monitor. He sat back in his chair, breathing heavily, his heart pounding, and waited for his boss to arrive.

Chapter Ten: Silent River and Opaque Orb

George Huit knew that he was going to have to do something about the Caperton situation. It was getting out of hand. First, there was that Sloan guy who refused to be hushed up about the events of that summer, now came this report from his on-site agent that the town drunk claimed to have been off flying in a "UFO" and had seen that missing Paige kid. Huit stood in his spacious office, staring out his window at the U.S. capitol in the distance. If he didn't do something soon, he'd be in deep water with his bosses.

And they would be in even more trouble with...Huit wiped the thought from his mind before even daring to complete it. As he tried to calm down, he removed his glasses and cleaned them with a soft cloth. When he had finished that and replaced the glasses, he sat back against the edge of the desk and began to breathe more slowly as he stared through his office window at the distant Capitol Building.

A small, blue light began to blink on the corner of his desk. Huit caught the blinking out of the corner of his eye and ceased gazing out the window. He removed a chain from around his neck and seized the key that dangled at the end. Inserting it into a small, hidden lock beneath the blotter pad on his desk, he gave it a turn and the blotter slid aside to reveal a panel of blinking lights. He glanced around nervously as he reached into the space to retrieve a small cell phone. He immediately clicked on one of the blinking lights and put the phone up to his right ear. He listened for a few seconds, then removed it from his ear and punched in some numbers.

"Silent River," he whispered into the receiver.

A voice from the speaker responded, "Opaque Orb."

Then it paused briefly and asked, "Any progress on the problem?"

They were pressuring him, Huit realized. He had expected it, but it was still a bit of a shock.

"Not yet," he responded. "I will re-visit the site myself and take care of the glitch."

"Time is short, Silent River. Soon things will automatically happen. Our friends don't understand patience. If they act, you understand how hard that will be to cover up. We've been able to hide some events when only a few individuals were involved, but any town, even a small one like Caperton, would be difficult to explain."

Huit knew that already. Such action had only been taken twice during his involvement with Orb. Once, it was a village in a remote part of the Nevada desert. One other time, a landslide had been listed as the official cause for the disappearance of a small town in the Rocky Mountains. Word of that disaster had attracted some media attention and an investigative reporter from New York had even come to investigate. THEY took care of her, though he wasn't sure how they did that. He knew that THEY were rumored to sometimes kidnap people and perform medical or genetic experiments on them, but no human knew why.

Caperton was small, but not remote and there were no mountains around that could make it easy to pass off a rockslide as the cause. There weren't even any rivers close to the town that could be caused to flood and wipe out the village. A tornado might serve the purpose but wiping out the entire population with a simulated twister seemed a bit too hard to believe. Just going in to kill all the townspeople by hand or with some craft-based lasers could be too easily detected by witnesses driving along the highway.

Finding the ideal time when no one was around would be tricky.

Huit had recruited someone as a plant to infiltrate a local militia group that operated near Caperton and since the members hailed from several nearby towns, word of any *special action* might get out. His plant was someone nobody would suspect of being a mole.

First of all, it was a young woman who worked in a nearby town. She wasn't the type. But, if she thought the local "militia" that she had infiltrated was close to interfering with the PLAN, she was authorized to eliminate its members. That made Huit feel safer, but it wouldn't be enough to satisfy THEM.

He would have been shocked to learn that his mole wasn't who he thought she was.

But, he had a second plant in case the first was exposed. Nobody would expect her, either. Her cover story was that she was a teacher.

Before Huit could state the difficulty he anticipated, the receiver clicked, and the line went dead. That was the style of the mysterious contact person known only as Opaque Orb. No small talk, only business and very little of that.

The contacts were quite infrequent, escalating every few years when activity increased. In between, when THEY felt it better to lay low, Huit was able to relax a little.

THEY arrived in waves, every few years, staying for a sort of tour of duty. Huit had no idea when they would appear or what they were up to. But, when they did arrive, it was his job to plug any leaks.

He pondered the purpose of the UFO visitors. He had concluded that they weren't simply from somewhere else in the galaxy or universe. That was too simple an explanation.

He had the impression that they did not share the emotions of humans, but they seemed to have a superior understanding of behavior, though they didn't care much about it, except when they needed to use it to force cooperation. They did not understand morality or compassion and apparently thought these were inconvenient attributes that merely got in the way of more important things.

Huit, however, wasn't sure what those things might be. Or, rather, he wouldn't admit to himself that he had an idea. He'd wipe those thoughts from his mind. The one thing he could acknowledge was that there was no choice for him or anyone else. Everyone on earth was a molecule to be studied or ignored...and, perhaps, discarded.

Back to the problem at hand. Caperton had to be effectively silenced. The financial persuasion Huit had provided in July and August had not been enough to accomplish that. It might have worked if not for the difficulty involving the village idiot. Apparently one weakness THEY had involved not being able to control someone with no inhibitions.

That is why THEY had had to counter his behavior by curing his alcoholism and giving his intellect a boost, which they did manage to accomplish prior to shoving him out of their vehicle. THEY had erased that part of his adventure from his memory.

But THEY still couldn't seem to control this Lapley guy.

Now, with his raving about taking a ride on a UFO and seeing that missing boy on board, the entire town was beginning to become restless. It had taken all of his unit's influence and power thus far to counter those rumors.

It was lucky that this Peter Lapley was known to be both a drunk and slightly demented; the story could be deflected from wider exposure by making that information available to any reporters who came upon the story.

But Lapley wouldn't keep quiet. He had quit drinking and, at the same time, had become serious about his story. The townspeople were beginning to listen to him. The story wouldn't die.

Peter Lapley would have to.

Chapter Eleven: The Glyphs

Tyrone Williamson had become intrigued by the recent medical events he had encountered in Millardville. First, there was the problem with Nicholas Dunbar and Jay Brashear, whom he had learned had disappeared without a trace, after his stop to seek medical care. Then came Kathy Fellner and her mysterious non-pregnancy. There was also the recent disappearance of that Fraley kid. All had developed the strange mark at the base of their skulls and had complained of buzzing in their ears.

Ty was sure there must be some connecting link among those four cases that would help him solve the medical puzzle. He just had not been able to find it.

Then, Ty was surprised to find that the wife of Jay Brashear was hospitalized right there in the Millardville hospital. Strange coincidence, he thought, but maybe he could find a clue if he could just talk to her. He had gone to the hospital to do that, but she had still been unconscious. He returned daily for a week, without success. However, he was able to speak at length with the mother of Deke Fraley. Then, Deke had vanished. First Brashear, then the Fellner baby, then the Fraley boy. There was something extremely strange about this whole situation.

It was Thursday morning and Ty, again, had to wait for Wally Hunter to put in his appearance at the Bluebird Café. Wally always seemed to be late. Renee, the ever-present waitress, flitted about the room, but was always close at hand before a cup was empty. Finally, just as she poured coffee into Ty's cup for the third time, Wally threw the door open, strode across the room and fell into a chair next to Ty and waved nonchalantly at Renee, asking for "the usual". Wally didn't notice that she gave him a warm smile.

As soon as his friend was seated, Ty leaned toward him. Wally noted the serious expression on his face.

"What's up, buddy boy?" Wally said with a bit of annoyance.

These get-togethers were supposed to be relaxing and fun, with no discussion of medical matters or other sobering topics. Lately, they had become too work-related.

"Listen, Wally," Ty began, frowning, "I've begun to wonder about these strange medical incidents that we have seen lately. First, Dunbar, then Jay Brashear..."

"Yes, I know," Wally conceded, running his left hand through his thick, slightly graying hair, which was, as usual, disheveled. "They all had those head problems, that constant buzzing, etcetera. But there haven't been any more reported cases and the state health department says we're the only area to experience all this."

Wally had put in a phone call to the State Department of Public Health.

"Apparently, the patients themselves haven't had any previous contacts with one another, so they didn't catch it from each other. Other family members don't have it, so it is not likely contagious through the air. Maybe it's a parasite or a fungus. We've talked to some of the patients and their families. None seem to have taken any trips to areas where they could pick up some infection or fungus."

"We haven't talked to Jay Brashear or Deke Fraley," Ty pointed out to his friend. " It's just been the family of Nick Dunbar, Kathy Fellner and her husband, plus Mrs. Fraley. They..."

Wally took his turn at interrupting.

"We should talk to that psychiatrist who has been treating Kathy, Dr..."

"...Charles Keller," Ty completed his friend's sentence.

As Wally frowned, Ty continued, "I checked with him, but the rules of patient confidentiality and the privacy of medical records kept him from telling me anything useful. I did emphasize that this mysterious malady may have something to do with Kathy's psychiatric problems, but..."

"Wouldn't talk, would he? You might as well drop the idea, Ty."

"Well, he did point out that I needed Kathy's okay to even contact him, but he would explore issues related to possible health problems and see if he could get a signed release from Kathy. He said it might be helpful for her to learn that she is not alone with whatever this is."

"Enough shop talk," Wally added. "Let's see what we can do for recreation over at the Y."

As the physicians departed, Renee glided over to clear their table. Then, the cell phone in her apron pocket began to vibrate. She took it out and looked at it. Looking around, she noted that there were no other customers, so she signaled the cook that she was taking her break and exited through the back door of the café, placing the phone to her ear.

Paul Sloan faced a dilemma. Now that he had identified Deke Fraley, should he try to get him to return to the hospital in Millardville?

That had been his initial instinct, but almost at once he had begun to worry. The boy had fled the hospital as the result of some sort of fear of the lights. To send him back would subject him again to face the same threat.

Paul had begun to develop a suspicion that his tormentors had some sort of purpose in mind in their ongoing harassment. After all, they had followed him everywhere, but had never actually harmed him, even though they clearly had that capability. Now, Deke had been literally chased to his house. Was there some reason for this?

Paul felt ethically obliged to ask Deke his preference. Deke recoiled at once at the idea of leaving the house. His fear was overpowering and now that he sensed he had an ally, or at least a fellow victim, he didn't want to leave. He couldn't remember where he came from or who he was, but Deke also begged Paul not to try to contact anyone to let them know where he was. Deke seemed paranoid, Paul thought.

But then, he had a reason to be paranoid. Someone really was after him.

The morning following their meeting, Paul arose early to work on a new project involving a computer program for the University Hospital. He had been plugging away at it for a couple hours when Deke emerged from the first-floor spare bedroom to which Paul had assigned him. Paul pointed to the kitchen, where he had scrambled some eggs. A couple minutes later Deke returned, wiping his face with a paper towel.

"You're some sorta computer whiz?" Deke asked. He was amazed at how easily he was able to speak with this stranger who had taken him in.

"I seem to have a knack for this stuff, yeah," Paul replied. "Besides, there aren't too many NBA teams that have been after me since my accident."

Deke wasn't sure how to take the last remark, since it seemed to be intended as dry humor. It was tossed out by Paul in the flat tone in which he did most of his speaking.

There was a small part of Deke that didn't understand humor. Though his memory was incomplete, he knew that it was not his strength. Besides, Deke didn't recall having been around any people with physical disabilities. In fact, he just had the vaguest memory of being around anyone before escaping to this former orphanage. He had a foggy recollection about the political appropriateness of the term *disability*.

At any rate, though Deke felt quite relaxed around Paul, he was less comfortable with his wheelchair, so he didn't respond to the comment about the NBA. He barely even knew that it had to do with sports.

Paul had become accustomed to the discomfort of others. He remembered his own difficulties as a child when encountering strangers who were physically different from him in some way. He thought back to his maternal grandfather's need to use a wheelchair in the last few months of his life. He had long ago concluded that the best way to address such discomfort was by providing information.

"Want to know how this happened to me?" Paul asked, without even looking over his shoulder at Deke. "Well, it happened when I was in the Army. I had a job as a truck driver at a base in Colorado. I was doing very sensitive work, top secret, actually. I didn't know the full scope of what my unit was doing; only the upper-level officers knew much about it and even they were kept in the dark about some details. Even my immediate superior, Lt. Webber, didn't know much."

"My duties consisted of driving a truck out into the highly restricted areas to retrieve parts of crashed experimental aircraft. Some of it was very strange looking. A few of the crash sites were littered with very unusual sheet metal or foil, and very strong, lightweight rods, and electronic devices. There was a thunderstorm one night and I was driving..."

Paul halted in mid-sentence. He hadn't thought about the strange crash site debris in years. He had always considered it not much more than slightly sophisticated junk from flying devices that were still in their beginning stages of development. He had assumed that the wreckage was from crashed American prototypes that were being tested at the base. But there was something about that junk, something that just now seemed very important.

Paul whipped his chair around and propelled himself across the room in two quick spins of the wheels, clamping his hands down simultaneously to bring the chair to a sharp stop next to the stack of computer printout paper in the corner.

Deke stared at his host blankly as Paul began digging through the pile. With an uncharacteristic shout of glee, Paul pulled free a thick bundle of papers, waving it overhead and almost tipping over his chair. He then dropped the stack into his lap, spun the chair back around and was back to his point of origin next to Deke almost instantly.

"Look at this!" Paul exclaimed.

Deke peered over his shoulder, seeing only pages of white paper with thick, black squiggles. "These are exactly the kind of symbols that were stamped on those pieces of aircraft wreckage! Now I know why they seemed so familiar that one night when my computer went berserk and began spewing these out."

Deke finally found a chance to speak. "So, what's the deal? What's all this mean?"

"It means," Paul began, "that those wrecks I was salvaging during Recovery were actually wrecks of these UFO aircraft, not ours. It wasn't experimental U.S. aircraft I was cleaning up after, it was crashed flying saucers!"

Paul slapped the heel of his right hand against his forehead. "I had my spine broken in some stupid attempt to chase down flying saucer souvenirs!"

Paul realized that he was actually expressing suppressed anger for the first time in years.

Deke was staring intently at the papers that were spread across Paul's lap. Something about these black hieroglyphs looked familiar to him, also. He knew he had seen them somewhere. A fleeting image of a chain link fence and a blinding light zipped through his mind. Brief images of other colored lights and strange, oval faces flashed into his mind, followed by a panicky feeling that he was being hurt in some way.

Paul sensed Deke's sudden discomfort. "What is it, Deke?"

"I, I think I've been on one of those UFOs! I've seen that writing before. They tried to hurt me, kidnapped me from my job, attached something to the back of my head, did something to my nose. That's when the buzzing in my head started, I think."

Paul had the uncomfortable feeling that his new friend was about to snap. He hated being put in the position of trying to calm other people. Over the years he had become such a loner, responsible for his own actions and emotions, that he hadn't the patience for dealing with anyone who was less self-reliant.

Then, as abruptly as he had begun to experience panic, Deke stopped. Paul noted that his body seemed to suddenly relax, and his face lost its look of fear. In the deflected early morning light, Deke's face seemed to take on a paleness that almost shocked Paul. And his eyes, now in the shade as the outside source of light was obscured by a sudden cloud cover, seemed to have narrowed and become deeply sunken in his face. Deke's mouth was clamped shut so tightly that his lips had the appearance of a slit in his face.

"Deke?" Paul wheeled himself back a few feet. His friend remained still. "Are you alright?"

The cloud that had obscured the sun passed and the room again was fully sunlit. Paul took another look at the slender kid and realized that his face was back to its regular shade and his eyes and mouth were normal. He scolded himself for letting his own paranoia distort his reasoning.

"They need your help," Deke said quietly.

Paul looked at him quizzically. "What? Who? What are you talking about?"

"The writin' on them pages. I can read it."

"You can what?" Paul wheeled himself forward and stared up into Deke's face.

"Yes, I look at those markings and I can tell what they mean. I don't know how, but the meaning just comes to me."

Deke reached down to pick up a few sheets of paper that had fallen to the floor when Paul had wheeled backward. He held them up with his left hand and pointed at the slightly crumpled pages.

"It says that they must ask you to help them. They are running out of time and do not understand why you haven't done what they wanted you to do."

Paul wasn't sure whether to laugh or scream. The idea seemed so absurd. His houseguest was able to read this stuff? This scrawny kid was bilingual in a most unusual way! This couldn't be happening. Once again he questioned his own reasoning.

Paul wheeled back a few feet and looked down at the floor, resting his chin in his hand. Then, after a few seconds, he frowned and placed his hands on the armrests of his chair, pushing himself to a fully upright sitting posture.

"You must be joking, Deke..."

"No, I ain't kiddin'. I realize how weird this sounds, Mr. Sloan, but I'm just readin' what it says. I don't know how, but I just can."

"Alright, then, Mr. Fraley. Supposing you can do this. Take a look at these pages and tell me about them."

Paul dug through the pages on his lap for a few seconds, finally freeing a half dozen from the stack and shoving them at Deke.

His houseguest took the sheets in his left hand and looked at them for a few seconds. Paul noted that his eyes again seemed sunken and for a second he thought he detected a red glow within his squint.

For his part, Deke saw that the marks on one page seemed to form a picture of a face. On the next page was a note that indicated the picture was to demonstrate that the senders of the messages knew who Paul was, sort of a confirmation that their request was genuine. Paul observed him in an effort to determine if he really was "reading" and not just scanning the mysterious markings and inventing their meaning.

After a few seconds Deke looked up. "They say that they know this picture will verify to you that they are for real. It's someone you know, and they want to tell you that they know she is important to you. Also, they say that this person is in danger and that, if you agree to help them, they will help you save this person."

"Cheryl is in trouble?" Paul sensed a rush of adrenalin. He forgot his skepticism about Deke's ability to read the symbols.

"Not from the writers of this message..." Deke added. "They want you to know that it is the others who are placing this woman in danger...and the whole world!"

Deke's face went even paler than usual as he related the message. He looked at Paul and shrugged.

The two stared at each other for several seconds. Their silence was broken by the ringing of the telephone in the hallway to the kitchen. Paul turned to the computer monitor on his desk and punched a couple of buttons, activating the speaker phone.

"Paul Sloan here."

"Yes, Mr. Sloan. I am Dr. Gene Baines from University Hospital." The voice came from a speaker on the big oak desk.

"Ah, yes. I remember you. You contracted with me for some programming related to your sleep disorder clinic. Is the system working okay?" Paul wheeled himself closer to the desk.

"Umm, well, that's what I'm calling about. There has been some sort of problem with a patient and the various monitors. The system seems to have shut itself off. I wonder if you could come up here and take a look at some of our readings and the accompanying video footage to see if you can unscramble what happened."

Paul pushed himself back from his desk. "Alright. I have nothing urgent on my schedule today. I can be there in a couple hours."

Deke was a little confused that Paul could just talk into the open space of the room and still be heard. He had never seen a speaker phone before.

"Very good, Mr. Sloan. We'll be waiting for you." There was a click, followed by a hum after the connection was broken.

Paul looked at Deke. "Well, partner, I need to attend to some business. Do you want to ride along?"

Deke shook his head; a look of near panic spread across his face. "I really don't want to go outside. Those lights may be waiting,"

"I understand. Maybe you can stay here and begin translating these pages of hieroglyphs."

Paul lifted his chin in the direction of a small desk in the corner of the room where the stacks were heaped.

Deke glanced toward the pile, shrugged, and nodded his agreement.

Chapter Twelve: Kathy's Ordeal

A week after the Thursday morning meeting with Wally, Ty received a call from Dr. Charles Keller. He had obtained Kathy Fellner's permission to discuss her case with Ty, her family doctor, and Wally, her obstetrician.

The two arrived at his office that afternoon and Dr. Keller escorted his two visitors into his warmly paneled office, motioning the two men to a pair of well-padded chairs in front of his desk. The tall, slightly balding man in the well-pressed light gray suit moved to the further chair and stood in front of it. His shorter and somewhat crumpled companion with noticeably ruffled hair and a loosened necktie collapsed heavily into the closer of the two chairs.

As soon as Keller moved to seat himself behind the desk, the taller man sat down stiffly, placing a manila folder on the edge of the desk.

"I am Dr. Tyrone Williamson," stated the taller man, extending his right hand to Dr. Keller. "I haven't actually been professionally involved with Ms. Fellner, but her husband Lee switched their medical care to me after I met them in the ER. This is Dr. Wallace Hunter." Wally, who was slumped in his chair, pulled himself upright and nodded.

"Just call us Ty and Wally," the shorter man commented as he extended his own hand to meet the one Dr. Keller had offered him as he turned from Ty.

"I believe we have all run into each other from time to time," responded Dr. Keller, "at the hospital or perhaps at the Riverview Country Club. Please feel free to call me Charlie."

Before Wally could speak up to point out his personal dislike for the country club scene, Ty shot him the disapproving look that Wally knew meant "*Shut up.*"

Ty could tell when his friend was about to launch into a spiel about his personal distaste for such signs of social status. Wally complied sheepishly. He didn't like it when Ty did that, but he knew that he should trust his friend's judgment this time, so he closed his mouth and fell back again into the chair. Though Wally had always been outgoing and sociable, he conceded that his friend was much more adept at formal and professional interactions.

"Yes, we were introduced at the reception when you first came to Millardville." Ty glanced at Wally, expecting him to protest that he had gone to the reception only because Ty had pressured him to do so, but Wally just smiled benignly.

"How's your novel coming, Charlie?" Ty knew that changing the subject was another way to silence Wally when he wanted to say something inappropriate.

"I'm working on it, a little bit at a time. If it weren't for the business we're here to discuss, I probably would have spent much of today working on it, but, as you will soon agree, this case has been so intriguing that I just haven't been able to devote time to routine fiction."

Ty saw that Wally was about to speak, so he cut him off.

"It's about forgiveness, if I recall."

"And the importance of family," Keller added.

Wally had always been a bit jealous of Ty's ability to navigate so well in all situations, whether formal meetings or pick-up basketball games at the Y.

He vaguely remembered that someone had told him that Charlie Keller was an aspiring novelist. Leave it to Ty to recall such small matters in order to break the ice during an occasion such as this.

"So, uh, Charlie, what do you have on Kathy Fellner? I've really been worried about her mental health during the past few weeks. She's suffered a really incredible shock." Wally straightened himself in his chair as he spoke.

"First, let me make it clear that I have consulted with Kathy and her husband to explain why I wanted to share this with you. I explained to them that there might be medical implications in Kathy's hypnotized responses and that I felt it was important to obtain the input of both of you. She had no problem with agreeing. Her husband did seem a bit perturbed that I asked them to waive any right to also attend this session, but Kathy calmed him down. You see, she is not aware of what I am about to share with you. She has no conscious memory of this."

With that statement, Keller inserted a cassette tape into the small tape player on the edge of his desk and punched the *Play* button. "Please forgive my reliance on ancient technology. Some things are just easier for me to use. Call me old-fashioned."

"What you are about to hear is Kathy speaking under hypnosis. I have already put her under and gone through some preliminary questioning at the point at which this begins. The male voice, of course, is mine."

Keller adjusted the volume and leaned back in his high-backed swivel chair, hands clasped behind his head. The tape began to roll.

"Tell me about that visit to the Mayes family, Kathy."

"I had planned it for some time. It was routine follow-up to make sure that the family was following through with things. I had sent Lola a letter telling her to expect me that morning."

There was a pause, then Kathy added, "They don't have a phone, so I had to contact her by mail."

"So, Kathy, you're on the front porch of the Mayes' house. What is happening?"

"Davey meets me at the screen door. He seems to be in a happy mood. We go inside and Lola and Kimmy come into the room." Kathy's voice pauses for a moment. "Ouch! My baby is kicking me really hard, so hard it hurts. But Kimmy, she comes up to me and places one hand on me, over the baby, and she's making sounds."

"What sort of sounds?" the male voice interjects gently.

"A sort of cooing. I can't describe it. It doesn't sound like a sound that a child would make. 'Coowoo-coo' or something like that."

"Is the baby okay now?" Keller prodded.

"The baby seems to have quieted. Kimmy did it! How did she do that? Wait, I don't feel well. I feel weak, faint. It's growing dark! Please, help me! What's wrong with me?" The voice faded into a plaintive wail.

Keller pushed himself forward and hit the *Stop* button.

"This next part is in a low monotone, hard to make out. You will need to listen very closely." He hit the *Play* button again.

The wail subsided suddenly. "I see green light everywhere. I feel so calm, so relaxed. Everything is warm. But where am I? I think I'm moving, moving up quickly."

The female voice began to pick up a hint of concern. "I'm in some sort of room. It's bright and I can see a silver ceiling above me. No, the color is light purple. Pink. Green. It keeps changing, but everything stays so calm. Now there are faces. Odd faces. Long faces. Dark, narrow eyes. I see Kimmy's face, but it is changing, becoming a lot like the other faces. Her eyes, they seem to be on fire..."

"On fire? The eyes are on fire?" Keller interjected.

"A sort of glow. The rest of the eyes are dark, but the middle part is bright and red. The eyes are so scary, they have always scared me, ever since I was a little child."

The voice intensified. "So dark and deep. The eyes are looking at me. The eyes tell me to rest. They say, '*It will all be well.*' Kimmy/not Kimmy is cooing again."

The voice pauses for a few seconds.

"I am on some sort of table. I can't move. I can't see what is happening, but I remain motionless. I feel calm. No, wait! I am scared! What are they doing? They, they have cut into my abdomen and are attaching something to my baby. I'm scared. They are taking my baby! No! No! Stop!"

There is a short pause, then Kathy resumed in a calmer tone. "The Kimmy child is cooing some more."

Then, the monotone returned. "The eyes look at me. '*It will all be well. You have been told it will all be well.*' I feel calm now." Kathy's words stopped abruptly.

Keller leaned forward to switch off the recording. He looked expectantly at his guests. Ty sat upright, a perplexed frown on his face. Wally was perched on the front edge of his chair, his head still cocked to one side, as it had been while he concentrated on the taped words.

At last, Ty spoke. "Charlie, would you say that Kathy Fellner is rational? This seems like a very bizarre story."

"She seems normal in all other respects, Ty. And I am convinced that she believes that this is what she experienced."

"That she was kidnapped by some sort of creatures with glowing eyes? And these 'people' took her baby from her?" Wally was skeptical. "Kathy Fellner is one of the most level-headed and sincere patients I've ever had. I don't get why she would tell this sort of nonsensical story."

"This story is hidden within her subconscious. It seems to be the root of all her fear and anxiety. I need to accept its emotional impact, at least, in order to help her work through this. Even if it is some sort of fabrication, she believes it." Charlie began to tap the edge of his desk with a pencil.

Ty leaned forward. "I've read about this in a medical journal. People think they are being chased or captured. They seem to have genuine fear." He stood up and began to pace.

Charlie interjected, "Mass paranoia? Did they think their problems were really happening?"

"Yes, that's what the journal article indicated," Ty responded.

"I've heard of such reported events. In the Middle Ages they were reported as demonic attacks. I think it has something to do with the occipital lobes," Wally offered.

This time Ty let him speak and even nodded approvingly.

Charlie ran the tape ahead for a while, then punched *Play*. Kathy's voice began again.

"I see their faces and the ceiling. The ceiling is purple and silver. I am floating again. Now, I look to the right. There is a room. We are passing a room. Wait! I see people in the room. A man. A boy. Why are they there? Why are they on tables? The eyes answer me. *'It will all be well.'*"

"You see a man and a boy. What do they look like?"

"Hmmm...man has light colored hair, partly gray, yellow tee shirt. Boy is young, maybe nine or ten. Ruddy complexion. Freckles. Somewhat overweight."

"Yellow tee shirt?" Ty had been listening by the bookcase, with his back turned, stroking his chin with one hand, his brow furrowed. Now he turned to face the desk.

"That's what she said, Ty," Charlie confirmed, clicking off the recorder. "Does that mean something to you?"

Ty took three quick strides that brought him to the edge of the desk.

"Yes. Yes, as a matter of fact. Jay Brashear was wearing a yellow tee shirt when he came to my office in July. And Jay has light brown hair. But, who's the boy?"

Ty paused in mid-step. "Have there been any reports of missing children in this area?"

"I recall a missing kid from over in Caperton, reported missing sometime in mid-July," Wally added. "Kathy said he was overweight. I recall that the newspaper report described that kid as being a bit overweight."

Keller looked on mutely as the two discussed something that seemed to make sense to them but was not clear to him.

Ty spoke next. "But what are we talking about here? We can't possibly be taking her story as truth, can we? We're getting caught up in some sort of fantasy!" Ty leaned forward with a look of shock and disbelief.

Wally at last caught some enthusiasm for the discussion.

"There may be some truth in this, even if it's layered with fantasy. Let's assume that Kathy Fellner has seen Brashear and a kid. Maybe it was in some normal place and she transferred them to an unusual setting in telling this story."

"The human mind is a wonderful and mysterious thing," Keller mused. "There may be something in what you say, Wally. Let me pursue this further. Maybe we can help you solve those mysteries at the same time I help Kathy with her problems."

Later that day, Ty and Wally stopped again at the Bluebird Café to order lunch. As usual, Renee waited on them promptly.

"You're unusually quiet," Ty mentioned as he doused his hamburger with ketchup.

"I guess I'm just thinking about Keller's tape. It's so weird, what Kathy had to say, that I know I should just laugh it off, wipe it out of my mind. But she's my patient and I know her. And I *know* she was pregnant. There is no doubt about that fact. She's a really down to earth person, capable of dealing with that horror of a social work job she has."

"Now, this happens, whatever it is, and she's all ripped apart. I want to get to the bottom of this. I want to do something, not just wait around and wonder what it all means."

Chapter Thirteen: Alvin Selkirk, Doctor of Divinity?

Caperton was a part of a consolidated school system, along with the similarly small towns of Bond and Reginald, each about seven or eight miles from one another. It was consequently labeled the Triangle School District. While the high school was located in Bond, and the younger students attended elementary school in the small building that had housed all the grades in Reginald before the merger, grades five through eight were located in the large, old, three-floored building that had once held all the school children of Caperton from kindergarten through high school.

In late summer there was an open house at the school in Caperton, so the students who had advanced from Reginald and their parents could meet their new teachers and tour the building. Town officials, including the Mayor, were there to help the principal welcome the newcomers.

There were a few speeches given by school staff and local officials. Ralph struggled through his address, sweating nervously. Joe Paige, still deeply depressed by Joey's disappearance, didn't attend. When Ralph was done, and after a few closing comments by the district superintendent, the crowd moved to the lunchroom for coffee and cookies, prepared by the Parent-Teacher Organization.

Ralph was standing off to one side of the group of milling parents, students, and teachers, when he felt a hand on the arm of his new suit coat. He glanced around and saw that it was an attractive young woman.

"Mayor Osgood? I'm a new teacher here." She held out her hand. "Sandra Romer; everybody calls me Sandy. I'm the new fifth grade teacher. May I speak to you briefly?"

Ralph smiled nervously, gripping her proffered hand with his moist, chubby fingers. She led him to the far corner of the room, chatting cheerfully. After a few minutes, they rejoined the other adults.

"What was that all about?" asked Carl Johnson, sidling up to the mayor.

Carl had been strutting around the room proudly in his new police uniform. Previously, he had just worn whatever he felt like. Thanks to Mr. Huit, he now had three complete uniforms. He also had a shiny new police car with all the modern gadgets, such as flashing lights, several types of sirens and a loudspeaker. He even had a shiny new badge. He also was able to hire two part-time deputies.

"Uh-huh..." Ralph stuttered. "She just wanted to say how pleased she was to meet me."

Carl nudged Ralph in the ribs with an elbow, giving him a knowing grin. Ralph immediately began worrying that Carl would start some rumors that would get back to his wife, but he couldn't help feeling pleased that he had received the attention of an attractive young woman. Still, he was also puzzled by the attention. Ms. Romer had even reached around to brush an errant strand of his hair off one of his ears, touching his ear lobe in the process, giving it a gentle squeeze. Ralph blushed just to recall that.

Meanwhile, the town began to benefit from the government gifts that were promised at the time of the town meeting in July. Carl Johnson had already received a brand new, high powered Lexus for use as the town patrol car. He tended to use it for what seemed to many others to be personal purposes.

Joe Paige, Water Commissioner, received the new water

pump, which was installed in the shed at the base of the same water tower on which Peter Lapley had found himself that eventful night of his claimed ride across the sky.

Nobody had thought to ask him how he got down safely from the top of the tower. Since people didn't believe his story, there was no need to question the details.

The streets had all been repaved, providing Peter with steady employment for the first time in several years. Street signs were installed after the community voted on actual names for the streets. *School Street* and *Church Street* were obvious choices. New street lights were installed.

Sidewalks and curbs were replaced, including the crumbling curb in front of the old Community Center. Work was begun on a new Community Center across the highway to the north of town, beyond the abandoned railroad tracks. Mayor Osgood received regular payments from the government to cover the cost of these improvements.

The City Council began to receive inquiries from businesses about establishing retail outlets and factories in the town. Mayor Osgood was suitably impressed at the prompt action that occurred just as Huit had promised back in July.

There was still one person in Caperton who did not enthusiastically endorse all these government financial benefits. Reverend Alvin Selkirk, minister of the True Faith Believers Church, reminded his parishioners nearly every Sunday that they should not rely on the government, but upon their Heavenly Father for the meeting of their true needs.

He preached repeated sermons on the topic that love of

money and what it could buy would grease the path to hell. His frustration that the message did not seem to be sinking in grew with every new government sponsored improvement. All of the City Council attended his sermons, yet they would often engage in some of the evil against which he railed during the days between scheduled Sunday services.

Alvin Selkirk had come to the ministry by a round-about path. He originally wanted to be a mechanical engineer, since he had heard they make a lot of money. When he applied for a scholarship by completing an essay and gave that as his reason, he was turned down. He tried to get the degree anyway, but the classes were much too difficult. He had come to hate Isaac Newton, physics in general, and every other science that had anything to do with engineering. He had never liked mathematics, either. By the second semester he had dropped out of college and gone back to live with his parents.

Then he learned that his cousin Gene had become a minister and was making good money. Gene informed Alvin that, if he developed a good preaching style, he too could be a minister and also get rich.

So, Alvin enrolled in the local junior college and majored in speech. He learned that he had a gift for composing convincing arguments and, with Gene's help, he also learned to write inspiring sermons. He became a lay preacher in his hometown and the congregation was so impressed that they arranged for him to get a scholarship to a school of divinity.

His first assignment as an assistant minister at a church in Iowa didn't seem to be making him any richer, but then the much beloved and elderly senior minister died. Alvin took over. He began to dip into the collection plate in an effort to fulfill his goal of gaining wealth but was caught.

After much begging and pleading for forgiveness, no charges were lodged with the police, but Alvin was forced to resign. That left him with no income, but also kept his resume clean, since he had resigned.

The experience actually shocked him deeply and he became much more careful, vowing not to get caught again. After that, he bounced around from church to church, never finding a chance for monetary gain.

He finally came to Caperton. He learned of their search for a new pastor when he found a newspaper on his doorstep, opened to a want-ad mentioning the opening. The ad was even circled in red ink. He didn't know how the newspaper got there; he wasn't a subscriber. It was almost as though someone had placed the paper there, turned to that page.

He applied and was accepted after a couple of interviews.

He credited his hiring to his ability to speak fluently, which he had polished at college and other churches. After a few months, he decided to quit and leave town with the collection money, but his car wouldn't start. It was like someone was trying to keep him there. He decided to stick around to see if anything better came along.

Weeks turned into months and after a few years he actually found himself liking the community and the people. He realized that the townspeople from this small town were very friendly and trusting. Alvin decided to refocus his efforts, aiming for fame and prestige, which he knew would eventually bring a better assignment and then more income.

Alvin resented George Huit's intrusion upon his bailiwick.

These were his people, not the federal government's.

When Peter Lapley, not a churchgoer, began to rave about UFOs and flying around with space aliens, Reverend Selkirk's patience at last reached its limits. He had to keep the parishioners focused on their faith and not allow them to be distracted by such nonsense. He would never find a more lucrative assignment if he couldn't tamp down this whole alien excitement.

The Bible included no references to such matters, regardless of what programs on the History Channel posited, and it seemed to the pudgy minister that this was a most ungodly intrusion by the forces of secularism into the realm of religion. The Bible indicates that God created man and other creatures of this planet; it says nothing about creatures of other planets. There was also, Selkirk reminded his Sunday audiences, no mention of God sending his only Son to save little green men who seemed determined to defy his natural laws.

Paul Sloan's claim that he was followed by a UFO the night of the town meeting was another shock to Selkirk. Paul had grown up near Caperton and his family had been regular worshipers at the church before Selkirk had arrived ten years earlier. Selkirk understood that Paul had attended church regularly before he left for college and the Army. Since his parents' deaths and his return to Caperton, Paul had attended sporadically, it was true, but Selkirk had somewhat excused his absences because of his spinal cord injury.

Paul was, moreover, perhaps the only person in the entire area who could be classified as some sort of intellectual, aside from Selkirk himself, who also claimed that title.

Most local kids who went away to college did not return to

settle in Caperton, but Paul had. Alvin knew he had to keep a watch on Paul, just in case he began to challenge the minister's teachings. Paul was well-read and Selkirk and Paul would on occasion find an opportunity to get together, usually after one of Paul's rare church appearances, to discuss or argue, in a friendly way, a wide range of topics, from theology to chemistry, history and philosophy.

By keeping in regular contact, Selkirk could keep an eye on Paul, try to retain some sort of positive relationship. He recognized that Paul was one of those rare people who seemed to be able to relate to everyone, from small town shopkeepers to bigwig government officials. That made him a potential threat to the minister.

Paul's open confrontation with George Huit had greatly pleased Selkirk, at the same time as his claim about the flying saucer had distressed him. Despite their friendly rivalry, the minister sensed that Paul had some definite anger issues lurking below the surface that might someday doom their friendly relationship.

Paul was one of the leaders of the community, though he lived somewhat reclusively out in the country. Actually, Selkirk mused, maybe it was the rarity of his appearances that gave weight to his pronouncements whenever he came to town and expressed a stand on some issue. Or maybe it was the fact that Paul's injury was military-related.

Paul may not have been in a war, but his service-related injury was evident whenever he appeared in town. His wheelchair was almost the same as a medal since it always reminded the locals of his service to his country.

The minister found himself bemoaning the fact that the town drunk and the town hero had somehow combined unwittingly to launch an assault on God's Holy Word.

In spite of his reaction to Paul's UFO claim the night of the town meeting, Reverend Selkirk strove to remain on good terms with him. They had formed an odd relationship. They had even begun to communicate via e-mail to discuss less controversial issues. Each seemed to find it advantageous to keep close tabs on the other's activities.

They even developed a somewhat grudging respect for one another.

Chapter Fourteen: Tara the Invisible

The farmers' complaints had died down and for a while no one had reported any more of those strange lights since the episode involving Peter Lapley. Several farmers who had complained about damage to their crops and livestock had received new farm equipment, paid for by the generous federal government.

Alvin Selkirk's congregation calmed down as the month of September approached.

Labor Day saw a traditional celebration in the intersection in front of Paige's Bar and the Highway Café, which had relocated from its place along the state highway to one block south, across from Paige's. They kept the name because that's what it had always been called. There was a big barbecue pit, a huge metal tub full of ice and bottles of various sodas and teas. There was the usual parade around the streets of Caperton, featuring tractors and flatbed trucks loaded with produce and smiling children.

The following Monday, school began.

Doug McGee and Lindsay DePriest were now in fifth grade in a room that, before the school consolidation, had been used for seventh graders. They no longer had to contend with a daily bus ride to Reginald. Doug felt proud to finally make it to the middle school of the system, after five years at the tiny school in Reginald. Also, he could now walk to school, rather than take the school shuttle, which also meant he could leave his house twenty minutes later, which therefore meant he could sleep longer.

Lindsay, on the other hand, was excited to meet new teachers and face more advanced academic challenges.

There were forty-four children assigned to the two fifth grade classes, twenty-two in each. Doug and Lindsay were in Ms. Romer's classroom. Joey Paige was to have also been in that same classroom.

In fact, the first day Ms. Romer called his name when she was taking roll. She was new to the area and had not heard of his tragic disappearance. Josh Tooney, the nephew of Dale Tooney, who had spoken up to George Huit at the town meeting, spoke up to enthusiastically enlighten the young teacher.

"Ms. Romer! Joey Paige isn't here. He seems to have been kidnapped by aliens in a UFO. Just ask Tara. Her father even rode on the flying saucer and saw Joey!"

Josh snickered and pointed at Tara Lapley, a slightly built girl with curly light brown hair, who was crouched down in her seat at the rear of the room, trying her best to be invisible. Josh's taunt caused her to slouch even further down in her chair. All this stuff about her dad and the aliens had just been one more embarrassment for her and her brother and sister.

While her father had changed completely since the incident involving his story of the amazing flight, had quit drinking and was now more serious, still his children had to face the other children of the town. Even worse, now they also had to deal with their classmates from Bond and Reginald, who had heard about the event from some of the Caperton children.

Tara worried that the sporadic teasing she had faced from the children of her hometown during the final two weeks of summer vacation would now be multiplied as the story spread about her crazy father and his claim that Joey was a prisoner on board an alien spaceship.

At least when Petey was only the town drunk, his antics seldom surprised anybody and the other children had long ago tired of teasing Tara about him, but now his changed behavior supplied new fuel for the fire.

"Now, Josh, let's be more tolerant," Sandy Romer gently upbraided him, before continuing with roll call.

Doug felt a pang of guilt about what Josh had said. He didn't know why, but he had a vague feeling that Joey's disappearance was his fault. He didn't think it was something to laugh about and he didn't much like Josh making fun of Tara Lapley.

Josh and Doug had never gotten along and had even had a playground fight back in third grade. Doug considered Josh to be an idiot and a bully. So, Doug was immediately annoyed by Josh's comment. Even if Tara's father was weird, Doug felt, that didn't mean *she* was weird. So what if the UFO story sounded strange, it was so far the only explanation anyone had come up with, besides the suggestion that he had just run away or been kidnapped by some crazy person, such as Mr. Dunn or someone who would have had to take a major detour from the main highway to even find Caperton.

No body or other real clues had been found, aside from his backpack, Doug's father said, so it remained a wild guess that Joey had been kidnapped. Maybe it was a UFO, Doug thought, but the idea of UFOs triggered a vague sense of déjà vu in Doug. He couldn't figure out why.

(Nobody had heard of the cell phone that Steve Muncie had found near Calvin Dunn's farm. Steve had figured out the password, *Password 1,* the most obvious possible one. If it had been anything more complicated, he would never have been able to use Joey's phone. He had charged it and used it to send poorly worded and insulting texts to other kids but hadn't bothered to check the photos that were accessible through it. The messages were sent out with Joey's name attached, which puzzled his classmates who knew Joey as somewhat of a nonentity with no obvious animosity toward others. Steve Muncie wasn't skilled with electronic devices.)

During the lunch break, when all the town kids who lived within walking distance of the school went back to their own homes to eat, Doug saw Tara shuffling along a few yards ahead of him and hurried to catch up with her. She was walking alone, as usual, with her head down.

"Tara! Wait! I want to talk to you!" Doug called out when he was only a few feet behind her.

Tara, surprised, turned to see who had spoken. She expected that it would be Josh or some other boy waiting to make fun of her again. She was surprised to find that it was Doug McGee, whom she couldn't remember ever talking to her before, though they had each lived in Caperton since birth and had been in the same classroom every year except two, when they had randomly been assigned to different rooms.

Tara crossed her arms and stared down at the sidewalk, awaiting the taunt that she was certain would follow. Doug felt another surge of pain when he saw the look on Tara's face as she turned around. It reminded him of the dog his mean cousin Matt used to tease. The poor animal would always slink around, nearly crawling on its belly as if anticipating a beating any second and as if any blow received must be punishment that was deserved for some reason not recognized by the poor creature. You couldn't even reach out to pet the dog without her whimpering and crouching low to the ground. Doug had been relieved when the authorities took the dog away from Matt. He half expected Tara to whimper when he spoke to her.

"Uh, Tara. Nice to be in school again, huh?" Doug wanted to say something kind of neutral to put her at ease.

Tara raised her eyes to look at Doug, though she still kept her head down. "I guess it is...Doug." She could barely hear her own words. She hoped that would be the end of the conversation and she could go on her way.

Doug couldn't think of any more small-talk that wouldn't sound totally stupid, so he got to the point. "I didn't like what Josh said to Ms. Romer. That wasn't very nice."

Tara felt a trickle of relief. Perhaps Doug was trying to be nice. He really did sound sincere. She uncrossed her arms and looked up. She still wished she could just end the conversation, though. She wasn't accustomed to other kids being friendly and she had no idea what to say. It would be so much easier to just turn and walk away. She felt a strong urge to do so.

Doug had caught up to Tara. "Uh, look. I, uh, well, that wasn't nice of him to say and I didn't want you to think everyone was like Josh. I've always thought your father was a nice person, always trying to be nice to kids and he sometimes even plays baseball with us and stuff. So, don't pay any attention to people like Josh, okay?"

Tara felt a smile tugging at the corners of her mouth. "That's because Dad is just a big kid himself. At least, that's what Mom keeps telling him." Maybe, Tara realized, her father's worst faults had some good sides.

"Lindsay and I were the ones who found out that Joey was gone. We talk about it sometimes and we both feel that there was somethin' weird about it. Joey never would drop a backpack full of candy and chips unless he was in trouble, so we don't think he just ran away. And, since his father called him from the tavern about nine o'clock that night, he knew that Joey left at night."

Tara squinted quizzically at Doug. "So what? I don't get what you're saying, Doug."

Doug had been standing with his feet close together. Now, he took a step to the left with his left foot, shifting his weight. He shoved his hands into his pockets. "What I mean is, my mother and sister did see some weird lights out west of town past that cornfield behind my house. Maybe Joey was going to check it out. Maybe something was out there."

For a second Tara feared that a taunt was being prepared, after all. She took a step back and put her fingers up to her mouth, clenching her teeth in preparation for an insult.

Doug sensed the girl's returning discomfort. "No, no. I just was about to say, we think that maybe your father's tellin' the truth."

Tara gasped, half in relief, half in amazement. "You think that a UFO came down and grabbed Joey Paige?"

Now Doug suddenly felt like he was the one being made fun of. "Coulda happened. There's a lot of stuff they don't tell everyone about. But, we just don't want anyone makin' fun of the idea, 'cause Joey was our friend and if people make fun of something, they won't believe it's possible and they'll give up tryin' to figure out what happened. We might never see Joey again."

Tara realized that Doug was serious, and she began to believe him. "So, what can you do about it, anyway?"

"Nothing, really, I guess. We just hope he comes back somehow."

The two began walking along the sidewalk, side by side. Suddenly Tara turned to Doug with a smile that Doug felt changed her whole face. He realized that he had never seen her smile before. He stopped walking and turned to face her.

"Why don't you try to trap them?"

"Huh? Who?" Doug was taken aback by the question.

"Trap the aliens! Save Joey! Don't you get it?"

"Yeah, right. How could we do that?" Doug frowned. Tara's idea sounded goofy, but he didn't want to hurt her feelings by saying so.

"I think there may be a way. Nobody seems to believe him when he tells them, but my Dad came back from that flying saucer with some sort of tool or knife. It belongs to the alien people. My Dad says he's sure they really want to get it back. They chased him all around the inside of that UFO thing trying to get it back. My Dad has it hidden, but I think I can find it if my parents aren't around. We could get it and use it to trick the flying saucer into coming back."

"Why would they come back? Just to get that thing?" Doug's words were skeptical, but the tone of his voice implied interest.

"Dad said they tried to pull it out of his hand, chased him around the whole spaceship just trying to get it, but they couldn't make him let go. He thinks they are afraid of him because he's the only human they haven't been able to make do what they want. He thinks that, as long as he is around, they won't come after the tool. But, he says he knows they want it real bad."

Tara's words sank into Doug's mind. He began to catch not only her meaning, but also her enthusiasm.

"If we take the tool out somewhere and wave it around, they might see your Dad isn't with us and come after it!" Doug's eyes widened. Maybe there was a chance.

"Yep! And we could get some people, maybe just other kids, if no grown-ups believe us, to wait and trap the aliens and make them let Joey go!"

At last, Doug's commitment was complete. This was the beginning of a plan and he loved to make big, secret plans.

"Let's go get Lindsay and tell her. Then, we'll meet after school and begin to figure out just how we can do this."

Tara smiled. She knew that if they could actually trap an alien, then everyone would see that her father wasn't some sort of loser. Then, she and her brother and sister would have a hero for a father, and everyone would treat them better.

Lindsay had band practice after school, so they agreed to meet on Friday instead. When that time arrived and Doug and Tara offered their proposal to Lindsay she was a bit skeptical at first, but her natural inclination was to take charge of things, so she quickly picked up on the others' enthusiasm, and then she took charge.

Lindsay asked in her take-charge voice where the tool was.

This led to the first obvious snag in their plan, since, as Tara explained, Peter kept the metallic instrument locked up. Tara saw him put it in a small metal box, lock it with a key and take it into his bedroom, but she didn't know what happened after that. And, since he had now given up drinking and the wild nights roaming the area, he was home every night and getting to the locked box would be a problem.

It seemed that Tara didn't have any easy opportunities to get hold of the box, since whenever she was home, her father was usually there, or at least her mother was, and she would be very suspicious if she knew Tara was snooping around her parents' bedroom. The plan would require a great deal of patience on the part of three fifth graders.

They would need to wait for a good opportunity.

Chapter Fifteen: The Caperton Lights

As the weeks went by, the town as a whole began to forget the entire UFO uproar. Farmers were busy with harvesting crops, kids were busy with schoolwork, and life began its familiar cycle again.

Then, without any warning, the entire controversy reared up again. It happened the night of the Homecoming football game late in the month. All of the Triangle Consolidated School District's games were played on the field at Caperton, because it had the best field of the three towns. Home baseball and softball games were played in Reginald and the excellent high school gym in Bond hosted basketball and volleyball games.

The homecoming football game was just getting underway on that Friday night in Caperton. The large lights that were atop a series of tall poles that surrounded the field were turned on for only the second time in nearly a year as Triangle had hosted and lost one home game three weeks earlier. The entire northeast portion of the town shared in the brightness that easily overcame the darkness that pervaded the area in late September after seven PM.

The teams were warming up on the field and younger kids were crowding around the wood-frame concession stand, the real reason they wanted to attend the game. Suddenly, just as the teams were lining up for the opening kickoff, all the lights simultaneously extinguished, leaving the expectant fans, players, and officials frozen in total darkness.

Complete silence also engulfed everyone a few seconds later. Only Coach Jepson's voice was heard as he instructed his players to remain where they were, so they wouldn't injure themselves or anyone else while wandering around in the inky darkness.

Before the usual buzz of voices could rise amidst the power failure, a woman's voice was heard clearly as she gasped and shouted, "Look!"

The person, still hidden in the dark, pointed toward the sky, but no one could tell in the dark that she was pointing or where she wanted everyone to look. Someone else in the crowd then added, "In the sky!"

With that elaboration, every eye turned toward the heavily overcast nighttime sky. Four bright lights seemed to be holding perfectly still, directly overhead. The lights didn't move for a few seconds; then, they abruptly began to circle, spreading farther apart as they did so. All at once, without a sound, they shot off in different directions. In just seconds, they had vanished into the heavy clouds. Almost immediately, the lights around the field came back on.

The crowd remained hushed. People stared open-mouthed at the sky, then at one another. The younger children who had been playing around the base of the bleachers were the first to break the silence, pointing toward the sky and screaming, nearly in unison, "UFOs!"

The hum of adult voices followed soon thereafter, as those in the bleachers began to compare their impressions with those of their neighbors. Eventually, the spell of awe and confusion was broken by a no-nonsense referee who blew his whistle and started the game. Still, during lulls in the on-field action, eyes would turn skyward and, here and there among the crowd, an elbow would nudge someone, or a raised arm would point to the spot where the strange lights had circled. To many it seemed that what they had seen was too much to believe.

The hubbub that followed that evening eventually came to the attention of Reverend Selkirk. His hopes that all would return to normal were dashed at once. Word of the occurrence reached the newspaper in Milllardville and a facetious article appeared on the sports page under the title, *"Alien Sports Fans Attend Game."*

The preacher read the article with great dismay. He feared that this ridiculous fantasy about flying saucers would bring unwarranted attention to the town, further distracting his parishioners from the True Word, as passed on to them by the Most Reverend Alvin Selkirk.

And, as he feared, things grew worse. A week later, a rumor began circulating that a reporter from the Spring City Sentinel was coming to Caperton and would be asking questions. Someone would surely be flattered enough by the attention to tell him all about the events of midsummer and Petey Lapley's absurd claims. Selkirk called Ralph Osgood and requested a chance to meet with the City Council.

Thus, it was that a few days later Mayor Osgood waited at the door of the Town Hall for the other members of the town's governing group to arrive. The meeting had been switched from Paige's Tavern to satisfy Reverend Selkirk, who was averse to meeting in such a den of corruption. The tiny brick municipal building occupied the space between the bar and the Old Community Center, as people were beginning to call it in anticipation of completion of the new one.

Osgood had smiled to himself at the thought of the somewhat stuffy minister sitting in the back room of the tavern, amid the pool tables and the smell of stale smoke and spilled beer, but finally acquiesced to Judy's suggestion of using the Town Hall.

He checked his expensive new wristwatch. It was almost seven. He brushed a few wrinkles out of his brand-new suit and checked the shine of his brand-new shoes. Municipal elections would take place in the Spring and a mayor running to retain his office should look mayoral, he thought.

Soon the Council members began trickling in and all were seated around the card table that served as the City Council dais. The Mayor noted that all were better dressed than usual, almost as though the presence of the minister required a church-like deference. Selkirk had asked to speak at 7:30, so they had half an hour to dispense with usual business.

"Pretty spiffy duds there, Ralph!" Carl Johnson remarked, elbowing the Mayor in the ribs with a conspiratorial smile. "Come into some inheritance, did you?"

Osgood chuckled nervously and looked away from Carl and at Judy DePriest. "Let's have some reports on the progress of the various departments. Selkirk will be here soon to gripe about everything."

Judy DePriest frowned. "He is a minister, Ralph. You should show more respect. What's gotten into you, anyway? You never acted like this before."

This response from *Gentle Judy*, as she had been dubbed in high school after she saved an injured fox that had gotten into the gym, annoyed the Mayor, but it wasn't as irritating as Carl's comment.

"It's just that he doesn't like our town improvements. He's always harassing me about them every time he sees me. He even preaches against them in church almost every Sunday. I'm going to quit going if he doesn't stop."

Of course, Ralph couldn't do that; Minnie would never let him hear the end of it.

"It's the money we've taken that he doesn't approve of," Judy replied. "We sold out to that Dr. Huit and Reverend Selkirk has become our conscience. Look at you, Ralph! New suit, new shoes! And you, Carl, and that uniform! You never dressed the part before you got that car. Now, you're even giving speeding tickets to many of the people around here and those passing through on the county road. You've changed!"

Carl's smile slipped from his face and he stared down at his very shiny shoes.

Ralph looked at his hands, which were folded in front of him on the card table. He coughed nervously. He had begun to perspire. Sometimes he wondered why he even wanted this job. Then, he would always recall that his wife Delores and her mother Minnie would never let him hear the end of it if he quit political office. Also, he didn't have any other job skills, so he really had no choice.

As Ralph pondered his troubles, he absent-mindedly tapped the lump behind his left ear. He had discovered it that morning and hoped it wasn't anything serious, but at his wife's urging he had already made an appointment with Dr. Williamson over in Millardville.

"Well, I've decided not to run for reelection," Joe Paige suddenly blurted out. "Ever since Joey disappeared, I haven't been able to get much done. It's all I can do to just open up the tavern every day and lock the door at night. Nothing is worth doin' anymore."

Judy patted Joe on the shoulder. "It must be so hard, Joe. The whole town feels for you. My daughter Lindsay was

Joey's friend. She says the kids all miss him."

Joe smiled weakly, his eyes watering. He knew that Joey wasn't really very popular, but he appreciated Judy's effort to cheer him up. Joey spent most of his time playing video games and watching TV at home and seldom, actually never, spent time with other kids.

"I guess I may as well face it that he ain't comin' back. First, I lost his mother and now him. For a while I even sort of hoped that what Petey was saying was true, that some UFO had sucked him up into the air and he is being held prisoner by some little green men."

He looked down and wiped away a tear that had started down his right cheek. "Man, I hate that Lapley fool now! Why did he ever start talking all that crazy talk?"

"Did you hear that he plans to run for mayor?" Carl blurted out, hoping to change the mood to something less serious.

Osgood's mouth dropped open. "What!? Petey for mayor? Why, he's a complete idiot for sure, now!"

"Well, he flagged me down one day to ask to see my new patrol car, since he never gets to ride to jail in my car anymore, because he went sober. He started talkin' and told me he plans to get your job, Ralph. He was real serious. Y'know, I don't think he's near as stupid as we all have always thought."

"What has gotten into him?" Osgood gasped, beads of perspiration forming on his forehead. Being mayor wasn't much of a job, but it was all Ralph had.

"Now, Ralph, you have nothing to worry about," Judy responded. I'm the town clerk along with being street commissioner, and he hasn't even filed for the election yet. But I don't think, with his reputation, that he has a chance."

Judy had an ability to reassure anyone, which she had developed in junior high as part of her successful long-range plan to be elected Homecoming Queen in high school. Caperton wasn't much, but she had some ambition.

"Good. You're right, Judy," Ralph responded with visible relief. His face rapidly faded back into its usual paleness as his anger subsided. "Now, let's get down to business and file our reports."

A few minutes later, promptly at 7:30, there was a tapping on the front door. Before anyone could respond, it opened, and the paunchy form of the minister lunged into view. He was dressed in a dark suit, despite the late summer heat wave and had his grayish hair neatly slicked back.

"Come on in, Reverend," Carl called out, motioning with one hand to the empty folding chair that had been placed at one corner of the card table. Ralph frowned. He was mayor and should have been the one to respond to the knock at the door. Since that opportunity had eluded him, he merely pointed to the empty chair.

"Actually, I would rather stand. I have come before this, this distinguished grouping to speak on a topic of utmost gravity."

Selkirk paused to look around the table and make sure he had everyone's attention. It was the same approach he took with his Sunday sermons. Then, satisfied that the mood of the room had become somber enough, he sat in the vacant folding chair.

"As you know," he resumed once he was satisfied that he was in full command of the floor, "we have all had to deal with the ramifications of the so-called UFO episodes that we have experienced the past couple months. You all know my stand on the government largess with which Dr. Huit has corrupted, or, that is, *blessed*, our community."

"Now I understand that we are to become the subject of an investigative reporter from Spring City. We will be the laughingstock of the state, my friends. We will be plagued by tourists. We'll turn into another, what's that place in New Mexico? Roswell! We will be another *Roswell*. There will be unsolicited publicity. How can my simple flock deal with all this big city hedonism? I say that we must stop it in its tracks!"

The minister knew, deep inside, that his personal pride was based on his ability to control his parishioners. If he didn't have his flock, he had nothing. The thought was too painful to consider, so he tried to avoid thinking it.

"You mean that reporter from The Sentinel?" Osgood replied. "Ah, he'll just come and interview a couple of us on the Council and maybe the football coach over at Bond. It's not a big deal."

"I hope that's true, Mayor Osgood. I just want to put a stop to what's happening here. We must remove ourselves from temptation's path. This flying saucer hoopla is ungodly and must be put to rest. If there is anything at all to this, it is clearly the work of the devil. We are a town in need of repentance, not reporters." Selkirk's lips curled up slightly; he was pleased with the alliteration.

"Well, I don't see any big problem with talking a little to a newspaper reporter. We'll just make sure that it's kept light and frivolous, Reverend. No need to get all excited."

Ralph found himself relishing the chance to get a bit of a needle in the minister's hide as a minor revenge for all the chastisement that had been sent his way from the pulpit the past several Sundays. The minister was in *his* bailiwick now. He smiled triumphantly.

"Alright, then," Selkirk replied. "Let me change my approach to one that can be understood by one in your position of responsibility. If this reporter makes us look like a town of fools, how many of those businesses and factories that you told us about would still be interested in the possibility of moving here? Here, amidst the hicks of this backwater town?"

The implications of what the minister had said struck Ralph Osgood with a nearly physical impact. If there was one thing he didn't want, it was for all this recent affluence to be curtailed. He had become accustomed to it and was also becoming quite fond of the credit he was receiving for bringing prosperity to the small town. Two or three new families had already moved to town, for which Ralph, as mayor, took credit. Minnie had quit nagging him about providing better for his family. He had even begun to think about the state legislature and who could tell how far he could go?

"You don't really think that one small newspaper article could do all that, do you, Reverend?" The mayor's voice had lost all its smug self-assuredness and was once again a plaintive whine.

Joe Paige had by now regained his composure. "I'm a businessman, Ralph. There just might be some truth in all that he says. Bad publicity can hurt."

Judy DePriest rose to her feet.

"A few questions to the right people and we'd start seeing some attention to all the street improvements we've been doing. A smart big city reporter would have no qualms about making us look like we had somehow done something wrong to receive all this government money,"

She didn't take note of Selkirk's knowing smirk.

"Remember that town in California where the city council gave itself big raises? They got away with it for a while, until word leaked out."

"No other town 'round here has a fancy new police car," Carl muttered. "I don't want to lose my car...or my deputies!"

Osgood was again perspiring. His hands, folded in front of him on the card table, began to shake. He began to twiddle his thumbs nervously. Finally, he gulped loudly and looked up at Selkirk.

"But what can we do, Reverend? We can't just tell the reporter not to come here. That would really make him suspicious about what was going on."

"That is something we need to think about. We need to find a way to dissuade him; he needs to be either talked out of coming here or else be shuttled away from these UFO stories to something more interesting. If we don't divert him, we'll just attract more attention, which will be bad for the town and a distraction to my parishioners. We would all lose."

"Maybe," Judy suggested, "we could divert him to Petey. Make the whole thing look like the wild stories of the town drunk."

"I don't know about that," Joe commented. "Lately, he's been pretty straight. I haven't seen him in the tavern for weeks. Business is suffering a little since he went on the wagon."

Carl chimed in, "He might just persuade the reporter that he's telling the truth. It's too risky."

"What we need is someone to stay with the reporter, escort him around town, make sure he sees only what we want him to see, that he speaks only to those folks we want him to talk to." Judy's voice had its usual self-assuredness, a quality Ralph envied. "And we need to get Petey out of town that day, just to be safe."

"But who could accomplish that? Who do we know..." Osgood's voice was quavering.

"Paul Sloan is the smartest person in the area. Maybe we can get him to give the reporter a guided tour, emphasize how much we've worked to earn all these things ourselves."

Ralph nodded to acknowledge Judy's idea. He wasn't sure Paul would be willing to bend the truth that far, though. He was a pretty straight shooter.

The minister cleared his throat. He didn't want to risk this assignment to anyone else, especially not Paul. Also, he doubted that Paul would be willing to do it. He put his hands on the edge of the table and leaned forward.

"Let me do it. A minister can be quite persuasive. I think I can handle a reporter, convince him it's all crazy rumors."

Selkirk despised the corruption he had seen around the town, but he feared even more the impact exposure of the whole UFO thing would have on everyone in town, especially his congregation. And his long-term goals of fame and fortune could be jeopardized.

A few blocks away, in a small, rented mobile home a young woman listened. Then, she made a call on her secure cell phone.

"This is Outpost Four. Per your instructions, I planted the story about a reporter from Spring City coming to town. I am now ready to neutralize the minister. I need your permission to take special action."

Chapter Sixteen: Into the Forbidden Zone

Meanwhile, far to the west, Sergeant Theodore Rader found himself sitting morosely in a small locked room constructed of concrete blocks in the middle of a huge airplane hangar. He'd been there for the two days since the incident with the flare gun. He still didn't know what was going to happen; as far as he knew, he hadn't been charged with any crime.

The ambulance crews at the site had rushed past him with stretchers and struggled back up with a half dozen or so bodies covered in Army blankets. The stretchers were loaded into the backs of the ambulances, which then rushed off at top speed, lights flashing. There was no need for sirens in the middle of the Forbidden Zone.

As the ambulances careened back down the rutted path, other soldiers began the recovery operation involving the vehicles, a process in which Rader had always been a participant. There had never before been any bodies involved. At least not any non-human bodies.

Colonel Webber had made his way to the top of the hill to attempt to fathom the extent of the problem. He had edged his way back down to where his driver leaned with both hands on the hood of his jeep.

Rader looked up, noticeably pale. "What will happen now, Colonel?"

Colonel Webber, noted for his military brusqueness, stared at the ground for a few seconds, and then pulled the cap from his head.

"We will not know until it happens, Sergeant. For now, you will be kept locked up back at the base, for your own protection. Then, we'll wait to see what THEY want to do with you."

As Webber turned away, Rader couldn't help but notice that Webber, speaking for the U.S. Army and hence for the US government, admitted that he had no control over the situation. A shiver shook his whole body.

Rader had been taken to this small room, big enough for only a cot and one chair. It wasn't exactly what Rader would call a "room"; it was clearly a jail cell. The door was steel and had a decided *clang* when it was slammed shut. Rader was allowed out of it twice a day for exercise, which consisted of walking under armed guard around the inside perimeter of the huge hangar in which the cell was located.

There was a barred window in the door, from which the sergeant could see little more than the backs of the heads of the two MPs who were stationed there continuously. There was a slot in the door for insertion of a food tray. A commode occupied one corner of the room. A water pitcher and a plastic cup for drinking rested on the chair. He was told that once a week he would be taken to a corner of the warehouse and allowed to use a makeshift shower.

He was allowed no visitors; at least he had had none, not even Lieutenant Lundy. Even the guards said very little to him and refused to respond whenever he attempted to engage them in conversation. There was no doubt that Rader was a prisoner.

He was puzzled by the fact that he had not received any notice that he had been charged with a crime. Everyone who was present knew that the shooting was an accident. He had a high-level clearance and had never been disloyal, so the top brass had no reason to fear that he was an escape risk.

The fact was that no one was talking to him, not even Colonel Webber. He had asked several times to speak to them, but the MPs to whom he addressed his requests would not even acknowledge his pleas. He had begun to think that a deliberate attempt was being made to drive him crazy.

And, Rader pondered, exactly what was he being protected from—or whom? He tried not to think too much about that, since he feared the answer. And Rader didn't fear much of anything.

Then, early one morning, while it was still dark, the door suddenly opened, and the MPs entered. One of them guarded the open doorway while the other walked briskly to Rader's cot and prodded the sleeping prisoner awake with a baton. The MP motioned for him to stand and his hands were shackled in front of him, and a blindfold placed over his eyes.

Someone he couldn't see swiped an alcohol swab across his left shoulder and inserted a hypodermic needle into his deltoid muscle.

He was physically dragged from the cell and was placed in the back of what he assumed to be a van, by the sound of the sliding door. An MP, again, Rader's assumption, sat on each side of him. They drove for such a length of time that Rader, despite his concern for what was happening, found himself dozing off. He was too disoriented to connect the drowsiness to the injection he had received.

Suddenly the van jolted to a stop.

The two guards seized Rader by the elbows and knees and yanked him bodily from the vehicle. He groggily realized that they were unlocking his shackles just before he felt a sharp pain in the back of his head and he sensed himself dropping. He lost consciousness before his body came to a stop.

Rader didn't know how much later it was when he again became fully aware of his surroundings, but a splitting headache centered in the back of his head was his first sensation. As he felt the base of his skull in response to the pain, his hand brushed against the blindfold that was still in place. He tugged it loose with one hand while he dabbed tentatively at a patch of dried blood at the base of his skull.

Night was approaching. Rader dazedly realized that he must have been unconscious for over twelve hours, maybe much longer. As his thoughts swam through his brain, it occurred to him that his confusion was probably the result of the shot he had received. He tried to blink away the pain and focus on his surroundings.

A large moon lit the surrounding hillsides. He was outside, somewhere far from the military base, apparently. It was growing cold, and he was not dressed for the chill of the night desert air. He shook his head in an effort to clear his mind to focus on his options. He tried to keep from his mind the obvious question. Why was this happening? What had he done to be punished so severely? He couldn't fathom why the military wasn't following its own code of justice in this situation.

He had the uncomfortable impression that the so-called THEY were calling the shots and his team's officers were neither able to question the decisions nor even explain to him what was going on.

Rader bit his lower lip and shook his head vigorously again. He first had to think of his survival. If he could somehow accomplish that, then he could focus on the whys and hows of all this.

One thing, however, merited a bit of consideration. If his superiors wanted to get rid of him, it probably didn't make sense for him to find his way back to his barracks. He could follow the van's tire tracks until he got his bearings, then veer away in another direction to avoid returning to the base. Then, since there was only one town anywhere close, he would have to try to find his way to Edgemont.

At that point he would need to figure out what to do. If he started exposing the secrets related to the crashed UFOs, maybe he could gain enough notoriety that the government would have to protect him. Or he could just keep going on to some other town, some other state, maybe even some other country.

The Army was such a part of him, though, that going AWOL was nearly unthinkable, no matter what the Army was trying to do to him.

Rader briefly pondered why, if they wanted him dead, they didn't just shoot him. It could be that this whole thing was just Webber's way of covering himself. Perhaps the colonel had gone rogue and the Army itself had no official involvement. Or, if Webber wasn't trying to avoid blame, maybe it would just be better for those behind all this if it appeared that a disoriented soldier had wondered away from the base and died of exposure. There would be fewer questions.

Rader decided he had better focus first on surviving the night. He was grateful for the bright moonlight. He would be able to follow the van's tire tracks for some distance. If he could determine the direction to the base, he could then figure out the route to Edgemont.

His early training for the recovery operations had included information on how to follow tracks in a desert-like setting. At first he couldn't find any tire prints, but he began to carefully and slowly walk in an increasingly larger circle until he at last came across them. He could see that the van, after dumping him out, had circled around and then backtracked along the path from which it had come.

With a small surge of triumph, he began to follow the tracks. However, after about half an hour of walking, Rader came upon a separation, indicating that the van had turned sharply away from its original path on the way back. Rader halted to ponder the possible reasons for this.

Other thoughts went through his mind as he stumbled along. Ever since the incident that landed him in custody, he had been wondering why the Army base was so close to a town. Sure, there was a fence and guard posts and warning signs that the area was off limits to civilians, except for those who had been cleared by security to work there in the battalion office, close to the front gate. And, the recovery operations were always deep in the Forbidden Zone, where crashes always seemed to occur, so civilians wouldn't see them, but why was that the case, anyway?

And why did anyone crash in the first place? There must be something dangerous in that area, some sort of radiation that interfered with flight. Or maybe the Army was testing new technology designed to bring down the visitors from other planets.

Maybe, then, the aliens were in on the process and encouraged it in order to develop their own technologies to overcome the humans' new inventions.

Were the Army and the aliens staging war games? But that would mean that the Army was in collusion with the aliens and that Americans were being sacrificed at the whim of the aliens. And, if the Army was involved, was the government also in on the scheme?

Rader was astounded at these possibilities and had to deliberately wipe them from his mind. He needed to survive the night first and he could consider all these crazy ideas later if he survived.

A shiver shook his body. He realized that he didn't have time to debate which direction to go, if he wanted to avoid depleting his energy reserves shivering out in the open at night. It probably didn't matter which path he pursued, since he assumed that the driver of the van was returning to the base and had decided to take a different route back than that used on the way out.

From the tracks in the semi-darkness of the early night, Rader couldn't decipher which tracks represented the trip out and which were the return tread tracks. So, arbitrarily, he chose the path that led to the right.

The sergeant had been plodding along steadily, concentrating on the tracks in the dirt, when he became aware that darkness was nearly complete. The realization shook him. He had been so intent on following the path left by the vehicle that he hadn't been paying attention to his surroundings.

He looked up. He had entered a ravine and the slopes around him were sharp and the hills blocked the moonlight. Also, a thin fog had settled into the depression between the slopes. Rader didn't recall ever seeing fog in the Forbidden Zone.

He looked down again, noting that the tire tracks were now more difficult to see. He had to kneel down every few steps to make sure that he was still on the correct path. The ground had become harder, and the tracks weren't as deeply etched into the dirt as before. A slight feeling of panic began to twist in Rader's stomach. Without the tracks he would be hopelessly lost. He gritted his teeth and concentrated on staying calm.

The ravine widened as he edged his way along. A shaft of moonlight broke free of the hills and reflected on the ground just ahead. Rader could see the tracks again, but his momentary elation was abruptly cut short when he observed that the tracks began to weave sharply back and forth, as though the driver had been swerving to avoid an obstacle. Then, as he half-sprinted forward, he saw that the tire marks seemed to drag suddenly through the dirt, as though skidding out of control. Straining his eyes to the utmost, Rader tried to follow the skid marks as they formed a circle in the dirt; the van appeared to have spun totally around. But no tracks led away from the site of the skid.

Odd.

Rader stared at the ground as the fog continued to gather around him, diffusing the moonlight and obscuring his view of the skid tracks. He shivered once more, though he didn't know if it was from the deepening cold or the fear that seemed to be creeping up his spine from the soles of his combat boots.

He tried to gather his thoughts, regain his focus. Again, he could not take time to dwell on the sudden disappearance of the tracks. He had to formulate a plan, in spite of the increasing shivering and the hunger that had now begun to gnaw at his gut.

Should he just continue straight ahead, the direction the van had been going before it had apparently skidded, then disappeared? Or should he backtrack and try to pick up a different trail? Did he even have time to do that before his body gave in to the exposure to the cold?

The thought of stumbling ahead in the darkening mist was discouraging but taking time to go back to where he first discovered the tire tracks would just use up more time and further exhaust his body. He tugged his shirt collar up around his neck and buttoned the top button. Despite these efforts the damp coldness seemed to seep through his olive drab fatigues.

Ahead, the ground continued the pattern of undulation it had begun at the ravine. It would be hard to keep a straight path, Rader realized, so he gathered some small stones together, as many as his fatigue pockets could hold. He walked forward to the next rise, placing the stones in the shape of an arrow that pointed to the next hill. When he was satisfied that he would be able to find it if he needed to backtrack, he again moved on. He gathered more rocks as he went. He felt a sense of satisfaction that he was at least making progress, though he was fighting fatigue, hunger, and a new foe—dizziness, and a ringing in his ears.

Each hillock he crested gave him a view above the thickening, low-lying fog. He still could not identify any signs of the base or the town. The sky had clouded up again, making it even darker. His shivering continued, unabated. He tried to ignore it. He clenched his teeth together until his jaws ached, but still the shaking continued.

Suddenly, as Rader rose to his feet after arranging more rocks to form another arrow, he spotted something just beyond the next ravine. He couldn't quite make out what it was, but its profile in the dark stood out unevenly from the surrounding landscape. Rader descended the incline to the base of the next rise and then scrambled to the top.

It was a van, almost certainly the one he had been tracking, the sergeant figured, and it had been flipped onto its top. There were no tracks leading to the overturned vehicle. As he edged his way down the slope he stared at the van in disbelief. How could the van have skidded way back where he had seen the last tire marks and then end up here? There weren't even signs of damage to the hillside near this site.

It appeared that the van had somehow been lifted into the air and then transported to this spot and gently set down on its top.

The angle of the hill was narrow, and Rader slipped on some loose pebbles as he descended toward the upside-down van. He lost his footing and skidded, sliding helplessly downward, bouncing over jagged chunks of rock and small, stiff bushes as he went. He groped desperately for a handhold but was unable to slow himself before he slammed at full force into the side of the van.

He sensed that he had incurred several cuts and he began to feel warm blood seeping down his left shin. A spot at the base of his skull stung. Realizing that at this time he couldn't do much about any gashes or abrasions, he chose to not look at them. Perhaps it would be best to not know the extent of his injuries. What worried him more was that he could no longer think clearly, likely because of his hunger or maybe because of blood loss.

Rader attempted to focus on the object that had just brought his downhill slide to such an abrupt halt. He found himself staring into the passenger side front window of the overturned van. The glass was unbroken, he noted at once, for he had expected that the force of the van crashing to the ground would have broken all the windows.

Glancing quickly around, he realized that, not only were they all intact, but the body of the van itself showed no signs of damage, not even a dent.

What of the military police whom he assumed had served as his guards in the van? Rader peered into the shadowed interior, searching for movement or the shapes of bodies slumped inside.

At first, he could see nothing. Then, slowly, he shifted his view to the middle of the car's interior. There, suspended upside down by their fastened seat belts, were two figures. They weren't moving. Their arms, dangling straight down, gave Rader the chilling assurance that they weren't going to ever move again.

Rader frowned. It seemed odd to him that the two MPs were strapped into their seats in the middle of the van, but there were no signs of the driver. If the driver was able to walk away from whatever kind of accident this was, why would the seat-belted passengers be killed?

This seemed doubly odd when his further scanning of the interior showed Rader no further damage to the vehicle.

He pondered what could have led to this situation. Had the driver somehow killed the passengers before deliberately flipping the van into the ravine, and then exited?

Rader edged his way around the vehicle on his hands and knees, searching for a clue to the unusual accident. When he reached the driver's door, he noted that there were footprints in the sandy surface of the hillside, leading away from the van. Perhaps his theory was correct.

Keeping his face close to the ground, he scrutinized the prints carefully. They seemed to be unusually long and narrow. And the boots worn by the maker of these prints did not bear the imprint of regulation military boots. In fact, the soles of the boots must have been totally smooth, Rader surmised. In addition, there was no heel print. If these were the driver's prints, he must have been out of uniform. Even the shoes worn with a dress uniform had heels.

Rader began slowly to follow the prints away from the driver's door. It was not easy in the dark and the steadily thickening fog. He continued to crawl slowly back up the hill, which is where the path led, using his fingers to feel for each new imprint in the dirt.

Perhaps the driver had been injured or dazed in the overturning of the van and needed help. Perhaps the driver could help him right the van and the two could form an alliance to drive away from this place. Together, at least, the two might be able to figure out what to do next.

The sergeant had just reached the top of the hill when he began to notice the fog. It continued to thicken, hugging the foot of the slope behind him. As he pushed himself to his feet, he could see that it covered all the lower ground in every direction, blending into the inky darkness.

The moonlight was once again shrouded by clouds. The mist had taken on a dark gray-green tint, though it was hard to assign a color in the gathering darkness. As he watched, it filled in more of the low spaces between the hilltops until Rader was left with the impression that he was on a small island, surrounded by a dark and lifeless ocean.

There were other similar lonely islands that were also protruding out of the gray-green sea of fog. Glancing back down the hill, he discovered that the mist had nearly engulfed the overturned minivan.

And, as he observed it, he was shaken by the sudden realization that the van was disintegrating before his eyes; the fog was dissolving it!

With a shockingly audible sizzling sound, the van was slowly but steadily collapsing before his eyes, with different sections crumbling off and falling to the side, only to disappear in the olive-colored mist.

Rader backed instinctively toward the middle of the hilltop, trying to remove himself as far as possible from the corrosive cloud that was edging upward toward him. As he did so, he tripped over a jutting rock and fell backward to the ground, automatically putting his arms out behind him to break his fall.

He quickly spun around to all fours in order to scramble back to his feet. But, as he did so, his eyes caught sight of something white or light gray on the slope of the hill opposite to that of the van.

As he focused on it, he came to the conclusion that it was a body, probably that of the missing driver. Despite the rolling upward progression of the acidic fog, Rader couldn't leave someone to be eaten alive by the mist.

He scampered down the hillside. The figure was prone with its feet pointed downhill amidst the stunted shrubbery that hugged the lower part of the incline and was already being lapped by the corrosive mist.

The sergeant began to hear the sizzling sound coming from his own boots as he hurried toward the figure. He quickly bent and placed his hands under the arms of the immobile body and hoisted it over his left shoulder. Surprised by the light weight of his burden, he made rapid ascent back to the crest.

The soles of his boots fell apart as he advanced.

Rader, glancing over his shoulder in nervous awareness of the advancing cloud, carefully lowered the body to the ground in a spot clear of rocks and other debris. As he rose to his feet, he had his first good look at the unconscious individual he had rescued.

"Damn!" Rader gasped. "It's one of THEM!"

Like the injured survivor he had seen atop the hill at the site of the earlier crash, the body was slender, though taller. The fingers were better formed. The head was large, but not excessively so. But there was no doubt in his mind. It was an alien.

He stared down at the pale, thin humanoid. There was no sign of breathing. Then, through the swirling fog, barely visible, he noticed a phalanx of figures moving in his direction. As they came closer he realized that they didn't look quite human. They were tall and very thin, with eyes that seemed to glow red. Their skulls seemed larger, even longer, than what Rader knew to be normal.

They were marching in silent precision, in a perfect line, resembling the Nazi stormtroopers that he had seen on a documentary on television. Rader decided that he had better get away from this spot.

The fog swirled closer. Rader didn't have time to contemplate his options.

Seizing the slender body, he again lifted it over his shoulder. Looking around, he caught sight of a hill rising high above the others nearby. If only he could get to it, he might be able to stay above the deadly fumes and ahead of the intimidating figures. He would have to make a dash through the dreadful mist, but it seemed to be his only option.

He took a deep breath and plunged down the hill. Almost immediately, as he descended into the first wavering wisps of the greenish vapor, he felt a tingling sensation around his ankles. He could smell the leather beginning to burn. The legs of his fatigue pants felt like they had caught fire.

Suddenly, even as the remnants of his right boot seemed to dissolve and drop away from his foot, Rader's toe caught the edge of a jutting rock and he felt himself falling forward. This is it, the end, he realized. The fog would certainly eat him alive before he could get back to his feet.

Even if it didn't, he was sure that the approaching figures meant to harm him. He clamped his eyes tightly shut and prepared for what he hoped would be a quick death.

Instead, as he fell, he felt himself rising, weightlessly floating upward. Then, still expecting pain, he felt his body becoming relaxed, then numb.

Rader opened his eyes for just a split second before he lost consciousness, long enough to see that he was enveloped in a bright green light.

His last thought, though it seemed like someone else was speaking, was *"It will all be well."*

Chapter Seventeen: To Catch an Alien, Part One

Paul Sloan sat before the computer screen, wearing a look of glum acceptance. Greg Bowie was rewinding the tape one more time, while Dr. Baines paced the narrow aisle between the door and the electronic gadgetry of the Sleep Center monitor room. Paul shook his head in resignation and pushed his chair away from the desk.

"Well, Mr. Sloan, what is it?"

Dr. Baines had hunched low beside Paul as though the view that Paul had would somehow give better results than what the professor could see while standing. He remained crouched while looking at Paul.

"Some sort of bug in the equipment? Do you think it's some sort of practical joke?" He glanced at Greg, who felt guilty, even though he had done nothing to warrant it. "How did Dunbar stay in that deep level of sleep for so long?"

Paul glanced at Baines's face. "I'm afraid this is indeed bad news. The equipment is fine. The problem is that Mr. Dunbar doesn't have a sleep disorder. It's something else, something worse."

"Worse?" Baines again stood up. "What could possibly be worse than sleep deprivation?"

It occurred to Paul that the doctor was so focused on his own medical specialty that he couldn't consider anything else as more important. "You saw that face, didn't you?"

"Well, yes. But, it must have been someone wearing a mask. I've asked that hospital security check all the staff lockers and offices to see who pulled this prank."

Greg finished punching buttons at the control panel. "It wasn't a joke, Dr. B. What about the missing two hours? I didn't imagine that. I know that something happened. The computer just didn't register it."

"The computer was interfered with by an outside force," Paul stated matter-of-factly. "I've checked everything I can, and I must conclude that there was some sort of electromagnetic interference that interrupted the program and caused it to shut down, then restart two hours later."

"So, you think that Mr. Dunbar did it somehow? Or his family? They came to us wanting answers, so why would they sabotage the testing?"

Dr. Baines' voice was taking on a tone of desperation. He appeared confused, running his fingers through his already disrupted hair. He stared blankly at Paul.

"My guess," Paul replied, ignoring the question, "is that this is not your first 'visit'.

"Visit?" Baines echoed back. The puzzled look on his face deepened.

"Yep. That wasn't the face of a prankster, my friends." Paul paused.

He was never sure that anyone else would accept what he already knew was the truth. He recalled his initial skepticism, and his months of denial.

"This may be hard for you to accept, but the computer was disabled, and Mr. Dunbar was kidnapped for two hours by…"

Bowie interrupted. "Aliens, right?" His tone and face revealed that he was serious.

Baines was about to laugh deprecatingly at his lab assistant, but Paul nodded his agreement with Greg.

"Dr. B., I've been reading some of those magazines in the lobby. One had a feature story on just this sort of thing. I wouldn't have believed this myself if that face didn't appear on the videotape. But it all matches with what some people in that article said happened to them."

Baines folded his arms across his chest and stared at Bowie. "Alright, then, I guess I can accept that as one hypothesis. But, unless you can find some corroborating evidence, I'm not going to be able to keep using this computer system. I would really hate to go back to our old, outmoded equipment."

Paul was surprised at the doctor's easy acceptance of the explanation he had been about to advance. Dr. Baines again brushed one hand through his perpetually disheveled hair and looked at him quizzically.

"I'd hate for you to have to dump my system, too, Dr. Baines," Paul replied to Baines's comment. "But, I have a suspicion that Dunbar wasn't your first patient to go through this while at your center. I think your previous programs probably showed some missing time periods and that video monitoring has been full of unexplained glitches for some time."

Dr. Baines shrugged. "You're right on that, Mr. Sloan. But that's why we decided to buy your system. It appeared foolproof. Still, I want some hard evidence."

"Here's an idea," Greg volunteered eagerly. "Have Dunbar

come back and go through this again, but this time set some sort of trap. Catch yourself an alien."

"I don't know if that can be done," Paul replied.

He debated with himself whether he should reveal his own experience with the lights, which had educated him to the almost limitless powers of the beings he had to deal with, then decided against such a revelation.

"Anyone, or any *thing* that can do what was done to the monitoring system here can surely defeat any simple trap we could set. It would need to be something highly sophisticated."

"Do you think they can read our minds and know what we are planning?" Bowie asked. "Some of the people in the magazine article said that they thought they could. Or are they able to watch us from afar and see everything we do?"

"I don't know," Paul replied with full honesty.

He had been in rather close contact with the lights for several months and, including his military experience, for several years, but he still did not know anything really solid about them. He didn't know where they came from or how they got here. He wasn't sure whether they were friendly, neutral or intent on destroying him. Based on what Deke had told him, he thought they might be described in all three of those ways at different times.

"Well, I still think this is pretty strange stuff," Baines commented.

"Yes. But keep an open mind and I'll work on a plan to prove it to you," Paul responded. "Just start by getting Dunbar back here and I'll take it from there."

Paul knew just what he needed to do. He had heard about a special door that could be installed that would make it impossible for someone to break into, or out of, a locked room. It involved something called a *glass re-locker*.

A pane of glass was placed in the middle of the door between the front and rear metal panels. If someone tried to pick the lock or break through it, the slightest vibration would shatter the glass and trigger steel bolts that would slide in place to firmly lock the door.

It was something often used on large safes in banks and Paul decided to try it in this situation. Only, in this case he would arrange for one door for each entry to the sleep lab area. The doors would be open until the alien passed through them.

Then, a photoelectric device would trigger a closing mechanism. When the alien tried to exit, the door wouldn't open easily and the glass would be shattered, locking the alien in with the patient.

He had some qualms about subjecting Dunbar to this, but he also knew that if he didn't do something like this, Dunbar would be even worse off.

Paul borrowed Dr. Baines's computer and placed an on-line order for the device, one for each of the three doors that accessed the sleep clinic, including with the order the dimensions of the doorways.

The security company with whom Paul worked would construct the doors and have them installed.

Chapter Eighteen: The Communication Conundrum

Alvin Selkirk had returned to his parsonage, a large frame house that had been built at the same time as the adjacent church. It had a large basement and big rooms on the main floor, plus five bedrooms on the second floor. The attic was huge, one gigantic room that took up the entire space on the top floor. He enjoyed the fact that the two structures were so appealingly laid out on a large tract in the center of the small town.

The Church should be at the center of the community and the lives of the people and this fine location served to emphasize that fact. He often mentioned this in his Sunday sermons. The minister told his congregation of how much he enjoyed climbing the internal stairs to the top of the steeple, whence he could see most of the town. He often pictured the warm fantasy that, on any Sunday, he could see his entire flock making their ways loyally and with humility to his late morning services.

How pleasing that must be to the Lord, he liked to think. In actuality, however, Selkirk had only made the strenuous climb one time, just to see what was there: he found it so physically exhausting that he had never tried it again. A small, worshipful village bathed in sunshine and eager to hear the Word was his ideal.

But this entire UFO hassle had dimmed his imagined view. Now he had nightmares that his church steeple was being buzzed by saucer shaped vehicles that used sizzling death rays to mow down the church members as they fled in panic in all directions.

He had this bad dream at least three times that he could recall; by the number of times he had awakened in a cold sweat, he guessed that it might be even more than that. He had to deliberately push aside these thoughts and a shudder of dread that engulfed his body and turn his attention to the task of contacting Paul Sloan. Maybe he would have some thoughts on how to deflect the reporter.

Selkirk hit a switch to turn on the power to his computer components, which rested on a large desk in the corner of his study, a room at the rear of the first floor. Normally, he used the computer to compose church bulletins and to print his sermons which he carefully saved with the secret thought that someday he might publish them in a book.

He used the electronic mail component infrequently, but he liked to think of himself as somewhat of a computer enthusiast, so he did keep in touch with a few fellow ministers whom he knew to have computer capabilities.

As the equipment clicked and hummed to life, he pulled up the large, padded swivel chair to the desk and clasped his hands thoughtfully together in front of his pursed lips. He did need to word this right. Everything depended on it. He felt e-mail was therefore preferable to a phone call. It would give him the chance to edit his comments, whereas using the phone might allow the message to be garbled.

He clicked on the e-mail icon option. He referred to a notepad by the keyboard and entered Paul Sloan's e-mail address. Then he paused again, trying to compose just the right beginning.

"Paul, may God be with you at this time. I have an important topic to discuss with you if you are available."

There was a long pause after Selkirk finished his message. It was a bit unusual, since Paul almost always left an automatic reply for times when he wasn't home.

The minister impatiently tapped his fingers on the desk beside the keyboard. He began to wonder if he had made some procedural error or misspelled part of Paul's address, but he double-checked and found everything to be correct.

Suddenly there was a response:

paul aint here right now.

The reverend was quite surprised by the poorly worded reply. Paul Sloan's written comments had always been written with correct, though sometimes sparse, grammar. But, it appeared to be an auto reply, after all, Selkirk thought as he prepared to sign off. No use pursuing this if Sloan wasn't there.

But the message continued:

he went to some hospital in spring city this is his freind can I help df.

Paul never seemed to have any close friends, Selkirk thought, despite the fact that he had the ability to get along with almost everybody, but maybe this was some distant relative who was visiting.

"When will he be back?" Selkirk typed, using his usual hunt and peck style.

soon i think i can take a messidj df

Again, the poor grammar and spelling. It was unfortunate that Paul wasn't there. The minister paused to consider what message would most likely elicit a prompt response when he returned.

Suddenly, however, before Selkirk could begin to enter an additional comment, a new message appeared.

The Reverend scanned the text immediately, hoping that Paul had just entered the house and had composed a response.

im not good with computars but i did lern some things in a class at scool i hope you can read this df

Relative or not, Selkirk figured, Paul's friend must not be too bright, since the punctuation was almost nonexistent and the grammar poor.

"I'm Reverend Selkirk of the True Faith Believers Church here in Caperton. Who are you?" Selkirk poked out with his index fingers.

im a frend of paul i jest got here wait i think sum one is hear now may bee paul

There was a pause of a few seconds, followed by a series of repeats of the last letter, "l" as though someone had inadvertently rested a finger on the key while being distracted. Then, the message resumed:

sounds in kichen butt no one is thar here footstops sumone combing strainge voce weerd wurds sumwhare im scered help hellp hel

The message stopped abruptly. "DF" had obviously pecked out the last words in a hurry.

The minister stared at the message, not knowing what to do. Then, in hopes that his correspondent had regained his or her composure, he tried again.

"Please acknowledge you are okay."

There was a long pause with no response. The minister eventually gave up. He'd need to try again, later.

The young woman in the mobile home noted all this through the tiny camera in Selkirk's study, which she had been able to plant during the previous Sunday's service.

But, first, she texted a short message to someone in the nation's capital: "Starting next phase." George Huit immediately contacted his crew and headed for his private hanger at the airport.

Deke Fraley, sitting before the computer in Paul's living room, in an old swivel chair once belonging to Paul's grandfather, that Paul had allowed him to bring up from the basement, had heard a sound, a sort of low hum, behind him in the living room.

Ever since that occurrence at the warehouse he had been deathly afraid of any sounds he didn't immediately recognize. Some of his memory was returning, mostly the things that had made a visceral impact on him.

He had started to respond to the last message he had received when that sound and an eerie feeling caused him to pause, then whirl around in the swivel chair. Everything blurred and then went black.

The next thing Deke realized was that he was no longer in front of the computer, nor was he even inside Paul's house.

He found himself strapped onto some sort of metallic table. He couldn't make out anything in the room he now occupied, except for the rounded steel gray ceiling above him. He tried to talk, but his words wouldn't come.

He no longer felt scared.

A voice seemed to appear in his head. *"It will all be well. You are here with me now and I have so much to teach you to counteract what my foes told you."*

Chapter Nineteen: Laurine Meets Dr. Keller

Dr. William Garris had always been a compassionate man. That is why emergency medicine had appealed to him as a field of specialization. Thus, when Deke Fraley had disappeared from the hospital, Dr. Garris had gone out of his way, on his own time, to stop at Laurine Fraley's house to see how she was doing. Finding that she was, in fact, extremely distraught, Dr. Garris had persuaded Laurine to make an appointment with Dr. Charles Keller, the relatively new psychiatrist in town.

A couple of weeks later, Laurine arrived for her appointment with Dr. Keller. After speaking with her for a while, he found her to be quite depressed and had planned to prescribe an antidepressant for her, when something she said captured his attention.

"Deke has left me, Dr. Keller, just like his father did. Gone. Vanished."

"You did tell me that his father died of cancer right in the same hospital here in Millardville where Deke had been...?"

Keller was curious about her use of the term "vanished." The doctor had never heard anyone refer to a deceased loved one as "vanished."

"I do apologize, Dr. Keller. It was actually Deke's stepfather, whom I married while pregnant with Deke, who died. You see, he wasn't Deke's actual father. I've kept that a secret all these years. It's been such a huge pressure, keeping that fact hidden from Deke and everyone for all that time. I thought I had overcome my feelings of guilt and, well, abandonment, but Deke leaving has brought it all back full force. Can you help me? I mean, why can't I stop feeling bad about something that happened so long ago?"

Laurine's thin lips quivered as she fought to hold back a sob that was ready to burst free.

"I see. Well, could you tell me more about Deke's actual father and what happened?"

Laurine, swallowing hard, held up her left hand, palm out, a wordless request for time to get her emotions under control. Finally, she began. By her third sentence, Keller knew he would need to look deeper into what she was revealing to him.

"He said his name was Attir, a foreign sounding name, maybe Middle Eastern. He was tall and thin with eyes that seemed to peer deep into me. We met one night when I was eighteen years old and had gone to Lake Patton to be alone and cry and maybe find a way to deal with all my pain."

She paused. "You see, my parents were divorcing, my mother didn't seem to care about me, and I had no close friends. My father had left that day, without even saying goodbye. I walked, crying, all the way to the lake, not really sure what I would do. I walked way out on the boat dock and looked into the water. It looked so dark and tempting. I guess I was really about ready to jump in..."

"And that is when you met Attir?"

"Yes. I don't know how long I had stared at the water; maybe it was hours, maybe only minutes. Suddenly, I noticed that a greenish light was reflecting off the water along the shore across the lake. I think I may have slipped on the edge of the dock and began to fall into the water."

"I really don't remember jumping. I just remember that I had looked over toward the light on the shore and then I was falling. The next thing I knew, I opened my eyes and there he was..." Laurine's voice trailed off until it was inaudible.

The reference to a green light registered sharply with Keller. He penciled it on his notepad, then looked up again at Laurine, who was leaning back in one of the padded armchairs, with her eyes squeezed shut. Her hands gripped the chair's arms with white-knuckle intensity.

Why so much despair? Keller wondered.

When at last Laurine's story resumed, she relaxed. "I don't know why, but this stranger seemed to be so reassuring to me. He used to always just look at me and say, '*It will all be well*'. I found that so soothing."

"We met several times after that first time, always by the lake. I knew I was in love. Then, one night, he was gone. He never came back. It hurt so much, but I no longer thought of ending it all, Doctor. His love had cured me of that and when I discovered that I was pregnant, well, I knew I had a reason to live, and I owed it to Attir and the baby inside me to survive."

"It was soon after that when I met Deke's stepfather, who had just moved to town. He was also alone in the world, so we decided to face life together. I had this funny feeling that Attir had sent him, or at least that Attir would approve."

"So, we got married and that was that. I never told Karl about Attir. He never knew that Deke wasn't really his son. Deke was born small and pale and with such thin arms and legs, he did appear to be premature and sickly."

"But he survived. Karl did love him. I think he would have, even if he found out Deke wasn't his. So, I never told either of them."

"But you still feel hurt that Attir left? Deep inside?"

"I suppose I do. It all seems so long ago and far away. Sometimes I feel like it didn't happen, like I imagined it. But I'm positive it did. I couldn't just dream this all up, could I?" Laurine leaned forward and stared intently at Keller.

"Dream?" Keller responded. "Dreams can tell so much about a person and what they feel. Have you ever dreamed about Attir?"

"I-I think I have, often. But I can never remember those dreams. I have always felt that he was watching over us, me and Deke. And Deke is so much like Attir, a loner, always most comfortable in the dark. At times Deke even had that far away deep, dark stare."

"Laurine, I'd like to try some hypnosis with you. I think we can perhaps help you identify more completely why you feel the way you do. With your permission, we will do that the next time you come in, next week. Would that be okay?"

Laurine nodded her consent. After summing up the day's session and saying goodbye to her, Keller sat alone at his desk. Words that she had used kept dancing through his thoughts as he prepared to dictate the notes for the session into Laurine's record.

"Green light." "It will all be well." The description of the deep, dark eyes, and Deke's appearance at birth all brought clearly to mind the case of Kathy Fellner. Only, with Laurine Fraley, the opposite experience had occurred, it seemed to Dr. Keller. Kathy had lost her baby to the beings of the green light; Laurine had received hers from the same source. Why? Why? Keller stared at his notepad and frowned.

Chapter Twenty: Tonya's Tale

Tonya Belding was in a probationary period at the Millardville office of Family Services. She was impatient, wanting to advance to a permanent job. She hated the uncertainty of not being permanent. The Family Services job was her first job after graduate school. She had chosen social work as a career because she wanted something easy and her parents had been pushing her to either go after a master's degree or get a job.

It turned out that grad school wasn't as easy as she had hoped it would be, but she feigned interest in the head of the department, whom she had heard was a secret womanizer. Once she had become close to him, she gradually let him know that if she didn't get good grades, she would get in contact with his wife. This same trick had worked well for her when she was an undergraduate and even in high school. The department head was also easily persuaded to find her a job after graduation, so here she was in this hicksville town.

"Millardville! What kind of name is that?" She had spat out when she first heard about the job opening.

She would have to make it through the six months' probation. She was determined to work hard, for a change, in order to impress her boss. She had spent several months as an unpaid intern in a Spring City office of this same state agency and she had been frustrated when she was unable to blackmail her supervisor, Frank Dorman, into giving her a great evaluation. Tonya was angry that the evaluation was worded in such a way as to make it clear to anyone reading it that she had problems relating to the families on her caseload.

While Kathy Fellner was on medical leave, Tonya had been

given the chance she wanted. She was temporarily assigned Kathy's caseload.

Tonya's first real assignment after taking over for Kathy was to follow up with the Mayes family, but Kathy's experience there on her last day of work had confused the picture. Kathy claimed the family was there, but neighbors and the landlord claimed they had moved out days or even weeks before Kathy's visit.

Tonya felt it would be a really positive point for her personnel file if she could get the credit for locating this missing family, since the children were considered to be at risk for neglect, possibly abuse, even abandonment. It might also look good on her record if she could file a report of neglect or abuse with the state's central abuse-neglect registry. So, as opportunity presented itself, Tonya began to collect clues on the family's current location.

The first solid clue Tonya uncovered was from the woman who lived next-door to the Mayes family, Mrs. Haker. Tonya had stopped by on the way to another house in the neighborhood and had taken advantage of a few extra minutes in her schedule of visits to knock on the door of the mostly gray, paint-peeling house to the north of the one in which the Mayes family had resided.

Mrs. Haker, a woman in her mid-fifties, had come to the door with an unusually sour scowl that almost caused Tonya to recoil physically.

"How may I help you?" snapped Mrs. Haker, wiping her hands on a kitchen towel as she pushed open the battered screen door. Her scowl intensified.

"I'm from the Family Services agency," Tonya began, avoiding eye contact with the annoyed woman, fighting back her rising revulsion at the appearance of what she saw as a frumpy old hag.

"I was wondering if you have any information on how or when the Mayes family moved. They were our clients."

Tonya knew that it was a breach of rules to identify a family as being known to her agency, but she added, "We think the mother may be abusing the kids."

"That don't hardly surprise me. I didn't much care for that bunch. But I can't help you none," growled Mrs. Haker, letting the door swing shut as she turned back to the darkened interior of her small house.

"Wait, though…" she remarked, turning back to face Tonya, who was trying not to reveal her disdain for this old woman.

"Yes?" Tonya responded with her most pleasant smile though she didn't feel like smiling. She actually wanted to retreat to the comfort of her car.

"Just something that little boy, Davey, said the last time I saw him. He was a nuisance and always trampling my flowers and making noise with his rowdy little friends. I remember one time when he…"

Tonya interrupted. "What did he say, that last time?"

Doris Haker stopped in mid-sentence and gave Tonya a withering scowl, even more intense than her usual one. "I was about to say, darling…" the word 'darling' oozed with contempt… "that Davey boy told me that his sister's daddy, they all had different fathers, you understand, was going to come get them that night and they would be moving somewhere out in the country. Of course, with that sort of trashy people, you can never believe anything they say. They really made the neighborhood a worse place to live, I say. I sure don't miss them none."

The novel realization hit Tonya that this disheveled old crone actually thought of herself as being better than the Mayes family!

Tonya had always assumed that poor is poor. Worthless, unmotivated people were all pretty much the same. Mrs. Haker must have some sort of delusions that she is better than other people, Tonya surmised. Maybe she was senile.

"Did he say where in the country they were moving?" Tonya asked through a rigidly fake smile.

"Somewhere over by Reginald, I think. I guess that Dubold character, that's the little girl's father, though she goes by her mother's last name, has family over that way. He used to live here with them. Worthless drunk, woman chaser. Ain't none of 'em no good."

Tonya felt a surge of triumph at having drawn this potentially useful information from this obviously unsophisticated woman. She thought to herself that this demonstrated that she knew how to relate to people. Take that, Frank Dorman!

"Well, if you do see any of the family or this Dubold person, call me," Tonya said, before Mrs. Haker had a chance to add further to her comments.

Tonya shoved her business card into the old witch's hand. Then she spun on her heels and strode off toward her car, leaving Mrs. Haker staring after her with a perplexed expression. As Tonya opened the car door, Mrs. Haker's expression changed back to her usual scowl, she rumpled up the card and threw it disgustedly onto the ground next to her front porch. She allowed the screen door to slam hard as she retreated into the darkness of her living room.

Then, one day in late September, Kathy Fellner finally felt well enough to return to work, part-time. Tonya had been using her office, but a small desk was placed in the corner of the room for her use when Kathy returned, and the two became office mates.

It was planned that Tonya could eventually have her own room when she passed probation if an opening occurred. Meanwhile, she would continue to work full time until Kathy could regain her strength. Tonya seethed inside at not being respected enough to be allowed to have a room right away. After all, how hard could it be for her boss to convince someone to retire to make room for a more capable employee?

Kathy was still not fully recovered, physically or mentally. Tonya could see that right away. She could also tell that Kathy was quite vulnerable and would probably be someone with whom she could readily build a relationship which might be of use professionally someday.

It was clear to her that Kathy didn't have much ambition and didn't seem to care much for success, at least the way Tonya defined it. Tonya felt that she would be able to use her as a stepping-stone in her own career advancement.

"You've worked here for quite a while, Kathy?" Tonya inquired, using one of her most ingratiating smiles.

"Yes. This breakdown I had was the first time off I've had in years. My husband Lee thinks I was just working too hard. My doctor has been very cautious in letting me return to work. That's why I'm only working mornings."

"Oh?" Tonya had been standing in front of Kathy's desk. She put her hands on it and leaned forward, working hard to show concern. "Your doctor must be really concerned about his patients. I'm new in town; maybe I should get him to be my doctor."

Kathy's face darkened for a second. "I do have a very good obstetrician. Dr. Hunter. Everyone calls him Wally. But, I meant my psychiatrist, Dr. Keller. I doubt that you are in need of either's services, Tonya."

Kathy was able to finish her response with a brief, but warm, smile. "You might try that Dr. Williamson. He seems like a nice guy. Lee and I are going to make him our family physician."

"You're going to a shrink?" Tonya blurted out, immediately rebuking herself for not showing more restraint. The one lesson she had learned in life was to never show other people your true feelings.

"I mean, that experience with your baby you told me about must have been very difficult. I'm glad you're getting some good help."

Kathy had told her younger co-worker about losing her baby but had not gone into any detail about the fact that it had been a very strange experience, involving an apparently false pregnancy, the disappearance of the Mayes family, and so forth.

For herself, Kathy still, even with Dr. Keller's help, had not been able to speak or think of her baby as someone who never existed. She had even felt the baby moving! She would always be real to Kathy.

"Was it a boy or girl?" Tonya sensed that Kathy would be grateful for being asked. Gratitude can be used for manipulation.

"A girl," Kathy responded.

Even as she did so, though, she realized that her quick answer wouldn't match with the fact that no baby existed. So, why did she continue to deny what everybody told her was the truth?

Kathy had no doubt whatsoever that she should have been the mother of a beautiful little girl by now. It was as if she was living two lives, one in which she was the real mother of a real baby she and Lee had named Stephanie, and another, a nightmarish dream in which the whole pregnancy had been some sort of hallucination.

"Has it been hard on your husband?" Tonya asked with apparent concern in her voice, while the thought of Lee, whom she had seen drop Kathy off at work, prompted her to think that he wasn't a bad looking guy. If Kathy totally loses her sanity, maybe he would need some comforting. Tonya filed this thought in the back of her mind for possible future action. At this time, though, she had other options she needed to pursue.

"Well, Lee has been worn down a little from having to deal with all this. After all, he lost a child, too. But, he's been very supportive, really. Seeing the psychiatrist was his idea. He even had a few appointments of his own."

Tonya turned back toward her own desk. "Well, scratch that previous thought," Tonya said under her breath. "I don't need a crazy person in my life."

"That's so nice of him," Tonya remarked aloud to Kathy, sitting back down in her chair and smiling what she hoped was a warm smile.

At that moment Kathy's phone rang and the conversation was interrupted. Tonya turned to a stack of folders on her desk and pretended to read the first page of the top one. Her mind was moving ahead fast, though. Shrink, eh? Maybe Kathy wasn't really ready to come back to work. Maybe, if she couldn't take the stress, there would be all the more reason for Tonya to pass her probation, since the administration wouldn't really want to have to replace too many workers at once.

Tonya smiled to herself as she pretended to start reading the second page; this time the smile was genuine.

With Kathy back at work, the agency was able to assign Tonya a few additional cases that had been in need of attention, but on which action had been temporarily deferred.

One of these involved Marla Brashear, who had been recently discharged from Millardville Memorial Hospital to a nursing facility. She had regained consciousness, but her physical recovery was slow, and she had limited speech. She was experiencing amnesia. Also, she became very agitated whenever the medical staff mentioned sending her back to her home. She seemed to believe that she had to stay in Millardville for some reason.

Her physician didn't think she was ready to be transferred; she still had some broken bones that weren't quite healed, and she had only recently emerged from a coma.

Tonya was given the task of arranging a visit by Marla's children, their first since she recovered consciousness.

They had come with their maternal aunt twice before, but this would be the first time they would be able to interact with their mother.

Tonya would need to prepare Marla for the visit, since it was clear that she had no memory of her own children.

Tonya felt this was absurd; who could forget her own family? Tonya could understand, though, why someone would want to; her family had not been anything to brag about.

This woman was putting on an act and just didn't want to be stuck with those brats. That was a response Tonya could understand. Kids were nothing but trouble. She herself never got along with her older siblings and was bitter about her parents' obvious favoring of them. That was her primary motivation in getting a college degree, to escape her family.

After getting her Bachelor's Degree, she didn't feel ready for a job, so after her parents told her to either continue her education or get out, she applied to the nearest University School of Social Work. She had chosen social work because she had heard it would be easy.

Tonya was lukewarm about trying to set up the visit, but she found herself at the door of the Millardville Care Center one sunny afternoon in early October. She checked in at the front desk and got directions to Room 108.

As Tonya entered the room she was surprised to see that Marla already had a visitor. A rather worn looking woman whom Tonya estimated to be in her mid-forties was sitting next to the bed occupied by the woman matching the photo attached to the agency file of Marla Brashear. The visiting woman had clearly visible graying streaks in her hair. Tonya wondered immediately why anyone would let herself go like that; she surely wouldn't.

Marla Brashear appeared frail and small amid the rumpled sheets, blankets and pillows that had obviously been heaped carelessly atop the mattress by some dull-witted member of this dump's housekeeping staff, who was doubtlessly some illegal immigrant from a third world country.

Neither the Brashear woman nor her rumpled visitor appeared to be on a first-name basis with a qualified hairdresser, either, Tonya noted with disdain. Maybe Marla Brashear had some excuse for her appearance, since it was doubtful that this dump employed anybody who would know anything about beauty, but the frumpy looking graying lady could obviously use some pointers.

"I am Tonya Belding," she began, interrupting the limited conversation between the two disheveled occupants of the small, dingy room. "I need to speak with the Brashear lady. Please excuse us, whoever you may be."

The slender, slightly stooped older woman stood up and turned toward Tonya. "I am Laurine Fraley," she said in a rather flat manner, extending her right hand, which Tonya ignored until the frumpy woman let it drop back to her side. "I became interested in Marla's situation while she and my son Deke were both in the hospital. She may not remember much, but she knows that she has been through some tough times and so have I."

"Well, fine. But I have some important things to discuss with her, so why don't you hurry on your way now, Noreen...or Maureen or whatever. You see, I am her social worker and I have some things I need to talk about with her and they are confidential, so you have no right to hear them. Go on. Scoot."

Tonya made a short motion with her hands to indicate that Laurine should leave.

Laurine frowned slightly at the taller woman's inability to recall the name she had just given her, but chose to ignore that, along with the demeaning tone of her voice.

"Then, if that's who you are, you must be aware that Marla has lost her husband and she can't even remember her own children. I've lost a husband and I don't know where my son is, so I find that she and I have a lot in common."

"Yes, well, maybe you should find yourself a social worker, too. Come back later. Okay?"

Laurine gathered up her purse and coat that had been hooked over the back of the wooden chair by the bed and turned to leave. Marla, throughout the brief exchange, stared blankly at the two.

"Now, Ms. Brashear..." Tonya began, turning toward the bed and seating herself daintily on the edge of the chair Laurine Fraley had just vacated. "We need to talk about why you don't want to take care of your own children." She stared intently at Marla.

Marla blinked a few times and shifted her focus from her departing visitor to the well-dressed stranger with the dyed blond hair who had just taken a seat at her bedside.

"You realize that your kids are coming to see you, don't you?" Tonya continued, shooting an accusing stare at Marla.

Marla smiled weakly. "Oh yes. I know. I don't remember having children. They tell me that they are really nice children, though. Their pictures have been placed on my dresser here by the bed. See?"

Tonya turned her head slightly in the direction to which Marla had pointed one bony finger. "Yeah, yeah. Nice children." She didn't really know why anyone would want children, but these poor slobs seemed to breed like cats.

She put her purse in her lap, so it wouldn't have to touch the germ ridden floor and leaned toward the bed. "So, why do you want to ditch them?"

"All I remember is that my husband Jay disappeared near here and I came out to find him. I know I'm married to Jay, but that seems to be my only solid recollection."

"Well, Ms. Brashear, you are not the first woman to lose her husband. And, if I may say so, your unkempt appearance today may actually provide a clue as to why he found some other woman more attractive."

Tonya was amazed at her own ability to cut through to the core of the whole problem. Marla Brashear was obviously such a bad wife and mother that her husband had fled the relationship and now she just had no use for the brats. It was that simple and the sooner this poor old hag accepted it, the sooner the kids could be placed in an adoptive home, etcetera, etcetera.

Marla closed her eyes and frowned, then turned directly toward Tonya and opened a withering stare upon her, which startled Tonya. It was such a look that she felt like she had been physically struck.

"My husband did not leave me, of that I am certain. He

was coming out here to visit an old college buddy, Paul Sloan, in Caperton, a town near here. That much I do remember..."

Tonya blinked, taken aback for a couple seconds. Then, recovering her command of the interview, she hit upon what she knew was a very insightful observation.

"So, your husband left you for another man. That must have been a terrible blow, perhaps enough to cause amnesia."

Marla sat bolt upright, her face reddened, and her fists clenched. Tonya, who had been leaning forward on the edge of her chair in order to better drive home her therapeutic point and also to decrease her exposure to whatever disease-causing parasite might be waiting on the chair, was not able to react quickly enough to avoid what happened next.

Marla seized her by her ruffled collar with both hands and yanked her toward the bed. Tonya's face went white with fear as her purse's contents spilled onto the floor.

"I may not recall much about my life," Marla hissed through her tightly clamped teeth, "but I do know two things! My husband loves me...and I love my children even if I don't remember them. Now, either you arrange that visit or I will be sure that your supervisor hears of your absurd and unprofessional behavior! Got it, Goldie?"

Marla released her grip on Tonya's collar and pushed her back onto the chair. Tonya's face turned pale. She gathered her purse's contents together as best she could and scrambled screaming for the door in sheer panic. She dropped a few items that she had tried to scoop into her purse, and lost one shoe, but only paused long enough to make sure she had her car keys.

A nurse's aide rushed by her as she left, hurrying to try to calm the bedridden patient. The aide bent to retrieve the shoe, expecting to hand it to Tonya when she returned for it, but she didn't come back.

In only seconds Tonya was safely in her car, panting heavily, doors locked, her head leaning on the steering wheel. Even as she gasped for air, her mind was racing.

Her brilliant career was at risk. This frumpy Brashear woman could ruin her career if she complained to her supervisor, Bob Peate. Tonya needed a plan. She wasn't sure how she could pull it off, but she would make it so that frumpy old lady was discharged from the nursing home straight into a mental institution!

Plans of action were always a big part of Tonya's approach to life. She had learned early that it was best to not leave things to fate, if it was at all avoidable. She knew that her intelligence, charm and beauty would take her far, but that wasn't always enough, and she wanted to be sure that she herself guided the direction of her progress.

She had slipped up during her field placement by not having an alternative plan to dating her supervisor to assure that her evaluation would be glowing. That had been a mistake. She should not have neglected the fact that Frank Dorman was one of those stiff-collared do-gooders who actually tried to give her what he thought was an objective evaluation and had an unfathomable attachment to his family.

So, now she began to form a plan to anchor herself securely in this job. She would solve the mystery of the missing Mayes family. That would put her in good standing with

Mr. Peate. Also, she would see to it that Kathy Fellner's fragile emotional state would stay that way. That would assure that the agency would have a vacancy to fill.

Proving Marla Brashear an unfit parent might be a challenge, but Tonya figured that if she accomplished it, it could only improve her chances of passing probation.

Tonya decided that she would take a field trip out to Reginald to wrap up the first part of the plan. First, though, she decided that there must be some way to assure herself that Kathy Fellner would lose her precarious balance and tumble from the shaky tightrope of emotional stability upon which she obviously swayed. Something Kathy had said about a psychiatrist had been simmering in the back of her mind. Perhaps Dr. Keller would be willing, or at least able, to help with the plan.

Step One: Tonya overheard Kathy on the phone one morning with her husband, who obviously was explaining that he wouldn't be able to pick her up from work that day for an appointment. Tonya's sense of opportunity was activated when she realized that Kathy was speaking about the need to cancel an appointment.

"Kathy, I couldn't help hearing the disappointment in your voice during that discussion ..." Tonya volunteered as she glanced to her left at her office mate.

"It's Lee. We only have one car today and he's using it, but he can't get away from his job in time to take me to my two o'clock appointment with my psychiatrist, Dr. Keller. I'll have to cancel it."

Kathy looked tired, as usual; it was nearly noon, and she was running out of steam. She was still on half-days and her day was supposed to end at noon. Tonya was amazed that Kathy didn't mind talking about the fact that she was seeing a shrink, since that clearly indicated she was crazy.

"You seem quite disappointed, Kathy," Tonya smiled as sweetly as she could. "Don't worry about it. I'll take a late lunch break and give you a lift."

Kathy didn't make any fuss about accepting the offer. She was very grateful, she told Tonya, since she really felt so much better after each session with Dr. Keller.

"I'm just glad to help," chirped Tonya.

Step Two: Find out Kathy's true mental state.

So it was that Tonya found herself seated in the warmly comfortable waiting room of the psychiatrist's office, glancing with curiosity at the paintings of western landscapes that hung on two of the walls. A small metal sculpture of a cowboy riding a bucking horse, which was located on the desk of the receptionist, confirmed that Dr. Charles Keller had a taste for the "wild west".

Tonya's mind whirled as she began to plot how she could use this fact to get in good with the doctor, whom she hoped would be of use to her in her plan to force Kathy to retire, thus making it more likely that Tonya would make it past the probation period.

At 2:50 PM the heavy oak door to the psychiatrist's office opened abruptly and Kathy exited, following her therapy session. Kathy looked much more relaxed exiting than when she had entered. Dr. Keller stood at the door for a moment and Tonya had a chance to size him up.

He was medium-to-tall in height, with a slightly receding hairline for which he seemed to attempt to compensate by allowing his sideburns to grow into his thick, well-trimmed mustache. The hair at the back of his head overlapped his collar. He was wearing a string necktie. Tonya also noted that the shiny shoes that he wore were actually cowboy boots, which were mostly hidden by the legs of his somewhat faded blue jeans.

Yep, she thought to herself as she turned on her most engaging smile, his thing is The West.

Tonya smiled brightly at him, but Charles Keller merely nodded somewhat shyly and began to close the door. This was not in Tonya's plan. She reacted swiftly, taking one step toward the closing door and then abruptly putting her hand to her forehead and collapsing to the floor.

A perfectly executed faint, she told herself, aware that her swoon had left her gracefully displayed at the doctor's feet.

A minute later Tonya had been helped into a chair by Dr. Keller, who, of course, expressed his concern, as did Kathy, but that was of no relevance to Tonya's plan, so she disregarded it.

"I'm afraid I just sorta sprung up too quickly there, Dr. Keller," Tonya commented in what she hoped sounded like a passable western drawl. "Got a bit dizzy."

"Are you alright now?" Dr. Keller inquired. Tonya was surprised to find that his accent was more Eastern than she had guessed it would be, not even Midwestern.

"I am fine. Please forgive my clumsiness. Growing up on the ranch in Colorado I could lasso a buckin' bronc, but out here I can't seem to walk straight some days."

"You're from the Centennial State, then, Ms...?"

"Belding. Tonya. Uh, I'm from Colorado. At least I lived there back in my early days." Tonya wasn't sure what the doctor meant by *Centennial State*, so she worded her response carefully.

She could see that she had a bite on her hook by the way the doctor smiled at her. He wasn't bad looking, she thought. Maybe she should make a serious try for him. After all, there was a certain status in being the wife of a doctor, even in this hick town.

She didn't know if he was married; but, that didn't really matter. It might just take longer if he was. These thoughts passed through Tonya's mind, but were chased out when she realized that wasn't a part of her long-term plan. She could dally with Doc Keller for a few weeks, maybe, but she had to keep her mind on her long-term goals.

Just at that moment Tonya's thoughts were cut short by the opening of the front door to the office, followed at once by the muffled sound of a woman's voice. Keller's eyes pulled free from Tonya's to take note of who had just entered. Tonya followed his gaze.

It was the frumpy woman from the nursing home, the one who had been visiting Marla Brashear, Doreen something-or-other.

With one glance, Tonya's opinion of her was reinforced: she was nothing but trouble. Her lack of make-up and fashion sense clearly showed that she was of the same lower social class as that Haker woman. What was she doing here?

"Excuse me, Tonya? I have an appointment," Keller commented quietly as he turned toward the reception desk.

Tonya did take some solace in the note of disappointment that she thought she detected in his voice.

As the new patient finished checking in with the receptionist, Kathy and Tonya gathered their coats and purses and prepared to leave. Tonya was nearly to the door when Kathy, smiling slyly, turned toward her and whispered, "He's not attached, you know…"

"Excuse me?" Tonya responded, turning toward her with a look of surprise.

"Dr. Keller isn't married. It was quite obvious that you took a quick interest in him, Tonya. He's a great guy, just a bit shy and unconventional. I think you should go for it, girl!"

Kathy was aware of transference, the tendency of patients to fall in love with their psychiatrists; she figured that the next best thing to acting on these feelings would be to urge Tonya to act on them for her. Kathy could sort of live her romance vicariously through Tonya.

Tonya was shocked to find herself actually blushing.

Keller had scheduled Laurine's hypnosis session for this day. He was pleased with how easily she fell into a relaxed state. He asked a few questions, then brought her back to the time she met Attir.

"Tell me about meeting Attir."

"He was so perfect. He came along just when I needed someone."

"But he also left you without warning?"

Laurine's face twisted into a look of pain. "Y-yes he did."

"And how did you feel about that, at the time?"

"Devastated! I almost went back to the dock again."

"What stopped you?"

Laurine's face took on a new look, anger. "I wanted to kill him! He left me worse off than when he found me!"

Then, her face relaxed and she commented, "I would never do that, of course. The day I thought about going back to the dock at the lake, that's the day I met Karl, my future husband."

"Tell me about Karl…"

"He was older than me by fifteen years. He told me he had been married before and had a daughter from that marriage. His wife refused to give him a divorce, so he and I couldn't actually marry. I kept my birth name, Fraley, and gave Deke that name. Karl hadn't seen his daughter in years. After he'd heard that she had become a reporter, he occasionally saw her on the TV news."

"So, Karl died of cancer?"

"Yes. His first wife heard about it and came to the funeral."

"But his daughter didn't?"

"No. She had disappeared while covering a story about a landslide in the Rockies. Very sad."

Chapter Twenty-One: Tonya, Part Two

After a week, Tonya encountered Dr. Keller in the parking lot after she got off work. He had taken that long to work up the nerve to ask her out, he explained shyly, and he didn't have her phone number, so he thought he would just drop by in person to see if she would be interested in going to Spring City to attend a concert by some country music star.

This was definitely not Tonya's idea of entertainment, but she figured it could work into her plans and she could tolerate it for a couple of hours. She surprised herself when she agreed to his awkward request, however, and was again genuinely surprised to find that she actually enjoyed the performance. She had never really listened to such music before, but each song seemed to tell a story and deal with realistic emotions. She could understand deceit and betrayal and lost love. She still thought the singers sang with an ugly twangy sound, which marked them as real hicks.

Charles, on the other hand, seemed to be actually transported and was markedly more at ease than any doctor she had ever met. He sang along with a couple of songs when the rest of the audience did so and cheered enthusiastically at the end of the performance. Tonya had been wondering if he was a real bumpkin, but on the ride home he was able to discuss rock and classical music with equal fervor, turning his car radio to different stations and remarking on whatever type music was playing.

He also discoursed at some length on football when his radio picked up a college game in progress. Eventually he abandoned the radio and asked about Tonya's life and interests.

No one Tonya had ever dated had ever expressed more than a cursory interest in her life. She suddenly felt aware that her own life was somewhat shallow. She invented a couple of interesting points of family history in an effort to impress Keller. She was intrigued that he did not seem to question her truthfulness, though she was unsure whether he actually believed her. He seemed to simply accept her story and occasionally ask a question that led her to elaborate further. Tonya was unaccustomed to that.

However, after Keller had dropped her off at her apartment that evening and she had some time to reflect, she reminded herself that no one can be trusted. She had learned that from experience. Charles Keller was just a smoother, much more convincing version of all the men she had ever known. Down deep he too must be as worthless as all the others.

She had to find a way to keep his trust long enough to use him for her own purposes. She must remain constantly focused on her goal of discrediting Kathy Fellner and, she hoped, shattering her fragile sanity. If she could slip in a little fun and pretend romance at the same time, then that was just frosting on the cake. Staying close to Keller might even help her figure out how to reach her goal.

It took her nearly two weeks to accomplish that. It was actually much easier than she had anticipated. Charles had to take a trip to a psychiatry symposium in New York and he asked her to drive him to the airport in Spring City. He had her take his car back to Millardville, since he didn't like having it exposed to the weather in the parking ramp at the airport.

He had an obsession with keeping his four-wheel drive vehicle clean and safe. Whenever he was going to park his car for more than a few minutes he would pull a plastic tarp out of the back seat to cover it. He even parked in the far corner of the parking lot at his office to decrease the likelihood of another car accidentally dinging his vehicle, even though he had a reserved spot in back of the building. He called this his "acknowledged neurosis" and he claimed that every psychiatrist had a right to one.

So, Tonya had his car keys and the keychain also had his office keys. She only had to find a good time to put her plan into operation and she knew she would reach her objective: a chance to review Kathy Fellner's file. With the knowledge she gained there, destroying Kathy's life would be as simple or complex an orchestration as Tonya chose to make it.

Once Kathy was out of the way, who could tell what options would open up? Maybe she could even allow herself to pursue the relationship with Keller. Maybe she could launch a brief diversion with Lee Fellner. Maybe she could do both. Tonya liked to have options.

At precisely 5:00 PM on a Wednesday evening, Tonya parked Keller's SUV in the far corner of the parking lot behind the building in which he had his office. She pulled the tarp out of the back and threw it over the Bronco just as Charles had shown her. She partly wanted to keep the car far from the view of Keller's receptionist, but also needed to deflect suspicion, since people from the building would be accustomed to seeing it there and covered with the plastic tarp.

She had studied the routine of Marsha, the receptionist. She always left work at exactly 5:05. The office cleaning service always began its work at approximately 6:00. This gave Tonya roughly three-quarters of an hour to complete her mission.

Tonya enjoyed the suspense of the situation, even as she felt the stress from the danger she was courting. That was a part of the thrill and Tonya Belding was nothing if not a thrill junkie.

5:07: Rita at last exited through the back door of the office building. The additional two-minute delay in Marsha's routine had left Tonya breathing deeply as she crouched low behind the SUV. Keller was due back in two days and Tonya had to attend a social work seminar sponsored by her agency the day before his return, as though she needed any additional knowledge or skills, and this would probably be the last chance she would have to complete her mission.

Marsha's car was close to the building and she probably wouldn't notice Tonya hunched down by Keller's car in the darkened far corner of the parking lot. Still, she was quite relieved when the receptionist's small SUV pulled away from the building and turned onto Pulver Street.

Tonya had already studied the many keys among Keller's collection on the Denver Broncos key chain. She had identified which were for the front and back doors of his house and the one that opened his garage door. Another fit the padlock on the gate to the fence around his back yard.

Tonya had placed small pieces of masking tape on the remaining two large keys and four small keys, just to identify which ones could possibly be used to gain entry to the office building, to his suite and the filing cabinets inside. In this way she wouldn't have to fumble with all the keys until she found the right one for each door and cabinet. She had thought about removing the excess keys, but she feared that she would fail to return them to the ring in their correct order and it was possible Charles would notice that his keys were not in the correct order.

Tonya decided to take no chances. A perfect plan required perfect execution and she wanted no imperfections.

Tonya approached the back door of the building, clutching the two large keys firmly between the thumb and index finger of her right hand. She reminded herself to remain calm and to not look around in what to an observer might appear to be a nervous manner.

She quickly tried the first key; it was the correct one and the heavy door opened with a tug. Tonya smiled. Past the door, she found herself in a long hallway. She carefully pulled the door shut behind her as she turned to move down the corridor. Luckily, Keller's suite was on the first floor, at the end of the hallway, so she wouldn't have far to go if she had to exit in a hurry.

She had pulled a small flashlight from her jacket pocket, but the doorway was lighted by a recessed ceiling bulb, so she didn't need to use it right away. Since she knew that the remaining large key had to be the right one, she promptly inserted it into the keyhole and a couple seconds later she was inside.

The office was dark, so she turned on the flashlight. She slipped quietly across the reception room, glad that she had worn rubber soled canvas shoes, which she had always found to be an indispensable part of her wardrobe whenever a bit of discrete snooping was called for.

This wasn't her first effort of this sort; she had tried unsuccessfully to use the same approach to obtain incriminating information on Frank Dorman back in Spring City. She had found his personnel file but was amazed to find nothing she could use for blackmail. He was squeaky clean.

A row of heavy metal drawers lined one wall of Keller's paneled outer office, behind the receptionist's desk; Tonya had noted their location the time she took Kathy to her appointment.

Though he had sworn to convert to electronic records, Keller had yet to get around to it. The drawers were therefore aligned in alphabetical order, so the only real problem was finding the correct key with which to unlock the appropriate one. Tonya jingled the smaller keys and began to try them one at a time on the drawer marked with the letter F. This time she had to go through all the keys to find that the last one was the correct one.

The drawer lock clicked mechanically as she turned the key, so loud that she paused to look around, switching off her flashlight to be safe, in case anyone heard the sound. Though her heart was now pounding forcefully, she congratulated herself on the cool and confident success of her plan thus far.

Again turning on the flashlight, after listening in the dark for a full minute, she opened the drawer, thumbed through it and pulled out the one with Kathy's name typed along one edge, last name first.

Now came the challenge. Tonya would need to make a copy of the file. Otherwise, it would be her word against Kathy Fellner's if she had to verify any claim she made to Mr. Peate about Kathy's mental stability. In actuality, she would need to show it to Kathy in order to blackmail her into quitting her job, though, as a last resort, she wanted to be able to anonymously leave the copied pages on Peate's desk.

The copying machine in the receptionist's office would make some noise and give off some light. There was not enough time to read through the notes and copy only the useful parts; Tonya would need to copy each page and sort out the best information back at her apartment. She paused long enough to gain an idea of the approximate number of pages. If she could copy them in about five minutes, there would be sufficient time to re-file the chart, lock the drawer and make her escape even if the cleaning crew came a few minutes early.

Tonya wanted to be sure that she had enough of a time cushion to avoid any possibility of a problem. If anyone outside the building happened to see the glow from the copying machine, it would take only minutes before police might reach the building.

Breathing as steadily and quietly as she could, Tonya carefully approached the copier with the file. In a few seconds the machine was humming steadily as it sucked up the pages from the feeder tray and spat out the copies.

Suddenly, the machine stopped.

She felt a chill passing through her body and had to make a deliberate effort to calm herself. What if one of the pages had become jammed in the interior of the machine?

However, a careful glance at the lighted message displayed on the top of the machine indicated that the old machine was out of paper. It took a few precious moments for Tonya to locate the drawer that held extra reams of paper and fill the tray. She was careful to use only a few pages, in case Rita might have been aware of how low the supply in the machine had been when she left the office. It was probably unlikely, but Tonya could not take chances. She berated herself for not checking on the paper supply before she started. She vowed to be more careful in the future.

As the final page was expelled from the machine Tonya checked her watch. Not much time remained. She would need to grab the copy, secure the originals back into the folder, place the folder back in the drawer, lock the drawer and make a hasty exit.

Just as she prepared to catch the original as it was about to be expelled from the machine, it again came to a halt. She knew it couldn't be out of paper again. She began to scan the various messages that would light up to describe the problem, but the lights all suddenly went dim and then blinked out.

Somehow the power to the machine had been shut off. She pulled out her small flashlight and began to check out the area at the base of the copier to see if she had accidentally dislodged the power cord, but her flashlight abruptly died just after she turned it on.

From behind her came a sound of something moving, a barely audible sound that Tonya wouldn't have heard if her senses weren't heightened as she tried to avoid detection. She felt her strength suddenly drain from her body, precipitously, like water spilling from a badly cracked cup.

She spun around as she began to fall, wondering without any real concern if the cleaning crew had suddenly caught her, or maybe even the police. Even as these thoughts flitted through her mind, though, she realized that she didn't really care. She didn't care about anything.

She felt relaxed and calm. *"All will be well"* was her last thought before she lost consciousness. It had not occurred to her that, while she was focusing on Kathy's file, some deep, glowing red eyes had been focused on her...eyes belonging to someone with a strong interest in maintaining Kathy's current recovery.

Tonya awoke to the glare of sunshine blazing through the windshield of Keller's SUV. She instinctively moved her right arm to block the sunlight, but a sharp pain in the back of her head caused her to scream out and pull her arm back as she grabbed her head with both hands. A loud buzzing suddenly erupted in her ears, rising rapidly to an intensity that nearly split her skull. She collapsed forward against the steering wheel, grimacing and gritting her teeth to stifle further sounds.

At last, achieving a degree of comfort or at least a lack of steady pain, she opened her eyes to see where she was. She found herself back in the far corner of the parking lot, behind Dr. Keller's office building. The protective tarp had been removed, but Tonya didn't recall having done that.

The sun was shooting early beams over the horizon, slicing between the building and a clump of trees to the west of it. The trees were nearly bereft of foliage in the midst of autumn. She tried to recall what had happened, how she ended up here. She vaguely recalled that she had come here for some purpose, but every time her mind seemed to touch on a fragment of memory, her head began to pound, and a buzzing began in her skull and she would feel faint.

After a few minutes she carefully moved her arms down to her sides, leaned back away from the steering wheel and extracted the keys from her jacket pocket. She started the car and pulled slowly onto Pulver Street. She took the most direct route home and stumbled into her apartment after parking the car as close to her own door as she could. She didn't even consider pulling the tarp over the car. She tripped a couple times as she made her way to her bedroom but managed to throw herself onto the bed and soon she was deep in sleep.

That's when the recurring dreams began, misty and

terrible dreams. Tall, thin, shadowy figures all appeared somewhere off to her left and began to slowly circle around her. Each was holding a small, metallic instrument of some kind, about the size of a pencil or screwdriver.

The figures gradually tightened the circle until finally halting and reaching out toward her with the shiny objects. Rather, Tonya noted, they were reaching down toward her, for she found that she was immobilized and lying flat on a cold surface, apparently some sort of table or cot. She wasn't restrained, but she couldn't move.

The objects in the hands of those around her reflected an array of colored lights, each device pulsating with a different hue. Then she would feel a cold terror inside. The strange and silent figures began to touch her with the lights from the objects they held, focusing on various places at the same time. She sensed, without actually seeing, that she was being poked and even pierced by the lights.

Then the dream, actually a bizarre nightmare, would end. She would drop into a deep sleep and awake to the blinding light of morning slicing through the blinds in her bedroom.

Tonya missed the next two days of work. She even missed the evening seminar she was supposed to attend. She did manage to drive her own car to the airport in Spring City, since it was easier to drive than Keller's SUV, to pick up Charles on his return from his out-of-state trip.

During the drive she felt no interest in his efforts to make conversation. She stopped at her apartment and Charles switched to his car, which he was annoyed to discover was not covered with the tarp and was parked amid other vehicles outside the apartment building.

Keller asked her to join him for dinner at his favorite steakhouse, but she declined without feeling any need to offer an explanation. She said goodbye with no particular emotion. Charles was puzzled by her behavior, but Tonya felt only a dim relief that she had accomplished what she had previously promised by returning him to Millardville.

For his part, Dr. Keller was disappointed with her changed attitude toward him, but he noted with clinical precision that Tonya seemed to be clutching at her forehead frequently and complained of insufficient sleep. He wasn't sure that this meant anything specific, medically, but he knew that he had heard of those symptoms recently.

He had a busy schedule for the next few days, but he decided to look into Tonya's behavior more closely as soon as he could. Someone else had mentioned similar problems. He needed to remember which of his many patients had those same complaints.

Back at work, Tonya felt somewhat listless. For no reason that she could grasp, she no longer had the drive to get ahead that she had always felt. She recalled having pledged to herself that she would somehow discredit Kathy in order to more firmly establish herself within the agency, but now she couldn't recall why she would want to do that.

She found copies of psychiatric reports on Kathy in her kitchen but didn't know how they got there and she didn't feel it important to read them, so she fed them into her paper shredder. She also couldn't figure out why she ever had a paper shredder.

She found herself performing her daily tasks routinely, well enough to be acceptable, but not well enough to merit praise. She just didn't care all that much anymore.

Eventually the Mayes case had come around to Kathy for routine review. There had been no further leads in relation to the vanishing of the family. Kathy had just resumed working fulltime, but she and Tonya continued to share an office until an upcoming retirement would make a separate office available.

When Tonya learned that she no longer needed to push Kathy into quitting, Tonya didn't care. In fact, she only vaguely recalled that she had planned to sabotage her co-worker. Thus, when Kathy saw Tonya's notation about the information gleaned from Doris Haker, she remarked on it to her office mate.

"What did you say?" Tonya asked, looking up blankly from the case record she had been reviewing in preparation for a home visit. Her job performance no longer reflected her desperate efforts to succeed, but she somehow managed to perform adequately.

Kathy, seated at her desk on the other side of the room held aloft a manila folder. "The Mayes file, Tonya? I see by your record note that you had visited their next-door neighbor and you learned something about their possible location."

"Oh, uh, yes. Not much, though," Tonya responded in a flat tone. "I think that old lady said the children may have gone to live with the father of one of them, the little girl's father. Kimmy, I think it was Kimmy's father."

"Well, that's a lead. I think we should call him and tie up this loose thread, make sure the family is okay. It's still an

open case and the county where he was last known to live is within our district, so we should follow up on this."

"I guess so," Tonya responded softly. "It's your case, again, so you can do what you want."

"Well, the town of Reginald is in Mary Sue's area, so I could ask her to check on it, but the truth is she's transferring into Gayle's area when Gayle retires, and it looks like they will be giving that part of the district to you after your probation. You should take this opportunity to begin working the area, getting to know the resources in that county. I will try to get through to this Jeffrey Dubold by phone, but then I'm going to see if Mr. Peate wants you to follow this one."

Tonya nodded numbly. She didn't really care. Even the reference to the passing of her probation didn't strike the spark that Tonya herself knew it would have a few weeks previously. Kathy seemed so sure that Tonya would pass probation that she was speaking of it as an accomplished fact, but Tonya was not even sure she wanted to keep working. She had been having difficulty focusing lately, mentally, and the buzzing inside her skull had never really gone away and it would grow more intense each time she tried to concentrate.

But, two days later Kathy exited from a short meeting with Mr. Peate and marched straight to Tonya's desk. She tossed the Mayes folder on top of the stack of files that were already there.

"It's yours, Tonya. Mr. Peate sees no reason to have Mary Sue try to pick up on this one when you already know it pretty well. Oh, I tried to reach Dubold by phone, but he doesn't have a listed number. The school people in that district don't know anything about the children, nor does the county health department or the Medicaid office. So, maybe the kids aren't there anymore, but Mr. Peate suggested that you and I both take a drive over that way, just in case. You need to get out of this office and you can familiarize yourself with the area. You've been so sullen lately. I know the children by sight, so I will be able to identify them if we locate them."

Tonya didn't argue. She was only vaguely aware that going to Reginald had been part of her master plan to secure a fulltime job. She had barely been able to make it out of bed that morning and she agreed that riding along with Kathy to another county might help her break out of what she was now beginning to recognize as a deepening depression.

Somewhere in the depth of her psyche she had at last recognized a faint glimmer of concern about what was happening to her. The buzz in her head was growing stronger.

They took Tonya's car, but Kathy did the driving. Tonya seemed distracted and Kathy convinced her that it might be better if she drove, since she was familiar with the county roads. Actually, Kathy didn't think Tonya was a very safe driver since her personality change.

Kathy was becoming quite concerned about Tonya's recent descent into apathy, which seemed to increase even as her own depression was beginning to lift. She recognized that Tonya had always seemed to possess a certain drive that seemed to animate her, almost to the point of being too aggressive at her job. Now that drive had disappeared and Tonya, who could ill afford it, seemed to be losing weight. Kathy thought she would try to find out what Tonya was experiencing during the trip to Reginald.

"I'm alright," Tonya responded to Kathy's inquiry about her

health as they drove along the state road just west of Millardville. Kathy glanced at her coworker slumped weakly against the passenger side door and concluded that she was definitely not okay.

"Tonya, I've come through a rough time myself these past few months, as you know, and I can tell when someone is not alright. You don't seem to have your usual energy and you are definitely losing weight. You have told me that you are no longer seeing Dr. Keller, but you gave no reason."

"I'm dieting." The words seemed to leap from Tonya's lips before she even had time to think them. She immediately realized that this was a lie and only addressed part of Kathy's concern and she briefly struggled to care about that fact. She had no problem with lying, but she always knew why it was necessary. In this case, she couldn't identify the reason. Then her voice again betrayed her.

"I needed to get rid of a few pounds in the usual places." Another lie.

Kathy frowned. She stared at her passenger's face in an effort to detect obvious signs of deliberate deception, but Tonya's head was tilted down and away from her. Kathy was sure that Tonya didn't believe the words she had just uttered. She did note that Tonya's hands were both tightly clamped around her knees.

Reginald was a forty-minute drive from Millardville, involving only one turn from the state highway onto a blacktop pavement that led the remaining five miles to the village. Kathy observed that the little town consisted of a small grocery store, a post office, gas station and a pool hall. She stopped at the post office to ask directions. Tonya remained slumped in the front seat, appearing to be asleep. After a couple minutes Kathy returned to the car.

"Got the directions, Tonya. I think we should be able to locate Mr. Dubold's farmhouse. It seems he lives at the end of the first gravel road just past the edge of town."

The small foreign car drew some curious glances as it rolled along Main Street. Everyone in Reginald pretty much knew who drove what car and no one in town drove a bright yellow car with a spoiler and sunroof. Tonya had never been of a shy or conservative nature, as far as Kathy knew, until recently, and her choice of automobile reflected her personality. Kathy surmised that the debt Tonya owed on the car was one piece of her drive to find secure employment.

The turn onto the gravel road was not as easy to find as Kathy had hoped. It was obscured by a gathering of scruffy looking evergreens that edged the blacktop and Kathy had gone nearly two miles before she gave up looking and turned around to come back to town for better directions.

On the way back, she finally noticed the thin graveled path that led to the south. The clump of evergreens left a deep shadow at the entryway to the road, which had made it hard to locate. It occurred to her that someone wanting to hide would find this to be an ideal place. Kathy frowned and looked at Tonya, who was now gazing blankly at the path ahead. She didn't seem to care at all, Kathy thought.

The road was quite meandering with many curves for some distance, and it became increasingly bumpy. Large potholes would suddenly appear, and the edges of the pavement were often crumbling. The condition of the surface was especially challenging when it occurred right after one of the many sharp curves in the road. The dead corn stalks in the farm fields that lined the untended road added to the desolation that pervaded the entire area in which the two social workers were traveling.

Kathy found herself driving very cautiously, gripping the steering wheel so tightly that her shoulders began to ache, and she became aware of a cramp in her neck.

Suddenly, after barely saying a word for the entire trip, Tonya spoke in a voice that sounded odd to Kathy, a flat, low tone with no apparent energy behind it to give it force, but the message startled Kathy nevertheless.

"We are near the destination. All will be well."

She hadn't shared the directions with Tonya, so how did she know they were close? And why did she add that same phrase she had heard at the Mayes's house in Millardville? Very strange, she mused.

A moment later the car crested a hill and Kathy was almost startled to see a quite large, faded gray farmhouse and a large, dilapidated barn at the top of the next rise. A lone, giant oak tree, bereft of leaves, loomed over the house as if to hide it from view. In the midst of summer when it was leafed out, Kathy noted, it would be nearly impossible to discern the house. Next to the house there was an older model pickup truck with a gun rack in the back window. A broken-down satellite dish lay collapsed by the back porch.

There were no people visible from the road. There was a sudden bone-shaking drop as their car hit another hidden gulley; Kathy's attention had been diverted to the farmhouse and she had momentarily neglected to scan ahead for craters. The car lurched right, then left as Kathy tried to steer her way out of the rut and suddenly the vehicle went into a spin.

Kathy panicked and reflexively tried to brake to a stop, but the car slid twistingly on the gravel pavement and then bounced down into the ditch on the right side of the road and, with a sickening crunch, slammed into a concrete culvert at the bottom.

Dazed, Kathy sat immobile behind the wheel. The car rested steeply on the bank of the ditch; the passenger side settled against the concrete. Kathy shook her head to clear her mind. She glanced down to her right, toward the passenger seat, worried about Tonya's safety.

Tonya wasn't there.

Pulling her left arm up closer to her face in the gathering darkness, Kathy was shocked that her wristwatch showed it was nearly 6:00 PM.

With a jolt, Kathy realized that it was no longer morning. She must have been knocked unconscious by the impact with the culvert. Tonya may have experienced a similar impact, maybe even worse, or perhaps she had managed to get out and had gone for help at the farmhouse on the nearby hill.

Kathy poked the release button on her seatbelt and promptly slid up against the gearshift; if it hadn't been for that she would doubtlessly have ended up against the passenger side door. She struggled to sit upright and scanned the dimming countryside around the car. Dried and brittle weeds obscured the front and back windshields.

Kathy fought to push open the driver's side door. Since the car was tipped on its opposite side in the ditch, she found this more difficult than she had anticipated. In addition, she discovered that her entire body ached. After two tentative shoves against the door, it finally gave way on the third try.

She pushed against the steering wheel and headrest with

her feet and was able at last to scramble free. Once out, she climbed onto the side of the car and was able to take a short step from there to the edge of the pavement. She pulled her cell phone from her purse and tried to call for help, but she couldn't get a signal.

The nearby farmhouse caught her attention. It was just a short walk, but Kathy's head throbbed painfully, and she found that she had to stop to rest twice before she even reached the dirt path that served as a drive alongside the large, faded structure. She had lost one shoe while kicking against the steering wheel and the sharp-edged gravel in the road caused her to grit her teeth in pain with every other step.

The evening had become chilly, and she quickly felt the cold in the toes of her unprotected right foot. She considered returning to the car, but her headache convinced her to put that plan aside. She rapped lightly on the porch door of the old house after mounting the four crumbling concrete steps.

While knocking, she noted that there were no lights on inside. Nevertheless, she pounded even harder, a sudden sense of her own helplessness fueling her effort.

Kathy was about to abandon hope when she detected a distant humming sound. Carefully descending the steps, she limped her way down the brick path that edged some lifeless rosebushes along the west side of the porch until she reached the corner of the house. The sound seemed to come from somewhere in the back of the property.

She glanced around the corner, gripping the loose-hanging downspout, which was missing the clamp that should have connected it to the side of the building. She quickly abandoned this effort to keep her weight off her sore right foot when she felt the downspout beginning to pull loose from the gutter it was attached to at the edge of the roof above. It crashed to the ground and made a loud and sharp *clang* that pained Kathy's ears.

The broken-down barn, in the same need of paint as the residence, loomed about a hundred yards behind the house. She could see a glimmer of yellow light that escaped through the space between the two halves of the huge barn door.

She felt a sudden surge of fear but didn't know why. It was a brief reaction, quickly overcome by her desire to seek help and to find Tonya. But, though she promptly pushed the twinge of hesitance to one side, a gnawing ache of discomfort settled into the pit of her stomach as she began to limp along the clearly worn path left in the now dormant grass between the side of the porch and the ramshackle barn.

The humming grew in intensity as Kathy slowly edged carefully past the house and along the overgrown and neglected vegetable garden at its rear. She just barely avoided bumping her sore foot against a medium sized pumpkin that seemed to have been trying to escape the garden by tugging the leash of its still attached vine, much like a dog on a chain.

It was only as she dodged this adventurous gourd that she began to realize that the humming she detected was not a sound thrumming in her ears, but vibrations that reflected against her entire body. What's more, she now noted that the yellowish light was really more of a green and it seemed to strobe with the same rhythm as the vibration she was feeling.

Kathy shuddered involuntarily. Though the thought of turning and escaping the farm clearly entered her mind, she found that she was continuing to place one foot ahead of the other in a slow, but unaltered limping approach to the barn.

There was a sudden rustling among the dried vines, plants and leaves of the long-neglected garden. Kathy's heart pounded against her chest as she whirled to see who, or what, was approaching. She hoped it was Tonya.

As she turned, the heel of her remaining shoe tangled in another pumpkin vine and she lost her balance, crashing hard to the ground amid leaves, sticks and gravel. Seconds later, before she could get her bearings and climb back to her feet, the source of the rustling became clear to her.

A young girl was standing next to her, dressed in some sort of one-piece outfit, it appeared to Kathy, but in the growing darkness she couldn't make out anything else. The girl, appearing to be only three or four years old, stood silently, hands at her sides. Kathy having come to a kneeling position, was on a level with the child.

"Hello," Kathy ventured in a soft near-whisper. She didn't want to alarm the girl. "Do you live here?"

The girl remained motionless, an arm's length away from her.

"My name is Kathy. Are your mommy and daddy home?"

Again, silence. Then, a cloud that had blocked the moonlight drifted on, providing enough light for Kathy to at last make out the child's features. Kathy caught her breath, for the little girl's eyes didn't appear normal. They were tight squints of darkness, with bright red glows buried deep within them. They also seemed wider than eyes should be.

Another chill shook her body. She had seen such eyes before! As that shock hit her, she collapsed back to the ground.

The child then stepped forward and reached out with both hands. Almost involuntarily, Kathy held out her own hands. The child, so small and frail in appearance, pulled her to her feet with no obvious effort.

As this occurred, Kathy's eyes remained riveted on the girl's face, which revealed no hint of emotion. The face, however, despite its unusual appearance, held a trace of familiarity. A second and only slightly lesser shock hit Kathy as she realized that the little girl with the unusual eyes was Kimberly Mayes.

The child turned toward the barn, still gripping Kathy's hands in hers, and gently tugged Kathy in that direction. Kathy's mind had become unfocused, a gray numbness. She couldn't resist; she didn't want to resist.

"All will be well," she heard.

Was it a voice she heard with her ears? No, she decided, it was just a thought that entered her mind.

As they drew close to the dilapidated barn, the structure began to throb with greenish-yellow fluorescence. Kathy realized dully that the glow and the throbbing sound, were somehow familiar, disturbingly so, in fact. She experienced an unwelcome rush of emotions, one upon another: longing, loneliness, distress, anger, fear, sadness. They seemed to swirl through her head and drain into her heart and soul.

But, she could not concentrate on this internal swirl and the feelings fell away, with only an overall sense of dismay echoing after them.

As the pair neared the barn, its unevenly constructed doors slid apart, as though they were activated by an electronic sensor. That is the explanation Kathy told herself, though she also realized that this was not likely.

She began to feel like she was stumbling into a foggy, dreamlike world and her thoughts seeped away even as her mind formulated them. The barn was aglow with the pulsating green Kathy had already noticed. As the child pulled her through the doorway, she was at first unable to focus in the strange light, but then, as if adjusting to bright sunlight after leaving a darkened room, she became aware that the interior of the barn was nearly filled with a very large, disk-shaped object that was emitting the throbbing light.

A number of short, slender figures were attending to the object, some on the outside, others entering or exiting its interior through a slit in one side. Kathy still couldn't focus her mind. Somehow, this all seemed to be very familiar. She felt calm. Even as Kimmy Mayes tugged her toward the slit entryway on the side of the object, she knew that she would be taken inside.

She did not resist, though in some deep chasm of her mind, she knew that she should, that she had resisted before, but also that it would be futile. She again heard the voice telling her, *"It will all be well."*

Even the discovery that Tonya was there, apparently unconscious and supine upon some sort of small table, did not arouse any surprise or any other reaction in Kathy. Kimmy seemed to speak, giving that same calming assurance over and over.

Kimmy led her to the far side of the interior. A panel of large, long, dark tubes lined the wall. The child pulled

Kathy to a stop before these. A slender person dressed in what Kathy felt vaguely resembled a lab coat stepped forward from somewhere to her left, touched one of tubes and the top half slid upward.

At that instant Kathy's veil of dulled sensation lifted. She felt that she was emerging from a dense fog. Her heart seemed to vault into her throat, and she let out an involuntary, though muted, shriek.

The top of the tube had lifted to reveal a glasslike inner unit, which was filled with a pale blue fluid. Floating in the liquid, slowly rotating, was the body of an infant, its arms and legs clasped tightly against its body.

At first the child's back was next to the glass, but as it revolved it came to a fully frontal presentation before her. Kathy gasped when she realized that its eyes were open, eyes much like those of Kimmy, deep and dark, staring into her soul. Its hands were closed in fists, but what she could see of the fingers seemed unusually slender. The arms and legs began to twist randomly, as if straining against the transparent enclosure, but Kathy barely noticed, for she found herself transfixed by the face. It seemed so familiar.

She felt a deep longing to reach out and hold the baby. An involuntary moan escaped her lips.

The Kimberly child tugged at her elbow. "Is yours," the small voice said, but the message wasn't necessary.

Kathy had already figured it out.

The peace of that moment was interrupted by a sudden, muffled cracking sound. It was an unwelcome intrusion upon Kathy's emotional focus on her baby. She tried to reach out to touch the tube, but Kimberly Mayes gave a violent yank on her elbow.

Almost instantly Kathy found herself hurled through the slit in the wall of the disk object, landing painfully on the hard dirt floor of the ancient barn, in the dark corner furthest from the door. The force of the impact caused her to roll over and over until she smacked solidly into the wall.

She found herself facing the direction from which she had come, her senses at once fully restored. She realized that the slit in the object was closing up. The small figures who had been swarming around on the outside of the object streamed quickly through the opening and it zipped itself shut without a sound. The object itself had begun to shudder with a rapid increase in the green glow's rate of pulsation. The light evolved into a pale blue, then a violet, then magenta. The object began to lift off the bare ground it rested on in the middle of the barn.

There were more of the cracking sounds, much louder. Kathy raised herself painfully with her right arm in time to see a group of perhaps a half dozen men, some dressed in mottled tan and dark green camouflage fatigues, others in plaid hunting jackets and jeans, burst through the double doors of the barn.

They were carrying a variety of firearms and were shouting and whooping as they rapidly cracked off shots that were deflected from the glowing object in the center of the barn. The glowing, rotating object seemed to be unfazed by the onslaught of gunfire as its aura altered to a bright red.

It rose to the top of the huge barn, then, with an earsplitting crunch, broke through the top of the building and vanished in a split second into the night sky.

Some of the intruders continued to fire uselessly at the gaping hole above them. Two suddenly stopped and pointed toward the back of the building, as the darkness of night took the place of the pulsating lights. A spattering of flashlights clicked on.

"Look! Look!" one of the men shouted in shrill excitement. "They left one behind!"

The loud cracking ceased as the small crowd of men focused their attention on the darkened rear of the barn, which was at once lit partially by a few flashlight beams. Kathy pulled herself to a sitting position against an adjacent wall and followed their gaze.

At first she saw nothing, then she began to make out what the men were focused on. Against the rear wall of the barn, several yards to her right, partially hidden behind a low stack of baled hay, huddled a figure clad in a light colored, one-piece outfit.

It was one of the slender people Kathy had noticed outside the object before she entered it, though this one was much taller. It, since she knew not whether it was male or female, if indeed such classifications even applied, was half crouching, almost as if unsure whether to stand and face the attackers or attempt to hide.

"This one's mine!" growled the man who had first sighted the figure.

"Aw c'mon, Dale!" pleaded one of the fatigue-clad men, waving a small handgun. "Let's all blast it at once!"

"Now, hold on!" interjected a third man, dressed in a plaid coat and baseball cap. "It's my farm and I'm the one who told you about this, so I should get the honor!"

"Dubold has a point, Dale," added a tall, heavyset man near the back of the group.

"Maybe we should just take our time, kinda kill him slowly," drawled a short man standing next to the first one.

Kathy realized that the men had not noticed her propped against the wall to their right, where the flashlights weren't shining. She was afraid that they would fire their guns wildly at her or the slender person if she startled them by speaking. She knew she had to do something before they cold bloodedly slaughtered their helpless prey at the rear of the barn.

However, as she attempted to change her position in order to speak, she inadvertently bumped her right arm against an ancient whipsaw that was hanging on a large nail in the barn wall behind her. It slithered from its precarious perch and hit the dirt floor with a high-pitched twang that reverberated loudly through the structure. Kathy gasped.

The men all spun around simultaneously with their weapons raised and pointed at her.

"It's a woman!" shouted the chubby man with the red face, pointing at Kathy.

"The alien must have kidnapped her. He was gittin' set to drag her into that flying saucer, probably to do terrible things to her," blurted the short man as he stepped toward Kathy, pointing his rifle upward.

"Could be, Chip," said Dale. "We arrived just in the nick of time."

Kathy recognized one of the men as Andy Pendleton, from her caseload. He was waving a handgun and had a crazed look on his face. "Let's torture that rotten alien!"

A small figure at the rear of the men moved quietly away from the others, toward the shadows, as the men debated their next move. Unseen by the armed men, the figure motioned to the crouching figure in the shadows, who cautiously edged toward him.

Kathy had been watching this and saw that the men with guns hadn't noticed. She observed that the small person was wearing a ski mask and goggles. She saw that both the "alien" and the ski mask wearer were edging gingerly toward a small door in the wall of the barn. The men continued to yell and mill around as they tried to decide what to do next.

The man first addressed as Dale, whom Kathy sensed was the leader of the group of armed men, suddenly wheeled back to face the rear of the barn. "He's gone! We looked away for a couple seconds and the alien escaped!"

Dale made an awkward lunge for the stack of hay bales as the others scrambled about around the edges of the building. It took them only seconds to confirm that their prey had vanished.

"Quick! He must have gone out that rear door!" shouted Dale. "Coach, you stay here and keep an eye on this woman."

The tall, red-faced man nodded obediently as the others clambered through the rickety doorway. He turned to Kathy, not sure whether he was supposed to protect her or hold her prisoner, since the tone of Dale's order seemed to imply that she wasn't to leave the barn.

"Uh, wh.., what are you doin' out here?" stuttered the perplexed man, holding his shotgun pointed neutrally at the ceiling.

Kathy struggled to calm the shivering that had now taken over her entire body. "I, I was in an accident and, and, I came back here looking for help, since I saw the barn all lit up."

"You weren't kidnapped by these alien beings?" Coach inquired, gaining a measure of confidence when he realized that Kathy was also nervous.

Normally, Coach Jepson was the one in control; the kids on the football team had to listen to him and do what he told them to do. His membership in this vigilante group put him in an unfamiliar situation, having to take orders from Dale Tooney, who seemed to have no problem with being in charge.

Of course, since his football team had had a losing record for four straight years, his self-confidence was beginning to dissolve. That, he guessed was why Dale asked him to stay behind and guard the woman. Dale didn't even trust him to hunt aliens.

"No. I just came in here and then you all arrived a second later."

Kathy decided it would do no good to tell him that she had actually been in the barn for several minutes, though she couldn't quite recall what had happened during that time.

"Hmmm. We had this place staked out tonight from out in the woods. We saw that UFO settle down here and float in through these double doors, but I don't recall seeing you walk up."

Coach paused as he gave Kathy an inquisitive glance. "I'll bet you was kidnapped, and they clouded your mind so you wouldn't know it! I'm not sure you should be told this, but I'd bet they did some awful experiment on you and then let you go!"

His eyes grew wider as he began to get carried away with his own wild theories. Then, his face relaxed as a look of sympathy spread across his face. He lowered the shotgun to rest next to his right leg.

Kathy felt the blood drain from her own face. Her memory of recent events was gradually returning to her, like something viewed through a dissipating fog. She realized with a jolt that there was some truth to her guard's words.

Tonya had been kidnapped and the "aliens" had been doing something to her. But Kathy couldn't quite pinpoint what else had happened after she saw Tonya. She knew she had been inside the UFO; that's where she had seen Tonya. She felt a strange tingling sensation as the memories fought their way into sharper focus. She remembered the long tubes along the wall, the way the top part of one slid up to reveal something that had caused her both joy and pain.

Then, she at last retrieved the final bit of memory. Her own baby had been inside the UFO.

Suddenly her world seemed to go black, and she felt herself falling.

Chapter Twenty-Two: Dale's Dilemma

Dale Tooney had always been a peaceful man, with the exception of the aggression he had displayed on the basketball court thirty years previously. At least, that's how he had tried to promote his image among the neighboring farmers and townspeople. But he was a man who knew himself well and he had always been aware of a certain degree of inner rage that he had to struggle to control.

There had been that one incident at the end of the sectional tournament championship game when he was a senior. He had been ejected from the game for retaliating when the opposing center had deliberately shoved him into the wall as he went in for a lay-up after stealing the ball. It was an incident that the town had quickly forgiven.

It was funny, Dale thought, that some people could lose their tempers and never be forgiven, while others, himself, for instance, would always be forgiven without even having to ask for it.

Dale recognized four types of forgiveness: the kind needed to preserve the status quo, as in his marriage, in which his wife Molly had always forgiven him to keep the peace in the family; the unwanted kind of forgiveness, when someone forgave someone who didn't believe they needed forgiveness, which was just disguised aggression in Dale's mind; the sincerely begged-for kind, which Dale had never felt he needed; and, finally the kind that wasn't requested or needed, but was given anyway.

That was the kind his neighbors had always given him. He accepted it but told himself he didn't need it.

The other center had suffered a broken collar bone and

shattered jaw, but Dale was applauded by the Caperton fans as he was escorted from the court by the men in the striped shirts. Forgiveness unrequested, not needed.

But now Dale was angry. He had been angry for several weeks, ever since the town meeting with that Washington bureaucrat. He resented the slippery self-congratulatory East Coast cleverness that Huit had displayed.

Then, the next day, came the news of the disappearance of Joe Paige's kid. Kidnappers, perverts. Dale knew better from the start. None of those usual scapegoats were responsible.

It was THEM. It had to be. THEY were making a mockery of this Huit's explanation, THEY were laughing at the people of Caperton, laughing at them in their helplessness, laughing at him, laughing at Dale Tooney.

Dale had become obsessed with this explanation. All his life he had fought, mostly successfully, to restrain his own urges to get even with anyone whom he felt was mocking him. Dale Tooney was not a forgiving man. That center from Kelly Bend had taunted him throughout the game and Dale had felt that his unseen elbow into his opponent's diaphragm was justified retaliation for the verbal abuse he had taken.

Smalltown hick? Take that! Next trip down the court, a crunching heel to the top of the toes. Further justice! Then, the Kelly Bend center shoved him. Well, he had been asking for it, so Dale gave it to him.

Caperton and the farm fields around it, made up Dale's world, the one place where he felt at home, felt like a hero, even. He had been welcomed home from the war in the Middle East as though he had been John Wayne from one of those old WWII movies, when all he had really done was get in the way of shrapnel from a roadside explosive device.

The town had really let loose that day. People from all the surrounding towns and even Millardville had lined the streets during the parade, which, in the small village of Caperton began a mile west of town, weaved around all the streets in town twice and then out to the three-mile corner to the east of town and then back to the Caperton gym.

Dale had still been on crutches and the outpouring of warmth had done much to confirm his loyalty to the community. He vowed to never leave Caperton, though it was also partly because deep inside he knew that outside of this farming community he was just a nobody, an acknowledgment that only reinforced his anger.

He eventually took over his father's farm, married his high school girlfriend, and settled in to enjoy life. Only these problems with UFOs had so far interrupted his peace.

Well, that is, until the recent difficulties with his wife. She was spooked by the lights and the rumors of UFOs. She wanted Dale to sell the farm and move with her and their son, the only one of their kids still at home. She also blamed Dale for his constant, brooding anger. She said he had changed.

Dale couldn't explain to her how he felt. If he didn't admit to the anger, he could control it. Admitting anger is letting it loose and Dale could never do that. He had to stay in control. But he felt he could do something to satisfy that anger, just as he had with the Kelly Bend player.

Night after night in the deepening autumn, Dale sat in the loft of his barn, surrounded by his growing arsenal of firearms. His neighbors knew him to be an occasional pheasant hunter. What they didn't know was that Dale was a devoted defender of his race, a subscriber to several vigilante and white supremacist publications, an outpost member of a group of modern minutemen who had formed in the next county.

Dale had a growing collection of automatic and semi-automatic weapons with which to defend his farm and community when the time came. And it was coming. He knew it. His growing roster of like-minded contacts, who were also concerned about the way things had been going lately, were ready to help change it all for the better.

So, Dale sat in the barn and watched the skies. Let them come, he thought. Small town hick? Dale sighted through the scope of his most powerful rifle and squeezed off an imaginary round. Take that! Justice! And now, Dale had his chance to take vengeance on real-life aliens.

Dale's followers were perhaps less angry, but equally devoted to settling things with anyone who seemed to think they were better than them.

Jeffrey Dubold wasn't a farmer, but he rented this old farmstead on the outskirts of Reginald. He was hiding out from the mother of his child Kimmy, who was always trying to cause him trouble about child support and his "fatherly responsibilities".

In frustration, he had gone into Millardville intent on having it out with Lola Mayes, the pea-brained harpy who wouldn't leave him alone. He clutched a handgun in his right hand. But, as he approached her house, he had been stopped in his tracks by the sight of something bright, floating in the sky overhead. He suddenly had no idea what he was up to. His mind went blank. The next thing he knew he was back in his farmhouse living room and Kimmy was asleep on the couch.

His first inclination was to throw her in his pickup and drive her out in the country and abandon her in a cornfield, but a voice in his head warned him not to do that, but to care for the child until further notice.

He made his living from selling whatever illicit drugs he could get hold of; any legitimate business would put him on the grid and make it impossible for him to hide from the authorities...or Kimmy's mother. The voice in his head told him to take care of Kimmy. He did have funds enough to feed her but was happy to learn that she required no additional parental care.

She spent her days sleeping, rising to eat whatever was available and going out to the barn to explore. Dubold would occasionally awake in the middle of the night and look out the window at the huge, gray barn, where he would see Kimmy wandering around, sometimes staring at the sky. Weird kid. Takes after her mother. He had no reason to do anything more for her.

Dubold had been recruited by Hugo Massingall, another drug dealer, to join the secret vigilante group that included Dale Tooney. Dubold assumed that Massingall had connections in the group who could help him with distributing his products, but after attending a couple meetings in order to see if he could find some customers, he found that he liked the members, especially the charismatic Tooney, and decided to study the literature they eagerly pressed upon him.

Before long, he was hooked on the idea of "defending the

white culture," though there were no non-whites living in his community, and eagerly met with the group on a regular basis. He also joined the others when they practiced with firearms and was pleased to find he had a knack for marksmanship.

Gordon Jepson was known as "Coach", since that was what he was. He was tall, over six feet, and wore his graying hair in an inch-long flattop that had not been stylish in decades. He had been a marine in one of the recent wars.

He wasn't a very good coach, but it was all he knew. He had applied for a job with the Triangle School District staff which already had some part-time coaching staff. After a couple of years as an assistant, he was promoted to head football coach when his predecessor retired. The part-timers quit in protest, since they felt their contributions had been overlooked and they were not too impressed with Jepson's skills.

Nevertheless, Coach, as he now insisted on being called, had a couple of non-losing seasons and the former assistants' reservations were ignored. Like Dale and Dubold, he lived alone and began hanging out at the local bar for companionship. There he met Hugo Massingall and it wasn't long until he was also recruited to Dale's team. He wasn't skilled with firearms, but he was a loyal supporter who readily welcomed the others to his house for team meetings.

Another rather odd choice for membership was Ricky Borntrager, a married man with seven children. He had been an athlete in high school, but his early marriage after graduation had made him feel compelled to get a job to support his new family. The babies began arriving almost yearly.

He knew that he and his wife didn't have a good relationship, though they put up a good front in the Reginald community. He felt trapped by his life and his feelings of anger grew until he began to take it out on his wife and children. He truly regretted that and searched for an outlet for his pent-up frustrations.

Hugo Massingall met him at a shooting range where Ricky had gone to get away from the suffocation of his family life. When Dale's wife left him, Ricky was very understanding and supportive. He became Dale's best friend as a result.

Chip Josephson was the Reginald version of Peter Lapley before his life-altering experience with the UFO. He was not thought of as bright and had trouble connecting with others. Hugo sought him out because of his reputation and Chip fell right into line with the others. Every team needs good followers who don't challenge the group decisions.

The final member of the small group was probably the least likely of all—a young woman who only gave her first name as Nora. She turned out to be a crack shot and was welcomed by the others when she was able to outshoot them all at their shooting practices. Dale couldn't see past her ruse and wasn't sure about her loyalty, but her shooting skills might come in handy, so he kept her on the team. She always wore a ski mask to meetings and would only pull it back on her head but never fully remove it. No one even knew the color of her hair.

There had been one other member, a farmer from Caperton named Calvin Dunn. He hadn't been coming to the group's mandatory weekly gatherings and hadn't even shown up for the town meeting with that government stooge Huit in Caperton.

Dale worried about him; not about his safety, but about his ability to keep his mouth shut about the group. In late summer he had sent Borntrager and Josephson on a mission to find and silence Dunn, but they reported back that no one knew where he was. As a result, Dale decided he should replace Dunn with a long-time acquaintance whom he could trust.

Andy Pendleton was an old high school buddy and basketball teammate. Andy had led an uneven life since graduation and had been in and out of prison twice, once for armed robbery and then again when he violated probation for that offense. Dale liked to keep his own reputation squeaky clean but felt a lot of respect for anyone who had been able to deal with the criminal justice system. He believed that Andy's experience would come in handy when the inevitable war with the aliens began.

This is the group that were scouring the woods just south of the Dubold farm.

Coach, however, was not in the group. The others found him an hour later, unconscious in the barn after abandoning their search. He seemed to have been hit over the head with a brick that was on the ground beside his body. When he began to stir, it took several members of the vigilante group to get him to his feet, since he was a big man. They were puzzled that his boots were missing.

"Where's that woman you were supposed to be guarding?" Dale demanded, prodding Jepson with the barrel of his shotgun. Coach just blinked and stared blankly at the leader.

How much later it was when Kathy awoke, she couldn't tell. But she realized she was outside, and it was cold. It was dark. She was moving, being gently buoyed along as if on some gentle wave. But it wasn't a wave. She recognized abruptly that she was being carried. Someone dressed in a lightweight, silvery fabric, rather than the heavy hunting jackets and camouflage fatigues of the men she had seen in the barn, was transporting her quickly along, seemingly without any effort.

The sky above was clear, a bright moon bathed them in a dim light. Tree branches intruded peripherally into her view, and eventually they blocked out the moon. She was being carried through a wooded area, probably the one to which Coach had referred. She tried to see who was carrying her so effortlessly through the woods. She knew it wasn't one of the armed men from the barn; this individual was much too light on his feet.

However, her face was pressed against his shoulder and she could not pull back far enough to see more than the underside of his jaw. She felt that she was safe with this person, but as her curiosity increased, she became determined to learn who he was and what was happening to her.

She pushed her palms hard against his chest in an effort to pull away from him and get a view of his face. His arms, though seeming to be rather thin, were as strong as steel, and her sudden violent twisting did not accomplish what she had hoped. Instead, she merely caused a shift in the balance of the pair.

The stranger stumbled suddenly to one side and both came crashing to the ground. Kathy rolled free, landing amidst a clump of soggy leaves and brittle branches at the base of a large tree. She quickly scrambled to her feet, emitting a small gasp of pain when she tried to put weight on her left knee.

Kathy glanced around to locate the person who had been carrying her. She found her rescuer flat on the ground a short distance from where she had landed. It was the alien the armed men had wanted to shoot.

But was he trying to kidnap her as the men claimed? Or was he actually trying to rescue her?

Kathy didn't know the answer from any logical consideration of the facts, but she sensed that she needed to protect the "alien" from the men and that only evil could transpire if the men caught the two of them. As he pulled himself to his feet, a beam of moonlight revealed that he was not an alien at all.

"We must keep going," he spoke gently, extending his right hand. "My name is Deke Fraley."

Suddenly there was the sound of someone crashing through the brush behind them. Kathy whirled around to find it was the short person with the ski mask from the barn. Her first thought was to run, but the pursuer stopped and immediately pulled off the mask.

It was a slender woman with light colored hair. The night was too dark to tell the exact color. She seemed vaguely familiar to Kathy. Then she remembered where she had seen her before. She was the waitress at the Bluebird Café. That observation only raised more questions.

The waitress whispered just loudly enough for Kathy and Deke to hear, "I'm Renee. I've seen you in my café a couple times."

Then, in response to Kathy's puzzled expression, she added, "So you will trust me, let me confess that I'm working undercover for the government. I've infiltrated this vigilante group to learn what they're up to. I had no idea there would be a real UFO, but in this line of work you have to deal with whatever comes up."

She paused briefly to study the faces of Deke and Kathy to be sure they understood her and to determine if they trusted her.

"I'll distract these morons, which won't be difficult. You two continue in the direction you were headed."

Renee's expression didn't change as she made these pronouncements. "You need to get going. Those men will be coming after us."

The sound of men's shouts revealed that their pursuers were indeed catching up. With a motion of her hand, Renee urged her two companions to head deeper into the woods.

Kathy and Deke wasted no time in continuing their escape. As they plunged back into the dark woods, Kathy heard Renee's voice: "They went west. Hurry!"

Kathy and Deke continued going south.

After a couple of miles, Renee dropped back and let the men charge ahead. She needed to discuss the strange turn the situation had taken with her contact person in the Spring City office and get further instructions.

Chapter Twenty-Three: Return to Hilltop House

When Paul Sloan had returned to Hilltop House after his journey to the sleep lab in Spring City, he found no sign of Deke. After he bought the old orphanage, he had an elevator installed that took him to the second floor, the attic, and the basement, but he couldn't find his guest anywhere. He had reluctantly concluded that Deke had moved on to another place of refuge, though he knew from recent experience that there might be a more chilling explanation.

Then he noticed the half-eaten sandwich peeking from an overturned plate next to the computer on his desk. Odd. Deke had been quite fastidious so far, behaving like an overly conscientious houseguest. Deke even insisted on doing all the dishes. It wasn't like him to leave anything in disarray.

Paul wheeled up to the desk and reached for the plate. Just then, he noticed that the computer was turned on and there was a message on the screen. Looking closer, he noticed that the message seemed to be incomplete. Paul scrolled the messages downward, searching for the earliest entry until heavy black figures of ominous hieroglyphs hit his eyes with an impact that knocked him backward in his chair. He took a few seconds to regain his equilibrium.

He then started to read the messages in order from that point until he came to Deke's last message, the somewhat garbled plea for help that had been sent to someone. Paul then printed all the messages that had been sent or received since he had left for Spring City that morning. As he rolled himself back a few feet from his desk he glanced through the sheets of paper until he found Reverend Selkirk's opening message.

Paul turned back to his desk. He tapped out a quick message and added *Urgent* to the title of the electronic missive. He then sent it, hoping that the minister would have some useful information about what had transpired.

Several seconds passed. Paul could feel his heart pounding.

He didn't like the way things were going. He felt uncomfortably like he was being watched. He had a growing fear that Deke was in deep trouble. Though he had been exchanging messages with Selkirk for several months, he didn't fully trust him. That lack of trust added weight to his apprehension.

Suddenly the computer screen blinked off. Then, just as quickly, it returned, but the background of the screen had become a pale yellow. As Paul stared into the screen, he had the strange sensation that he was peering into something deep, three dimensional. His fear slipped into a distant corner of his mind as he felt his concentration being drawn not just to the screen, but into it.

"*It will all be well.*" A voice seemed to gently insert this thought into the mix of emotions that he was now experiencing. It superseded fear. It outshone confusion. It triumphed over distrust. It threatened to overcome his judgment. But, still, Paul had instinctively gripped the arms of his wheelchair as he felt the soothing calmness engulfing him.

As his senses seemed to surrender one by one to the voice in his head, he managed to maintain his grip on the chair and on reality. The chair became his lifeline to existence. He had overcome so much since his injury that he seldom accepted any comment at face value. He held on to just enough distrust to allow him to fight away the calm words he perceived but didn't actually hear.

His caution saved him again. He fought off the urge to give in to whatever was pressing him to relent.

Paul found himself looking into a room within the computer screen. At the far end stood a tall, spindly being, its back to him. It seemed to be ignoring him while its hands flew rapidly above a panel of glowing lights.

After about a minute, it stopped what it was doing with the lights and turned toward him. The face seemed to be very sinister. The eyes were deeply recessed and glowed red. There was what appeared to be a scar along the left side of the face, which drew Paul's gaze. The individual's mouth was small and clamped shut, surrounded by deep creases, but it was the scar that captivated him, though he couldn't figure out why.

He felt a growing anger as he stared at it. Paul didn't hear any voice, but he was receiving a communication from the alien. He remained calm, gripping his armrests tighter and glaring at the being, trying to convey the anger he was experiencing.

"I notice you are having negative thoughts..." the alien began.

"I want you to leave me alone and leave all of us alone," Paul responded.

"That cannot be done. The mission is not finished. You must abandon your useless emotions and assist us."

Paul checked again on his contact with the wheelchair. "What is your mission?"

The being turned back to his panel of lights without responding. Paul felt like he was being brushed aside, unworthy of a response. Apparently humans had no right to question the aliens' intentions.

Paul leaned forward and released his grip on the armrests. He did so purposefully and immediately found himself drawn fully into the room with the alien.

He was amazed to discover himself able to move forward without a wheelchair. The feeling was intoxicating, being able to walk again after all these years. This feels like a dream, he thought. He was strongly tempted to surrender himself to the feeling. But he couldn't shake his innate skepticism, bred of years of distrust that began with his Army experiences. He knew that he shouldn't let his emotions—either euphoria at walking or mistrust and a rising feeling of hatred—control his actions.

But, after a tremendous attempt to suppress what he felt, he decided to physically confront his tormentor. He told himself that it was a well-considered choice. He may not survive the experience, but he had to try.

Slowly moving forward, since he had to accustom himself to being able to walk after all these years, he crept up behind the alien, who seemed not to notice him. He was just about to hurl himself on his prey when the room dissolved and Paul collapsed back into his chair, in his living room. His thoughts were clouded by a swirl of emotions.

Had it all been a dream?

Chapter Twenty-Four: Marla and Laurine

In the Millardville Care Center, Marla Brashear's children had arrived for a visit. Marla found it frustrating since she still couldn't remember them. The nursing home had offered to arrange her transfer to her hometown, but Marla knew that Jay was somewhere around this area and she refused to leave. After an awkward visit of two hours, the children had left with their aunt to return home. They were disappointed, but their aunt explained that it would just take more time for their mother to recover.

Then, late one overcast afternoon about a month later, Marla Brashear suddenly sat upright in bed, screaming out her husband's name. "Jay!"

Her memory had been gradually returning and now she had all she needed to act on her situation. When the staff came running to see what the problem was, she was calmly dressing herself. Despite the efforts of the various nursing aides and attendants to return her to her bed, she finished dressing and pushed past them on her way to the door of the room.

As she raced down the hallway, she was aware that the nursing home staff would be pursuing her with the aim of returning her to the room she had just escaped, probably carrying some sort of physical restraints. Some facilities can be odd that way. They seem to think that they own their patients. They would never just let her go. She had to out-think them.

They would expect her to head for the parking lot. She had headed that direction when she left her room. However, she instead veered to the right as she neared the front door and ducked into a supply closet. When she heard the staff run past, she slipped out and headed toward the rear of the building, carefully dodging other staff.

As she passed a vacated nurses' station, she saw a phone book on the desk and grabbed it, quickly tearing the city map out of the front. She was lucky enough to find a family group on its way to visit someone. She tagged along close at the rear of these people until they passed the back door of the facility, then she dropped back and exited the building.

She hurried through the streets of Millardville as fast as she felt it was safe to do; she didn't want to attract any attention. She was looking for the address Laurine Fraley had given her just prior to Tonya Belding's visit interrupting their conversation.

At last, she located Adams Street and turned north. After passing a couple houses and checking their street numbers, she glanced at the crumpled phonebook page in her hand and reversed her course, since the numbers were getting larger and she was looking for the eight hundred block, not the nine hundred.

She also crossed the street, glancing carefully around first, since she needed to find 827, which was on the side of the street with odd-numbered addresses. It didn't take long until she located it. She glanced around as she tried the door. Finding it unlocked, she hesitantly pushed the door open.

Just as she pushed it open, she noticed the nursing home ambulance rounding the corner a couple blocks away. She quickly slipped inside. She glanced back toward the window in the door and saw the ambulance rumble past.

Then she called out, "Mrs. Fraley! It's me, Marla Brashear from the nursing home! Are you here?"

It occurred to her immediately that this was an unnecessary question. Jay would often point out such things, to her irritation. He could be a bit pedantic at times.

After she had checked the kitchen, living and dining rooms, she heard a board creaking upstairs. She began ascending the stairs to the second floor. She paused for a few seconds and felt the silence again surround her. She had a bad feeling about what was going on. Still, she continued upward.

Whatever might be up there wasn't any worse than returning to the street and having the nursing home orderlies catch her.

When she reached the top of the stairs, she found herself standing at one end of a hallway with four closed doors, two on each side.

Suddenly the door downstairs opened, and she heard several heavy footsteps. A voice called out, "Mrs. Brashear, we know you're here! Please come quietly. We don't want to have to sedate you or use this straight jacket..."

A second later she heard the first heavy boot upon the bottom step. In near-panic she glanced around. She didn't know what else to do, but she was determined to find a way out. She just needed a couple seconds to think.

Noting a dim light emanating from beneath the last door on the right, she hurried toward it as quietly as she could. She assumed that Laurine Fraley was inside. Marla grasped the doorknob and gave it a quick turn.

The door opened a few inches, and she was able to glance within.

Laurine was indeed inside. She was standing stiffly on the far side of the room, staring out the window toward the back yard. A large, iron-framed bed stood between the two women.

Marla heard the footsteps behind her, nearing the top of the stairs. She could hear heavy boots hitting the hallway floor and when she tried to slam the door behind her, someone stopped the door before it could close. Marla took one last glance back and saw a heavily muscled and hairy arm pushing the door back open; a second man holding a syringe and straight jacket crowded in behind the first one.

In panic, she backed toward the center of the room, bumping into the rickety bed. She fell onto it just as the door flew open. A scowling and bloated face appeared in the dim glow from the light as the first orderly lunged toward her.

"Gotcha!" yelled the stocky man as his right hand tightened on her left arm.

Marla recoiled from his touch and squirmed free. She desperately rolled away from the grasping hand and ended up tumbling to the floor on the far side of the bed, landing with a thud. She quickly sprang to her feet and turned toward Laurine, who had not reacted at all to the scuffle occurring just a few feet away from her.

Marla called out, "Laurine!" as she took a quick step toward her, but Laurine showed no sign that she heard it.

The room was suddenly bathed in a green glow that flooded through the open window. Laurine continued to stare blankly out the window as she was tugged upward in the light.

Marla reached frantically for her friend, but the next thing Marla knew, she was also rising from the floor and slipping soundlessly through the window out into the misty day.

The shocked orderly made a tentative grab for Marla, but a pencil-thin red beam of light struck him in the forehead, and he fell to the floor. The second man also fell as a second ray of light hit him, but Marla didn't see that, since she was already out the window and being pulled skyward toward a floating grayish oval.

After the two women were pulled into the rotating craft, the green light vanished. There was a brief *whooshing* sound and the vehicle vanished in a second. Then everything became still except for the writhing bodies of the barely conscious orderlies.

The next morning the nursing home orderlies stumbled into their place of employment. Both drew a blank when asked about what had happened, though they did complain about splitting headaches. Millardville police put out a missing person report regarding Marla.

Her sister was notified but decided not to share the report with Rosie and Richie. She didn't want to upset them further.

Chapter Twenty-Five: Escape from Edgemont

Sgt. Rader awoke in a cold, damp place. The last thing he remembered was the creeping, acidic fog. He didn't know how much time had passed; it could have been minutes or days, maybe even weeks, though he didn't think that was likely, since he hadn't eaten anything and would have starved or died of thirst if it had been a significant length of time.

He couldn't see, but he couldn't feel a blindfold over his eyes, either. He could tell that he was propped against a wall of some sort. He felt around, trying to see if he could pick up by tactile means any clues to his location. He noticed that he was wrapped in some sort of cloak, nearly weightless, but sufficiently warm. He tried to stand but tumbled to his left. His legs were bound in some way. He struck his forehead on a solid object as he fell, almost losing consciousness again.

In the distance, somewhere, he could hear indistinct sounds, perhaps voices, perhaps the hum of an engine. The sound was monotone, but steady. Teddy twisted his body sideways until he was able to roll over once, then twice. In this manner he eventually found himself closer to the unidentified sound. He tested his voice, but also learned he was gagged in some manner, though he couldn't feel anything restricting his mouth or tongue.

Eventually, he began to see small slices of light, but not enough to gain a full picture. The indistinct sound grew clearer. It was the hum of a motor running very smoothly.

As Teddy twisted around some more, his vision cleared further. A slender, pale figure wearing some kind of hooded jacket or cloak was bending over some sort of device that emitted various lights, which were dim. The lights would sort of flare up as the figure's hands paused above each light, then they would dim again. Rader tried to speak but couldn't.

"I am running a test of my vehicle."

Rader became aware of the words without actually hearing them spoken.

"Telepathy." The word also appeared to just enter Rader's brain without being heard.

The pale figure at last removed his hands from the panel of lights and they died down completely. The humming sound also ceased.

"I had to put you into physical suspension. I was afraid you would see me as an enemy and either run off or attack me. You people of this world have a rather sad tendency to run from anything that is unfamiliar or fight what you cannot comprehend."

Rader suddenly realized that he could move his feet and his mouth was no longer gagged. "Who are you?" he called out.

The pale being turned to face the sergeant, who remained seated on the ground. Rader realized they were in some sort of cave.

"We do not use individual labels as your people do. However, for the sake of your convenience and comfort, you may call me 'Kattor'. You saved my physical being when the acidic fog had almost overtaken me. You also saved me from the enemy hunters. I am grateful. Most of your kind would have saved only themselves. Most of my kind would not be grateful. That's one way you differ from the others of your kind. That's one way I differ from my own kind."

It wasn't really a verbal exchange. Rader started to frame a question, but the pale being continued to speak.

"I am an outsider. I am the product of genetic experimentation by those whom you call aliens."

Rader didn't know if this elaboration was in response to his unspoken question, or just something the alien had volunteered.

"The last thing I remember..." words formed in his mind finally escaped through his mouth before the slim figure could anticipate them.

"The last thing you remember is feeling like you were falling and then a green light. Correct?"

The sergeant felt a bit annoyed by the interruption. The alien wagged his top-heavy head from side to side.

"My way of communicating is making you uncomfortable. I will try not to anticipate your next words." Rader felt some reassurance.

"I regained consciousness as you picked my body off the ground and carried it up the rise. I retrieved my...".

He paused for a few seconds as if searching for the correct word. *"My device. My 'wand'. Our word for it has no easy translation into your language. We'll call it a 'wand' if that is alright with you."*

Rader started to respond vocally, but Kattor again read his thoughts despite his pledge to speak. *"I see that you agree."*

Then, though Kattor's facial expression didn't change, Rader understood that the alien was somewhat perplexed.

"I apologize. It is nearly as difficult for me to adapt to your way of communicating as it must be for you to use our method."

Then, he resumed his narrative. *"The wand emits lights with different functions. The green light is used mostly for transportation. I used it to lift both of us above the fog and to move us to this cave, where I have hidden the parts of my damaged vehicle that you see before you. My repair efforts have been futile. The damage from the crash is too extreme."*

"Like Roswell, huh?"

The stranger paused, perplexed. *"That had nothing to do with my people. We aren't all from the same place."*

Rader had struggled to his feet. He turned toward Kattor, a bit stunned by this information. He had assumed that all the UFO sightings were connected.

"In the vastness of space and time, are you surprised that there are so many intelligent civilizations that are coming here for a thousand different reasons? Your race is so limited in its thinking."

Kattor stared straight at Rader.

"And don't be surprised that they don't all come in peace. Mine did. We are called the Fifths since we are the fifth planet out from our star. The ones for whom you recover wreckage are here for much more sinister reasons. They call themselves the Dominants. They are from another galaxy. They are the ones who created that acidic fog and sent out their hunters to make sure I didn't survive. They were not actually coming after you, but they did want you punished for killing one of them, so, since you hadn't succumbed to the elements or the fog, they would have given you the same

death they gave the vanload of soldiers and expected to give to me, as well."

Another pause to let that message sink in.

Then, *"A war is coming. A war among several distant civilizations. A war in time and space. I am here to warn you. Your planet will be caught in the crossfire."*

Rader sank back down on a nearby boulder as he tried to absorb this information. Kattor took several strides toward him and then, using his telepathic communication, told Rader, *"They are near this cave. We must hurry to escape. I have provided foot coverings for you, so you will be able to proceed quickly. Come!"*

Kattor reached down and took Rader's arm and pulled him up. Rader glanced at his feet and noticed for the first time that he was wearing some sort of boots that, like Kattor's, had no heels.

He shrugged and hurried after the alien. Soon Rader and the alien stranger were hurrying through the woods that surrounded the base of the mountain where the back entrance to the cave was located. The sergeant had no idea where they might be going, but it occurred to him that their pursuers probably had highly sophisticated tracking devices, so he figured all he could do was try to keep up with his new comrade.

After a few minutes he heard a loud scraping sound. He looked over his shoulder in time to see the alien's wrecked vehicle being dragged from the front opening of the cave in a green glow, higher up on the mountainside. Their pursuers seemed intent on salvaging the craft, he thought, but at that moment there was a blinding flash of white light, which was accompanied by a force which tumbled both Rader and his alien companion to the ground.

When Rader was again able to open his eyes and focus, he realized that their pursuers and the spacecraft they had been trying to extract from the inner part of the cave were gone. He and his companion were sprawled on the side of the mountain, among rocks and a few trees.

Actually, Rader realized, they were in some sort of ravine. He didn't know if the salvaged vehicle had exploded or the enemy aliens, the Dominants, had fired some sort of explosive at him and Kattor.

Rader pushed himself up to a sitting position. "What was that all about?" he asked, looking at the emotionless Kattor who had apparently just saved him.

"I left an explosive device on my ship. It doubtlessly killed some of them, but others will be back to pick through the pieces. I am now stranded here, just as you are."

"I don't understand why they are concerned about your actions. You are only one..." Rader paused, trying to decide on the correct word or term but abandoning it to save time, "you are just one...er...person," he finally concluded.

"I am not the only one who opposes them. My entire civilization believes they must not rob your planet of..." the next words didn't reach Rader's ears or his brain. Rather, he just received a general impression of what the alien was conveying.

"What I'm trying to say is that they want an...an element that is found on your world. It is used to boost their craft's

power and speed and is essential to interstellar and inter-dimensional travel. Without it, travel to this place would take generations to accomplish."

The actual message didn't include pauses or structured sentences or even adjectives, but the sergeant understood the message.

"So, that's why they came here?" Rader wore a concerned look as he tried to get the full picture. "As far as I'm concerned, they can have it, if we don't need it. Then, they can just go away and leave us alone."

"The element is indeed rare and is unknown to your scientists. It is located below this..."

Again, a brief pause as the alien tried to find the words and again Rader noted that he was only hearing what his mind supplied in the way of vocabulary and grammar.

"...below this mountain and in lesser amounts around your world. It is also present in small amounts in your atmosphere. If the Dominants remove it, your world will deteriorate. Your air will be unbreathable. They have been scouring the galaxies for eons to find this one rare element. Now that they have located it, they can mine it and send it back to their home planet. Meanwhile, your world will be thrown out of balance ecologically."

Rader wondered if Kattor's people also used that element.

The alien's thoughts explained that the inhabitants of his world relied on time travel and inter-dimensional techniques which their foes didn't understand.

When Rader used his mind to ask why the Fifths didn't share their technology with the Dominants, the answer seemed to be jumbled so much that Rader couldn't understand it. His best guess was that Kattor thought it was an was an absurd question, not fit for an answer.

But Rader had the answer to his main question. If Kattor was telling the truth, then clearly the world of humans was at great risk. They would need to find a way to resist the Dominants.

First, though, Rader and Kattor would need to escape their pursuers.

They made their way out of the ravine, Rader with some difficulty, the alien with no obvious effort. At the top, they discovered another cave opening that Rader assumed had been uncovered in the same blast that had thrown him and Kattor to the ground. In fact, it crossed his mind that the ravine may have also been caused by the explosion. Then he wondered if these were even his thoughts or if Kattor was supplying this information.

The alien signaled the sergeant to follow him into the cave. *"I have not seen this cavern before."* This time Rader was sure Kattor had communicated these words to him telepathically. Kattor did not explain why he was interested in the cave.

The pair edged their way into the narrow opening. It appeared that this was a cave that had been closed off by a landslide; there were boulders of varying sizes piled about the mouth, with a few apparently toppled away with the recent blast. After 20 or 30 feet, the space widened out and it was possible for the two to walk fully upright.

It was almost too dark to see until Kattor held out his wand and a pale orange light was emitted. A few steps later, off to the right, was what the sergeant assumed was another tunnel. His companion held his wand up at the entrance and Rader noted that it wasn't a tunnel, but just a deep recess.

As Kattor moved the light around, Rader was shocked to see a motionless body propped against the wall at the far end. Kattor, as usual, showed no emotion. He simply altered the light to green and bathed the body in the glow.

Gradually, the person was lifted from the ground and Kattor skillfully pulled it toward the two. As the body cleared the cavern he settled it carefully on the ground again. Rader suddenly realized it was a human, a female.

He wondered if she was dead. Kattor responded wordlessly to assure him that she was only in some sort of suspended state, apparently having been put into that condition by Kattor's foes. He informed Rader that he did not know what reason his enemies would have for doing this. Their motives were unclear, but always reprehensible. Rader was struck by his companion's total contempt for his enemy.

With a start, the woman's eyes suddenly flew open, and all her limbs jerked spasmodically. She turned her head from side to side with a look of dread. Then, the phrase "*It will all be well*" formed in her mind and a look of peace replaced the fear and she relaxed into a foggy stupor.

Nearby, in the foothills town of Edgemont, Cheryl Hunter had gone to her job the day after the bad storm and the events involving Sergeant Rader's disastrous mistake which was, of course, unknown to her.

She hadn't seen John Lundy that morning or for several days afterward. It seemed that whenever she looked out, John's car was gone.

One afternoon, after work, she sat inside her apartment's front door and waited. Around 6:00 PM she heard the sound of a car pulling into the parking lot and looked out in time to see John leaving his car and heading for his apartment.

To create a reason to go see him she had baked a pan of brownies and when she was sure John was home, she headed out to offer them to him. She knocked on the door and waited a few seconds before she heard the sound of footsteps.

John opened the door. He appeared rather distracted, Cheryl thought, and he took the brownies with only a short *thank you* before he closed the door. Cheryl, not to be discouraged, knocked again. John appeared again, still holding the pan of brownies.

"Say, John. I'm really tired of hanging around this boring apartment building. How about going with me for a ride into the mountains? The leaves are changing colors and it would be really relaxing. How about it?"

John didn't seem enthusiastic, but he finally agreed. A few minutes later he and Cheryl were winding their way up a mountain in Cheryl's dark red Dodge. They had left behind the carefully groomed vegetation of the small foothills city's well-kept yards and were now surrounded by evergreens and small bushes. Cheryl had the windows rolled down and the mountain air was really refreshing.

She looked at John. He was just staring straight ahead, with no apparent emotions. Cheryl was worried about him. Finally, she pulled to the side of the road, turned off the car, and faced John.

"Something's bothering you, John. I can tell. You've hardly been at home for days now. Something's going on. I haven't told you before, but I overheard that Sergeant Rader begging you to go in to the base that one night a few weeks ago. What's up? We're going to sit here until you tell me what's going on."

Cheryl set her jaw firmly and stared straight at him. At first, John refused to look at her. Then, she leaned over and put her hand on top of his. He looked up. Cheryl saw that he had tears brimming in his eyes. Finally, he looked into her eyes and began to sob. Cheryl put her arm around his shoulder and hugged him.

"Tell me," she said firmly.

John knew he was violating his oath of secrecy, but he couldn't take the stress anymore. He explained his job to her. He told her of the night that Rader shot the alien. He told her that Rader had apparently been taken away to be left to die in the Forbidden Zone.

Cheryl's mouth dropped open when she heard all this, first when she heard about John's job, and she had barely begun to accept the possible truth of all this when John told her about Rader. And the aliens.

"This just sounds incredible. And horrible, John, but I do believe you. That poor Sergeant Rader!"

Then, she suddenly thought of Paul. He had been working as a *Recovery Specialist* when he was injured. He didn't tell her more than that, but for some reason Cheryl made the connection in her mind. Paul may have been investigating aliens when he had his accident!

John gulped hard and continued. "There is more..." He paused for what seemed like a couple minutes. "After Rader shot the alien, my team was sent back to check out our original site. When we arrived, we were shocked to find..."

He paused again and looked at Cheryl to gauge her acceptance of his story thus far. His eyes scanned her face imploringly. Cheryl merely nodded.

John resumed. "The sky was dark when we got there, but then we saw lights rising from behind a ridge. It was an alien spacecraft. It rose into the sky a short distance, paused and began moving slowly toward us. It stopped above our trucks."

"I...I have never been so terrified. I knew they were looking at us. Every soldier knew that. Then it began to glow a bright red and shot a beam of light straight down into the ground. It hit some of the trucks behind my jeep and then moved on down the column. Every vehicle exploded when the light hit it. My driver had the presence of mind to gun his engine and we drove away as fast as we could. We kept looking back, afraid that they would follow us, but we just saw their aircraft shoot up into the sky."

John began to shake.

"We drove until we reached our headquarters building. The members of Team A were already there. We told them what had happened. They just stared at us like they didn't believe anything we were saying. Colonel Webber called us into his office and told us to never again mention anything about our experience that day."

Cheryl again leaned over and hugged the sobbing Lieutenant. He pushed her away gently and looked her in the eyes again.

"This morning they sent us out to retrieve the bodies and the damaged trucks. When we got back I got permission from the colonel to take a few days off and I drove home again."

Cheryl had one question, but she was afraid to ask. After a few seconds, though, John calmed down a bit and she ventured to inquire about Rader.

"They arrested him and kept him locked up in a makeshift jail somewhere on base, I heard. I think they were going to turn him over to the aliens. That's all I know."

John sank back into the car seat. Cheryl felt so sorry for her neighbor. But John had more to add. He turned his sorrowful face toward Cheryl. "And, when I left the base this afternoon, I was followed by something on my way home, something in the sky." He gulped hard and began to sob.

The two sat there in Cheryl's car, each trying to deal with the shocking truth.

Eventually both calmed down and Cheryl decided to begin driving again, mostly to clear her mind.

Suddenly, three figures stepped out of the tree line and started to cross the highway a few feet in front of the car. Cheryl slammed on her brakes and skidded on some loose gravel, but she was able to stop just short of them.

In the growing darkness, she realized that one of the figures was Sgt. Rader. The second individual was wearing a dark colored flight suit with what appeared to be a sweatshirt over it, with a large hood hiding most of the person's face. The third member of the small group remained briefly in the shadows of the pine trees alongside the highway.

The sergeant approached the car.

"I know you," Cheryl began.

Rader glanced at the passenger seat and recognized John Lundy, who just stared back in amazement. Teddy turned to Cheryl. "We need a ride," he began, glancing around nervously. "We are being chased by some really bad...er...people who want to kill us. Please, help us!"

Cheryl was shocked that the same self-confident soldier she had overheard the night of the big storm when he came to get John was now pleading in a voice that reflected fear and uncertainty.

"Of course," she responded and hit the unlock button on her armrest. The sergeant and the figure in the metallic clothing climbed into the back seat. The third person shuffled uncertainly toward the car, finally wobbling unsteadily for a few steps, and then collapsing across the hood of the car.

Cheryl and the sergeant immediately rushed to offer assistance. As Cheryl neared the figure now sprawled on the pavement in front of her car, she realized it was a woman. As she reached to help her to her feet, she felt a sudden shock of recognition.

It was Dana Warrick, her cousin!

Cheryl was about to ask her cousin where she had been and what had happened to her, but she could tell by her flat affect that Dana was in no condition to discuss anything. Cheryl helped Dana into the back seat on the right side, next to Rader. The hooded figure was on the left side, with the hood concealing his face.

Cheryl prepared to turn around and drive back into Edgemont, planning to get Dana to a hospital and wondering frantically where she had been for the past three or four years, but the stranger with the hood in the back seat objected, though not in a verbal way, she realized.

The words just seemed to appear in her brain, telling her to get away from the city as fast as she could. Cheryl might have normally protested, or asked a lot of questions, but for some reason she felt an urgent need to comply with these instructions. She did as she was told and gunned the car away from Edgemont, into the mountains.

It was a strange ride. John and Dana were non-communicative. The stranger seemed to communicate without speaking. Only Rader and Cheryl were "normal," but Rader seemed to be physically exhausted, and she felt a legitimate fear that something bad was about to happen.

She drove on along the twisting mountain road with a feeling of impending doom. After twenty minutes there was a sudden flash of light that blinded her when she looked in her rearview mirror.

"It's gone," Rader commented without emotion. "Edgemont is gone."

Chapter Twenty-Six: To Catch an Alien, Part Two

The Dunbar family arrived at Dr. Baines' clinic before 9:00 P.M. as they had been instructed. While the doctor's nurse, Gloria Jones, updated Mr. Dunbar's recent health history which basically consisted of Clint and Lou confirming that things continued to be as bad as before, perhaps even worse, Dr. Baines and Greg Bowie made last-second adjustments to their equipment and inspected the newly installed doors with the glass re-lockers. The company had been very prompt in responding to Paul's order, since he had told them it was an emergency. He had been one of their best customers over the past few years, so they wanted to keep him happy.

"Do you think Sloan's doors will work?" queried the technician. He himself was skeptical, since he knew from reading the magazine article that the so-called "aliens" seemed to be able to go wherever they wanted, whenever they wished, regardless of anyone's efforts to stop them.

"Well, Greg..." Dr. Baines began, once again running his hand through his thinning hair as Greg had seen him do so often that he was becoming rather annoyed by the act, "we can only try it and see. I think Mr. Dunbar's life may depend upon our stopping whatever is causing his insomnia. As a man of science, I think that even aliens must obey the basic laws of physics."

Greg was surprised that the doctor seemed to accept the possibility of alien abduction without any equivocation.

By 10:00 P.M. all the preparations were complete and Clint and Lou Dunbar had departed for Millardville. Greg seated himself before the various dials and switches while Dr. Baines sat on a stool near the door to the room, from which he had a clear view of the hallway leading to the sleep study room if he cracked the door just a fraction of an inch. He hoped to maintain a human view of the room in case the electronic equipment somehow failed, despite Paul Sloan's precautions.

One hour passed, then two. Greg, accustomed to these late-night stints, was still alert, but Dr. Baines was obviously drowsy. Greg stood to stretch and was about to nudge the nodding physician when a loud clanging sound pierced the air. Dr. Baines responded by leaping to his feet, knocking over the stool, and scrambling into the hallway. Greg took a glance at the monitors and saw that they were all inactivated. Then he hurried after Dr. Baines.

It took only seconds for them to reach Nick Dunbar's room. They were startled by what they saw through the window of the door.

On the other side of the glass, in a half-crouching position, was a slender figure of medium height, dressed in what appeared to be a suit of dark but flexible copper-colored foil. The figure's narrow slit-like eyes seemed to regard the two men without emotion, though Greg had the definite feeling that it was shocked to encounter the two humans and to discover that the door had locked firmly behind it.

The alien's deep-set eyes began to glow a bright red, which so startled Greg Bowie that he halted in mid-stride. Behind the figure, Nicholas Dunbar appeared to be suspended in air above the bed, bathed in a green glow. Some of the electric leads dangled from the unconscious man. The crouching figure's left hand held a pencil-shaped device that was emitting the glow that encompassed Nick Dunbar.

For just a moment the three stood still as though none of them knew what to do next. Suddenly the figure transferred the wand to its other hand and pointed it at Dr. Baines.

The green glow suddenly dissolved, dropping Nick Dunbar roughly onto the floor, after which a blue glow began to grow around the end of the wand. A streak of blue light then shot from the glow and, passing through the window glass, struck Dr. Baines in the forehead. He crumpled forward and smashed into the metal door.

Greg rushed to his side as the figure on the other side of the door fumbled at the latch, at last moving away from the door and pointing the wand at it. There was a bright red flash, temporarily blinding Greg, but when he was able to look again, the steel door remained securely in place, though there was a noticeable bulge in the lower part of the door. The alien pointed his wand again.

Nick Dunbar, meanwhile, had begun to emerge into consciousness to find himself on the floor with a strange, crouching figure shooting colored lights at the door from a metallic tool of some kind. He ripped the remaining electrodes from his skin and managed to pull himself to his feet.

Being quite drowsy and unsteady, he fell forward, striking the slender being and knocking him to the floor. As the metal rod hit the floor, the light went out. Then the stranger regained his balance and picked it up.

At first, the blue light resumed, but it then morphed gradually into green as it was focused on Dunbar. As it bathed him again in the green glow, Dunbar once again became unable to move his limbs. He felt himself floating. He tried to scream, but no sound came from his mouth.

The intruder seemed confused, turning back toward the

door and shooting a blue light at it, but again letting Dunbar drop.

Nick suddenly realized that this floating experience had happened to him before, night after night. In the morning, he would awake exhausted, and his memory would fade rapidly, leaving a vague, uneasy feeling of dread, but at this moment he was totally aware of what was happening.

With a sudden red-hot rage, Nick Dunbar leapt to his feet and hurled himself at the alien, knocking the wand from his hand and slamming him hard into the metal door. Within seconds, he was straddling the intruder and pummeling him without mercy. All the built-up rage and frustration from what he now recalled had been happening to him for many months escaped at once.

Watching from the door's window, Dr. Baines, who had recovered from being hit in the head by the blue light, and Greg Bowie saw their opportunity and opened the door using the key Baines had kept in his pocket. As they pulled the door open, Baines saw the wand on the floor, still glowing blue. He reached down to grab it.

Greg pulled Dunbar from atop the alien and hustled him out of the room. Baines followed, re-closing the door and making sure the latch caught. The alien remained motionless on the floor of the sleep chamber. The humans glanced at one another. It seemed that they had caught an alien, maybe even killed one.

"Now what?" asked Greg Bowie, looking at his boss.

There was a loud crash at the end of the hallway as the door to the parking lot blew open. The three men watched as a green light appeared.

"Oh crap..." thought Nick Dunbar. "Not again..."

Back in Millardville Lee Fellner was frantic. Kathy hadn't returned from work the day before. He contacted the police, but they did little more than check the hospital and her place of employment. Lee had already done that.

In desperation, he decided to see if Dr. Keller had heard from her.

Charles Keller had his own missing person concern: Tonya Belding had not been at home when he went to pick her up for their longstanding date the night before. Her car wasn't even in her driveway. Though their relationship hadn't progressed too far recently as Tonya had never actually broken up with him, he had been looking forward to their trip to the capital city to see the rodeo. He called to confirm the date, but the call went straight to her voice mail.

Lee convinced Dr. Keller to accompany him to Kathy's and Tonya's place of employment. Mr. Peate escorted them into his office.

"Tonya and Kathy went out on a home visit yesterday," he stated. "I believe they were on their way to Reginald. They didn't report back in before closing time, but that isn't necessarily unusual."

He was interrupted by his secretary who told him the police were on the phone. He spoke briefly, then turned to his two visitors.

"They found Tonya's car in a ditch on a rural road. No sign of her or Kathy."

A look of dread froze on Lee's face. Charles Keller grimaced.

Chapter Twenty-Seven: Flight to Hilltop House

Late the previous evening, Kathy and Deke had hurried through the woods a few miles west of Millardville after heeding Renee's advice. Kathy was still limping. It had been a long night and the two had only stopped to rest a couple times. Deke had urged Kathy to get some sleep when they reached a dilapidated farmhouse along the way, while he would stand guard, but she was too keyed up to rest. They resumed their flight until they saw a large building some distance ahead, atop a hill. Deke recognized it.

"That's where I was when the aliens captured me," he told Kathy. "I've been hiding out there for a coupla weeks. The guy who lives there calls it Hilltop House. He's really nice and he's not a bit scared of the aliens."

He grabbed her by the hand and began tugging her up the hillside, through the last of the trees, and into the clearing that was dominated by the old mansion. She was wearing oversized boots that belonged to Coach Jepson and that made it difficult to walk.

Deke was a bit hesitant in opening the front door, since he didn't know if the aliens might have returned there, maybe to capture Paul. But, just as he began to turn the doorknob, it was jerked open from within, throwing Deke off balance.

He landed in a heap at the foot of Paul's wheelchair, but promptly jumped back to his feet.

"So, Deke, where have you been? And who is this with you?" Paul inquired.

Deke explained and introduced Kathy, who appeared to be in danger of collapsing. The stress of the night was catching up to her.

"I think I know some of the aliens' plans," Deke began. "They were discussing them in front of me; I guess they didn't know that I could hear what they was thinking. I came to understand that they was after me because I'm part alien."

He paused and glanced at Paul, expecting him to be shocked by that last comment, but, when it became clear that Paul was unphased, Deke resumed.

"They was thinking that my father is their enemy and had escaped somehow out in the mountains out west. I guess they don't know our words for states or mountain names."

"I think they just wouldn't care about that sort of thing," Paul commented as he ushered the two into the computer room.

Paul pointed to one of the couches and Deke and Kathy shuffled to the closest one. She was now limping and visibly shaking. As she collapsed onto the sofa, Deke dropped down next to her and Paul wheeled himself over to where they were, executing a crisp spin to face them.

"So, they were chasing you because they knew that your father was their enemy? Why would they need you?" Paul looked deeply worried.

"I'm not sure, but I think it had something to do with holding me hostage as a way to get my father to surrender. He seems to know a lot of their secret plans and has been trying to warn the people here on Earth and they are afraid that their plans will be wrecked if he does that."

"What plans?" Paul asked in his usual unemotional manner.

"Some of 'em have come to Earth to steal something we have here, buried in the mountains, I guess, something that they can use to make their flying saucers fly. They also have some sort of plan about making half-alien babies that can grow up and fight for 'em."

This last comment drew Paul's attention. "Please explain..."

"They are thinking way into the future. They are planning to take their time to dig up the stuff they need and will be staying on Earth for as long as it takes to do that. By the time they are ready to leave, the babies will be grown up and can stay here to guard any of the stuff that they leave behind. And...they will blow up Earth after that."

Deke glanced at the piles of computer paper that were strewn across the desk and floor. "You had me see if I could translate these writings that you printed out. I was busy doin' that when the computer started making noises. I looked to see what it was and found out that it was someone named Sell-something. He asked a couple questions and I had been writing answers to say you weren't home. It takes me a lot of concentrating to do that, since I never learned to use a computer very good at school."

"I looked up at the last second to see a bunch of those alien dudes standing over there by the hallway to the kitchen. I typed 'help', but then a green light hit me and the next thing I knew I was in one of their scout machines...that's what they call the littler ones. They call the really big ones 'sky machines'."

"They put me on a bench thing in the middle, next to some sort of thing, er...engine, I guess you could call it, that I think gives them UFOs power to fly. It was making a humming sound that I couldn't hardly hear. I tried to stand up, but something seemed to be holding me down. They just sorta ignored me while they talked or thought about what they were gonna to do next."

"I couldn't really tell that we were moving, but then the scout machine began to go down toward the ground; I could hear the thoughts of the one guy who seemed to be driving the thing. He was worried about something not working right or something like that. Another guy was saying they needed to get someone who was on the ground. After just a couple minutes I was able to sort of see through the wall of the UFO. I guess they can make them, uh, tran...tran..."

"*Transparent?*" Paul suggested.

"Yeah, that's the word. They could change their walls to make them see-through when they wanted to land. When we came to a stop, I could tell that our machine was sorta floating into a big old barn. When we stopped moving, part of a wall in the scout machine opened up and several of the little guys got out with some sort of tools to do something. A couple of the tall ones went out, too. After a short while they came back, floating a woman with blond hair in one of their green beams."

Kathy, who had been listening intently, had regained some of her strength. When she heard Deke mention the aliens in a barn transporting a woman onto their scout machine, she gasped. "Tonya!"

Deke and Paul glanced toward her briefly.

Deke continued. "I think the short ones are sort of like workers and the tall ones are soldiers…"

Paul rested his chin in his cupped hands, still staring at Deke. "Sounds like ants or bees. Different ones have different jobs." Paul leaned back in his chair. "Please continue, Deke."

"Well, they floated the lady to the part of the scout machine behind where I was still sitting on the bench. A wall there opened up. I hadn't even seen there was a wall. And they used the green light to drop her onto a sort of table in the middle of that room. They had other people in tubes, I think. I guess a few hours passed. I'm not too sure how long, but we were in that barn while the short ones worked on something outside the scout machine. Then, a slot slid open, and a little girl came in with Kathy here and showed her a baby in one of those tubes. The little girl, I think, was like me, part alien."

"Anyhow, there was a gunshot or something loud and all the little guys came rushing back in and the aliens shoved Kathy out. Something musta hit the machine behind me or something, 'cause whatever was holding me down seemed to quit working; I think it was a bullet and it messed up their machinery a little. I jumped up and ducked out before they could stop me. They was in a awful hurry, I guess, so they didn't come after me."

"While the shooting went on, I hid in a dark corner of the barn and the scout machine began lighting up and whirling up off the dirt floor until it crashed out the roof of the barn and then the men who had been shooting saw me and started after me. I think they thought I was one of the aliens. I made it to a small door along the wall and escaped, but I ran back around to the big front doors while the men with the guns ran off toward the woods."

"There was still one guy inside. I knocked him out with a brick I found on the ground outside. Kathy had fainted, I guess. I noticed that she was missing a shoe, so I took the boots off the unconscious guy and put them on her feet, figuring she might need them when she woke up, if we needed to run in the woods."

At that statement Kathy looked at her feet, realizing for the first time that she was wearing camouflage pattern boots.

Deke continued, "Since she was still knocked out, I scooped her up and took off through the woods with her. After a while, some short lady showed up and told us which way to go while she tricked the men with guns into going the wrong way." Deke paused and looked at Paul and shrugged.

"So, here we are, Paul."

Things were beginning to make sense to Paul. The tall ones are in charge and that was why he encountered the tall, smug one in his recent fantasy-like computer confrontation, the one with the scar, who was so dismissive of Paul and definitely felt superior to humans!

While thinking about his recent experience, Paul felt a surge of anger. The sight of the scar made him shiver. He wasn't sure why, but he actually hated this particular alien. He made a conscious effort to take his mind off these feelings.

Now he knew why they might be coming to Earth: to steal resources. But there were, as he had suspected for a while, some benevolent ones. The good ones were the ones who caused his computer to display all the hieroglyphs and Cheryl's picture and were asking for Paul's help.

When it became clear to her that the two men had finished their discussion, Kathy asked Paul if she could use his phone. She wanted to call Lee, let him know that she was okay. He must be worried sick. Surprisingly, Paul declined the request.

"The aliens seem to monitor my phone calls and computer messages. They may be able to find you here. It's best that we wait until we are among a larger group of people. I don't think they will bother you two if there are many witnesses. That seems to be their pattern; they like to keep things quiet."

Paul decided he had one more task before he could leave for Caperton. He had to contact Dr. Baines at the hospital in Spring City to see if he and Greg Bowie were able to capture the alien. When he was transferred to the Sleep Center by the hospital switchboard, someone informed him that no one knew where the two were. They hadn't reported for work the previous day. In addition, the family of Nick Dunlap had been phoning to ask where Nick was, since he hadn't been released to them when they arrived to pick him up.

Paul grimaced. This was very disturbing news, but there was nothing he could do to help. Paul decided that he should go into Caperton when the sun was up all the way, partly to get his guests into the relative safety of a larger group of people and also to see what Selkirk wanted. As he had told Kathy, he could no longer trust computer or phone contacts.

He asked Deke and Kathy to come along with him. First, though, he fixed them some breakfast and gave them a chance to sleep on the couches in the computer room.

While they slept, he stayed alert and on guard, but kept thinking about Cheryl Hunter. The early hieroglyphs on the computer, according to Deke, said she was in trouble. Paul wanted to help but didn't even know how to find her.

The computer screen suddenly lit up, again a pale-yellow color. Paul knew this wasn't a good sign, but he rolled himself up to the desk and prepared to respond. As he began to survey the screen, it dissolved into the same scene as before.

Once again, Paul found himself inside the three-dimensional spacecraft that appeared. He didn't have any idea what was happening, so, once again, he gripped the armrests. The same tall figure was leaning on the control panel at the front of the room. Paul decided he'd keep quiet and see if the alien spoke first. After a few seconds, the tall figure pushed himself to an erect stance and spun around to face Paul.

"Do not go into the small village called Caperton", he commanded via telepathy.

"Why not?" demanded Paul with a glaring countenance, concentrating on the contempt he felt for this being.

He had the feeling the alien wasn't hearing his words, that he was watching a prerecorded message. Then, as before, the image vanished, and Paul fell back into his chair. Again, he had noticed that ugly red, pulsating scar. He was puzzled by his own reaction of pure hate.

Chapter Twenty-Eight: A Rough Ride

The car with Cheryl, John, Rader, the hooded stranger, and Dana sped through the mountains. Cheryl had been gripping the steering wheel with such white-knuckle intensity that her shoulders began to ache, and she was nearly exhausted. All the time, she kept checking her rearview mirror to see if they were being followed. At last, she came to Interstate 76 and headed northeast, away from the mountains. Maybe they weren't being pursued.

That hope was suddenly dispelled when they crested a hill and found a huge, brightly lit triangular object looming in the sky in front of the little car. Its multicolored lights flashed in rapid succession. Cheryl knew it was what people would call an unidentified flying object; she herself didn't recall ever seeing one, but the sight elicited a gasp from Dana in the back seat.

The UFO just seemed to hang in mid-air, not moving up, down or side to side.

Cheryl had never believed in such things, but she suddenly revisited a childhood discussion she had with her cousin during a family get-together perhaps twenty years earlier. The two cousins had been watching a television show on unsolved mysteries about possible alien visitation when Dana had nonchalantly commented that she was scared to death of such things.

Now that John had confided in Cheryl and she had this object almost blocking the car's path, she was a full believer. Her heart pounded so powerfully that she thought it would burst. She was just about to slam on her brakes so she could turn around, when a voice seemed to appear in her brain: *"It will all be well."*

Though she tried to press the brake pedal, she found that her foot wouldn't do what her brain commanded. In fact, the car seemed to pick up speed. Just as the car was directly under the huge UFO, a bright light reflected in the car's passenger-side rearview mirror.

Cheryl glanced over her shoulder. A small internally lighted disk-shaped object was gaining on the Dodge. John took one look at it and pulled his knees up close to his face and began to shake.

A red beam of light shot down at the car from the trailing object, but the huge one, which was now directly overhead, responded instantaneously with a bright red light of its own that intercepted the beam from the smaller disk.

Then, the large vehicle's light followed the path of the smaller one's red beam until it reached the disk itself. There was a huge flash of blinding, white light much like the group had witnessed outside of Edgemont. Rader gasped out an expletive. John's face turned ashen. Dana remained in a daze. The hooded person didn't move. Cheryl closed her eyes because of the dazzling reflection of light off the mirror. When she opened them again, both the small UFO behind the car and the huge one overhead were gone.

"My people have solved the problem." The unspoken words again came across in Cheryl's mind in a completely soothing manner. *"As I said, it will all be well. And it is. Drive on."*

Cheryl felt compelled to do so. When she was certain that there was no more immediate danger, she asked, "Why are they chasing us?"

"They are after me, their enemy," was a telepathic reply from the back seat.

"They are after me for killing one of their comrades," Teddy Rader offered flatly.

"I don't know what they want, but I'm sure they're chasing me," commented the lieutenant in a barely distinct voice. He was visibly shaking.

"I believe they are after me," responded Dana, who had awakened from her slumber as a result of the bright lights.

"I discovered their secrets while investigating the strange disaster that buried that village in the mountains. I believe they are after me because they fear I will reveal them to the world."

"Aren't you worried they'll try to kill you like they tried to do with Sergeant Rader?" Cheryl responded to her cousin's statement.

A mental message from Kattor supplied an answer. *"They still have plans for you. It was far too easy for me to find you. They allowed it. They know that you wouldn't cooperate with them but thought you would reveal yourself to me. You have a gift or talent they want to put to use for their own evil purposes. Since my people have located the place we need to reach and they haven't, they must follow us to find it. It's important for us to get there as soon as possible to set up defenses against them. We must prevail and reach our goal before they can determine where it is, in order to foil their plan."*

"Are they responsible for those frightening nightmares I used to have as a child?" Dana asked, shaking her head vigorously to try to dispel the remaining cobwebs. "I used to dream that I was taken aboard a mysterious aircraft...scary monsters did something to my head."

"They must be aware of how valuable you would be to the cause of my people and want to stop you or turn you against us."

Dana spoke again. "So, both your people and the bad aliens want me to reach some place up ahead?"

"Yes. My people want your help in stopping them because you have special qualities."

Dana looked perplexed and a bit frightened. "What qualities could I possibly have that could help either side? And why did the small UFO try to blast us if they want to follow us to our destination?"

"You will understand at the appropriate time." Then, he added a comment. *"If you need to know these things, you will be told. But, you don't need to know at this time."*

Rader noted that Kattor had not really answered Dana's question. His suspicions of Kattor started to grow. What was he up to? It occurred to the sergeant that Kattor might be lying about a lot of things. How could the sergeant be sure Kattor was a good alien? Teddy wondered if he had just accidentally tuned in to thoughts the alien didn't intend to share.

John still had a concern that the conversation wasn't addressing. "Did the small flying saucer also destroy the one with your people in it? Both disappeared."

John was worried that the large UFO had disappeared and would not be able to rescue them if they were attacked again. Kattor read his thoughts and recognized that John's overwhelming emotion was a blinding fear. That would not be helpful to their mission. Something would need to be done about it.

"My people merely re-entered another dimension of existence. In terms that earth beings can understand, time is a dimension in which our vehicles can travel."

"Is that what they do when our military or others see them suddenly vanish in the sky?"

John was still not sure about the answer. His fear of alien spacecraft remained as high as it had been at the time of the team alert when Rader had to come get him. The recent destruction of Team B and the city of Edgemont had magnified that fear exponentially. His shaking intensified.

"My people have the ability to switch dimensions in an instant. It is not that hard for advanced civilizations such as mine, though it can be understood that you Earth beings do not have the intelligence to accomplish such simple feats."

Kattor turned his face to the car window and put a hand up to his forehead. To John alone he transmitted a telepathic message: *"You will learn more soon."*

John's face turned even paler.

Rader, sitting next to the hooded passenger, was the only one to be concerned when Kattor turned his head toward the window, a seemingly benign motion. Kattor seemed almost contemptuous of Earth people. The sergeant also felt that his explanations sounded a bit dubious. Teddy decided to just not let it worry him for now, but he would stay on guard and try not to think any thoughts that might upset the alien. He switched the topic of discussion slightly.

"So, what is this great place we are driving to?" he inquired.

The answer came back: *"Caperton."*

Cheryl and Dana exchanged quizzical glances. The town's name meant nothing to John and Rader, but it brought up all sorts of memories for the two cousins. Conversation then faded out. Each passenger seemed to be lost in his or her own deeper thoughts.

Cheryl recalled her trip across the country on the way to Edgemont. She wondered what would become of all the people she met on the way if the aliens came after them. She thought of her parents and Jay and his family. Would she ever see them again?

Teddy was exhausted. He began to doze. His mind entered a twilight between wakefulness and dreams. He recalled his childhood. He was the youngest of five children. Images of family get-togethers passed through his mind. His thoughts took him back to the times he had been bullied as a youngster.

His oldest brother had taken him aside to teach him to defend himself. He was a rather puny child, but his brother inspired him to get into sports. At first he wasn't good at anything, but he stuck with it; Ben wouldn't let him stop. After a while he began to have some success.

He always thought he was too short for basketball, but he learned to dribble extremely well and discovered to his surprise that he was a natural point guard. He tried football; again, his size was an impediment. But his determination won him respect among his teammates.

He was never the best athlete on any team, but he won several *Player of the Year* awards based on his effort and attitude. His academic performance improved as he gained confidence on the basketball court, gridiron, and diamond, but he didn't feel suited for academic pursuits.

He joined the Army after high school and planned to make it his career. The incident in the Forbidden Zone likely ruined his prospects, to say the least. He couldn't rule out being court martialed when this was all over. If the aliens got ahold of him first, he might even be executed. With that thought in mind, Sergeant Rader drifted off to a fitful sleep.

Sitting to the right of the sergeant, Dana remained groggy and was still having trouble focusing on events around her. She felt like she'd been drugged. She now fully recalled her childhood and the abductions, though precisely what happened afterward remained a mystery.

She knew she should be frightened and/or angry. The aliens had not only ruined her childhood by frequently kidnapping her, which she still couldn't fully accept had happened, but also her marriage to Ty. She had thought throwing herself into her journalism career would keep her mind off the nightmares she had been having, but her first big break had only taken her away from Ty.

Then she had found herself being rescued from that cave with no recollection of how she got there or how long she had been there. Also, there was something else going on in her head, a memory that she couldn't pull to the surface of awareness. Trying only led to increased buzzing. The fogginess swooped back in as she rode along in the back seat and she dozed.

John continued to be seized by intermittent paranoia, though it receded as they got farther from the mountains. He had learned to hide his nervous constitution from his superiors in the Army, but now it was on full display.

He'd led a rather unhappy childhood, an only child in a single parent household. Like Rader, he had been bullied relentlessly, initially because of his reddish complexion, but later because of his lack of social skills. Unlike Teddy, though, he responded to that experience by turning inward.

A raw, unfocused hatred grew within him, but he never found an appropriate release for it. He imagined himself to be a great athlete and scholar, but down deep he knew that he was only fooling himself. Worse than being a failure, he had become a nobody, a nonentity.

After a decidedly mediocre stint at college, he had joined the Army in the hope of adding clarity to his so far unfocused existence. He had met and married the daughter of the base commander, though she had her own issues and was trying to punish her father for a lifetime of being forced to move from base to base. The marriage was a solution to her father's filial demands on her and it gave John shelter from criticism by his superiors.

Transfer to the recovery team had been a way to keep him out of the view of the intermediate brass. He was deemed to be very compliant and thus was a good fit for the recovery squad. He had been befriended to an extent by Sergeant Rader, whom Colonel Webber had secretly given the mission of keeping an eye on the nervous lieutenant.

On the surface Lundy showed enthusiasm for the Army; he refused to take leave except when his superiors ordered him to do so. Underneath he couldn't deal with the issues that arose related to his position of authority and his fear that he would be exposed for the phony he knew himself to be.

Jolene had grown increasingly aware of his inadequacies and had taken their two sons and moved out, filing for divorce. This had exacerbated John's condition. It was shortly after the divorce was finalized that Cheryl Hunter had moved into the apartment complex and John had decided to try to build a relationship with her.

This temporarily lifted his mood, but the night of the thunderstorm had again shattered him. He would occasionally rally and was hoping things were headed in the right direction that night in the Forbidden Zone, but it was a fleeting hope.

When Rader had been arrested after the Forbidden Zone incident John knew he should try to do something to help Teddy, but his confidence had again been shattered and he couldn't bring himself to take the action that would be required. He drew within himself and refused to even visit Rader. Since the escape from Edgemont John had not been able to bring himself to even look Rader in the eyes.

This was made easier by John's place in the front passenger seat of Cheryl's car and Teddy's place in the middle of the rear seat. The sergeant was quite aware of John's emotional problems and chose not to reopen that can of worms while dealing with this whole alien situation. Let the lieutenant handle his own problems for a change.

Cheryl drove nonstop to the east through the night. When they hadn't seen the UFO for an hour or so, they made a quick stop at a fast-food drive-through restaurant at an exit. Kattor ate nothing; he told the others that earth food was not something his people could tolerate. They also filled up on gas, Rader performing that task while the others, except Kattor, who exhibited no apparent concern, scanned the skies nervously to warn him of approaching UFOs.

Cheryl continued on for another hour, then pulled to the edge of the road, intending to turn the wheel over to John who seemed to have calmed down after a couple of hours with no UFO sightings. For his part, John decided driving might be a change of pace that could take his mind off the fear that was ever near the surface of his psyche, or maybe he just wanted to convince himself that his behavior was under control.

Cheryl was exhausted. She opened her door as John did the same on the other side and the two strode around the front of the car. Kattor again put his fingers up to his forehead.

As the two were passing in front of the Dodge, Cheryl caught sight of a brightly lit object behind the car, in the western sky. She hoped desperately that it was a star or planet. John followed her gaze and his fears resurfaced immediately. He froze in his tracks. Cheryl halted by the opened passenger side door.

A green light shot down to the ground a hundred yards to the left of the highway and headed slowly but steadily toward the car.

Kattor responded, promptly exiting the back seat and circling to the front of the car. He reached out and seized John in a bear hug, pulling him toward the open driver-side door. John struggled, but Kattor assured him that "*It will all be well*" and he grew calm.

John ceased resisting as the light approached from across the farm pasture. When the light was about to engulf the pair, Kattor pulled out a small wand-like device and pointed it at the UFO. Crimson particles shot from its end into the path of the green beam. There was a sudden flash where the green and crimson collided. The small craft seemed to dissolve.

Kattor, still hugging John, turned back toward the car and released him. John stumbled briefly, grabbing the door for support.

Cheryl was relieved when she saw this. Rader was surprised. Maybe Kattor was actually on their side, after all. Teddy's doubts dissipated. John quickly regained his balance and started to get behind the wheel, glancing nervously over his shoulder. Maybe it would be okay.

Suddenly, however, the scout machine reappeared, and a blast of green light shot back toward the car, engulfing John. Cheryl screamed. She could see the panicked look on John's face as he was lifted up into the sky, at first slowly and then, with a sudden flash, he was gone from sight, along with the UFO.

Kattor exhibited no reaction; he merely turned away and reentered the car. Rader took a couple steps toward the spot where the light had struck Lundy. But there was nothing he could do to save the lieutenant. Rader observed that Kattor now showed no emotion and merely returned to his spot in the back seat, again turning his face toward the window.

It dawned on Teddy that, though it had initially appeared that Kattor was attempting to save John, he had effectively put him in harm's way.

Dana said nothing. She was the only one who had not exited the car during this occurrence. She seemed to be in shock.

Teddy circled around to the passenger side where Cheryl was leaning against the roof above the opened door, shaking and panting hard. He shoved Cheryl into the passenger seat. Then he raced back to the driver side and jumped in with the same agility he used to leap into his jeep and jammed the gearshift into Drive as he landed on the seat. He stepped forcefully on the accelerator. With a violent jerk and a squealing of tires, the Dodge rocketed back onto the highway.

The passengers rode along in grim apprehension. Interstate 76 dovetailed with Interstate 80 just over the Colorado-Nebraska border.

As Teddy drove, Cheryl nervously checked the passenger side mirror for any sign of a silvery reflection in the sky. Her fear of another attack alternated with her concern for John's fate. She developed a severe headache from the stress.

After a couple of more hours, they again stopped for gas and Rader rushed into the convenience store to buy some food, using Cheryl's debit card, since she was the only one possessing any form of currency. While she filled the tank, Cheryl nervously eyed the western sky, fearing that somewhere above the clouds their pursuer was watching. Finally, after not seeing any sign that they were being followed, she began to relax.

The small car continued to cruise east on the interstate, stopping when more gas was needed and grabbing food on the run, since most of the passengers were still concerned that the UFO would return.

Cheryl and Teddy were the only ones who could drive. Kattor had no interest in trying and Dana was still too disoriented to drive, so they rotated shifts behind the wheel. They napped when they weren't driving.

The car continued on across the state, passing signs for exits to places both large and small. Eventually they passed the first Spring City exit. Cheryl told Rader to pull over and they again switched places. Cheryl found herself looking for the exit to the highway heading south, toward Millardville.

She still hadn't seen a light in the sky for several hours. She didn't know why she felt the urge to leave the Interstate. Cheryl noted that the sky to the south was beginning to darken with heavy storm clouds.

Just after the Dodge exited the interstate at Spring City, a small jet airplane came in for a landing at a nearby private airstrip. Three men wearing suits exited and walked to a waiting limousine. Then, they also headed south.

Above the dark clouds, in the scout vehicle, Jay Brashear had gradually become alert. He had no idea how long he had been a prisoner. At first, he couldn't move his head and could barely move his eyes. It reminded him of the time he had awakened in the middle of surgery on his broken wrist, which was an incredibly uncomfortable experience emotionally, even if he felt no pain.

As he slowly emerged from a mental fog, he could tell he was in a brightly lit room, with a half dozen metallic tubes lining the walls. He surmised that he was in one such tube himself and, therefore, that the other tubes might also contain people.

His memory gradually cleared, and he could recall seeing a strange cloud of dust on his way to visit his friend Paul. He remembered, vaguely, visiting a doctor somewhere. There were brief images of a middle-aged man and a young boy floating in a green glow and then being deposited in cylinders close to Jay.

He also had the puzzling impression that, at some point, a short man had dashed around the room with several small, slender grey figures with large, glowing eyes in clumsy pursuit, at last subduing him and dragging him to a table on the far side of the room.

They appeared to be conducting some sort of medical procedure on their victim, who had ceased to struggle. Jay's eyes blurred and a buzzing sound seemed to block out everything. He struggled to avoid again drifting into oblivion. He couldn't bear to have that happen again! What else could he recall?

Focus, he must focus. Otherwise, he would again be lost.

In desperation he searched his memory, fighting the fog that seemed to be trying to invade his consciousness. Jay attempted to turn his eyes to the left, but he couldn't quite focus on the cylinder next to him.

Then, on the opposite side of the room, Jay discerned a young woman with blond hair. The grey figures were hustling about her, placing her into one of the metallic tubes. Jay surmised that her presence in the room was fairly recent and had something to do with his regained consciousness.

Shortly after her arrival there had been a sudden rush of activity among the pale beings, the distant sound of...was it gunfire? Something had bounced off Jay's tube with a metallic clang. He detected a hissing sound, like air escaping a punctured tire.

Suddenly he felt his arms move and he could turn his head. He considered trying to break free of the tube, but he was still too groggy to act. And, if he did gain his freedom, what would he do? He had no idea where he was.

Immediately after the gunfire, Jay felt the room shift and he heard a loud crunch sound. He had the impression that he was on some sort of flying vehicle and that it had just taken to the sky at a high rate of speed.

Sometime later, he couldn't tell if it was minutes or hours, there was a great deal of activity and different aliens entered the room and began shining green lights on the tubes, including Jay's, and moving them out and onto a different, larger vehicle.

Jay next found himself in a larger room, along with the other tube people, all lined up along the wall. A tall alien was hunched over a console of flashing lights.

Jay again drifted out of consciousness.

Chapter Twenty-Nine: Tara the Invincible!

In late October, Lindsay, Tara and Doug finally got the break for which they had been hoping. Ralph Osgood had asked Peter Lapley to ride with him to his medical appointment in Millardville, using the excuse that he might be too upset to drive back from there if he received bad news about the lump behind his ear.

Plus, it was rumored that the reporter from Spring City might show up unexpectedly and it was necessary to get Peter out of town, just in case.

Ralph picked him up at 7:30 a.m. on a Tuesday. Tara overheard her parents discussing the fact that Peter would be gone from the house for several hours. She phoned Doug and he contacted Lindsay. Today would be the day. Ralph was to arrive at 9:00 AM. Tara told her mother that she wasn't feeling well, and Margie reluctantly allowed her to stay home from school.

Ralph and Peter rode along the county highway on the way to Millardville. They exchanged a couple pleasantries during the first ten minutes of the trip. Then Ralph got down to business.

"Peter, do you understand the pressure I'm under since you started telling your story about riding on a UFO?"

"Sure. But that doesn't change the fact that it happened."

"But Petey, there's so much at stake here! We could lose all the help that the government is giving us: Carl's car and his deputies, the new water pump, the money for street repairs! That must be something you understand since you have had steady employment for a few weeks now."

"But, Ralph, I can't tell a lie! It happened and I think everyone should know about it so they can fight back against the aliens."

Ralph was again frustrated by Peter's refusal to cooperate. For a time, he drove in silence, a scowl on his face. He decided to change the subject and get back to the aliens later.

"Petey, what's this I hear about you running for my job?"

"*Peter*, Ralph. I go by *Peter* now. And I haven't decided for sure, but I just feel I need to do something more useful. I've wasted my life so far and it's time I made something of myself. I want my kids to be proud of me. I just can't go back to my old way of life. I don't understand how I ever started down that path in the first place, all the drinking and running around. I'm a changed man, Ralph, and I can't turn back."

Ralph sighed. He turned onto the state highway that led to Millardville, feeling like there was a heavy weight on his shoulders. After a few minutes, the small city came into view. The doctor's office was on the south side of town, five or six blocks from the hospital.

As Ralph turned into the parking lot of the one-story brick building, his mind shifted to the problem with his ear. Having, or rather, *trying* to have a discussion with Peter did at least accomplish one thing, making it so the mayor could get his mind off the possible diagnosis he could face.

Nurse Ruehle directed Ralph and Peter to the waiting room, promising in her always business-like way, "Dr. Williamson will be with you in a few minutes."

Ralph glanced nervously at his watch; a few seconds later

he did so again, since he hadn't really focused on the time when he took that first look. In just a couple minutes, Jean Ruehle returned and directed Ralph to the examining room.

Peter was absorbed in a magazine in the waiting room, something that had never happened before during any of his visits to a doctor's office.

The nurse weighed Ralph and had him sit on the edge of the examining table while she applied the blood pressure cuff. Ty came into the room with Ralph's file, which was quite thin, since Ralph seldom went for medical care.

Dr. Williamson always told the mayor to lose weight on the few times he did go for an exam and he was afraid that his cholesterol and blood pressure wouldn't please Ty, so he was reluctant to see the physician. And, when Ty came into the room and picked up the chart, he shook his head when he noted the weight and blood pressure, but he said nothing at that time.

"So, what seems to be the problem, Mr. Osgood?" Ty leaned forward, removing his reading glasses. He employed his sincere professional expression.

Ralph noted that he wasn't addressed as *Mayor Osgood* but chose to let it go. "It's this lump behind my ear. It doesn't hurt, but I'm worried about it."

Ty reached out with a gloved hand and took a close look at the spot Ralph had indicated. He also wasn't sure what to make of it, so he pressed on the lump just hard enough to see if it was solid. At first it was, then it suddenly collapsed as if it had been broken. Ralph yelped in pain.

A small amount of yellowish pus leaked out of the collapsed spot. That didn't surprise the doctor, but the small, hard thing that slid out immediately afterward did. Ty reached out with tweezers and tugged lightly on it and it slid out through the same hole from which the pus had oozed.

Ty called Jean into the room to clean and dress the wound.

"I'm going to put this under my microscope, see if I can determine what it is."

As the doctor peered through the lens of his microscope, he was surprised to see what appeared to be some sort of microscopic electronic device. It had several *legs* embedded in chunks of skin and fatty tissue.

Ty went back to the examination room to inform the mayor that he didn't think it was anything to worry about, probably just an infection. He said he would send it to the hospital for analysis and let Ralph know the results in a couple of days.

Then, Ty phoned Wally and arranged to meet him for a late breakfast.

Peter and Ralph stopped at the Bluebird café for coffee and doughnuts before leaving town. Ralph was surprised at how relieved he felt that his worries were resolved. He even paid for Peter's coffee and doughnut and left Renee a generous tip. He was so relieved at the good news that on the way back to Caperton he forgot to worry about Peter and his UFO nonsense.

Two hours later Wally arrived at the Bluebird Café, late, as always. He sat down at the usual table, across from Ty, who was holding something in a plastic container with a lid and staring at it with a furrowed brow.

"What's that? A sandwich?" he asked as Renee hurried to

the table to take his order.

Wally didn't notice that she looked very tired, as if she hadn't slept the previous night. Though he was very attentive during examinations of his patients, he had never been very observant in social situations. He asked for coffee and a ham sandwich. Renee sighed as she turned back toward the kitchen.

"It's what I was telling you about," Ty responded, sliding the plastic box toward his friend. He withdrew his hand and sat back, looking up at Wally. "See what you think."

Wally accepted the plastic container and very gingerly peeled open the lid.

"Careful, it's fragile." Ty warned. "I took this from behind a patient's ear. Look at it carefully."

He handed Wally a magnifying glass that he had brought with him from the office.

Wally squinted his eyes until the small, dark item came into focus. "Looks like some sort of miniature electronic device," he commented.

"But how did it get behind the man's ear? The patient had no idea how it got there. It was completely encased in human tissue!"

The two looked at each other and shrugged.

After the doctors left, Renee stood in the kitchen, thinking about the previous night. Her agency assignment had been to infiltrate a potentially dangerous militia group, not to deal with alien invasions.

Things were slow at the Bluebird and Renee told the cook that she needed to go home, since she wasn't feeling well. She phoned one of the other waitresses and returned home after Audri arrived.

Once home, the situation began to get to her. She hadn't been able to sleep the previous night. She tried again to report her experience to her headquarters office in Spring City. But what could she say? Her superiors might think she'd gone over the edge.

Instead of phoning as she had earlier, she sent a coded text message to inform her supervisor of what had occurred. Then she sat back and waited, and worried.

At last, she received a response. Decoded, it said, "Stand by for further instructions."

Renee was frustrated. She had just informed her superiors that a vigilante group had attacked a flying disk and tried to kill two civilians, but she was merely to "Stand by." She was exhausted.

Renee sat on the edge of her couch and mulled recent events. She had been in the agency for six years. The undercover assignment in Millardville had been routine...until now.

When Ty and Wally returned to Ty's office, where they planned to use the computer to search out any similar medical incidents, they found Lee Fellner and Dr. Keller waiting.

After filing a missing-persons report at the police station, Lee had thought of going to see Wally and Ty, since they were present when his wife's phantom pregnancy was discovered. He wondered if perhaps Kathy had experienced a medical problem that she wanted to discuss with Wally, or maybe with Ty, who was now their family doctor. He was beginning to feel desperate. Mostly, he wanted to do something other than pace the floor waiting for news from the police.

Charles accompanied Lee, knowing Kathy had signed a release to permit exchange of information with Ty and Wally. He had a nervous feeling that the disappearance of Kathy, and Tonya might have something to do with Kathy's dream of being abducted.

After Lee and Charles learned that Ty and Wally had no new information, they exited the physician's office. That might have been the end of the matter, but Wally had an uneasy feeling. He turned to Ty.

"Ty, ol' buddy...I just don't like what's happening. I know Kathy Fellner. I've been her doctor through three pregnancies. What if there is something to all this alien stuff Keller had in his file on Kathy? The police don't consider it their responsibility since no crime has been committed and a nonexistent baby isn't a missing person."

Ty ran his hand through his slightly graying hair. This time Wally wasn't irritated by his habit. He reminded Ty that Jay Brashear, Cheryl's older brother, had also disappeared. There was the guy from Caperton who swore that he was kidnapped and flown around by some strange looking beings. He had claimed to have seen a person matching Jay's description on the UFO on which he had been riding.

The two agreed that a short trip to Caperton to discuss things with this Lapley guy might offer some clues.

It was approaching 10:00 AM when Tara began to put the plan into motion. She waited until she could hear the distant clinking of bowls and silverware being carried from the dining room to the kitchen sink. She listened for her mother to click on the radio to the Millardville station that carried the *Swap Shop* show, in which listeners from all around the area called in to offer to buy or sell various yard sale type items.

Margie had bought a used freezer at a good price the previous summer. The twin bed Tara slept in was also purchased from someone in Millardville whose youngest child had outgrown it. Tara was convinced that her mother would be in the kitchen doing the dishes and listening to the radio for the next half hour, plenty of time for her to act.

Tara slipped noiselessly from between the covers. Her room had a hardwood floor, no carpet, so she would need to be careful. The floor was creaky and one wrong move could be heard by anyone downstairs. She decided it would be best to crawl around the edges of the room, where the boards of the floor were more secure and would make less noise.

Once she made it to the door, she would need to be additionally careful when opening the door, since the floor was a bit warped and the door always stuck on it, requiring a rather strong tug to open it. Tara's dad had been planning to fix it but hadn't gotten around to it.

From the doorway of her room, Tara knew that she could tiptoe to her parents' bedroom, the door of which was at the far end of the hall. She had practiced doing so several times during the past few days and she was confident that the hall floor was pretty much creak-less.

She was barefoot, so she would be able to make it down the hallway with a minimal amount of noise. Once in her parents' room, Tara would need to quietly and quickly search the room for the metal case in which she had seen her father place the shiny metal object.

Carefully, slowly, Tara edged her way on all fours along the wall by her window and then turned left, altering her path only to go around her dresser. She was making the final left turn and heading toward the doorway when the sleeve of her pajama shirt caught on the lever that controlled the opening to the air vent located on the wall, close to the floor.

Before she even realized that her sleeve was snagged, Tara had moved her arm forward, causing the air vent to slam shut. Tara gasped and froze. As she struggled to free her sleeve, she could hear the pounding of heavy feet on the stairs. Tara froze.

In panic, she made a desperate dive for her bed. Just as she pulled the blankets over her head, the door flew open, catching momentarily on the uneven floor and giving her time enough to burrow beneath the jumble of blankets and sheets. Tara expected to see her mother standing in the doorway, full of concern for her daughter's safety after hearing the crash of the vent.

Tara decided to lay still and feign sleep. She was afraid her mother would look into her eyes and quickly unravel the entire scheme. Tara had been amazed that her mother had so readily accepted the stomach pain story; never in her recollection had Tara seen her mother fooled twice in the same day. She figured that came from years of her mother listening to her father's excuses for staying out all night.

As she lay there, it dawned on her that the footsteps she had heard on the stairs were far too heavy for her mother to make. And, she recalled, her father had left with the Mayor earlier, so it couldn't be him.

With her eyes wide open with sudden apprehension, Tara positioned one arm across her forehead, lightly covering her eyes. Maybe it was her father, returning unexpectedly early from his trip to Millardville. She kept one eye slightly uncovered and trained on the doorway.

It took her several seconds to ascertain that the figure in the doorway was not that of her father; it was a larger person, a man too tall to be her father. From his stance, he appeared to Tara to be tense and possibly angry. The man glanced around the room for a moment and then stealthily approached her bed.

From somewhere Tara heard her mother's voice, very loud and shrill. Something was wrong, Tara realized. Her mother was screaming, in fear, rather than pain. The man glanced back toward the hallway.

He walked back to the doorway and yelled down the stairs, "You better shut your yap, lady, or you and your kid will both be sorry!"

The screaming stopped and the man took a few steps back toward the bed. Then, Tara heard the front door slam, which distracted the man for a moment.

Tara decided that she had to make a break for it, since she might not get a second chance. She didn't know what was going on, but she sensed that her mother and she were both in terrible danger. She had to get herself to safety and then do something to help her mother.

She screamed and threw the quilt off her bed, being sure that it landed on the invader's head. Then, leaping from the bed, she raced toward the window on the south side of her room, opposite the doorway.

The man, throwing off the quilt, now turned his attention to Tara. He spun around until he was facing the girl. When she broke for the window, he decided he would cut her off before she got there. He threw his bulky body in the direction Tara was headed, but the slender girl was very light on her feet and at the last split-second she changed direction and dodged past the stranger.

His mass carried him forward until he hit the window frame, shattering two panes of glass and cracking the others. Tara then threw herself to the floor and rolled under the bed. The man caromed off the window frame and fell to the floor with a heavy thud.

Tara could see that he had been cut in a couple places by the glass. Blood was dripping down his nose and into his eyes. One eye was partially closed. He was dazed for a couple seconds, but Tara saw that he was regaining his focus and would be coming after her as soon as he fully recovered. Even as she thought this, he turned from his back to his stomach, screamed in rage and began scrambling under the bed to catch her.

"Little girl! Do you know where the alien wand is? Tell me and you won't get hurt!"

Tara gasped. So that was why he was in their house! She was so scared she was shaking, but she knew she had to do something. She had to find the wand before the man in the dark suit could get to it.

As soon as she perceived that he was committed to trying to reach her under the bed, Tara rolled out from under it on the opposite side, jumped to her feet and dashed for the door, dragging it shut behind her before her pursuer could free his bulk from the cramped space under the bed.

Without wasting a second, Tara turned to the left in the hallway and scampered for her parents' room. She glanced over her shoulder just as she reached the door. Seeing that the man hadn't exited from her bedroom yet, she carefully eased open the door to her parents' room and began to quickly search for the wand.

She had seen her father place it in a metal tackle box with a lock on it and then take it into his bedroom. He had closed the door behind himself, so Tara didn't know where he put it. She checked the dresser, hurriedly tugging out each drawer and dumping the contents on the floor, while discarding the empty drawers to one side. She dug desperately through the piles of clothes, searching.

She had to find the box and the key before the bad man got to the room. She knew he was out to harm her and her family and she did not for a second believe his promise not to hurt her.

Tara could hear the man entering and exiting her brother's and sister's bedrooms, making his way down the hall, so she worked fast. He would reach the master bedroom in just a few seconds.

At last, having ransacked the final drawer without success, she turned to the closet. She and her sister had played hide and seek, and she had hidden in that closet. She knew there were shelves in there. Maybe the metal box was on one of the shelves!

She had just opened the closet when the bedroom door burst open. The large man, dressed totally in black, stood there, glaring at her with blood dripping down his forehead into his eyes. She stepped into the closet and closed the door behind herself. She heard the man's shoes scuffing the hardwood floor as he frantically tried to reach her before she could pull the closet door shut.

Then, she realized that there was no lock on the closet, so she pushed it back open just as the stranger yanked on the doorknob. This caused it to fly open and the man to lose his balance and trip backwards over a couple of the upended drawers. He landed on the floor with a crash and a bellow of rage.

A gun he had been clutching flew from his hand and slid across the floor until it reached the darkness below the huge old bed. Tara knew that she couldn't dodge around her pursuer, who was already struggling back to his feet, so she tried what had worked in her own bedroom.

She dropped onto her stomach and scooted backward under her parents' king-sized bed. She was able to propel herself back a fair distance under it as the partially blinded man stumbled to his feet and began to thrash around in the pile of clothes, searching desperately for her.

The bed was much lower than her own and, while Tara's small frame easily fit beneath it, the space was too cramped to allow the man to slide under it as he had done with her bed. Tara assumed that he had learned from that failed attempt and would try to reach her in some other way. She continued to tremble while pushing herself feet-first toward the wall at the head of the bed.

The stranger heard her clawing at the floor and dropped to his knees, stretching under the bed as far as he could in an effort to reach his handgun. Tara also began to search for the gun, not because she thought she could use it to defend herself but to deprive the man of the chance to use it on her. She was far too unwilling to harm anyone else to use the weapon on another person, no matter how much danger she was in.

Tara pushed herself back as far away as possible from the stranger's outstretched gloved hands, sweeping her arms from side to side as she went, in a desperate effort to locate the gun.

When he couldn't reach her, he fell on his stomach, pulling a flashlight from his heavy, black suit coat. When he clicked it on, the light blinded Tara. She covered her eyes with her right hand, but as she brought her hand to her face, it brushed against something cold and metallic. It had to be the gun.

She pushed it off to her right side as hard as she could. But, then her left hand brushed against another object, also metallic and cold. Tara reached back with her left hand and grabbed it. If it was the gun, what was the first object?

But the second object was a box. The tacklebox! She was able to spin it around so she could reach the clasp. Her fingers scratched at the clasp, but, as she expected, it was locked. The man made one more desperate stretch for Tara, who finally released the scream that she had managed to suppress up to this point.

Just as the man's hand seized a handful of her hair and began tugging her toward him, she grabbed the box with both hands. She knew that she only had one chance. With all of her strength, she shoved the box toward his leering face. Maybe she could break his nose, then grab the box and make a run for it.

The box slid smoothly across the wooden floor and came to an abrupt, crunching stop when it hit the man's face. He made a surprisingly muted grunt, released his grip on Tara, and rolled over on one side. She waited a few seconds, but he didn't make any more movements.

Tara shrugged her body free of the under-bed darkness and pulled herself out to the light, balls of dust rolling along the floor with her. The stranger lay on his left side, totally silent, not breathing. His eyes were half-open and unfocused.

Tara bent to pick up the metal box. As she did so, she noted a small hole in one end of the box, the end that had collided so solidly with the man's face. She stared at the small, circular opening for a couple seconds, noting that it looked like a pencil had somehow been thrust point-first through the end of the metal box from the inside.

Then, suddenly understanding, she glanced down at the immobile assailant. She choked back a feeling of nausea.

Stepping gingerly over his silent form, she bent to get a view of his face. Right between his eyes was a small hole, about the circumference of a pencil. She found a matching hole at the back of the head, then a couple feet further along the same path, she located the metallic blue wand. It had apparently slid along the interior of the metal box until it reached the end. Then, without being slowed at all, it had passed neatly through the metal box and into the skull of the bad man.

He was dead, no doubt about that. Tara had never seen a dead person before, and she gagged involuntarily.

She dropped the metal box, which made a loud *clang* when it hit the wooden floor. Shaking even more than before, she gingerly picked up the wand and carefully wiped off the blood and brain tissue on the bedspread, ignoring the wave of nausea she experienced. She rested the metallic instrument gingerly in the palm of her hand, the point away from her body, and headed for the hallway.

She hadn't heard her mother's voice since she had heard the front door close several minutes ago and she needed to find out if she was okay. She forced herself to stop shaking and descended the stairs as quietly as she could, carefully scanning ahead of her to make sure no other evil men awaited her.

At last, she came to the bottom of the stairs and tiptoed through the dining room toward the kitchen doorway. She could hear the radio, but it was mostly static, as if someone had spun the channel selector in a failed attempt to find another station.

Peeking in, Tara found a chair overturned by the table. Nearby, on the floor, was one of her mother's canvas shoes. Beside it, upside down and sputtering noisily, was the radio. Tara shut her eyes and made a conscious decision not to imagine what may have become of her mother. Maybe she was somewhere else in the house or out on the lawn visiting with a neighbor or something.

Tara made a quick search of the downstairs, finding the front door ajar. Her mother would never leave the front door open at this time of year when cold air could invade the house and trip the thermostat, turning the furnace on. She would always remind Tara, Johnny and Melody to close the door whenever they entered or exited the house. In addition, when Tara noticed the doormat overturned a few feet away on the porch, her heart sank. Her mother was obsessive about keeping the house straightened up.

As she pushed the door open a bit, the rush of cold air reminded her that she was still in her pajamas, so as soon as she was satisfied that no one else was in the house, she retreated to her room and put on her school clothes.

That reminded her that she was supposed to meet up with Doug and Lindsay to put their alien-catching plan into motion. Her friends—having someone to call *friend* was still a novelty to her, but that was how she thought of them now—would be waiting for her in Calvin Dunn's dried up cornfield on the western edge of town.

She had done her part in finding the metal object her father had left locked up in his bedroom and she didn't want to let them down now. She needed something to keep her mind from focusing on her mother's absence, so she concentrated on the alien-catching plan. She returned to the kitchen for a dish towel to wrap around the dangerously sharp object.

Then she went to the front door and slipped into the shoes she had kicked off there the day before upon her return from school and grabbed the jacket she had left draped on the coat rack by the door. With a look of determination, she took a deep breath, pulled the door all the way open and stepped out into the chilly fall air.

Lindsay and Doug were already waiting at the prearranged spot behind Doug's house. Doug had brought along the badminton net from his garage and Lindsay had grabbed a new roll of duct tape from the junk drawer in her kitchen. In typical Lindsay fashion, she had already partially unrolled it.

The plan was for one of them to hold up the device and wave it around on the assumption that the aliens would be monitoring the area in hopes of spotting their missing weapon. When they took the bait and came after it, the fifth graders would duck into the shelter of the cornstalks, still standing in the field since Calvin Dunn had vanished in midsummer, the same as Joey Paige, and there had been nobody to harvest the ears of corn.

When the aliens ventured into the midst of the dead cornstalks, someone would throw the badminton net over them and all three of the kids would wrap them up in duct tape. It was a simple plan and the three saw no flaw in it, as long as they maintained a firm resolve.

They had spread word of their plan among their schoolmates—the ones they thought they could trust. However, they were bitterly disappointed when word got out and three uninvited classmates showed up instead: Dale's nephew Josh Tooney, Steve Muncie, and Nancy Burrows.

"Hey, Dougie! We came to help you catch aliens and save the planet!" Josh, being the ringleader, spoke first with words dripping with derision as the three stepped out from the cornfield where they had been hiding.

Doug answered the challenge with equal disdain. "No one invited you, Tooney!" He sat his jaw and took a step toward his antagonist.

Steve Muncie stepped out from behind Josh and raised a cell phone over his head. "We heard about it from the kids you invited and we un-invited them! We're going to take photos to show what dorks you all are! Everyone is going to be laughing at you! Now...smile for the camera!"

There was a *click*, but Steve was holding the phone backward and just got a shot of himself with a goofy smirk.

Doug merely chuckled and held his ground. "Did you steal that phone from your mommy?" he taunted.

"Nah! I found it right here a couple months ago!" Steve spat back, pointing at the fencepost near where he had discovered the cell phone.

"But it ain't none of your business where I got it, Doggie!"

Steve knew that was one of Doug's most hated nicknames, used exclusively by people trying to insult him.

Doug's memory began to clear. There was something about that phone. At first he couldn't recall why it seemed so familiar. Then, it hit him!

"Muncie—that camera belongs to Joey Paige! Give it to me!" Doug didn't recall why he connected the phone to Joey, but he was certain that it belonged to his friend.

Steve pulled back and began trying to find the photo he had just taken. His sister had shown him how to do it. He stepped off to the side of the small group to see what he could find.

He was amazed to discover pictures of a UFO floating over Calvin Dunn's barn.

He turned to show Josh, but just then, Nancy, the third unwelcome visitor, pushed her way past the two boys and glared at Doug. He considered her one of the most unlikeable people he had ever met. She had been held back in school, so she was older and larger than most of her classmates. Her very appearance was intimidating. It was rumored that she always carried a knife and that she had used it to kill and skin her neighbor's cat.

The rumor may have been apocryphal, but Doug believed it. Lindsay often pointed out to him that he was too gullible.

Nancy turned with a sneer to face Lindsay, who had stepped forward to stand with her arms crossed beside Doug.

At this moment, Tara arrived. Doug could tell by her demeanor that she was in distress, even more than usual. She looked dejected and scared, Doug thought, much like she had when he had spoken to her on their way home for lunch the first day of school. She was crying quietly but trying hard to hide it.

"Well, well, well! Look who it is, Little Tara Lastly!" Josh sneered as he took a step toward Tara. She seemed to shrink as the bully who was nearly a foot taller loomed over her. Doug stepped between the two.

"Back off, Tooney!" Doug warned.

Steve, in shock tried to show Josh the UFO photos, but he was busy harassing Tara. Josh noticed the bundle Tara was clutching close to her body.

"Whatcha got there, Weirdo?" he challenged as he reached around Doug, who reacted too slowly, and swiped at the kitchen towel. The towel and the metallic rod inside fell from Tara's grasp.

"Josh—wait! Look at this..." Steve began.

Doug was quick to make up for his slowness in fending off Josh. He scooped up the bundle as it hit the ground. Josh responded by again grabbing at the bundle, but hit Doug's arm instead, knocking Doug off balance and causing him to trip over a clump of dirt. Josh managed to snare and yank one corner of the towel as Doug fell. The towel unrolled and the metallic shaft fell to the ground. The towel landed next to it.

For a moment everyone stared at the items on the ground.

Steve tried again. "Tooney, ya gotta see this!" He shoved the cell phone in front of his friend.

"What's this?" Nancy demanded as she pushed Steve aside to get a better view of the metallic object that lay on the ground in the midst of the group of fifth graders.

"Everybody stop and lookit..." Steve tried again.

Tara stepped up beside Doug. Josh reached down and gripped the device in his right hand and started to boast, "It's mine now!"

He squeezed it tightly and held it above his head triumphantly, but his victory was short-lived; he let out a horrible shriek and let it drop to the ground. He grabbed his right hand with his left. Large rivulets of blood began seeping out between the fingers of both hands.

As everyone stared in amazement at what had transpired, Tara stepped forward and bent to gingerly retrieve the blue object. She knew what it could do. She carefully rewrapped it in the towel and walked past Josh, who had fallen to the ground and was thrashing around in agony.

In a voice that was much stronger than any of her classmates had ever heard, she called out, "That's the thing my Dad stole from the aliens! It's dangerous!"

Josh moaned in pain as he stumbled to his feet, still clutching his hands together. Tears were streaking his face.

Steve Muncie tried again as Josh danced about, screaming. This time, he showed Doug the photos. Doug's eyes opened wide as he stared at the phone's screen. Doug grabbed the phone to show Lindsay and Tara.

Suddenly, there was a flash of green light from the nearby farmhouse. As the fifth graders turned to look, a disk-shaped object arose from behind the barn and in a second zoomed to a place in the low-hanging overhead clouds. The kids broke and ran in every direction among the dead cornstalks, with the exception of Tara.

The small girl, who had always been extremely meek, held her ground and calmly unwrapped the towel to reveal the device. She carefully rested it in her fingers and shoved her right arm into the air.

She defiantly shouted at the scout ship, "If you're looking for this, come and get it!"

A collective gasp came from the other fifth graders.

The UFO came to an immediate stop over her head, hanging in mid-air as if suspended from the clouds by invisible wires. It appeared that its occupants had taken Tara up on her challenge. Tara shoved the blue wand even higher into the air, jutting out her chin in clear defiance.

As the others watched, a green light flashed toward the ground, but was partially blocked by some of the cornstalks that were higher than Tara's head. The corn stalks were yanked from the ground and began to rise toward the scout machine with their roots dangling below them and clods of dirt dropping away as they rose.

For a second, the green light only hit the left side of Tara's body and she was lifted unevenly off the ground.

"Tara! Just drop it and RUN!" Lindsay screamed.

Tara's fingers parted and the rod dropped free and landed at Doug's feet. He quickly picked it up and turned it over, very gingerly, in his hands. His thumb rubbed a slight bump on the device. A red light suddenly shot out of one end and struck the hovering spacecraft, gouging a hole in its underside.

Doug was startled and instantly released his grip on the alien device. The green light from the hovering scout machine vanished at once and the UFO moved away slowly, wobbling as it rose in the sky.

Tara, who had risen about six feet, fell immediately to the ground and smacked into the cornstalks, which crumpled beneath her weight, but also broke her fall. The ground was soft from a recent fall rain.

She immediately leaped to her feet and shouted, "I'm okay!"

The others stared as the UFO continued its rise, stabilized itself, then shot away. The six children paused long enough to take it all in, then—as a group—cheered spontaneously.

Then, Doug pulled out the phone and the group gathered around to study the photos Joey had taken in July on the night he disappeared.

Their moods were dimmed when Lindsay reminded everyone, "We still didn't catch an alien..." and the cheering died down.

Chapter Thirty: "The Fortress is Ready"

Alvin Selkirk returned home after a trip to Millardville to get groceries. He parked his dark blue SUV in the alley behind the parsonage and began lugging the plastic bags to the kitchen, which was near the rear of the huge structure.

When he finished putting away his groceries, he moved on to another task. He still had not been able to get in touch with Paul Sloan. He pulled his desk chair up to the computer to try again. He wanted to talk Paul into handling the Spring City reporter who was expected to arrive within the next week.

He had barely begun to hit the keys when he suddenly felt a pain. He clapped his right hand over his heart as the world started going black. He collapsed sideways onto the oval area rug, gasping for air. He was perspiring profusely. He struggled to his knees, half lying on the couch. Then the view in front of him shrank down to a pinpoint and he lost consciousness.

Sandy Romer saw all this through the camera she had hidden in the minister's study. She knew the time had come. She took her handgun from the lockbox in which she had stored it, put on her specially adapted fall jacket with an inside pocket designed like a holster, exited her mobile home, and strolled nonchalantly out the door and down the street.

She had phoned the school switchboard to leave a message that she wasn't feeling well and would be taking the day off. She turned left on the street before the schoolhouse and took the long way around to the parsonage, so she wasn't worried about being seen by anyone at the school.

After going another block, she turned right and made her way to the alley behind the parsonage, approaching the back door very cautiously. She felt in her pocket for the copy of the key she had stolen, and then returned, during a Sunday sermon a couple weeks earlier. She looked around one last time and inserted the key.

She crept down the hallway until she reached the door to the kitchen. She glanced across the hall to Selkirk's study, where she found the minister passed out on the oval area rug.

Her agency had developed a time-released drug with which she had coated the computer keys during the previous Sunday's church services. It had done its job. Sandy dragged the hefty minister fully onto the couch. She then pulled out her cell phone and punched in some numbers. When someone responded, she merely said, "The fortress is ready. Now I will move on to the next target."

She paused, listening to the voice on the other end. "Yes, the attic of the parsonage is large with plenty of room for the expected arrivals."

Her Dodge was parked along the highway near Millardville so Cheryl could take another turn behind the steering wheel. Suddenly a bright light appeared in the west and a scout machine rose over the horizon. Kattor quickly motioned the small group to get into the ditch next to the highway. The alien vehicle seemed to be wobbling crazily as it approached.

"There has been damage," Kattor commented without emotion. *"This is the one my people dealt with back near*

*the mountains. They were not destroyed as I had hoped.
However, they did suffer damage."*

Working their way through the woods across the highway
toward the area to which the UFO was headed, several men
in Army fatigues, camouflage clothing and hunting gear,
carrying a variety of firearms, moved quietly through the
woods toward the highway. They had spotted what they
hoped was an alien spacecraft and were determined to
locate it.

Leading the group was Dale Tooney, deftly and soundlessly
moving between the fir trees that skirted the farm fields.
Trailing him in single file were Jeffrey Dubold, Coach
Jepson, Ricky Borntrager, Chip Josephson and Andy
Pendleton. Hugo Massingall brought up the rear, a position
assigned by Dale because he wanted someone reliable at
the back in case someone approached them from behind—
or if any of the others got cold feet and tried to abandon the
mission.

Hugo was dependably loyal. Dale was disappointed that
Rita wasn't available, since she was the group's best shot.

Suddenly Dale raised his left hand and the group behind
him stopped without a sound. Dale pointed to the east
where a bright light was climbing unsteadily toward the
clouds.

The seven vigilantes brought their firearms to the ready,
but before they could do anything more, the object began
wobbling downward, out of sight behind the surrounding
trees.

The man next to Dale, Jeffrey Dubold, lifted binoculars to

his eyes in order to try to locate it, but he soon dropped them back down when it fell from view behind the treetops. Dale tapped him on his right shoulder and motioned for Dubold to follow him. The remainder of the group trailed along after them.

After a few minutes, the small, armed band emerged into a clearing. Dale pointed toward the far side. There was the alien vehicle, propped against the jagged trunks of a few trees that were sheared off near the ground. It was obvious that the scout machine had crashed.

As Dale and his compatriots huddled amid some bushes, unsure what to do next, a narrow wedge opened in the side of the glowing object and half a dozen small figures emerged somewhat unsteadily and staggered out onto the ground among the tree trunks.

Dale felt a rush of exhilaration. Rising to his feet, he took a quick aim and fired his weapon. One of the figures collapsed to the ground. As the other members of his vigilante force followed suit, a crescendo of shots echoed in the early morning air. The vigilantes rushed across the open ground toward the UFO, firing and whooping wildly as they ran. The alien bodies bounced with each round that struck them.

By the time they reached the far side of the clearing, the pale bodies were sprawled out on the ground. Dale, leading the group, pulled up short. He used the toe of his combat boot to turn over the first one he reached.

"Yeehaw! We got 'em, men! Every freakin one! We killed us a buncha aliens!" Dale shouted, dancing around wildly, waving his rifle in the air and firing it in celebration.

The others followed his example and soon the air was full

of gunshots and whooping.

After a while their excitement subsided. They looked around, trying to figure out what to do next. Andy Pendleton knelt next to one of the bodies and lifted it.

"This alien don't weigh nothing!" he proclaimed loudly.

Jeffrey Dubold bent over another one and added, "The bullets went clean through the bodies, and there ain't no blood or guts. These things are like some sort of dolls!"

Dale checked on the first one he had shot. "I don't believe it. These aren't even living aliens! They're robots or somethin'..."

As Dale examined the body, the bullet holes suddenly closed up. Dale dropped the body and turned to the others with a look of utter bewilderment. Suddenly one of the prostrate figures stirred for a moment, then rose rapidly to its feet. In a couple seconds, all the others had done the same.

"My God!" shouted Dale, his mouth falling open, but it was the last thing he would ever say. A red light forked out from a device in the hand of one of the creatures with a single bolt striking each member of the vigilantes one at a time and a second later, all seven men were dead on the ground.

In the next few days people would hear that Dale Tooney had mysteriously vanished, as had the high school football coach and a few others. Rickie Borntrager's wife noticed that he was gone but didn't have any desire for him to be found. Andy Pendleton was the only one reported to the authorities. Nobody seemed to miss Hugo Massingall—or even know who he was.

George Huit waited in a large black car with the darkened windows. He was parked on the blacktop road that ran next to a large farmhouse just south of Caperton that belonged to a man named Dunn. He knew the farmer was not there, thanks to action taken during the summer. Some of the visitors would be lodged on the farm, though most would be on the upper floor of the large parsonage in town, once the town had been "pacified."

Huit was becoming concerned that he hadn't heard back from the agent sent to take care of Peter Lapley and his family. That was a bad sign. He typed out coded instructions to direct Sandy Romer to check into it.

As he waited, his mind drifted back to that time twenty-two years earlier when he first became involved in this madness. He was a young college graduate applying for a government job. After undergoing a series of tests that included a key psychiatric evaluation, he was placed into an agency, a secret one. This delighted him, since this implied that his superior talents had been recognized. As part of his training, he was informed he would have to undergo a "challenge." He wasn't told what that would be.

It had happened in the middle of the night. He was awakened by bright lights shining through his bedroom window. The next thing he knew, he was being physically lifted into the air as the light altered into a pale green. His heart was pounding, racing so hard that he was sure it would explode.

In just a few seconds, though he wasn't sure exactly how long it was but felt that it had happened very quickly and without any sound, he found himself pulled inside a large disk-shaped vehicle. Knowing that he was being tested, he forced himself to calm down and his heart rate dropped considerably.

He had been placed on a metallic table in the middle of a room. He found that he couldn't move any part of his body, except for his eyes. He detected a dozen or more tall, pale figures on the periphery of his vision. He realized that he was in the presence of non-human creatures. At first he wanted to scream, but he squelched the urge, again reminding himself that this was only a test.

From among this crowd of creatures stepped an especially tall one. His eyes were deeply set and glowed red, giving him a sinister appearance. His enlarged cranium had several long, prominent, vertical veins that appeared and disappeared, as if in response to each heartbeat. Huit had the impression that this was their leader.

He moved toward Huit without making a sound, as if they were in zero gravity. He stopped and stared into the agent's eyes. He spoke without a voice; the words seemed to just appear in the human's mind. Again, Huit began to feel panic rising in his chest, but the stranger told him, *"It will all be well"* and he immediately realized that it would.

There were no words spoken, they just seemed to show up in George Huit's mind.

"You have been chosen from among your people to be our official contact. You have passed the initial test by remaining calm. Henceforth, you will do what we command. To not do so, would result in extreme measures. We will expand our involvement with your world, seeking what we need, and we will tolerate no resistance. You will be helping us. We will come back from time to time to instruct you further."

With those words still echoing in the agent's mind, the room around him began to dissolve and he again found himself back in his own bedroom. He could barely believe what had just happened. And, as the tall alien had told him, there were more visits and more specific requests.

In the following weeks, Huit was given a private office with a view of the U.S. Capitol. A special telephone line connected him to another human. At least he assumed it was a human, at some unknown location, where that human was given direct instruction on what the aliens wanted to be conveyed.

Huit was given the code name *Silent River*. The human at the other end was labeled *Opaque Orb*. Huit eventually saw these code names as a sort of grim, but accurate, description.

Huit could tell no one about all these things. He was clearly supposed to be *silent* while his mysterious contact was definitely *opaque*, in the sense that Huit could never see through his cover to know the entire story.

In subsequent contacts Huit learned other things. He wasn't the only one working with the aliens. There were other units involved, other branches of government. He was told that the U.S. military was involved in a secret arrangement to cover up alien crashes, particularly in the Rocky Mountains where the aliens were perfecting their technology. They were trying to adapt it to the Earth's conditions.

Huit was eventually informed that they were preparing for a war with enemies from other planets and wanted to be ready when the fighting came to Earth. What worked well in space or on their home planet wouldn't necessarily work in the Earth's atmosphere. They intended to have a tactical advantage by being more familiar with Earth than their enemies were.

The humans had to provide their latest, newly developed weapons and machinery for the aliens to practice on. This often resulted in deaths of human pilots, whose bodies were recovered by special *Recovery Teams*.

Recently one of the alien crafts had been badly damaged in a lightning storm during a war game with the U.S. Army, and a human had killed one of the alien pilots. That unfortunate sergeant had been dealt with in the manner that the aliens instructed. Also, this Peter Lapley here in Caperton had been claiming loudly that he had been abducted and was immune to the alien technology.

He had also been marked for elimination.

Huit was aware that there was another individual in the area whom the aliens wanted to eliminate, Paul Sloan, who had challenged Huit at the Caperton community meeting. But, they hadn't asked Huit and his team to take on that project. They apparently considered him enough of a threat that they intended to take care of him themselves.

They were aware, however, that some of the opposing aliens were protecting Sloan, so the job had been difficult to complete; they didn't want to make too big a commotion by using advanced methods such as the explosive light wave technology that they possessed.

They were biding their time. They had, however, kidnapped a friend of Sloan's whom they also considered a threat, for some reason unclear to Huit. After his own difficult encounter with Sloan at that community meeting in Caperton, Huit was hopeful that they would make him pay painfully for his impertinence.

With his government job there was no time for a personal life. In fact, Huit was afraid to even attempt to have one. It was difficult enough just dealing with all this himself but having to worry about friends and family would be far too much pressure. A couple times he hadn't moved quickly enough to keep his overseers happy, and they had let him know that they would allow few failures before taking extremely negative action. He didn't have to ask what THAT would be.

Friends and family would just provide further targets for THEM to use to put pressure on him, or perhaps punish him. So, now, when they said *Jump,* he jumped.

He used to wonder what would happen if the government resisted and he wondered why they didn't try. Then, it became clear to him that the aliens had made a deal that didn't totally favor them but did buy the silence of the nation's leaders.

The U.S. government and, he presumed, other governments around the world, had been given some scraps of information on ways to develop advanced technology, mostly of a military nature. The aliens only shared a little bit, obviously not enough to permit humans to use it against them. Thus, silence was bought by both bribes and threats, the carrot and the stick.

In addition, there was a rumor going around, among his team members, mostly, since they had not received as much information about the alien agenda, that information on additional sources of energy could not be made known to the general public, since the powerful oil companies would be put out of business and the auto industry would be crippled.

Huit thought that this was merely disinformation to distract anyone who got too close to the truth. The aliens weren't about to share information that would allow humans to challenge them out in space or even on Earth. Huit had also come to his own conclusion that it was part of the alien plan to keep countries at war with one another so they couldn't unite to oppose the aliens.

With this current assignment, he didn't know what the aliens were going to do with the large house he had been sent to secure, but that's what he had been told he had to do. All he knew was that there was a place in this village that had special properties that the aliens in charge needed. That is why he and his team had come to Caperton.

It was such a small town that there was little chance that the operation would be noticed as long as they were careful. A person could sometimes walk down the middle of Main Street in Caperton without encountering anybody or being seen by the people huddled in their houses along the way.

Also, he had been ordered to eliminate this Lapley guy, whom the aliens had abducted. Huit was told that they had tried an experimental brain procedure to make him more compliant. The procedure had worked well on some other planets, Huit understood, but with Peter Lapley there was an unexpected side effect of increasing his intelligence. At least that's what Huit had been told.

There were also a couple of children who had gotten in the way. Children could be difficult, according to Opaque Orb, since they didn't always accept without question what they were ordered to do and, like Lapley, they weren't always easily managed.

Lapley was actually quite intelligent, they discovered, and the changes they made in his brain chemistry merely broke down his longtime resistance to learning. Huit wasn't sure about all this; it sounded preposterous. The aliens often began early to try to brainwash children and periodically returned to give them sort of booster shots, but Peter Lapley had never been one of their targets.

He had learned through Opaque Orb that there were many other groups of alien visitors. Some were allies of the one called Kattor and his Army, others were opposed to them and led by someone called Attir. There were also neutrals who just seemed to be observing Earth for scientific purposes or out of curiosity.

However, they had all been visiting Earth for decades and even centuries, maybe even millennia. Huit wondered if there were other *handlers* like him for each group of the visitors, but that information was beyond his *need-to-know* level.

Huit had also learned that the motivations of the aliens could not be analyzed. Maybe there were elements of the plan that had not been explained to him. Every time he thought he had the aliens figured out, they would do something that would totally surprise him, such as destroying a village in a landslide, which Huit didn't think was a safe thing for them to do, from THEIR standpoint. It created too much public attention.

It was lucky for them and him that the reporter investigating the incident had vanished and nobody else had really pursued it.

He could only surmise that they would prefer, if possible, to not be bothered by curious humans, but they had no reluctance to perform dramatic acts of violence, such as the landslide, when necessary to eliminate anyone who was too troublesome. Huit assumed that the aliens had somehow diverted attention away from that event. Or, perhaps, they had developed a way to induce mass amnesia.

He often wondered how much the government knew about the aliens. He knew there had long been a rumor that the President, whoever it might be at the time, knew the whole truth. He wasn't sure about that. Maybe there was someone in the Pentagon or Department of Defense who knew and maybe not involving the President provided for "plausible deniability". It certainly would be a burden for anyone to keep such a secret and, perhaps, the President didn't need that distraction.

Huit was convinced that there was nothing anyone could do about it, anyway.

Huit frowned. His reverie always led him to the same dead end. He didn't really like knowing what he knew, but there was no way out of this responsibility that he could see. His only choice was to continue to try to please the aliens and not think about possible implications and not try to look too far into the future. This had turned him into a practiced liar and even made him an accomplice in murder.

He'd started out wanting to help others by getting rid of bad guys. Now, he was one of the bad guys, perhaps the *baddest* of them all. Maybe he was helping mankind by keeping the aliens from destroying the planet. Again, however, he didn't really know if they were here to help or hurt Earth's residents. It may be to do one or the other or even both.

More likely, though, the aliens didn't really care. Huit's life had become an ongoing bad dream, even a nightmare. After all these years, though, he didn't know any other way to live. Maybe it was just as well that he was accustomed to this strange truth.

Chapter Thirty-One: Alien Communications

Sandy Romer approached the Lapley house. It was close to the parsonage, in fact, a block north of it, but most houses in the tiny village could be described as "close" to any other thing in town, especially from the viewpoint of a native Chicagoan such as Sandy Romer.

She knocked, but there was no answer. She tried the front door and found it unlocked. She chuckled to herself as she shook her head, wondering that the people in small towns were so trusting, so careless. Back in the neighborhood where she had grown up, nobody trusted their neighbors.

She pushed the door open and called out, "Mrs. Lapley? It's me, Tara's teacher. I just stopped by to ask how Tara is doing, since you phoned to say she was ill."

She knew it was unusual for a teacher to personally check on ill students, but she needed a cover story in case a problem arose.

There was no response, so she began exploring the house. She pulled her handgun from her inside jacket pocket and held it next to her face with both hands in a ready position, glancing around furtively as she entered each new room.

When she found nothing on the bottom floor, except for the mess in the kitchen, she began to ascend the stairs as quietly as she could; some of the steps, however, creaked loudly. She tensed and stayed close to the wall, carefully perusing the space ahead. She reached the top floor and found herself at one end of a long hallway. She checked each room as she proceeded, finding nobody, coming at last to the room at the end. The door stood open.

She took one glance and drew back involuntarily.

There on the floor at the end of the bed was her fellow agent, Walter Turner. There was a small, clean hole in the center of his forehead.

She hesitantly approached his body to investigate. She checked under the bed and noticed a handgun near the headboard. She pulled it out carefully and discovered it had a full clip of ammunition and had probably not been fired, unless Turner had reloaded. She hadn't seen any shell casings or holes in the walls or furniture, so that was unlikely.

Sandy wasn't too unhappy about his death, since he was a rather unpleasant individual. But this development was entirely unexpected. Having found no one else there, she knelt to examine the body. She couldn't see how this had happened. The entry hole and exit opening in the back of the skull were the same size; she had expected to find a larger exit wound. That's what a bullet would do. It must not have been a gunshot, but *what*, then?

Then she discovered the metal tackle box underneath some of the piled-up clothing that had been dumped on the floor. There was a hole in it matching the one in Turner's head.

Sandy made a mental note to do some research on what could cause the small wound to the front of his skull without blowing out the back of his brain, but she had other things to do right then. An agency forensics team could be called in, if there was time, but she needed to get on with her assignment.

She did briefly allow her mind to wander. She hadn't been with the department that long, since she was recruited immediately following her college graduation, much like George Huit. She was told that all her school loans would be covered if she joined a special unit of the government.

Her parents had both died while she was in high school and her aunt and uncle, who took her in, didn't seem to really care about her future and chose not to support her after graduation, so this offer came at a perfect time. She was interviewed by George Huit, who also interviewed several others in her graduating class including that mousy little nerd Renee Hanold, whom Sandy hated.

"Such a teacher's pet!" Sandy muttered to herself. "Always thinks she knows all the answers!"

Huit had apparently seen something in Sandy that would make her a good fit for this secret organization. She didn't know why she was chosen, but she found that her natural distrust of others seemed to match well with her career as an undercover agent. Also, she loved the adventure of it all. She knew how to deceive people and she enjoyed learning how to use a handgun.

She shook her head and tried to regain her focus on the current assignment. She finished checking out the interior rooms and moved downstairs to check the basement and garage.

Just as she exited through the back door and began moving toward the garage, a large car pulled into the driveway.

One glance told Ms. Romer that it was the Mayor's car, but why was he here and why had the microphone she had secretly placed behind his ear ceased to function? She had noticed while she was at the parsonage that the bug had gone silent. If not for that malfunction, she probably would have had more information on where the Mayor was, and she could have avoided being caught in the middle of this operation.

Then, she noticed that Peter Lapley was in the passenger seat. Sandy had met him at a parent-teacher conference for Tara. She quickly shoved her gun back into the inside pocket of her jacket. She glanced up nervously as she waited to greet Ralph Osgood and Peter Lapley.

Meanwhile, back on the highway just outside Millardville, the small group of travelers were shocked by the sound of gunfire from the woods on the other side of the highway. Rader motioned everyone to get down. He moved toward the edge of the pavement.

Kattor stepped forward to join Teddy as they carefully approached the road. At this time of morning, they were able to cross without concern about traffic. They soon were edging down into the ditch on the other side and climbing up the embankment on the far side. They approached the trees.

Rader heard Kattor thinking, *"Take care. They are just ahead."* Then he drew out his wand and entered the tree line with the sergeant following closely at his heels.

When they came to the edge of the clearing, Kattor held up his hand. Looking to the other side, they beheld the aliens hurrying around their crashed vehicle.

"They are attempting to make repairs," said the voice in Rader's head. Kattor pointed his wand device and a red light shot out, dividing into half a dozen forks, piercing each of the six bodies, which immediately collapsed to the ground. Rader's mouth dropped open in amazement.

As Kattor and the sergeant rushed across the clearing, they came upon the dead bodies of the vigilantes. None had any sign of injury, but all were obviously lifeless.

Rader's puzzlement was observed by his companion.

"These humans made the mistake of trying to kill my foes. They were not aware that bullets wouldn't work."

Rader realized that, like the other messages, those did not seem to be actual words, just the gist of the comments. The aliens likely didn't have a word for "bullets". If their species had ever used such weapons, it was likely centuries earlier.

Kattor continued. *"It is much too far and too dangerous to send living beings across light years of space, which is why my people use dimensional travel. Our enemies primarily use what you might call androids. They are not living beings, though they are imbued with what your people humorously call artificial intelligence."*

Kattor paused and then added, *"How can any intelligence be artificial? Intelligence just IS. It's a quality that is available to any animate being. That is why they are able to perform the functions needed to pilot their craft and do what they do with your people. Living ones were always sent as a safeguard, to ward off any kind of revolution. It's rare, but it does happen; the Dultog Planet incident, is an example."*

Teddy found this rambling history lesson extremely boring and was able to tune it out, but Kattor's thoughts suddenly exploded in his brain, shocking him back to awareness. The alien was apparently trying to be sure he paid attention. The sergeant experienced a searing pain in his skull, but it was brief.

"The androids are made with a safeguard chip that requires them to be accompanied by living beings. Without the presence of living ones, the androids do not function. The vehicles are pre-programmed to reach their destinations."

"*The androids are inactivated until they reach their objective, such as your world, and the living one is automatically revived from a suspended state at that point and activates the androids. They then begin their efforts to destroy your world. Those from my world, as I have informed you, use other methods of travel and we have solved all the dangers.*"

Kattor was examining the lifeless bodies. He turned back to Rader and added, "*My wand destroyed their intelligence centers and made them into lifeless shells.*"

Since Rader was worried that Kattor might again violently assault his brain, he managed to frame a question. "So, if a living alien is needed for these androids to work, where is he now?"

Rader thought this would block Kattor from again attacking his thoughts, since it would prove that he was paying attention. He considered that maybe he had found a hole in Kattor's explanation. "Did he escape?"

Kattor would not be deterred, however. "*No escape would be allowed. The living one must have been taken prisoner when my people blasted this scout machine back in the mountain part of this world. Since these androids were already programmed, they were able to continue on their mission up to this point.*"

The sergeant didn't believe all that the alien was saying. He was beginning to see the explanations as questionable, rather convoluted and self-serving. He found himself a bit annoyed that Kattor was bragging about the superiority of his own people, but he dropped the thought.

Kattor may have heard what he was thinking, but if he did, the alien didn't respond. The sergeant decided to focus on how glad he was that the threat from the "bad" aliens had ended and thus avoid thinking negative thoughts about this alien.

He had learned how to suspend judgment during his years on the recovery team where there was no room for questioning what was happening. It was an old habit, easily reactivated.

Back across the highway, huddled down to be sure they weren't exposed to gunfire, were Cheryl and her cousin Dana. Cheryl felt sorry for her cousin, who seemed to have had a rough time during the past few years. She looked Dana in the eyes, searching for any sign that her cousin was recovered from her ordeal and took this opportunity to hug her and ask what had happened to her.

Dana smiled weakly. "I don't really recall much about it. I was on assignment to investigate a landslide in Colorado, but when I reached the site of the buried village something happened, and I can't remember much else until the sergeant and his friend pulled me out of a cave."

"I think I had been captured by strange creatures who appeared somewhat human but were quite scary looking. I recall that one had a long scar on the left side of his face. They had long faces and large skulls with bulging veins. It was terrifying! Those memories stay with you. I do have memories of that much, but that's all."

Cheryl saw Rader emerge from the trees on the other side of the highway. He motioned to her to cross to his side of the road. She assisted Dana in crossing the pavement and the sergeant then led them into the woods.

Cheryl gasped when she saw Dale's body; she had known him when she was in grade school and Dale was a senior. Everyone in the school had considered him a hero. Now his lifeless body lay sprawled awkwardly amid the overgrown weeds that edged the copse of trees.

"What happened?" Cheryl asked.

"It appears that these humans came upon the occupants of that crashed scout machine and they were killed." Kattor's explanation, of course, was totally lacking in emotion. *"I have eliminated the scout machine occupants."*

"Now what do we do?" asked Cheryl. "Are we safe?"

She looked at Rader and Kattor. Kattor tugged his hood down lower over his head, carefully covering the scar that ran alongside his face, as he turned to the group.

"No. There are more of my enemies in the vicinity. These bodies can stay where they are. Some of their compatriots will be along soon to dispose of the debris. They will remove the androids as well as the human bodies and the scout machine. They will try to avoid having their presence revealed to the people of your civilization who reside nearby. That is why they act promptly when something like this occurs. That is also why their scout machines are most often present only after your world goes dark. Daylight activity would be difficult to obscure. We must move on before they arrive. They will not be friendly."

"Why does our government go to so much effort to deny that you people exist?" Rader had begun the question with his voice but stopped speaking partway through and let Kattor read his thoughts.

"You wish to know why your government would try to deflect interest in such things."

Kattor completed Teddy's thought as if deliberately letting the other humans in on the question.

"Did it ever occur to you that they have no choice other than to accept what their alien handlers demand of them?"

Kattor didn't use the word "alien" but that is how the sergeant interpreted it.

"It's the same reason your military was forced to help them develop better scout machines and light beam weapons. My foes, the Dominants, have so much power that nobody on your backward planet could resist them, though they are not yet ready to let their presence be widely known. But they are about to begin their conquest. That is why I directed Cheryl Hunter to transport us to this place. It will begin soon if I, with your help, cannot stop them."

"This is why I have chosen you and the other humans to be my underlings in this project. You will help defeat my enemies..."

Then he added, *"...even if it requires the death of some of your people."*

Rader detected some scrambling of the telepathic part of the message, as though Kattor had backtracked and edited his own thoughts.

"Strange," the sergeant whispered under his breath. Kattor shot him a sideways glance.

"Let's get back to the car," Rader suggested. He had to struggle to again avoid feeling some level of contempt or resentment of Kattor and his self-congratulatory attitude.

Rader had obeyed those in authority for most of his life. That helped him make the high school sports teams he tried out for, though it had never occurred to him that it also restricted his ability to improvise solutions to problems which had not been covered in his training.

Blind obedience also helped him survive in the recovery squad. *Just do your duty*. That was his motto. Then, when the flare gun incident happened and he was the one who was punished and even his commanding officer, Colonel Webber, failed to come to his assistance and had also aided THEM in trying to administer a death sentence, the sergeant's sense of duty evaporated.

Now, Rader knew he would have difficulty obeying or believing anyone, including the alien. He was aware that Kattor probably knew of his distrust. This mind-reading stuff was just too complicated.

Back in the countryside near Caperton, Paul was worried and lost in thought. The alien with the scar had told him not to go to Caperton. Should he heed this warning?

Putting his own life at risk was one thing, but endangering others was not acceptable under most circumstances. Nicholas Dunbar was a necessary exception. Kathy and Deke shouldn't have to pay for the results of Paul's difficulties with the aliens.

Suddenly, as if in response to his inner turmoil, the computer screen lit up, but it wasn't yellow as before. It was a pale blue. Paul cautiously wheeled himself to the desk, hesitated, then reached out to tap the *Enter* key. The screen went dark for a moment, then came back to the blue color. This time there was a different alien, one without a scar and who faced Paul directly.

"This is a short message, Paul Sloan. We know that Kattor has warned you not to go to Caperton. Our people ask that you go. Cheryl Hunter will be there soon, and you are the only one who can save her. Your planet's future depends on you. Your friends must also go."

Paul was about to reply, but the screen suddenly went black.

Paul thought for a moment, then wheeled over to the hall closet near the kitchen. He pulled the door open reached inside and retrieved the shotgun his grandfather had left him in his will. He also grabbed a box of shells. He stashed everything in his old Army duffel bag and hooked it over the back of his wheelchair. He had to be ready for any problems that might occur.

Then he wheeled around to go awaken Deke and Kathy.

Chapter Thirty-Two: To Catch an Alien, Part Three

The sky was growing dark with storm clouds, or so it appeared. There wasn't rain in the forecast, so many people who had been enjoying the mild autumn weather cursed the weatherman on the Spring City TV station for not predicting this event.

High in the sky the dark clouds roiled ominously, but they weren't actually clouds. They were generated by a simulator and emitted from a large triangular aircraft that floated noiselessly in the air. The "cloud" moved slowly and steadily toward Caperton.

A smaller, round scout machine dropped alongside it. Inside, Marla Brashear and Laurine Fraley stared blankly from the translucent tubes in which they had been encased. A childlike figure stood in the space between them, holding an infant and smiling grimly, rocking from side to side to soothe the baby.

At the top of Main Hill, Minnie Boyd looked out her screen door as she noticed that the sky was growing dark. "We're going to have a real sopper of a rain!" she announced to her daughter Delores, Ralph's wife, who was sipping coffee at Minnie's kitchen table. This was a daily ritual that Minnie insisted on.

Delores responded with a perfunctory, "Yes, Mother."

She did not really enjoy coffee, at least not with her mother, but needed to keep peace in the family. If Ralph ever found out that his wife and her mother didn't get along, there would be trouble; Ralph and his mother-in-law were very close.

Alvin Selkirk stirred groggily on the couch in his study. He couldn't recall what had happened, but he had a vague feeling of dread. He tried to shake himself fully awake, but all he managed to do was fall off the side of the couch. He lapsed back into darkness as he lay on the thickly braided oval area rug that covered the original wood flooring in the center of the room.

Renee was nearing Caperton. Her cell phone buzzed on the console between the bucket seats of her car. She picked it up and quickly checked the message. It had the attached photo of a young woman with long auburn hair. She knew without further explanation that she was looking at the visage of her target, forwarded to her by agency headquarters.

She also recognized that this was Sandy Romer, a former cadet at the academy. The two had not been friendly. Renee knew this would be a challenge. Both were technically working for the same federal government, but now they were on opposing sides. The message also said that ambulances and additional agents were being dispatched to Caperton in anticipation of casualties. That wasn't an encouraging comment.

Near Millardville, Kattor ushered the small group back across the highway to the ditch next to Cheryl's car. *"My enemies are coming. We must remove ourselves from sight. That dark cloud is not a cloud. It is a disguise for their main vessel,"* he reported calmly via telepathy.

"They will be dispatching a salvage vehicle down to clean up the crash site. They will not be happy if they see us."

Even as he spoke, a small, glowing disk dropped through the thickening mist above their heads, straight into the wooded area they had just vacated. In only a few seconds, the object arose from the clearing in the middle of the wooded area, followed by another object, which was towed in a green light emanating from the first one. Both vehicles accelerated and were gone from sight into the dark cloud above within seconds.

The cloud itself began drifting to the south and west, in the direction of Caperton, which was totally opposite the usual wind pattern for that time of year.

The alien androids and the bodies of Dale Tooney's vigilante group were also sucked up into the sky.

The group hiding in the ditch by the highway stared in amazement. Kattor hurried them back into the Dodge, with Cheryl again driving, and they resumed their mission with the alien providing telepathic directions. Just south of Millardville they turned onto an intersecting highway and headed for Caperton.

On the western edge of Caperton, Doug, Lindsay, Tara and the other three fifth graders had fled the cornfield and were huddled in the living room of Doug's nearby house. Both of Doug's parents worked in Millardville, so the kids had the house to themselves.

This wasn't normal, since Doug's parents hadn't been sure Doug could be left home alone, but they discussed it and decided that he was old enough to be left by himself, plus he didn't appear to be really ill or have a fever.

His mother was still a bit nervous about leaving her eleven

year old son alone, so she took the precaution of contacting their next-door neighbor, Mrs. Caddell, to ask her to check in on him periodically. Doug's mother was still worried, but she had something important to do at work, so she chose to risk it.

Doug's father pooh-poohed her for her doubts. Eleven-year-old boys were old enough to take care of themselves for a few hours.

Tara led a still-whimpering Josh into the kitchen, where Doug had told her bandages and antibiotic ointment were stored. Nancy also came along, saying she knew something about cuts.

After treating the wound as best she and Nancy knew how, and wrapping it tightly in a bandage, Tara looked at Josh.

"Do you believe me now?" she challenged him. "You saw the pictures on the phone, and you saw a real UFO up close."

"I...I...I saw it, but it can't be real" Josh stammered. Then, immediately contradicting himself, he added, "Your father must have been telling the truth." Finally, he conceded, "Yep. I was wrong. I'm s-sorry, Tara."

Tara put away the supplies and walked past Josh into the living room. Nancy followed her. Josh, holding his bandaged right hand in his left, trailed sheepishly behind them.

They found Doug and Steve sitting on the couch. Doug was still angry at the three intruders who had spoiled their plan and had almost gotten Tara abducted. Lindsay, however—in her typical manner—had moved past any desire for recriminations and was trying to decide what to do next. She was leaning against the door frame, lost in thought.

No one noticed the black sedan with darkened windows that was barely visible parked next to Calvin Dunn's farmhouse a couple hundred yards to the south of the McGees' house. The dried cornstalks no longer obstructed the view as they did during the summer.

George Huit had, however, noticed movement at the house and brought his binoculars up to his eyes and focused on the six children as they left the cornfield. He had been lost in thought about his past and missed the scout machine that had dropped out of the darkened sky just moments earlier, a major blunder on his part. The fact that they were children did not allay the uneasy feeling he now had in his stomach about what he was observing.

At the McGee house Lindsay was taking charge once more. "We need to try again with our plan. It almost worked the first time, so we're not giving up now! We made a mistake standing out in the open like that. It just made it too easy for them to swoop in and try to zap Tara—with the metal thing—up into their flying saucer thing. We need to lure an individual alien into the open where we can use the net and duct tape."

She turned to Josh, Steve and Nancy. "Will you help us this time?"

Steve had been huddled with Doug, looking at the cell phone photos. All three nervously looked up at Lindsay. The three appeared uncertain at first until Josh gulped and spoke up.

"If Tara can be that brave, so can I!" Josh sounded confident, but bit his lower lip, which he did on the rare times when he wasn't. The other two glanced at each other, then also nodded.

"Alright, then!" Lindsay turned to Doug. "You and Josh need to handle the net. Steve and Nancy will tape up the alien once he's in the net. I'll take the metal thing and be the bait this time. Tara, you stand by the back door and be ready to slam it after the alien chases me inside."

Then, she had another inspiration. "Let's make the place as crowded as we can so it will be hard for him to escape. Push all the chairs in the kitchen into the living room. We'll force him to follow the path we make. Just leave enough space for me to run in front of the couch. Doug and Josh can hide behind the couch and be ready to throw the net over the alien when he follows me. Nancy and Steve can handle the tape."

Josh protested that he might have trouble throwing the net with his injured and bandaged hand. Lindsay thought for a few seconds and said, "Just do your best." She didn't always remember that others might not have her positive attitude. "Doug can handle most of the net."

Doug was once again amazed at Lindsay's take charge attitude and bravery. Josh, Steve and even Nancy looked a bit fearful, but were afraid to admit it in front of the others.

Lindsay and Tara handed the net and duct tape to the designated individuals.

Lindsay turned to Tara, who had returned from the kitchen with the towel-wrapped device. Lindsay held out her hand and Tara carefully unrolled the towel, gently dropping the blue wand onto her palm, warning her, "Remember—it's sharp!"

Lindsay nodded silently in response, carefully cradling the metal rod in her right hand as she turned toward the back door. On the way out of the house, she spied Doug's Cubs' hat hanging on a hook and grabbed it. Placing it on her head, she announced to no one in particular, "For good luck."

Once Lindsay was outside, she noticed that the sky was growing very dark.

A sky machine drifted above the clouds, unseen by people below. On board were Jay Brashear and John Lundy, a recent addition. Both were immobilized.

In the driveway next to the Lapley house, Sandy wasn't sure what to do to get out of her situation. She had been caught exiting the house by its owner, Peter Lapley. Sandy had just shoved her handgun into her inside jacket pocket. Mayor Osgood and Peter had exited the mayor's car and were staring at her. Sandy tried to think of a way out of this dilemma.

Suddenly, a small, green car whipped around the corner from Main Street and slid to a stop on some gravel behind the mayor's car. A woman with short, blondish hair leaped from the driver's side. She had a handgun of her own clutched in her right hand.

"Stop right where you are, Sandy Romer!" Renee fixed a solid stare on Sandy. "Keep your hands where I can see them! Take that hand out of your pocket...very slowly!"

Renee leaned forward on her car, gripping her gun in both hands with her elbows resting on the hood.

Sandy knew she had two choices: comply and probably lose her job when Huit found out she had failed, or try to fight her way out.

She shoved her hand further into her jacket and yanked out her gun.

She pointed it at Peter Lapley first; he was her main target and she believed she could take him down and also get Renee. How she relished that opportunity! She squeezed the trigger.

Peter anticipated her action and moved surprisingly fast to duck out of the way, but Ralph, standing right behind him, wasn't so lucky. He was hit in the left shoulder. His face lost all its color as he glanced down at the blood trickling from the wound; with a shocked expression the mayor collapsed immediately.

Sandy swept her arm to her left and fired again. The shot missed Renee and lodged in her bullet-resistant windshield. Renee returned fire and the round from her gun struck the teacher in her right shoulder.

The force of the shot spun Sandy around. Her arm fell to her side and her fingers released the gun, which clattered on the driveway and bounced onto the grass edging the pavement. Sandy screamed in pain and collapsed. Renee was on her in a second, securing her in handcuffs while she writhed in the driveway.

Just then the two Millardville physicians turned off the highway onto Main Street. The gathering darkness made it almost impossible to see, but Ty stopped just a block into town and went into Joe Paige's Bar to ask the proprietor for directions to the Lapley house, as they wanted to talk to Peter.

"Go south one block. It's on the corner on the same side of the street as this tavern," Joe said. It was very clear and concise guidance.

While the doctors were getting directions, two ambulances from Millardville turned onto Main Street and headed south. Ty and Wally jumped back into the car and followed the ambulances, which drove to the back of the house where they were already going. They parked across the street from the Lapley home and got out to see if there was any way they could help.

As they approached the ambulances, Ralph Osgood regained consciousness and looked around. He was being given oxygen and looked very confused. His face was twisted in agony. His left arm was in a sling, but it was a nonlethal wound.

Wally found the waitress from the Bluebird Café in discussion with an EMT. He approached her with a quizzical expression on his face. His first assumption was that Renee must be a resident of Caperton who had witnessed a shooting in her neighborhood. Then he noticed that one of the two patients—a woman with reddish hair and a blood stain on her jacket sleeve —was handcuffed and being placed in an ambulance.

Wally approached Renee to ask for an explanation. As he neared her, he noticed that she was sliding a handgun into a holster inside her jacket.

Renee filled him in, describing how she had shot Sandy Romer after the teacher had shot the mayor. "I had to shoot her. She had just shot the mayor and was about to shoot another man, so I shot *her*."

Wally was surprised that she described all this as if it were the most natural thing in the world for a waitress to shoot someone to save someone else's life.

Seeing that Wally was still perplexed, Renee pulled her

identification badge out of her jacket pocket to show him. Then, seeing that the normally outgoing doctor was still stupefied, she held out her hand and smiled.

"Hi, I'm Renee. I'm a waitress." That broke the tension, and both smiled.

While Sandy Romer was being loaded into an ambulance, Renee realized that someone was missing from the crime scene: the short man who had almost been shot when the mayor was hit.

Also missing was Sandy Romer's handgun. This was important evidence. Renee had a hunch that if she could find Peter Lapley she would also find the gun.

She signaled one of the agents who had arrived at the same time as the ambulances, and he followed her toward the front of the house. Two additional agents climbed into the back of the ambulance carrying Sandy Romer.

As the ambulance departed, the two physicians looked around and noticed a small group of people huddled on the lawn of the house just across the street. They walked over to see if anyone else had been injured.

Carl Johnson's house was only two blocks away and he had just gone out to his front lawn to check out the darkening sky. When he heard the shots fired at the Lapley house, he jumped into his patrol car and slammed his foot on the accelerator. This was his first big chance to deal with real crime!

Spewing gravel and screeching his tires, he sped toward the Lapley house in the gathering darkness and promptly crashed into the large oak tree in their front yard. He wasn't injured, but he remained in his car for a minute. He wanted to do something to help, but first he wanted to be sure the shooting was done. No sense in charging into the middle of a gunfight!

He waited until the ambulance carrying the schoolteacher departed to get out and investigate. The sight of the crumpled front end of his beautiful new car almost made him cry.

Paul turned right from the highway onto Main Street. The sky had become increasingly dark, and it was becoming difficult to see more than a few feet ahead of the van. In the back seat, Kathy had been trying to reach Lee by phone, but the call wouldn't go through. Paul sensed her frustration.

"Don't worry. This fog can't hug the ground for long. When it lifts, the phone service should improve." Actually, Paul wasn't sure of this; he just wanted Kathy to stay calm.

Deke, in the front seat, suddenly grabbed Paul's right arm. Paul looked at him, discovering the same change in his countenance he had witnessed when he first found Deke in his house. Deke's skin became pale, and his eyes appeared to recede in their sockets until they were just glowing red ovals. This lasted for only a few seconds, then he returned to normal.

"I need to get out here!" Deke's voice sounded stronger than Paul had ever heard it.

He applied pressure on the hand-brake lever just as Deke opened the door and hopped out, before the van had completely stopped.

Deke stumbled forward for a couple steps before gaining his balance. With a perfunctory wave to Paul, Deke began jogging west on a side street. He had no idea why he had the overwhelming urge to do this, but he sensed that someone at a nearby house needed his help.

While the heavy fog made it difficult for Paul and Kathy to see, Deke found that it didn't impede his vision. It seemed to dissipate as he neared the western edge of town. He was able to discern a young child wearing a baseball cap exiting the back door of a house, holding something shiny and metallic. At the same time, Deke noticed something bright and glowing hovering above the house.

Suddenly, a beam of green light shot down from the hovering object, nearly striking the child, who immediately headed for the back door of the house. The object in the sky circled around to the other side of the dwelling and after barely a second, moved to a third position. Deke concluded that the pilot was seeking the child inside the house by looking through the windows.

The silvery craft finally settled in the back yard. A narrow slit opened on one side and a slender figure wearing a copper-colored jumpsuit climbed out. In its hand was a long, glowing scepter. Deke sensed that this was some sort of weapon. The copper-colored person was planning to use it on the child with the baseball cap.

Upon observing this, Deke decided there was no time to waste, and he bounded up the steps to the front porch. He began banging on the door.

Doug pulled back the living room drapes and peered out the window in response to the pounding. When he saw a rather pale person he didn't recognize, he considered that it might be an alien trap and refused to open the door.

Lindsay had rushed through the back door with the alien in pursuit, holding the scepter. Tara, braver than ever in her life, waited for both to fully enter the house and shoved the door shut. Doug turned away from the living room window when he heard the commotion behind him. He was unable to get back to his station behind the couch before Lindsay went charging by.

Despite their plan, the kids all dropped the things they were holding—the duct tape, the net, the wand—and scattered in all directions in panic, colliding with the jumble of furniture.

Lindsay, however, quickly regained her cool and stopped to pick up the wand. She lifted it high over her head and screamed out the rallying cry they had chosen: "*For Joey!*"

Lindsay's voice was powerful and shrill, an almost physical force penetrating the others to their bones.

Doug immediately snapped out of his fear-induced panic and grabbed the net from the couch where he had ditched it on his way to check on the pounding at the front door. Josh, again biting his lower lip, which he did habitually when under stress, moved to help Doug, though Josh wasn't much help because of his bandaged hand. Steve rejoined Nancy and again began to unwind the duct tape which they found harder to do than they expected. They did manage to tear off a strip about four feet in length.

The alien ducked as Doug and Josh threw the net in the air. Doug realized as they did this that they should have practiced it first, since it wasn't as easy as he imagined it would be.

The alien ducked and the net flew past him, with just part of it landing on his head as he turned to point his scepter at the boys, who then shrank back in fear. Tara and Lindsay, using her free hand, made a grab for the discarded net and threw it back over the alien.

Doug and Josh recovered their composure and seized the ends of the net, pulling down hard on it. This surprised the alien and knocked the scepter loose. It fell on the couch, where Tara was waiting to pounce on it.

Steve and Nancy tried to wrap the tape around the alien struggling with the net but were only partially successful. He twisted and thrashed about in desperation. As he did so, he noticed the stairs leading to the next floor and, with a sudden effort, shook free of the net and began scrambling up the steps.

Josh was willing to let him go, as was Nancy, but Steve and Doug raced after him. At the landing midway up the stairs, the alien encountered the window overlooking the back yard and—pausing for only a second—threw himself through the glass.

He was badly cut by the shards, something that truly shocked him since he had never encountered glass on his home world and didn't know the pain that being cut would produce. When he landed on the dead grass of the lawn, he was momentarily stunned.

Deke appeared from around the side of the house and with a couple long strides, threw himself into the air, landing on the dazed alien.

Lindsay, Tara, and Nancy had picked up the net and duct tape and made a dash for the back door. Josh, feeling guilty for his cowardice, trailed after them, but had the presence of mind to grab the scepter off the couch. He didn't know what exactly it could do or how to make it work, but he figured he could at least pummel their prey with it.

It was over fast. Deke pulled the dazed alien to his feet. Doug and Lindsay draped the net over his head and pulled it down to cover his entire body. Tara and Lindsay wrapped the tape around their subdued opponent's lower legs. Steve and Nancy managed to tear off a couple of more long strips of tape and handed them to Tara and Lindsay, who wrapped it around his torso, pinning his arms to his sides beneath the net.

For good measure, Josh reached over the heads of the others and swatted their victim with the scepter. It released a flash of blue light, startling Josh into dropping it, but Deke grabbed it off the ground and pointed it at the alien, who was again beginning to resist and had torn the length of tape that bound his legs.

A red light came out of the scepter and struck the alien in the forehead. He had begun to regain his footing but collapsed completely when struck by the red beam.

Deke stepped to the prostrate figure and bent to check on him. "He's not dead, just dazed. Let's keep wrapping the tape around him." Then, he added, "I don't think he'll be able to move for a while, but we should find someplace to lock him up before he does recover. His friends may come looking for him, so we need an out of the way place."

Tara had an idea. "There is a jail in the old Community Center downtown. That's where they used to put my Dad to sleep it off when he had been drinking too much. It's where they hold town meetings. We can take him there and lock him up in the one cell with the lock that still works."

"How will we be able to drag him all the way downtown? That will be so slow that, if the others come looking for him, we'll be sitting ducks!" Steve looked very worried.

The enormity of what they had done was beginning to sink in for all of them. They had already done more than enough to anger the aliens. Now, they were in danger up to their necks. They had no choice but to see it through.

Lindsay had a suggestion. "Doug's brother's wagon is in the garage. We can put the alien in it and pull him to the jail."

Doug felt a little peeved that Lindsay had come up with the idea when it was his family's wagon, but he swallowed his annoyance and left to get it. When he returned, he also had in the wagon a canvas tarp from the garage.

The six fifth graders placed the unconscious alien in the wagon and covered him with the tarp. They began pulling and pushing the wagon down the street. Since Deke, still carrying the scepter, could see in the darkness of the cloud that now lay over the town because of his innate sharp visual acuity which he had inherited from his alien father, he led the way with Tara giving him directions on where to find the Community Center. Luckily, she had gone with her mother many times to pick up Peter from the jail, so she knew how to direct Deke, even in the dim light of the shrouding fog.

As they hauled the wagon down the middle of 3rd Avenue, Lindsay, in her typical inquisitive mode, asked Deke who he was. Deke thought for a moment and decided he should explain some things to the fifth graders, since they were risking their lives against a common foe.

"First, my name is Deke Fraley. I grew up in Millardville

and graduated from Millardville High School last year...barely. I am..." He paused, not sure how or if he should share this information with a bunch of grade-schoolers, but he decided they had earned his trust.

"Well, I recently learned that I am half-human and half-alien."

He glanced around the group, expecting to find them shocked or at least skeptical, but they seemed to accept his revelation. In truth, their recent experiences had left them open to believing almost anything.

"As I was saying, I grew up in Millardville, about ten miles from here. Even so, this is the first time I've ever been to Caperton. I've always had trouble making friends, but that never bothered me. I didn't feel like I needed friends. I got a job at the carton factory as a night watchman. It wasn't much of a job, but I've always enjoyed the peacefulness of the dark."

"Then, one night this past summer something shocking happened to me. I was taken, against my will, on board a UFO." He paused again. "Are you still following me on this?"

Lindsay responded for the group, as was her habit, "Tara's father was also captured by a UFO, but some people didn't believe him when he told everyone about it." She shot a glance at Josh, who seemed cowed and stared at his bandaged hand.

"He brought back that metal rod thing with him and the aliens have been trying to get it back. That's why we decided we would show everybody that her father was telling the truth by using that thing to lure an alien into a trap."

"And you just helped us do that!" exclaimed Doug. Lindsay shot an irritated glance at Doug. She didn't like it when someone tried to steal her credit.

Deke nodded his understanding. He then resumed his story.

"I didn't recall my first abduction until later, after my second one, when I left the hospital. During the second time, I met my father Attir, who told me to be ready, 'cause his enemies might capture me to use against him. He has been their enemy for a long time. Then, as I said, I recalled the first time and knew Attir was right. They had kidnapped me during my nightshift. They took me on a UFO and attached something to the back of my head."

He paused again and lifted his left hand to the spot on the back of his head where the triangular scar still remained to show where the device had been attached.

"They hooked something to the place where my head and backbone are together. It hurt so much that I blacked out from the pain. I wanted to scream, but no sound came out. They told me they were putting something in my brain so they could find me again in the future whenever they wanted to."

"After I fainted, the next thing I remember is that I woke up in my own bed, with terrible buzzing inside my head. As the buzzing got worse, I couldn't concentrate on anything else. My mother took me to the hospital, but I didn't remember that part about them putting the thing in my brain until after the second time."

"They took you twice?" Steve asked in shock.

"That's what he said, you moron!" Josh shouted at his friend. Then he glanced at Doug to see if he approved of the rebuke.

Doug merely nodded, not wanting to get involved in the middle of a squabble between two bullies. That would be a no-win situation. Josh took Doug's silence to mean that he had approval from Doug, his new best friend.

"But why do they want to find people again?" asked Lindsay.

"I ain't clear on why they do that. I have a scary feeling that they want something from us. They didn't answer my questions about that, though."

Deke continued. "That first time it was my father's enemies, who are called the Dominants, who abducted me. The second time it was my father and his people, who took me to their home planet and taught me all about the struggle between them and the Dominants and how to read their writing. The third time was when the Dominants came back while I was hiding out in the house of a man named Paul Sloan."

"Wow! Three times!" Steve exclaimed, his mouth dropping open.

"Wait! About the second time: wouldn't it take a long time to get to another planet and back?" asked Lindsay. She wasn't trying to find a hole in Deke's story, but had to have it explained fully before she could believe it. That's the way she approached new information.

"Yes, it usually would. But, they all have the ability to travel back and forth in time, so the trip to their planet was like a snap of someone's fingers. I even came back to the same time I left. I know it sounds confusing."

"It sure does," Nancy commented under her breath. She rolled her eyes. She remained skeptical of the whole alien abduction thing. She checked her boot for her knife.

"So, whose planet did you go to? Your father's or the Dominants'?" Lindsay needed to be clear on this, also.

"It's the same planet." Deke paused to be sure Lindsay was satisfied with this answer, but she continued to look confused. "It will be clear to you after you hear the whole story later. For now, I just need to talk about how I got here."

Lindsay frowned slightly but didn't ask any more questions. She would be able to challenge everything after all this was over. She found that to be a comforting thought.

"Anyway, the Dominants chased me to Paul Sloan's Hilltop House out in the country not too far from here. When Paul had to leave to do something, they came for me again. They put me on one of their spaceships that they call scout machines. Their big ones are called sky machines, since they aren't meant for landing on the ground. That's what the scout machines are for, since they are smaller."

"They put me on one of the scout machines. They had some sort of problem and had to do repairs, so they landed on a farm somewhere near here. They found a large barn where they could work without being seen. I think some men found them in the barn and attacked their scout machine with guns. The aliens had to get out of there fast and I escaped when no one was watching me."

He paused, then added, "Being chased by UFOs is the most frightening thing you can go through!"

"Those aliens are so horrible!" Lindsay exclaimed. As she finished that outburst she realized how absurd it would have sounded just a few hours ago.

As soon as she said it, she also recalled that Deke had said he was half-alien and she immediately apologized to him, but he told her he wasn't offended by the remark. She smiled sheepishly, then regained her usual self-confident demeanor.

Deke looked directly at Doug, who had turned to listen to his story. Then he moved his gaze to look at Lindsay and Tara on the left side of the wagon. He also paused for a moment to make eye contact with Josh, Steve, and Nancy.

He wanted to be sure they understood the importance of what he was about to say. "The aliens will want their weapons back. They don't want to share any of their inventions with us. They will be coming after them. They will be coming after all of us. Stay alert. Stay together."

"They have ways of seeing everything we do. They are tricky. Things are not always what they seem to be. They lie constantly. They can disguise themselves. They can sort of see the future, but just real important things."

He looked down at the wand and scepter he was holding.

"We may need to use these to fight them off. We have captured one of them and they aren't going to like that."

All six elementary schoolers stared at Deke and nodded, even Nancy.

Deke and the fifth graders continued to roll their captive toward the Community Center, which was still being called that despite the fact that a new one had just been completed north of the railroad tracks using the money Huit had provided.

Chapter Thirty-Three: The Approaching Darkness

By the time Deke and the fifth graders closed and locked the jail cell with their prisoner inside, the dark cloud had nearly engulfed the town. Huit's remaining agent stood by the open window of the parsonage attic looking out on the billowing darkness.

On the first floor of the building, Alvin Selkirk again struggled to gain consciousness, at last stumbling to his feet and looking around in confusion. He could see a dark fog seeping in underneath the front door.

Cheryl turned her car off the highway onto Main Street. She didn't want to risk driving into the growing darkness, so she pulled into a parking spot in front of the bar, one block south of the highway. Kattor threw open the back door and stepped out.

Unlike the others, he had no trouble seeing in the darkness. He strode purposefully to the sidewalk and, as the other riders headed into the tavern to escape what they thought was an impending storm, immediately headed south, passing the Lapley house. His long strides took him further, finally approaching the parsonage three blocks down Main Street from Paige's bar.

Rader paused at the open door of Paige's bar and stared intensely after the alien until his vision was obscured by the heavy fog. He had a bad feeling.

Joe Paige had been in the tavern for a couple of hours, restocking the cooler behind the bar with light beer and diet colas. Then he went back to grab some regular beer and regular colas. He liked to have a routine. The tavern wouldn't officially open until noon, but he didn't have anything else to do. The chip man had just stopped by to refill the display of chips and candy at one end of the bar.

Joe was surprised when the bell on the door jingled and Cheryl, Dana, and Teddy stepped inside. Joe didn't recognize them. He stared at them as they approached.

"Uh—we're not officially open yet," he said with the fake cheerful voice he used with strangers. The three strangers looked very stressed, so he decided to let them stay until the storm passed. They all collapsed into a booth across the room from the bar.

After a minute, Dana rose to her feet and walked toward the restroom, which was on the way to the pool tables in the room at the back of the establishment. No one paid much attention. But, while they weren't watching, she continued past the door to the Ladies' room and past the three pool tables and exited through the back door into the alley. She then turned right and headed south. Her eyes were glazed over.

Paul's van passed by slowly in the dark mist just as Kattor strode past the Lapleys' house. By the time Paul carefully cruised to a stop in the parking area in front of the church, Kattor had reached the front of the parsonage just to the south of the church. He pulled the door open and vanished within. Paul caught just a glimpse of someone in a hooded jacket entering the building.

Within that large house, Reverend Selkirk awoke to the sound of the front door closing and footsteps on the stairs. With extreme effort he finally managed to stand and stagger to the doorway of his study.

From there he could hear a commotion from up above, on the second floor, or perhaps in the attic. A feeling of consternation evolved into a determination to act, though he wasn't sure what awaited him. He had a feeling that something bad was happening up above.

He began to move toward the staircase, bracing himself unsteadily against the wall, forcing his feet to keep moving. His mind was still foggy. Slowly, but with determination, he stumbled along until he reached the foot of the stairs. Seizing the railing with his left hand, he was able to vault himself onto the first step. From there he reached out with his right hand and gripped the banister to pull himself up to the next one. Using that method, he continued upward.

When he reached the landing, he could tell that sounds were coming from the attic, so he grabbed the railing leading up to the second floor. Once he got there he paused just long enough to listen for the sounds he had heard and confirmed that they were indeed coming from the attic.

Then, he turned the ancient doorknob, pulled open the door to the attic stairs and proceeded upward. The higher he went, the more his acrophobia took control of him. Still, he was determined to find out what was going on.

The climbing had caused his breathing to become very labored, and he had begun to perspire, despite the fact that it was a mild autumn day. Selkirk became aware that his heart was pounding; he could feel it when he put his hand against his chest. He knew that this kind of stress and strain could bring on a heart attack or stroke.

He had received his last physical nine years earlier when he was hired by the church. The physician had informed him that he had dangerously high blood pressure and cholesterol.

In response to these warnings, Alvin took steps to make sure he wouldn't ever again receive such a warning: he quit going to doctors.

Selkirk searched in the dark for the light switch, but when he clicked it on, nothing happened. He had not changed the light bulb that burned out the last time he went to the attic. He found that he couldn't make his feet take any more steps up the stairs to the top floor and he didn't feel safe trying to climb them in the dark.

He was desperate to get up to the attic, however, so he resorted to crawling up the steps on his hands and knees. He rose back to his feet for the last two steps but fell on his face in the uncommonly dark room.

He couldn't see anything, but he felt blood pouring from his nose. He also felt the rush of cold air coming from his right where the window overlooking the street was located. He was certain he had not left it open. He had only been up there a couple times, years ago; it was too difficult a climb.

Trying to pierce the darkness with his eyes, the minister got the impression that the darkness was actually flowing in from outside, just like the cold air, and filling every available space.

Selkirk began crawling toward the open window, but before he could reach it he became aware of the silhouette of a man standing with his arms at his sides in front of it. He discerned the shape of a handgun in the man's right hand.

Then, the minister realized there was one other person present, by the back wall of the attic. The figure lifted a small handheld item over his head.

In the violet light that it gave off, he realized that this wasn't a human. The head was large and bald, the eyes were two glowing red coals set deep in wrinkled sockets. Even in the dim light he could see that this creature had large pulsating veins running from its neck to its forehead.

Selkirk had risen to his knees and now tried to stand. He stumbled about, finally turning to face the monster he saw before him.

"It must be a demon come to do battle with me, the devout minister who had been preaching so effectively against sin all these years!" Selkirk muttered in his fever dream.

He began to tremble. If only he hadn't been so pure and saintly, if only he had been less of an inspiration to his flock, this demon would not have come to steal his soul and send it prematurely to burn in the fires of hell!

Selkirk was vaguely aware that he wasn't thinking clearly, but he couldn't snap back to clarity. He was still groggy from the chemical on the computer keyboard.

The "demon" turned his gaze on the shivering man cowering before him.

"I am Kattor, leader of the Dominants. We know all about you, Al-vin-sel-kirk. I chose you for this operation. I am the one who arranged for you to get your employment with this church, as you call it."

The minister's foggy mind raced back to the time when he found the newspaper opened on his front porch, with the position at this church highlighted. There was also the time when he had decided to abscond with the church treasury, but his car wouldn't start. Every time he attempted to do something like that, something always came up to keep him in Caperton.

Was it the demon who had brought Alvin Selkirk to Caperton and kept him there? If so, that demon had also kept him in the service of the Lord and brought him to this place and time to do battle with all the demons!

The demon's voice continued very clearly, very calmly.

"When we discovered this natural portal from our galaxy into yours, we needed a pliable human to help us secure it and give us time to open it fully. It had to be someone who had no family and would not often come into this room. We ascertained that you met these criteria. You preached that we did not exist so well that you convinced the fools who came to hear your words. You even convinced yourself. You diverted their attention elsewhere. This allowed us to accomplish our mission. You helped us to succeed."

"I—I—did no such thing!" the quivering minister protested.

"But you did! And your effort to deny our existence made it possible for us to complete this action without interference..."

Kattor made a broad sweeping motion with his free left hand. It was at this moment that Selkirk realized Kattor wasn't actually speaking words; the minister was just receiving them in his mind.

Kattor continued, *"Your efforts to convince the dull-witted rabble that we do not exist allowed us to succeed. If they had known what was true, our mission would have been impossible. You have made our task simple."*

The alien/demon sneered at the trembling human. *"You have been a very obedient and faithful servant!"*

This comment hit the kneeling man hard. He fell. He stammered, "You are a d-demon sent...sent from hell?"

Kattor responded, *"I am not familiar with those terms. I am from the world of the Dominants."*

Once again, Kattor's steady telepathic voice lent power to his words, but also motivated the minister. He began to regain his strength.

"But there is nothing in the Bible that says anything...about...Dominants."

"What is this 'by-bull' of which you speak?" Kattor asked mockingly. *"Are you referencing that collection of fairy tales you keep on a shelf and only bring out every seven of your days to wave at the brain-dead ones who come to listen to your foolish jabbering?"*

At this comment, Alvin Selkirk leaned forward and with a mighty effort stumbled to his feet, with growing anger that his life's work was being ridiculed. He began to regain his strength.

"We have no need for such superstition. The universe has existed always. Galaxies, solar systems come into being and blink out of existence. Sentient civilizations do the same. My people know they have only a short time to find a way to live forever. That is why we find ourselves on your puny planet; the key to eternal life is here! We may need to destroy all other beings, but WE must live on. Forever!"

Selkirk was dumbstruck. He had never doubted the existence of God. He had never questioned the Bible. Sure, there had been times when he was younger that he didn't feel the need to think about it, but once he became a minister, once he began preaching about it every Sunday, he had gradually begun to...*believe.*

Kattor again looked into the minister's eyes, where he saw fear and confusion. Selkirk felt a headache coming on. He needed answers.

"But why are you here tormenting me?"

"Because you have been of such great assistance to us, I will take the time to further enlighten you. Your people were placed on this tiny rock by our ancient ancestors, the original Dominants, to allow you to evolve to the point at which you could be of service to us in our war against the foolish 'Fifths,' as they call themselves. Your people have always sought to mine the crassest of elements—gold, silver, copper—without touching the most valuable element of all, which is buried deep within your world."

"It is the element that makes travel between dimensions possible. If only you had known! Such fools! We will force your people to mine it and then we will use it to destroy the Fifths. Of course, the element is extremely poisonous, so your people will die off as they perform that task. If any survive, we will always have use for slaves!"

"Are the Fifths angels? Why else would you demons want to destroy them? I don't think demons are able to destroy angels..."

"The Fifths are mortal. There are no such things as angels. There are just the strong and the weak, and the Dominants are strong. The element we seek will give us power to go anywhere and do what we want. The Fifths will not be able

to catch up to us as we expand our domain across the galaxies. They will wither and die on the home planet."

Selkirk stared at the sneering alien with both shock and contempt. Could all that he was saying be true? Or was this sneering demon merely baiting him. Devils are known for deceiving people, after all. Aliens exist? No God? Evolution was real? He felt insulted, violated.

The thought crossed his mind that, as a good Christian, he should forgive this creature, turn the other cheek, but he didn't think he could bring himself to do that. Demons don't deserve forgiveness. He fell back into a seated position on the attic floor as panicked thoughts raced through his mind. What could he do to save the human race from the ravages Kattor's soldiers had planned for it?

A quote from his high school history class, long lost to his memory, came to the forefront of his mind. It related to Theodore Roosevelt's 1912 presidential campaign: *"We stand at Armageddon and do battle for the Lord!"*

He gritted his teeth and began to rise. It was time to stand and do battle.

Back at Paige's Bar, Rader noted that Dana had not returned to the booth where he and Cheryl were seated. It had been an incredibly long time, he realized. He also realized that it had been a while since he'd heard from Kattor.

He turned to Cheryl. "Maybe you should check on your cousin. Something's not right."

Cheryl, who had begun to relax after the long, stressful ride from the mountains, suddenly snapped back to full alertness. The sergeant's words were like having a glass of cold water thrown on her face. She leaped to her feet and rushed to the women's restroom. Finding it vacant, she hurried on to the pool table room. Looking past the tables, she noted that the back door was open.

She turned to Rader, who had followed her, and the two headed for the alley. Once they got there, they were unsure where to go. Visibility was reduced to half a block.

"Caperton's small. If we split up maybe we can locate her faster." Cheryl headed north toward the highway; the sergeant headed south, toward Main Hill.

Rader's head was beginning to pound. He had become convinced that Kattor was up to something evil. He recalled the overturned van and the marching soldiers in the Forbidden Zone. He didn't know why that image came to him now, but he had become unsettled by the alien's increasingly insulting and arrogant telepathic comments during the recent trip.

The final one was, *"Humans are such fools. They never see clearly what is happening around them."*

Then there had been a pause. *"Things are not always what they appear to be."*

The sergeant felt that Kattor was openly taunting him. He didn't understand that cryptic last comment and it worried him.

Then Rader got a brief glimpse of movement in the alley ahead. He started to jog toward the figure who was now heading for the back door of the parsonage. He reached the door too late to stop the person who had just entered the building and he found the door locked. Glancing around, he saw no one else, so he assumed it must have been Dana. He circled around to the front door.

In the parsonage attic, Selkirk heard the back door open and slam shut down below. He felt a sudden cold breeze and the door to the attic stairs also slammed shut. He could hear footsteps ascending to the attic.

George Huit sat in his unmarked black government car in front of Calvin Dunn's farmhouse and began to worry. His agents should have reported back to him on their progress by now.

He was especially concerned about Sandy Romer. He had purposely given her what he thought was an easy task. There had been plenty of time to eliminate the Lapleys and the two problematic children. He was usually very patient, but the stakes were particularly critical this time. He had never felt so much pressure.

He could see the dark cloud descending on the town and knew that Opaque Orb would be closely monitoring today's events. Huit's neck would be on the chopping block if his part of the plan wasn't completed, and the plot was jeopardized because of that.

He punched a number into his phone and waited nervously for Agent Romer to respond.

The phone rang once. Nobody answered. Huit glanced skyward and realized that the UFO cloud was blocking his signal. He felt a panic rising in his gut. He started his car and pulled out onto the gravel road that led into town. He would need to do this job himself, he realized.

His car died suddenly, without warning, without sputtering, without making any sound. Huit frowned. He knew this was a part of the alien procedure, to restrict the number of witnesses while the work was underway. This meant that the mission was going forward without his okay.

He grabbed his handgun from the glove compartment, shoved it into his suitcoat pocket and started to walk toward town. He had to get there before anything else went wrong. Luckily for him, the Dunn farm was close to Caperton, though at the end of an extremely long lane.

Up above the dark cloud, in the small scout machine that hovered beside the large, triangular craft, the small figure that stood holding the infant began to move. She glanced at the two tubes, then looked around cautiously. Nobody was watching.

She slowly reached up toward a light that glowed on Laurine Fraley's tube. As she touched it, it slid open silently. A cloud of gas floated free. Laurine's eyes blinked open and she took a deep breath.

When Laurine saw the short female alien, she paused. At first she felt fear, but alien Kimmy put her hand out and Laurine gripped it. The girl guided her out and then turned toward the other tube. In a few seconds, Marla Brashear also found herself free.

Kimmy handed the baby to Marla; she knew that Marla had been brought on board originally to care for the baby and had been released when it was discovered that she couldn't adapt to the on-board atmosphere. She had been re-obtained after modifications had been made that allowed her to breathe on the scout machine.

Kimmy then led the two women toward a dark part of the interior and motioned for them to seat themselves against the wall. She returned to the part of the scout machine where the control lights blinked as a tall alien bent over the console.

"It's done," she communicated via telepathy. Actual words weren't necessary between the two. Kimmy's meaning was just conveyed from her mind to the alien's mind.

The tall alien glanced toward her and then turned back and waved his hands over the console. The lights flashed multiple times and the scout machine tipped to one side. It began to descend rapidly. The other aliens, who were in another part of the vehicle, were unexpectedly thrown against the sides of the craft, crumpling to the floor after the impact.

The tall alien had disabled the inertia-compensation mechanism.

Kimmy grabbed the bench on which the alien driver sat to keep from being slammed against a wall. In the back, Marla, holding the baby securely, and Laurine were propped against a wall and the momentum shift just served to hold them in place. The scout machine slowed and then settled gently onto the vacant football field on the northeastern edge of Caperton.

The tall one arose from the console and turned to Kimmy. *"Come, little one. We will now exit. Prepare the others."*

Kimmy quickly retreated to the room where Marla, Laurine and the infant were waiting. She held out both hands.

Marla grabbed the left hand, Laurine the right hand, and Kimmy pulled them to their feet. Marla rested the baby over her left shoulder.

Kimmy held out blindfolds. The two women received telepathic instructions to wear them to avoid damaging their eyes in the dark fog outside, so they complied without question. Kimmy then led them to the front of the scout machine, where the tall alien touched a light and a slit appeared in the side of the disk.

He then ducked through it, followed by the two women, with Marla holding the infant, and Kimmy. The tall one reached back through the slit and again touched the light. The opening closed and the scout machine again shot skyward, out of Earth's atmosphere and into space.

The small group headed west, in the direction of the church, led by the tall one, who could see in the dark cloud. Kimmy helped guide Marla and Laurine, since she could also see, and the two women couldn't.

Kathy had exited Paul's van and was watching as Paul began to lower the wheelchair lift. Paul caught a glimpse of a slim figure wearing a hooded jacket entering the parsonage. Then, as the figure reached back to pull the door shut, Paul saw his hand; those weren't human fingers! He had a hunch that this alien was up to no good.

Kathy tried again to reach Lee by phone, but still couldn't get a signal.

At that moment George Huit emerged from the swirling mist, striding purposefully toward the church after walking from his car, which he had abandoned in front of Calvin

Dunn's farmhouse. Paul watched as he turned and moved toward the parsonage. But, when Huit tried the front door he found it locked. He punched it in frustration. A frown crossed his face as he stood at the door, uncertain about what he could do.

After a few seconds, he pulled his gun from his pocket and pointed it at the doorknob. This wasn't an approved option, but he had seen it in movies. Maybe...

"Well, Mr. Huit...I see you have returned to the scene of your folly..." Paul rolled up the ramp by the front door.

Huit was taken aback by the voice of his antagonist. He returned the gun to his inside pocket and spun quickly to face Paul. He decided to try the back door and stepped to his left with the intent of going around him. Paul turned his chair to block him. Huit took a step back and tried again to elude the chair.

"Out of my way, Sloan! I am on official government business!"

Paul dropped his head to his chest, staring up at the agency man. "Government business? I don't believe you know what government business is."

"And YOU do?" Huit countered.

"Well—I'm certain that it's not turning our government over to alien invaders." Paul rolled his chair forward and struck Huit's shins with his footrests. Huit took a step back.

Huit glared down at Sloan. "If not for me the nation and maybe the world would have been destroyed by now. Get out of the way!"

Paul countered, "I think you have betrayed not only your country, but also the world." He rolled forward and bumped Huit again. Once more, the agent stepped back.

"I have only done what needed to be done! Why can't you understand that?"

"Because..." Paul retorted as he again rammed the man in the black suit, "...you should have done what's right, not what some alien overlord or his minions told you to do!"

Huit grabbed the railing beside the steps for support. "I have saved hundreds of lives, thousands! Maybe even millions!"

Paul gripped both wheels and gave them a spin, once more bumping Huit, who involuntarily retreated, almost falling down the concrete steps.

Paul continued angrily, "Even if we all die, we deserve the choice. Each one of us has to have the option to decide whether they will resist or just give up. You just gave up. Maybe the rest of us would fight. I know I would! Now, you are their puppet, and you must dance to their tune!"

Paul again put his palms on the top of the wheels of his chair. "I have never given up, even when I could no longer walk. I knew I would continue to live and live the way I wanted to!"

Paul again bumped his footrests into Huit's shins. He tumbled backward down the steps, landing on his back, but immediately rolled over and scrambled to his feet.

This brought his eyes to the same level as Paul's at the top of the steps. He pulled out his gun and pointed it at his opponent's face. Paul didn't flinch. He stared steadily at Huit.

Huit's face was twisted in pain, but it was emotional, not physical. He had been under nearly constant pressure for months while working on the Caperton project. He knew that failure, even if it was not his fault, would likely result in his own death. He couldn't take it anymore. He had no close friends in whom he could confide his frustrations. Agency policy forbade consultation with any kind of counselor in order to make sure knowledge of the aliens' presence didn't spread beyond the organization.

He locked eyes with Paul, his lips quivering. He slowly began lowering his weapon. "I only did what I had to do! I was just following orders!"

Even as these words left his lips he realized that they constituted the same defense uttered by Nazi criminals at Nuremberg. He suddenly realized that he had been wrong, totally wrong, all along. He felt a sharp pain in his stomach and doubled over, falling to the ground.

Paul turned his chair and wheeled himself down the ramp.

Huit remained slumped by the steps for a while, then gradually arose and stumbled away with his head bowed.

At the bottom of the ramp Paul was met by Peter Lapley. Paul didn't know him well but remembered him from the town meeting in July. As Peter shuffled toward him, Paul realized that he, too, was clutching a gun. He almost smiled; this was becoming absurd.

As Peter drew near, Paul noted that his demeanor was rather odd. Though he raised the gun and pointed it at Paul, his face betrayed no emotion. He just seemed...blank.

Paul suddenly realized that he still had the shotgun tucked into the bag hanging from the back of his chair. He'd not thought about it while Huit was threatening him, but now he remembered and reached back over his left shoulder to retrieve it. He didn't want to shoot Lapley, but he thought maybe he could use it to scare him into putting the handgun down.

Peter intoned in a staccato voice, "You have been a problem for too long. Now you must die."

Suddenly, there was a loud crunch and Peter pitched forward. Hitting the gravel that covered the parking area in front of the parsonage, he rolled over a couple times. The gun flew from his hand and slid into the street.

Peter lay on his stomach, head lifted and looking forward, a stunned look on his face. He shook his head vigorously from side to side.

Glancing at the few neighborhood people who had gathered around to see what was happening, he blinked a few times, then raised himself up onto his left elbow. He discovered that a slight woman with light colored hair was crouched over him, holding a gun.

It was Renee whom he had last seen in his driveway at the time Sandy Romer was shot, ready to strike him again with the butt of her gun, if necessary.

"I—d-don't know why I said all that," he stuttered, a look of confusion on his face.

Paul, like everyone, had heard of Peter's purported adventure on the UFO. "I think I know why. You were programmed to kill me by the aliens on that UFO. That was probably the entire purpose of them kidnapping you."

Peter struggled to his feet, rubbing the back of his head where the waitress/undercover agent had struck him with the gun.

"You—you're right! I-I remember now!" he announced, touching the scar that had been left just below his skull at the time of the abduction. "I didn't escape from those aliens...they just let me go after attaching something to the back of my head. They did something to make me want to kill you! I was supposed to use that blue wand thing they gave me. When I hid it in my house, instead, I think they decided they needed to get it back before I gave it to the government. Actually, I had thought about giving it to you. I figured you might know what to do with it."

While this was occurring in front of the parsonage, a lone figure had entered the back door. Dana Warrick moved as in a trance as she headed up the stairs on the way to the second floor and then the attic. She pulled the door open and ascended.

At the top of the stairs, she encountered a quivering man in a black suit facing a figure in the center of the room. That individual was holding aloft a glowing device emitting a blue shaft of light that seemed to be holding the man frozen.

Dana stood motionless, with a dazed look, next to Selkirk.

The alien turned toward the blank wall at the back of the room. A beam of violet light replaced the blue one, creating a small, rotating wheel of bright colors that expanded steadily until it was halfway to the ceiling. It held its size and position for a few seconds and then collapsed back to a speck.

The figure in the center of the room then turned to Dana.

She moved forward and stood facing the wall at a distance of about four feet, her arms extended to each side. Then, the light was again activated.

The small beam of light that had played upon the rear wall of the room now was aimed at Dana, striking her in the back of her skull. She screamed in agony and twisted from side to side.

After a short time, she quit moving and stood staring in a daze at the wall. A few seconds later her body began to glow, and a beam of light shot from her forehead and struck the wall. The light again began to swirl and grow larger.

Selkirk's vision had blurred when he fell to the floor, but he gradually regained his sight. His eyes focused on the swirling light, now seeming to form a pattern with dimly moving parts. He thought it resembled a kaleidoscope. As the minister watched, the jumble of pieces came together into a frightening scene: a phalanx of armored soldiers was marching toward Dana.

Their visages were terrifying, their eyes resembled glowing red coals. They carried some sort of spears or lances on their shoulders. They were about to reach the opening in the wall in front of Dana.

Alvin Selkirk shuddered. This was clearly pure evil.

Dana found her mind drifting away from the frightening scene before her. Memories of past experiences started trickling into her mind, at first slowly, then faster, until the stream of recollections became a raging, overwhelming river.

She recalled the first night she was taken, at age seven. She awoke to find three tall, pale men standing at the foot of her bed, staring at her with their glowing, evil eyes. She started to scream, but she heard a voice say, *"All will be well."*

This calmed her until she was transported in a pale green glow through her bedroom window into a huge, circular object floating silently above her house, which is when the effects of the calming message seemed to wear off. Dana remembered the panic she felt when she realized how high up in the air she was.

Then, the message came again into her mind as she was floated through an opening in the side of the object and into a transparent vertical tube. At that point she mercifully lost consciousness.

The next thing she recalled was being placed into some sort of chair with a number of flexible tubes attached to her head and neck. The same, horrible creatures who had brought her to this place stood around, apparently discussing her. She couldn't hear voices, but they kept huddled together and from time to time looked in her direction.

Dana had the impression they were congratulating one another, though she had no idea why.

In retrospect, Dana recognized that as the end of the easy phase of her contact with these monsters. They placed her face-down on a metallic table and attached something to the back of her head. She had never felt such overwhelming pain! It was both inside and outside her skull and was dispersed throughout her body.

She realized she couldn't move her arms and legs. She screamed repeatedly, hoping her parents would come rescue her and make the agony end. All she could think of was how much she wanted it to stop and how desperately she wanted to find herself back in the safety of her own bedroom, the one with the pastel fairytale wallpaper and her Strawberry Shortcake quilt. She wanted her mommy Elizabeth and her daddy Karl.

Recalling these events left Dana drained physically, mentally, and emotionally even all these years later. Another series of memories flooded over her, many involving the same horrific abduction scenario. She never remembered these events...until the next time it happened, which Dana now realized was three or four times a year.

It never became less intense or painful. In one of the memories, she recalled being lifted skyward, going higher and higher until darkness surrounded her. Then she saw below her a dimly lit ball that grew larger and brighter as she approached it, until she realized it was a planet.

She and her alien kidnappers were deposited there for what seemed to her to be days. In one of the more recent occurrences, she was introduced to another alien, who looked at her calmly and seemed to smile, which caused the scar alongside his mouth to spread open and leak a greenish fluid. Despite the smile, Dana felt only disgust as she stared at him.

Then the words entered her brain: *"I am Kattor. You are my child. When you have grown older I will come back to your planet to take you away. You will then help me achieve my mission. You are very special to my people."*

Dana thought that this implied that her tortures would lessen; they did decrease in frequency, but not intensity.

During subsequent abductions she received "training" on how to help her "father". These events involved painful injections that she understood would allow her to move more safely between Earth and Kattor's world. Many of these sessions took place on the aliens' smaller vessels.

They began to mold her thoughts and ambitions. She was guided toward a career in journalism during subsequent encounters. These abductions were comparatively brief and did not involve travel into space.

She was informed that she could best assist their cause by working in that profession. As before, she didn't recall these sessions at the time they occurred, but she found herself developing an interest in becoming a reporter. She was taught to shade her reporting to sow skepticism about UFOs and alien visitors.

That was why she had gone to the mountains, lured by the prospects of a story about a town that had been buried in an avalanche. Other reporters were beginning to mention reports of alien visitations prior to the disaster. Dana, however, wrote convincing stories that explained away the UFO sightings and emphasized the seismologically precarious substrata that had led to the massive avalanche.

After that, she was whisked away to Kattor's home planet for what seemed like years, though Kattor repeatedly made comments to the effect that time was a dimension in which one could travel.

At first, Dana didn't see the significance of those references, but she eventually realized that she was going backward and forward in time and the lengthy visits to Kattor's world were mere days back on Earth.

When Kattor and Rader retrieved her from the cave, she had actually just arrived there. Her mind went blank whenever she tried to speak of all this, which gave her a rather stunned demeanor.

The alien also made some comments that Dana didn't understand. Kattor at one time had said that his people couldn't permanently erase memories without damaging human brains beyond repair—and the Dominants needed intact humans to help implement their plans.

Dana's reverie came to a sudden end. She found herself back in the present, held in place by unseen chains, facing the rear wall of the parsonage attic. A cohort of frightening aliens was approaching steadily, now coming up a final rise toward what she had been taught was a portal between worlds.

Something was attached to the back of her head and she detected a low hum, a sort of buzzing. Kattor was standing in the middle of the room with a violet light emitting from a device in his right hand.

Against the wall next to the descending staircase a pudgy man with silver hair huddled in a nearly fetal ball, staring blankly ahead and muttering pompously to himself, "I am Reverend Selkirk!"

At the front of the room, standing next to an open window was another man, wearing a dark suit, with his arms crossed in front of him, not moving.

With a start, Dana recalled being shocked repeatedly over the years with nearly lethal bolts of energy. The bolts weren't electrical, Kattor had informed her, but were related to a power source found only on the alien's home planet. She was being infused with that energy to turn her into a kind of battery.

What she hadn't been told was that once the excess energy was drawn out of her, her body's atoms would be torn apart to continue to fuel the portal.

Kattor turned to address Dana. *"Your purpose is to use your built-up power to keep this intergalactic portal open long enough for my soldiers to make it into your world. It requires tremendous power to do so. It is only open partially at present. We need to utilize your excess energy to blast it fully open."*

Dana felt a strong suction coming from the back wall. Her shoulder-length hair whipped around her head as though she were caught in an oncoming hurricane. It wrapped around her eyes and she could no longer see the portal, but she could judge from the wind that it was still open. She wanted to stop this horrifying event. She knew the entire planet was in danger.

Alvin Selkirk regained his awareness in time to gaze in shock upon the activity going on at the back of the attic. Evil beings were about to cross into the Earth through his parsonage. He knew instinctively that something must be done to keep the marching soldiers from reaching the portal.

Alvin crawled on all fours to the wall by the stairs and rose to his knees by placing his hands against the wall, then struggling to his feet.

This movement drew the attention of the man by the window, who had thus far not moved. He raised his handgun and aimed it at the minister, who immediately shrank meekly back down to the floor.

But the anger inside Reverend Alvin Selkirk was growing.

Chapter Thirty-Four: The Impact

Meanwhile, down below, the tall alien from the scout ship led his small band to a yard across from the church. He telepathically told them to stay put while he checked things out. He crossed the street, then walked past the front of the church and on to the front door of the parsonage. After he departed, Marla and Laurine received telepathic instructions to remove their blindfolds.

At this time, Teddy Rader came around the corner of the parsonage. Cheryl came to the front of the same house from the north. After searching the area around the bar and finding no sign of her cousin, she decided she'd see if Rader had had any success. The sergeant told her that he thought Dana had gone inside.

Rader and Cheryl watched as the alien from the scout ship came closer. As he neared the door, he paused for a moment to tell them, *"I am Attir, leader of the Fifths Expeditionary Force. I have reason to believe my enemy Kattor and his minions are within this structure."*

He paused briefly to look at the two humans. *"It will be dangerous inside; do not follow me."*

He reached between Rader and Cheryl and seized the doorknob. The door opened easily. He strode inside, closing the door behind himself. Rader grabbed for the door but was too late. It was locked again.

Cheryl was desperate to find her cousin, so she looked around for another way in. She had grown up in Caperton and had attended children's parties at the parsonage.

Seizing Teddy's sleeve, she pulled him toward the south side of the building. She knew there was a low window there. When she had been in her teens, her best friend had been the daughter of the minister who lived there at the time. Sometimes they would sneak out of slumber parties via that window, which had a latch that didn't hold, and go to Paige's bar to buy colas.

There were laws against children being served in bars, but kids were good customers and always bought a lot of snack foods, so Joe had welcomed their business. Of course, he wouldn't sell alcohol to them. It was a small town, and everyone would hear about it if he did.

The slumber party girls never told anyone about Joe's collusion, and he appreciated it in a conspiratorial sort of way. After loading up on drinks, chips, and candy the girls would sneak back to the parsonage with their treats and enter through the broken window to share them with the other girls who were waiting up in her friend's bedroom. Cheryl marveled that they had never been caught. The danger made it even more fun.

Cheryl led Rader to that window and discovered it was still easy to open. She pushed the lower part of the window upward and the two were able to climb inside. The place looked much the same as Cheryl recalled it.

Hearing the sound of footsteps above them, she steered Rader to the flight of stairs leading from the first floor to the second. They paused, unsure what they might be getting into. Then, they plunged ahead.

As they reached the second floor, Cheryl recalled how it used to look when her friend Pam lived there. She glanced through the open door of a bedroom. Now, it was sparsely furnished without any flair—a typical bachelor's place with only a huge, old bed and a single dresser. Discarded clothing and shoes were strewn about the room.

She sighed heavily, thinking about what a great place it used to be. She suddenly recalled the time that her cousin Dana had been in town and attended a slumber party with her at Pam's house. In the middle of the night, she was awakened by a dim light. She had realized that her cousin was no longer in the bed next to her. She then had heard a scream from Dana that was cut short.

Cheryl tried to get up to check on her cousin but fell back on the bed in a deep slumber. When she awoke a couple of hours later, Dana was once again sleeping next to her, murmuring indistinctly in her sleep. Cheryl didn't know why that memory had popped up after all these years.

Up above them in the attic, Selkirk had continued to struggle to stand, but with no success. He gave up, breathing hard. Then, the door down at the bottom of the stairs had burst open, followed by the sounds of feet on the steps. The minister, lost in a fevered world of confusion, hoped an angel had been sent to save him.

Kattor also heard the sounds of someone climbing upward. He spun around to see who it was, concerned that someone might be able to thwart him when he was so close to final success. This resulted in him losing his concentration and allowing the glowing silver wand to shut off, which, in turn, caused the portal to shrink and Dana to collapse in exhaustion.

Just as the portal was almost closed, a lance gripped in an armored glove was thrust through it from the other side, propping it open. Nobody in the room noticed this because of developments in the middle of the attic.

There followed a series of rapid events. Attir reached the top of the steps and immediately saw Kattor standing in the middle of the room. Kattor was shocked to see that his nemesis had found him, and he allowed his arm to drop to his side as he readjusted his grip on the wand.

Attir raised the slender rod he gripped in his right hand and a bolt of red lightning shot toward Kattor, who anticipated Attir's shot and dodged to his left, returning fire in short bursts as he moved. Attir grabbed his right side and grimaced, though he managed to stay on his feet.

Kattor briefly grabbed his own torso before punching a button on his wand. He then whirled to face the large, open attic window, where Huit's remaining agent, the man in the dark suit, stood in confusion with his handgun clutched in both hands and pointed at the ceiling.

Huit's agency was responsible for cooperating with Kattor and his Army in accomplishing their goals in order to keep the peace. Huit had placed his agent at the attic window to make sure no humans interfered with Kattor's plans. The agent didn't know what to do when a second alien appeared and tried to stop Kattor.

Before Attir could return fire, Kattor moved toward the window and grabbed the agent. He gave him a shove toward the middle of the room just as Attir shot a red beam at Kattor. The agent fell into the line of fire and crumpled to the floor when the blast of red light hit him in the chest.

A green light lit up the area just outside the window. Kattor climbed out into the light. Suddenly a bulky figure hurled himself into the green light behind the alien.

It was the minister, Alvin Selkirk.

His hand touched Kattor's boot and he grabbed hold. The light began to draw both of them out and upward toward the waiting alien vehicle. Since the transport beam had the effect of paralyzing anyone caught in it, Alvin Selkirk couldn't move, but his eyes had been open when he lunged for Kattor.

The sudden realization that he was 40 feet in the air shocked the minister as he had a deathly fear of heights.

For his part, Kattor tried to shake loose this unwelcome human, but realized—since he was also unable to move—he would have to wait until they were both inside the waiting scout machine.

But as he looked up, he discovered a huge sky machine.

Attir had anticipated Kattor's escape attempt and had hijacked the scout machine that was assigned to this mission in order to escape with Kathy, Laurine, Kimmy, and the baby, and then he had sent it rocketing into space so it wouldn't be available for Kattor to use. Sky machines weren't made for planet-level tasks.

Attir had time to get off one last shot at Kattor, as he was pulled through the opening into a brightly lit room in the giant vessel, but Selkirk blocked his view, so he instead aimed through the opening at the android pilot he could see on the far side of the room.

His wand blast caused the android to crumple to the floor, brushing the navigation light panel as he fell. The sky machine lurched to one side and began to fall slowly toward the ground. The falling android pilot had inadvertently bumped the antigravity function to a "partial" setting, so gravity still had an effect on the sky machine, but not as much as it would if it had been fully engaged.

Selkirk, in his still-fuzzy mind, thought he was doing battle with Satan. The minister saw himself as the Defender of the Faith.

Back in the parsonage, Teddy and Cheryl had just reached the attic. They found Dana and Attir collapsed on the floor and rushed to help them. Neither noticed the alien soldier struggling to keep the portal open with his spear.

As they assisted Attir and Dana in carefully descending the attic stairs, he managed to jimmy the portal open several feet and he and three others clambered through to the attic. When the lance was removed, the portal collapsed.

In an interior room of the large spacecraft, Jay had finally shaken the fog that had filled his brain, after the final fumes inside the cracked tube had dissipated. He found that he had regained his strength. He pushed his clenched fists against the sides of the tube in which he was held.

With a loud, ripping sound, one side split open and Jay spilled out.

There had been an alien at the other side of this room, monitoring the safety mechanisms on board. The commotion in the transporter beam room, where Kattor and Selkirk now lay sprawled on the floor, caused this alien to leave his post to see what was happening. He discovered that the commander of this mission, Kattor, was fighting his way to his feet. A human was struggling on the floor next to him.

Noting that the alien in his part of the sky machine had abandoned his post, Jay turned to the tube next to his and began running his hands along its sides in search of a switch or latch that would open it. He noticed a small, yellow light glowing at the base of the tube.

When he touched it, the tube opened a couple of inches, so he clapped his hand securely onto it. The tube slid open from the middle with the top half disappearing into a slot in the ceiling and the lower part sliding downward.

The man who had been imprisoned within collapsed forward and Jay caught him before he could hit the floor. This was facilitated by the partial gravity.

As the man regained consciousness, he began to swear profusely. Jay tried to calm him down, since he was afraid of attracting more of the aliens to this room, but Calvin Dunn could not be pacified.

Jay glanced around and found that there were no aliens in sight, so he moved on to the next tube. When he touched the yellow light and opened the tube, he found a young woman with blond hair. Jay motioned her out and, finding her to be unsteady on her feet, seated her against the wall.

He then moved on to the final tube in the group. When he opened it, a chubby, red-complexioned boy fell out and began immediately searching in his pockets for candy and gum, not seeming to notice that Jay was there.

Once Joey Paige had managed to pull out a handful of gumballs, he tripped on a loose shoelace and dropped most of them. He got down on all fours to retrieve them, following a rolling one behind some metallic benches along the wall.

In a few seconds, they had all revived, but Calvin Dunn continued with his profane outbursts. Hearing the noise, the alien who had abandoned his post reappeared from around a corner.

Jay had seen aliens before, but the other humans had been unconscious when brought on board the spacecraft. The pale being standing before them had an elongated skull, deeply recessed, red-glowing eyes, and several long, protruding vein-like features beginning just above the eyes and terminating at the top of his head. The arms were very long and very thin, with large hands having only four digits.

Tonya gazed in horror at her first conscious sight of an alien and released a tremendous scream. Calvin Dunn ceased his profane outburst and stared in shock at the unfamiliar figure standing before him. All he could say was, "What in the name of...?"

The alien slowly approached Jay, Tonya, and Calvin as if he was uncertain about what should be done.

Just then, the slowly descending sky machine brushed against the top of the parsonage. The impact knocked the alien and humans off their feet. Jay pounced on the pale being and found that he wasn't very strong.

He and Calvin shoved him into the tube that Calvin had just vacated. Jay quickly found the release light that had allowed him to free Calvin. Touching the light caused the tube to enclose the alien, who only struggled briefly before the gases emitted within the tube rendered him unconscious.

Rader and Cheryl had begun descending the stairs from the attic. Rader was assisting Dana, who was having trouble standing. Cheryl did her best to support Attir, who was holding a hand over his injured side.

A few seconds later, the four alien soldiers who had stepped through the portal cautiously approached the top of the attic stairs and began to descend slowly, one step at a time.

Down below, Ty had crossed the street from the Lapley's house to see if any of the people gathered on the lawn were in need of medical attention.

As he glanced around he caught sight of the sky machine descending gradually to the ground one block to the south. He saw a lot of spectators fleeing in panic. Some were getting knocked down. There could be injuries. Ty headed south. As soon as Wally ascertained that there were no serious injuries among the group on the lawn across from the Lapleys' house, he followed his friend.

Inside the crashing sky machine, Selkirk had just managed to regain his feet after the green glow had vanished. The collision with the building threw him and Kattor against the wall, dislodging the wand from the alien's hand.

It bounced toward the minister, who seized it and turned it over carefully in his hands, trying to understand how it worked. He pushed a small bump on the device and a red light shot out, cutting a slice out of the wall of the transporter room.

Kattor dodged out of the way. He realized that he would have to neutralize this pesky human.

The sky machine continued its slide to the ground, tipping even further to one side. The alien touched a spot on the wall and the slit he and the minister had been pulled through earlier reopened. He and Selkirk slid down the sloping floor and back through the opening and dropped roughly to the ground ten feet below.

The massive ship crunched along the side of the building and finally settled at an angle, leaning against the church.

Selkirk and Kattor rolled free of the giant disk-shaped vehicle. The minister tried to stand but felt a sharp pain in his lower right leg and knew immediately that it was broken. He collapsed and dropped the wand.

Kattor saw his opportunity and hastily retrieved it before the growing crowd of citizens who had come out of their nearby homes to see what was going on could react.

At first, the onlookers were just curious, but the sight of the alien was very shocking to them and many turned in panic and ran screaming back toward their houses. Those who remained formed a circle around the alien. Their curiosity outweighed their apprehension.

When Teddy, Dana, Cheryl, and Attir exited the parsonage they found themselves amid the milling crowd of humans just outside the front door. They took Dana and Attir to a yard across the street where they saw a battered group of people standing around in a daze.

They lowered Attir and Dana to the ground. Cheryl went back to the church to see if she could find a way to get medical assistance for them.

Jay, Calvin, Tonya, and Joey stepped cautiously through the slit in the sky machine one at a time and slid down the slope to the ground. Joey had some trouble with sliding, so he sat down and scooted toward the edge.

The crowd tightened the circle and Kattor found himself trapped. His first thought was to blast the humans with his wand. Then, his eyes fell upon Cheryl whom he knew from their long trip and he came up with another plan.

He took a couple of quick strides and grabbed her by the hair on the back of her head. As he dragged her around the circle, he brandished the wand and shot short bursts from it at the crowd. The people backed away.

He glanced over his shoulder and noted that the humans who had been on board were vacating the sky machine. He pulled Cheryl's head back and held the wand to her throat and she ceased to struggle. The crowd gasped as they saw a trickle of blood run down the left side of her neck. They gasped a second time when they saw Kattor's scarred face as he walked Cheryl backwards to the sky machine.

The throng of humans split apart to allow Kattor and his hostage to pass through. He wasn't a trained pilot, but he knew enough to get the machine into the air. Kattor's one hope was that the crowd would stay back until he could enter the badly damaged machine and get it airborne.

Then, he would just need to keep it in the air long enough to come within reach of the rest of his squadron of invaders, who waited above the clouds for his order to join the soldiers from the portal in an attack. After they saved him from the damaged sky machine, he planned to transfer to another vehicle and resume the attack, with or without the phalanx of raiders who had been about to come through the portal.

Paul had just turned from his encounter with Peter Lapley when he felt the ground shiver and heard a huge crunching sound. His eyes had immediately been pulled to the sight of the sky machine smashing into the middle of the church.

As he wheeled himself past fleeing residents and dodged some flying debris, he heard a woman's painful scream. He frantically scanned the area in front of the church; it reminded him of a war zone.

Then, through the still-swirling dust and debris, he saw Kattor dragging Cheryl up the sloping side of the sky machine and through an opening in the side of the badly-damaged vehicle.

Paul shouted for everyone to move out of the way and gave his chair's wheels a powerful spin, propelling himself toward the same opening just as it snapped shut. Paul grabbed his wheels just in time to avoid smashing into the damaged vehicle.

He slammed his fist in frustration against the sloping exterior of the UFO as it began to rise unsteadily. At that moment he was angry. This was the situation that he had been repeatedly warned about on his computer. Cheryl was in trouble, but there was nothing he could do to help her!

The sound of the sky machine crashing into the church had reverberated throughout the small village, including the old Community Center, where Deke and the fifth graders had just deposited their unconscious and securely bound prisoner. While the others rushed outside to investigate, Deke remained in the building to guard the prisoner, firmly clutching the wand and scepter he had gotten at Doug's house.

As soon as the fifth graders were gone, he winced in pain as he heard the sky machine colliding with the parsonage. The fifth graders, who had just departed, drifted gradually in the direction of the crash until they stood on the perimeter of the circle of adults who had gathered to gawk at the crashed sky machine.

Lindsay noticed her mother on the periphery of the crowd. The family lived directly across Main Street from the church. Lindsey joined her there. The other fifth graders trailed behind her. She was their natural leader, though none of them were consciously aware of it. They lined up behind Lindsay and stared in shock at the scene before them.

On the lawn across the street to the north of the heavily damaged church, a small group of injured people had begun to assemble to avoid falling debris. Among these people were the group Attir had guided from the football field.

When she saw Attir approaching after he had exited the parsonage, Laurine turned Kathy's daughter Stephanie over to Marla and went to his aid. Wally came over to check him out while Ty paused to examine Dana, his long-absent wife. She was still dazed, and he couldn't get her to communicate with him.

Tonya Belding approached, limping and unsteady. Charles Keller recognized her and rushed forward to help her. She was confused, not knowing where she was or why Charles was there. Despite being disoriented by her recent experience, she recognized him, smiled, and put her arms around his neck, for balance. This surprised the psychiatrist, who misinterpreted it as an affectionate embrace and hugged her. She didn't mind.

Joe Paige's heart leapt when he saw humans exiting the badly damaged interstellar craft, but after the lady with blond hair, no one came out for a while. Then, a man in a yellow t-shirt exited. Joe waited.

No Joey.

His eyes welled up when it appeared that no one else was going to come out and he turned to make his way back to the bar. He had been hoping that something like this shocking event would bring his son back to him, but his heart sank when he realized that wasn't happening. Even this unimaginable invasion of aliens from space didn't portend a change in his luck.

Suddenly Judy DePriest called out to Joe, "Joe! Turn around. It's Joey!" Her daughter Lindsay took up the call.

"It's Joey! It's Joey!" The other fifth graders joined in cheerfully, even Josh, Steve, and Nancy who had a history of harassing Joey individually and as a group. Josh was amazed that he could feel positively toward such a loser.

As Joey slowly scooted down the slope of the sky machine, Joe heard the shouting and cheering and turned to look back.

There was his son, perched cautiously on the lip of the crashed vehicle, looking much the same as the last time he saw him, wearing the same clothing, apparently no worse for the strain of his ordeal. In fact, Joey didn't know what had happened and was mystified by the reception he was receiving.

Joe hurried over and reached up to help him to the ground, embracing him in a joyous bear-hug. After a moment, Joey shrugged and returned his father's hug while giving a thumbs-up to his fellow fifth graders while he looked over his father's shoulder. He had no idea why they were cheering. Joey just felt good to be part of something involving other kids.

As the minutes passed, other abductees began wandering out of the slit doorway. One was a slender man with thinning blond hair and a ruddy complexion, John Lundy. He had no clue about where he was, and he didn't recognize any of the others.

Cheryl, whom he would have recognized, was somewhere in the bowels of the ship.

Though she found the sight of Joey reuniting with his father very heartwarming, Tara Lapley realized she didn't know where either of her parents were.

During the battle with the alien at Doug's house and on the way to the jail cell in the Community Center with their captive, she had made a deliberate effort to suppress her worries, but seeing Joey reunited with his father brought home to her that she also wanted to be back with her parents and her tears began to flow.

At first, Doug didn't recognize the problem. Lindsay always said he was slow on the uptake in situations involving emotions. Doug recalled that Tara had been upset when she joined the other fifth graders in Calvin Dunn's cornfield. The reason suddenly dawned on him.

"Tara, we can look for your mother, now." He put a comforting hand on her shoulder.

She started to turn toward him, but then glimpsed her father standing with Carl Johnson near the pile of rubble that had been the church. She broke away from the others and rushed to jump into her father's arms. She started to blurt out the story of what she and the others had done, but part of the way through the story she broke down and began to sob.

"I don't know where Mommy is! I think the bad man took her—or maybe one of the aliens." It occurred to Tara that this was an astounding statement to make, but it was accurate.

Peter was no longer under the impression that the aliens feared him, but he hadn't told Tara that. He looked into his daughter's eyes and said with a touch of bravado, "Don't worry about it, Tara. She might still be somewhere inside this flying saucer."

He pointed to the narrow slit through which Calvin Dunn, Tanya Belding, Jay Brashear, Joey, and a few others had just emerged.

"If she is, I will save her!" He wanted to keep his daughter calm.

He lowered his daughter to the ground and reached out to grab the town cop by his left elbow. "C'mon, Carl! Let's go in and try to save some people!"

Carl wasn't sure it was a good idea but relented when he realized that some of his fellow townspeople were watching.

"Just let me get my gun from my patrol car."

After all, there was an election coming in the Spring and he couldn't risk appearing cowardly. On the way to his cruiser, he secretly hoped that Peter would change his mind before he returned or that someone else would insist on taking his place.

As the town cop strode away, Tara turned to her father and asked if she could go inside the sky machine with him. Peter smiled sadly and shook his head *no*.

"I've been in one of these and it may not be safe. You stay out here and watch to see if your mother comes back."

Tara was disappointed and feared for Peter's safety, but reluctantly nodded her consent.

Carl returned from his crashed patrol car with the ancient pistol, fumbling to put it back together as he walked. He had to stop a couple times to pick up parts that fell off, but at last he thought everything was holding in its place, so he shoved it into his holster.

He scanned the crowd of onlookers, hoping someone would offer to take his place. When no one seemed to be volunteering, he shrugged his shoulders and climbed up onto the sloping side of the sky machine. Peter smiled grimly at Tara, then turned and followed Carl up the slope and into the dark interior.

Tara plopped down on the nearby curb, pulling her legs up close, putting her head down and clasping her hands around her knees. After a few seconds, she jumped up and followed her father into the machine.

Following her earlier encounters with the man from Huit's agency and the alien captive, fear was not a factor in her decision, especially when her mother's and father's lives may be at risk. She was careful to not let Peter see her.

"Gosh, she's brave!" marveled Josh as he observed her action.

Peter's other two children, Johnny and Melanie, approached the crowd hesitantly. Johnny was the oldest sibling at age thirteen and he was trying hard to keep six-year-old Melanie from sobbing while fighting the same urge within himself.

Judy DePriest approached them and gathered them into a group hug with herself and Lindsay. Doug joined them.

After handing the baby to Kathy Fellner, Marla Brashear caught sight of Jay sitting on the remnants of the church steps. She was still unsteady from being confined in the tube on the UFO, but she managed to wobble and limp her way toward Jay, while calling his name. She collapsed before she could reach him but kept calling his name.

At first he thought he was imagining it, since he assumed she was still back at their home with their kids, but when he finally focused on her voice, he realized she was right there, just a few feet away. He had been immobilized even longer than Marla and when he jumped to his feet and tried to run to her, he fell flat on his face in the parking area in front of the church. Husband and wife lay facing each other on the gravel. They smiled at one another and began to laugh.

Kathy and Lee also found one another. Lee was thrilled when Kathy showed him his new daughter, Stephanie. Their long quest for parenthood was over though both were worried about what would happen next.

The citizens of Caperton continued to mill around, stunned and fascinated by the huge interstellar craft in their midst. Doug, Lindsay, Josh, Steve, and Nancy huddled together as a group, discussing Tara's foray into the interior of the monstrous machine that was propped awkwardly against the side of the church.

Jay spotted Paul sitting grimly in his wheelchair next to the crashed sky machine on which Cheryl was now Kattor's hostage. He pulled himself to his feet and approached his old friend, walking very unsteadily. Paul extended his right hand but couldn't smile. Cheryl was still in great danger.

"Cheryl's inside!" he informed Jay. "I need to save her! The aliens have been sending me messages saying I'm the only one who can help her! I need to do something!"

Jay had never heard Paul so distressed.

Jay hadn't been in the crowd surrounding the hostage taker and his victim and hadn't seen Kattor pulling his sister aboard the huge sky machine, but as soon as Paul informed him, he was also determined to save her.

Both realized that neither had much chance of getting inside the crashed vehicle, since Paul used a wheelchair and Jay was still unsteady on his feet. Paul glanced around until his eyes fell on the small group across the street, who were still being examined by the doctors.

Paul received a telepathic message. He looked up and noticed a tall, pale figure amid the huddled people. He recognized him as the alien who had urged him to drive into Caperton.

Attir's message was brief. *"I am injured and cannot physically enter the sky machine, but I can use my device to lift you up into it."*

He pointed the wand at Paul and a green light shot across the street and enveloped Paul and his chair in front of the parsonage and lifted them into the doorway of the crashed machine. Then Attir repeated that procedure with Jay.

Paul tried wheeling himself inside but found he and the chair together wouldn't fit through the opening. He received one more message from Attir.

"Leave the chair. Once you are inside, I will lower the gravity level and you will become weightless and able to maneuver yourself to where you need to go. As a trained pilot of the Fifths, I have the ability to adjust the gravity remotely. Kattor is not a pilot and never learned to do that."

Jay and Paul turned themselves toward the interior and discovered that Attir had indeed lowered the gravity. They pulled themselves through the opening and floated toward the back of the spacecraft.

Carl and Peter had already entered the darkened interior of the downed ship. Carl reached for the flashlight he wore clipped to his belt. He was so nervous that his hand was shaking badly, and the beam of light bounced all over the place and neither man could see very far ahead.

In a few seconds, Carl regained his composure and he and Peter began exploring the spacious interior of the sky machine, which consisted of both vertical and horizontal dividers, suitable for a vehicle designed to operate in space, where there was no gravity and rooms didn't require *up* and *down* orientation.

The two humans found weightlessness both exhilarating and frightening, but their inexperience hampered their ability to investigate the interior and their mission was far too serious to dwell on their new physical sensations.

Peter and Carl cautiously proceeded further into the dimly lit interior. They stepped over the body of the android pilot on their way to the next room. They encountered a table-like structure that—like the control panel up front–seemed to be an outgrowth of the floor beneath it, as though the material of which they were made had been poured into a mold. There was an array of objects resembling surgical instruments clipped to a panel above the table.

Peter shuddered, beginning to recall what had really happened when he was taken aboard the UFO. He remembered that he had indeed been rendered immobile and placed on the table, face-down. Something had been attached to the back of his neck.

His eyes locked onto a particular instrument that was clipped into place along with several others and wondered if that was the one to which he had been connected.

Carl noticed several jar-like objects of varying sizes attached to the wall. He floated closer and shakily raised his flashlight to get a better view. Then he pulled back with a gasp, releasing his flashlight, which floated in midair next to him. He reached out to grab it again but found that each time he tried to touch it, it drifted away.

In each jar there was a body immersed in fluid, each very different from the others, each frighteningly non-human, but obviously alive and moving. They ranged in sizes from miniscule to some that were as large as human toddlers.

Carl turned to Peter with a pale face. Peter looked grim; he realized he had seen them before. He recalled that the aliens had told him these were sample specimens from several galaxies. They had even pointed to a large, empty one that they said was reserved for him!

He had the impression that they were sharing a cruel joke among themselves, though they made no laughing sounds. They did make some mewing sounds, interspersed with clicks. Peter hadn't been amused; he had been terrified!

The two came upon a panel of lights. Carl reached up cautiously to touch one and a large section of the wall slid into the floor. On the other side were tubes holding larger "specimens." The exploring humans approached these tubes carefully, afraid that there might be more monstrosities.

One was clearly a human male, dressed in black clothing, floating lifelessly. In fact, none of the floating bodies appeared to be living. They were, however, at least human.

The tube next to the man in black was opened, but empty. A trail of fluid from the glass-like enclosure led back in the direction from which the men had come. Globules of the fluid were drifting through the gravity-free room toward the opening in the sky machine.

Suddenly, Peter and Carl heard a terrible scream from the direction of the doorway. It was a child's scream. The two men whirled halfway around. Carl pulled his pistol from its holster as he finally seized the floating flashlight at the same time. As usual the cylinder tumbled out but floated in place as he tried to retrieve it; every time he touched it, it floated out of his reach.

As they were turning, the two men found themselves facing the slot through which they had entered.

There stood a hideous figure, a tall alien with bulging veins, glowing red eyes and a scar on his left cheek that dripped a greenish fluid. The alien was gripping Tara by the neck with one long-fingered hand as she struggled to escape. He clutched a lifeless appearing Margie in his other arm. The trail of floating globules led to the alien and his hostages.

The foes stood facing each other, not knowing what move to make next. Obviously, the alien had hostages and Peter feared that he would be willing to murder at least one of them in order to secure his escape. Peter stood with clenched fists, but didn't know how to save both of them, or even one.

Seconds ticked by as memories of both played through his memory. Margie had always been there for him, even when he had been a drunk and a total fool. But Tara was a mere child. She was cute and funny and hadn't even really experienced life yet. Peter couldn't choose between them.

He began to perspire. He thought about asking Kattor to let him take their place. Kattor read his thoughts and Peter saw his eyes light up as an evil sneer spread across his face.

"*Choose...*" The word appeared in Peter's mind. It was a simple word, but its meaning was chilling.

"*Choose.*"

"No!" Peter screamed in agony. "I can't!"

Peter could hurl himself at the alien in an effort to free his wife or daughter, but he knew he probably wouldn't be able to save both. In the lowered gravity, it would be impossible to move fast enough, anyway.

Kattor's sneer turned into an evil grin.

"Choose..."

"I can't!" Peter repeated through clenched teeth. "I can't!" Kattor's grin became even more menacing.

"Choose...or both will die." The telepathic voice was devoid of emotion, but its meaning was sinister. Kattor, clutching Tara and Margie by their throats, pushed both hostages forward to emphasize his intent. Tara's small body began to writhe.

Peter was shaking. Carl just stood, trembling. He wasn't much help with his gun, and he was totally useless without it.

The light from the slit doorway was suddenly dimmed by someone stepping through it into the interior of the sky machine. The alien and his hostages blocked much of Peter's view.

All that he could see of the figure was that he was wearing the same kind of boots as the alien, boots without heels.

Peter gulped. "What now?" he muttered to himself.

His eyes filled with fear for his wife and daughter. There was no way he and Carl could overcome two opponents in time to avoid losing one or both of the hostages. The figure in the alien boots moved quickly from the doorway and reached out both hands. Peter closed his eyes, knowing he didn't want to see what happened next.

Tara screamed again, but it was muffled as Kattor's hand clamped down on her mouth.

But the booted figure didn't seize either hostage. He instead grabbed Kattor around the neck from behind in a choke hold. He gave the alien's head a quick twist and threw him to the side.

Kattor lost his grip on Margie and Tara as he went limp. Peter immediately pushed himself forward and floated over to help his wife and daughter.

Sergeant Theodore Rader stepped out from the spot where Kattor had been standing. He was still wearing the alien foot coverings Kattor had put on him back in the mountain cave.

Carl now felt brave enough to move forward to be sure the threat had indeed ended. He pulled out his handcuffs and moved to place them on Kattor. However, as he did so, the alien suddenly sprang up. He evaded Carl's effort to grab him. Kattor then turned around and floated deeper into the interior of the sky machine. Carl made a half-hearted effort to grab him.

As Peter tended to his wife and daughter, who thankfully were both now conscious, Carl and Teddy floated after Kattor, seizing handholds on the walls of the dim interior to propel themselves forward.

The darkness made it nearly impossible to follow the alien, but they glimpsed movement at the rear of the sky machine and continued their slow-motion pursuit. The two humans paused periodically to listen, but there was just eerie silence.

Then, after several turns, they were frustrated to find themselves back at the entrance. Though Carl seemed willing to abandon the pursuit, Rader was determined to keep going. He had his own reasons to want to stop the alien.

Suddenly, the sky machine gave a lurch and began to rise. Kattor had found the main controls and, though he couldn't pilot it, he knew enough to start the engines. With a bit of luck, he might be able to get it off the ground and into the sky.

But he had a problem. Jay and Paul were also trying to find him. He had glimpsed them down one of the passageways.

He pulled Cheryl from a metallic tube that rested against the wall and dragged her limp body toward a panel of blinking lights on a pedestal base in the middle of the chamber. If he could just stretch far enough to reach the lights with one hand he could lower the gravity further and increase the speed of the craft's ascent while he scanned the various corridors that led to the chamber.

At that moment, Rader floated into view. He was still receiving Kattor's telepathic messages. He tried to scramble after the alien, but Kattor shot a blast of red light in his direction and knocked him backward. He tumbled helplessly down the passageway toward the front of the sky machine.

Kattor spun around in time to sight Jay floating down a passageway toward him. He abandoned his effort to reach the lights in order to again press his wand against Cheryl's throat.

As he turned to face his opponent, Paul shot out of the darkened interior behind him and grasped him in a bear hug. Kattor thrashed around, still holding the weapon against Cheryl's neck.

"Allow me to go free or Cheryl Hunter dies!" The words appeared in Paul's brain, slightly scrambled, but he understood Kattor's intent.

Paul held on tenaciously but realized that he couldn't save Cheryl in this way. Sooner or later, he would have to release Kattor. When he did, he expected that Kattor would murder her anyway. He didn't know what he could do to stop that from happening.

Suddenly, a thought struck Paul. He had been told repeatedly that he was the only one who could save Cheryl. Was that true? The computer hieroglyphs, the aliens on his computer who wanted him to save her... Why did they keep insisting that he was the only one who could do it?

Obviously, others could do as much as he could. Even more. People who still had use of all their limbs were more likely to match Kattor physically.

He couldn't comprehend why the alien hated him so much. If he could figure out Kattor's motivation, maybe he could figure out how to save Cheryl. Then, the reason came to him! He concluded that he was the only one who could save Cheryl...because of his personal history with Kattor!

His long-suppressed memories rushed back. He knew he had seen Kattor before. He had seen him recently when he had the illusion of being pulled into the computer, but that wasn't what he was thinking about. No, there was another time, an earlier time.

His mind flashed back to an event that occurred years ago, when he had been part of the Army recovery team. He had been driving a jeep into the Forbidden Zone one night on a routine reconnaissance. Lieutenant Webber was seated beside him. Suddenly there was a bright flash of light, followed by a tremendous crashing sound, just over the next ridge.

The officer urged Sloan to step on it.

When they reached the top of the rise, their eyes were seared by the heat of a crashed and burning wreckage that came into view at the bottom of the slope, leaning against the hillside. Green, blue and white lights were alternating rapidly around its edges.

The two soldiers climbed down from the jeep and the officer told his driver to call for backup, including an ambulance. After Paul had done that, Webber told him to go down to the bottom of the gulley and see if he could help anyone. At that point Paul believed they were merely involved with the recovery of innovative U.S. prototypes, plus, unfortunately, American bodies.

Paul proceeded down, lighting the slope ahead with his flashlight and edging carefully among the loose rocks and sand. Suddenly, the ground gave way under his feet and he found himself sliding and bouncing down the hill until he slammed into the side of the wrecked vehicle. The flashlight bounced along beside him and landed underneath it.

When he opened his eyes, he found before him a gash in the side of the mangled wreckage. He got to his feet, brushed himself off and looked for the flashlight, but couldn't locate it.

He cautiously entered the crashed aircraft. At first the interior seemed very dark, but his eyes began to adjust. It was then that he realized that there were several small bodies scattered around inside, and they weren't human bodies!

He felt a surge of fear and turned to scramble out of the wreck, but a tall, very pale figure blocked his path. A beam of moonlight stole into the ship's interior, briefly permitting him to see the figure now blocking his exit. Paul lifted his eyes to the face.

To him the face seemed like pure evil. The squinted eyes resembled burning red coals. The cranium was long and sloped. There were bulging vein-like streaks that began just above the eye slits and zigzagged to the top of the skull.

Before Paul could make a move to go around him, the alien produced a pencil-like weapon and pointed it at him. Paul realized he was about to be shot and he had no way out. He felt a panicky need to escape, so he tackled the alien as hard as he could, like he used to do as a high school linebacker.

The two rolled against an interior wall, struggling as they went. The wand device bounced free. Paul grabbed it and took a swipe at his foe, cutting the side of his face. Bluish-green fluid spurted from the wound and flowed down the alien's chest.

The alien wrestled the wand away from the soldier, which resulted in Paul being sent hurtling through the gash in the side of the scout machine. As he lay there, partly outside the vehicle, the alien took a step toward him and stood over him, glaring. Then his narrow mouth curved into a smirk.

"You will pay for this, human!" The alien touched the wound on his face.

Then he pointed his weapon at the helpless soldier lying before him. Paul instinctively rolled to the side in an effort to avoid the expected blast. The light beam hit him in the lower part of his back. Paul felt a searing pain. Then, his world went dark.

That was the last thing he knew until waking up in the base hospital with no memory of what had happened. Lieutenant Webber was standing by the foot of his bed.

"What happened?" Paul asked.

The officer responded, "You were in an accident, Corporal, on the way to the recovery site. You should be up and about soon."

Paul accepted that story, since he couldn't remember the truth. But, Webber had lied about his recovery. He never saw the Lieutenant again. He also never walked again.

Now, Paul had the answer! Kattor had been the alien whom he had scarred and who had in turn crippled him. That was the personal connection, why Kattor loathed him. And why did Kattor bring Cheryl into the situation? As bait to lure Paul in, apparently.

"Release her and I will be your hostage!" Paul's thoughts reached Kattor's mind as he mouthed the words.

"I am the one you want. I have been the stumbling block in your path. If you have me, you can kill me as soon as you escape and you will win. I will no longer keep you from completing your mission."

He studied Kattor's face. He could see that the alien was considering his proposition. Paul knew that Kattor was doubtlessly reading his mind to gauge his sincerity. He maintained his hold on the alien but did not try to block Kattor from reading his thoughts.

At last, the alien moved the sharp weapon from Cheryl's throat and allowed her body to slip free. Jay moved forward to take his sister by the arm and float her out of the interior of the sky machine and toward the light coming through the opening up front.

Once Jay and Cheryl were safely out of sight, Paul released his grip on Kattor, who immediately whirled around to face him. He lifted the sharp device and prepared to thrust it into his longtime enemy's heart.

Kattor responded with a sneer. *"You don't even know why I hate you!"*

"Yes, I do," Paul responded calmly. Kattor began pushing the weapon into Paul's chest. Paul steeled himself for the inevitable. He felt calm. He had saved Cheryl. That was what mattered.

"I was gone from your world for many years, but I always planned to return to get my vengeance for what you did to me! Now, I will have it!"

Meanwhile, the front door to the parsonage opened and the four alien raiders stepped out, carrying long rods strapped to their backs like rifles. The crowd didn't notice them at first; they were focused on the crashed sky machine they had just seen several people enter.

The four alien raiders had frightened the crowd of humans as they approached the sky machine. People in the crowd took one look at the soldiers and scurried in all directions for the safety of their homes. The alien marauders ignored them and climbed on board, entering through the slit opening.

As they were going in, Jay was helping his sister to exit the dark interior. The four aliens ignored the humans and headed for the back of the ship. Jay feared that something terrible was about to happen to Paul.

There was a flash of light back in the darkest part of the sky machine. Jay gritted his teeth, fearing he would hear a scream of pain from Paul. He carefully lowered his sister down to Wally Hunter, who was waiting below. Then, he spun around and rushed back in to help his friend.

Before Jay could reach Paul, the four raiders and Kattor brushed past him on their way out. They continued to ignore the human. He also ignored them. He was desperate to reach his old friend.

Jay found Paul prone on the floor, not moving. His heart sank. It appeared that his old friend had paid the ultimate price for Cheryl's life.

Jay had thought a lot about friendship over the past few months since he was abducted. If only he had been able to reach Paul the previous summer, maybe this whole sad situation could have been avoided. At the very least, Paul would not have had to go through this alone. Jay bowed his head in sorrow.

Then a message appeared in his mind. He wasn't accustomed to telepathy as a way of communicating, but the message was undoubtedly there. It was from someone named Attir, whom Jay realized was an alien.

"I increased the gravity to hold Kattor down, but it also held Paul Sloan down. When the four soldiers entered, I lowered the gravity so they could take Kattor prisoner. I believe your friend is unharmed."

Paul stirred and pushed himself to a sitting position. He looked at Jay. "Is Cheryl okay?"

Jay lifted his head as a feeling of relief rolled over him. He looked at Paul and a grin spread across his face. "Yes, thanks to you, old buddy!"

Attir alerted the two that he was going to decrease the gravity to allow Paul to exit under his own power. Suddenly, Paul found himself floating up from the floor.

As Jay and Paul drifted toward the exit, the four soldiers emerged from the sky machine with Kattor's arms bound behind his back. While two of them held Kattor prisoner, the other two split off and headed for the Old Community Center. A few minutes later, they emerged with the alien who had tormented the fifth graders and hauled him to the front door of the parsonage. He was still groggy and wrapped in the badminton net.

Rader walked up to Kattor and stared at him. Kattor ignored the sergeant. Rader stood there for a moment, shook his head sadly, and turned away.

Jay wondered why the four raiders had turned on Kattor.

Attir responded. *"Our planet's governing council have long been concerned about Kattor's increasing belligerence. They decided to stop Kattor in his tracks before he could bring any more dishonor to our people. The raiding party sent to the portal was actually following orders from the council to arrest Kattor."*

Once he and his chair were safely out of the sky machine and on the ground, Paul wheeled up beside Rader, who was standing next to the immobilized Kattor.

One glance at the cowed alien shocked him. He felt a jumble of emotions: anger, regret, fear. But he didn't expect to feel pity. He saw that his enemy was thoroughly defeated.

For some reason, his long history of hating this alien seemed to be pointless. Hate was not a useful emotion. Paul's mind turned to forgiveness. It was a positive thing.

But how could he forgive this alien who had cost him the use of his legs? Kattor felt no positive emotions. His people didn't forgive their enemies. Only humans do that. With a feeling of sadness, Paul turned away.

The raiders hauled Kattor and the other alien into the parsonage and up the stairs to the attic. There, they pried open the portal and dragged their prisoners through to the alien landscape on the other side. Then, the portal closed.

By this time, most of Caperton's residents had come out of their houses to see what was going on. Doug's parents had returned from their jobs in Millardville. They were shocked by what they found on Main Street, but when they went to their home, they also found it in disarray. When they realized that Doug wasn't there, they went looking for him.

"I told you Doug was too young to be left at home alone!" Doug's mother remarked.
.
Minnie Boyd drove her daughter down Main Hill to the center of town to see what was happening. The road in front of the church was blocked, so they had to detour around the rubble. They saw the ambulances near the church and parsonage and also a block further north at the Lapleys' house. They found the mayor receiving medical attention from Ty in the yard across the street to the north of the church.

Delores and Minnie got out of the car and climbed over the concrete and bricks to reach Ralph, whom they were relieved to find out was not seriously injured. One arm was in a sling, but the bullet had just grazed him. The mayor's delicate emotional constitution had caused him to faint at the sight of his own blood.

Chapter Thirty-Five: Attir's Message

Attir, holding his side, sent a telepathic message to Deke. He asked his son to come to the area behind the parsonage and added that he wanted Deke to bring his mother, Laurine.

When Deke and Laurine arrived, Attir held up his right hand, palm out. *"What I am about to share with you has wider implications. I will ask the humans present in this town to join us. Please be patient while I contact them."*

Attir sent out a mental request to anyone in the vicinity to come hear what he had to say. They were puzzled, but intrigued, by the method and subject of the contact. Several grabbed at their ears or shook their heads vigorously, glancing at one another quizzically. After a minute or two, they began arriving in the yard behind the partially destroyed parsonage.

Rader and Paul Sloan, with his wheelchair pushed by Jay Brashear and accompanied by Cheryl Hunter and Marla Brashear, arrived first. Alvin Selkirk, his leg in a splint, was cautious and on guard in case it was a new demon attack, but he saw Peter Lapley, Margie, and Tara headed in the direction indicated by the telepathic message and asked them to help him. Still, he carefully peeked around the corner of the damaged building first since he didn't know who had put the message in his head. It could be the demons.

Doug and Lindsay told her mother that they needed to check on something and they trailed after Tara. Teddy found his way to the back yard, as did Ty, Wally, Tonya, and Charles Keller. Dana Warrick joined Ty and Wally. Lastly, Kathy, Lee, Stephanie and Kimmy showed up.

Once everyone stood before him, Attir placed one hand on his son's shoulder. He looked around the group and addressed them with his voice, which was calm and deep.

"I am Attir from a distant galaxy and this is my son Devtir, who is known to many of you as 'Deke'. This Earth woman Laurine is his mother..."

He paused briefly, motioning to Laurine.

"Kattor—the 'alien' as you might call him—tried to have his army invade your town on the way to conquering this planet. He and I are from the same planet, which our people don't reference with a name as you people do. We also don't have labels for each person as you do on this planet. We only started using them when our increased contact with you made it useful."

"Our world is locked in orbit around our star in such a way that one half is always in light, the other in darkness. Our people exist only in the gray borderland where light and dark meet. Light and darkness permeate our very existence and form our character."

He paused again, glancing around at the attentive faces before him.

"We are all related to one another. Because we are related, we feel each other's pain. The closer the relationship, the greater the pain."

The small crowd was formed in a semi-circle in front of Attir, amid piles of rubble. Some of the children were seated on chunks of broken masonry. They all were attentive to Attir's words. He continued.

"For what you Earth people call centuries peace reigned on our world. No one would want to do anything to harm another member of our race, since it would also result in pain that would ripple out to affect everyone. Therefore, we lived in peace with one another. All disputes were resolved peacefully by our governing Elders."

"When our people developed the ability to go out into the cosmos with the goal of spreading our message of peaceful coexistence, they learned that it was difficult to find sufficient fuel to make voyages to other planets. Eventually, my ancestors discovered an element that would fuel their peaceful mission. They would send out mining crews to uninhabited worlds to obtain this essential element. This sometimes resulted in the dying of those planets, but since they weren't inhabited we saw no harm in that. Sometimes, our mining so damaged a planet that it would implode. This took centuries, so it was thought that there were no real drawbacks."

Attir again looked around the semi-circle of humans. All were listening closely.

"We were aware that the implosion of a planet could affect the orbits of other planets in the solar system. The breakup of a planet flings large pieces of stone and debris into the space between planets. These became what you call "asteroids" and were a danger to the remaining planets. Still, we believed we were being careful, sweeping these free-floating bodies from the skies and launching them into our star."

"We thought we were being extremely careful in choosing planets to mine. Eventually, however, such planets grew more difficult to identify. We resorted to using worlds with lower life forms. That choice was justified by the belief that peace was worth the sacrifice of non-sentient life. When

those planets could no longer be found, we were faced with an ethical dilemma: was it right to use planets with higher level life forms?"

"Also, a dispute arose concerning whether the peace we sought to spread justified the taking of the element from inhabited worlds that wouldn't give it to us willingly. Our peaceful society began to fracture over these issues."

"Many fell under the influence of leaders who believed, as you people say, 'the end justifies the means'. Those who disagreed began to resist. For a few centuries, our society debated the correct course, as the mining crews continued to travel farther to locate the element. Peace became more expensive and harder to maintain as the element became more difficult to obtain."

"My brother and I grew up in the gray border zone between the two hemispheres of our planet in the midst of the continuing dispute. Our mother was from one of the families who were resisting, our father came from the group who advocated pursuit of the element no matter the cost. It was what your people would call an 'arranged marriage,' designed by the elders to try to bridge the ideological gap."

"It didn't work. My older brother eventually joined those who advocated taking the element forcefully. He then returned as an officer of the Dominants, as the supporters of that belief had started calling their militarized branch. I had, meanwhile, joined the opposition. A civil war was only avoided because everyone knew that physical fighting would be painful for every combatant. Therefore, our propensity to experience pain felt by those related to us led to a stalemate."

"Finally, the Dominants took another approach. They took the war to other worlds, without regard to the wishes of the

Fifths, which our opposition began to call themselves because we are on the fifth planet out from our star. If the native population did not capitulate, the Dominants would slay them and take what they desired. Once the element was exhausted on a planet, they would move on to the next one."

"The Fifths had only one acceptable option, to come to the aid of the victimized civilizations and help them resist the Dominants' invasion."

"That is what brought me to Earth. I was an advance scout to find someone on this planet who could help us set up resistance."

Attir paused again, as he fought back a strange emotion— shame—with which he had no experience.

Then he looked around once more and said, *"That alien being who tried to bring his army to this world was the one who was just arrested by his own army in front of this building. I am ashamed to admit that he is my brother, and his name is Kattor."*

He was going to mention that Dana was Kattor's daughter, but he received a telepathic message from Rader warning that to do so might subject Dana to a negative response from the crowd for being related to the individual who was the villain behind the recent terror.

Again, this suggestion surprised Attir, since such concerns did not exist on his world, but he concurred and said nothing about his niece.

He continued. *"The birth rate on our jointly occupied home planet began to decline, largely because the proxy wars took our most fertile residents away from home for so long."*

"To address this concern, both sides sought out planets with occupants that genetically most closely resembled those of our home planet to help revitalize our populations. This eventually resulted in what on your world is often referred to as 'alien abductions' and the mixing of our native genetic material with that of people from other worlds."

"Both sides have resorted to it. It would often take generations to complete the process, so our people would come back to..."

Attir paused, realizing that even this explanation might not be palatable to the former victims of the process.

"Our people would return periodically to monitor those who had been selected to further our genetic work."

Again, he stopped, once more feeling regret. *"I can only apologize for the error my people and I have made. We did not stop to consider how our choices would impact others. I am ashamed. I am sorry."*

Paul rolled his chair forward. "What is done, is done. Please continue."

Attir looked at Laurine. *"I was sent here as a scout to learn if the element we sought existed on your world. My job was to search for it and—if I found it—alert my people, who could then come here in force to train the humans to resist the Dominants who would inevitably be coming to steal it. I did find the element."*

"I did not expect to also find love with a human, but that is what happened. I had to return to my home planet to report on my findings. I learned that the Dominants were already on the way, so I had no time to spare. I had to leave immediately."

"On the way home, I was intercepted by the Dominants, who retrieved my findings by reading my mind. I was able to escape after that, since they had no further use for me. After a number of your years wandering the cosmos, I made it back here. Unfortunately, while I was struggling to get back here, the Dominants had found a natural portal between your world and ours, which they could use to transport the element back to our planet and also to transport their shock troops here to overcome any resistance to the mining of the element."

"My primary goal during the recent time was to stop the Dominants from opening that portal. The governing elders of our home world had finally taken a stand against the Dominants. So, today when the Dominants opened the portal briefly, the force of raiders waiting on the other side had actually come to arrest Kattor."

Attir paused and again surveyed the audience. "He and the Dominants will not be spreading their toxic philosophy further."

The crowd was silent, each person reflecting on what Attir had said.

Paul pushed himself back in his chair, a look of relief on his face. He began to clap. Jay and Marla followed his lead. Others joined in. Reverend Selkirk moved forward to clasp Attir's hand. Lindsay began to cheer. Doug and Tara joined her. Soon, the entire crowd was clapping and cheering.

Attir was overcome with another new emotion: gratitude.

The crowd eventually drifted away. Attir approached Laurine and Deke. "We will use my wand to travel to your place of residence, Laurine. I can recover there while you relate to me what has occurred since last I saw you."

Laurine smiled a rare smile and Deke did also. As they slowly made their way to the edge of town, a green glow came from Attir's wand and the trio rose skyward in it and moved to the north toward Millardville.

Ty watched them go. He then turned back to see if anyone else needed help. He assisted Josh Tooney to an ambulance to have his injured hand tended. Seeing that the various EMTs had everything under control, he decided to go look for Dana. He didn't have to look long. She rushed up and jumped into his arms.

Ralph was groggy, but alive. Peter came around the corner of his house and found Ralph attempting to drive his car with his good arm. He told the mayor to scoot over and started the car to drive Ralph up Main Street Hill to his home.

Ralph felt overwhelmed by the day's events. "Petey—er—Peter, you can have this job if you really want it. It's too much responsibility for me."

"Nah, you do a great job, Mayor Ralphie! If you decide to run for the state legislature, I'll be your campaign manager."

Charles Keller led Tonya, Kathy, Lee, and Kimmy to his Bronco. After placing her baby gently in her husband's arms, Kathy turned and lifted Kimmy into the back seat and joined them. Kimmy didn't know where her mother and siblings were, so Kathy and Lee decided to take her in until it could be sorted out.

Tonya looked at Charles Keller. She felt a tremendous relief that this strange event was all done. Keller opened the passenger-side door for her. She was pleased.

Maybe there was a future with this hick cowboy. After all, there was a certain status in being a doctor's wife. She smiled; for once it was a genuine smile. She had no ulterior motives. Well, almost none.

Jay and Marla met up with Cheryl and Paul on the nearby corner, then they all turned to make their way to Paul's van. Paul drove them to Hilltop House, where they stayed up all night discussing old times.

John Lundy found Teddy Rader on the edge of the crowd in front of the church. John was still groggy from his imprisonment in a tube. Teddy led him toward Paige's bar, where the two soldiers had a few beers as Joe Paige announced that drinks were free. He felt exhilarated at having his son back. When night came, they didn't know what to do. Then, Peter Lapley appeared and invited them to stay at his place.

Epilogue

Sergeant Rader awoke early the next morning. Peter was already awake and there was a pot of coffee ready in the kitchen. Rader took his mug of coffee out onto the back porch and leaned against the railing. For the first time in weeks, he felt calm.

Then, he heard a distant whirring sound and, looking to the west, he discovered a dozen helicopters flying toward the town. They were emitting clouds of smoke as they flew. Only, it wasn't smoke.

Rader looked on with dismay as the clouds settled to the ground. He knew it wasn't good.

By the time the sun rose in the sky, nobody could remember a thing about the alien invasion. They seemed to find convenient explanations for things that were different, such as the demolished church and parsonage that had been hit by a small airplane, and the reason Lundy and Teddy were sleeping on the Lapleys' downstairs couches: two guys Peter had met at Paige's who needed a place for the night. Which was true, sort of.

Later, word got out that Sandy Romer had been arrested for discharging a weapon in the middle of town and the school board had promptly terminated her contract and brought in another teacher who was told that some of the students were discipline problems, but the new teacher found no evidence of that.

Some children who had previously not gotten along with one another suddenly became friends, but none offered any reasons for their changed attitudes, nor did they understand the reasons themselves.

Reverend Alvin Selkirk understood that his church and parsonage had been damaged by a small airplane that crashed, though the pilot bailed out beforehand. The plane wreckage, Selkirk informed everyone, had been cleaned up, though he didn't recall precisely how or when.

Peter, Margie, and Tara had come home with Johnny and Melanie and found no bodies or blood anywhere. The family dog, Dippy, was blamed for knocking over the dresser in the master bedroom and the family cat, Mr. Purrfect, received credit for knocking the radio off the kitchen counter.

Tara didn't recall doing it, but she confessed to breaking the window in her bedroom.

Doug had some difficulty in explaining why the living room furniture was piled up in the middle of the McGees' living room and why the window on the stairs was broken. He cheerfully moved the pieces of furniture back into their original positions and dug some money out of his childhood piggy bank to pay for the window. As with Tara, he didn't recall causing the damage, but he didn't mind paying for it.

The descending fog wiped out the memory of the more stressful parts of the experience. A similar fog settled over Millardville.

A single scout machine followed the helicopters. On board the scout machine Greg Bowie found himself in a transparent tube between Dr. Baines and Nick Dunbar. He couldn't move or speak. He could think, however. He was terrified. Then he heard a voice in his head, a calm voice, a soothing voice. And his fear evaporated.

"It will all be well."

About the Author

Photo by Josh Renshaw

The author, Ronald D. Renshaw, grew up in a small Iowa town much like Caperton. He lived for a while in northwestern Colorado when he was eleven years old. He attended Morningside College in Sioux City and received a master's degree in Social Work from the University of Illinois in Champaign. He also spent three years in the Army and emerged as a sergeant. He spent 32 years working as a social worker. He is now retired from that and spends his days spoiling grandchildren.

Made in the USA
Coppell, TX
12 May 2021

55436257R00272